BOSTON BOLTS HOCKEY:
WAR
BRITTANÉE NICOLE

First Edition October 2024

Model Cover Design by Sara of Sara's PA Services

Trope Cover Design by Sara of Sara's PA Services

Illustrated Cover Design by Cindy Ras of cindyras_draws

Formatting by Sara of Sara PA's Services

Editing by Beth at VB Edits

CONTENT WARNING

Content warning: This book contains discussions of childhood illness and death of family members.

Too Sweet - Hozier
Please Please Please - Sabrina Carpenter
Scars To Your Beautiful - Alessia Cara
Someone To You - BANNERS
i am not who i was - Chance Peña
Little Bit Better - Caleb Hearn, ROSIE
I'll Be Waiting - Cian Ducrot
Belong Together - Mark Ambor
That Part - Lauren Spencer Smith
Put A Little Love On Me - Niall Horan
Stargazing - Myles Smith
Mele Kalikimaka - Bing Crosby, The Anderew Sisters
Breathing - Lifehouse
Sweet Disposition - The Temper Trap
Evergreen - Richy Mitch & The Coal Miners
Anyone - Justin Bieber
Where's My Love - SYML
False Confidence - Noah Kahan
Carry You Home - Alex Warren
Burning Down - Alex Warren

STUDIO VIBES

DEDICATION

For all my quiet girls:
Remember, you were not made to blend in.
You're made to sparkle and shine.
Don't be afraid to be a little vicious, boundaries are hot as well.
So are tattooed broody men who are absolute simps for their girls.
War is for you.

CHAPTER 1
TYLER

"GOOD MORNING, Boston. This is Beckett Langfield, along with my brothers, Gavin, Brooks, and Aiden. Today, we're bringing you another Langfield love story."

Gavin sighs. "That is definitely not what we're doing. We've been over this."

Brooks snorts. "Good luck with that. I don't know why you still try to stop him. He takes over every episode."

"Anyway," Aiden quips. "This is the Langfield Report, and today, we're here with Boston Bolts captain, Tyler Warren."

"To discuss how he fell in love because of me," Beckett interrupts, every word brimming with pride.

A laugh threatens to burst out of me, but I clap a hand over my mouth to stifle it. It's hard to be around these four and not laugh, but I've got a reputation to maintain—hard-ass enforcer, right winger, and yeah, captain of the Boston Bolts—so I don't want this interview to go off the rails.

Aiden tries again. "The purpose of this podcast is to give players a direct link to fans. To allow them to tell their own stories rather than be the subject of someone else's."

Pride fills me as I focus on my center's words. He's the best damn player in the league, and not all that long ago, he opened up to the world about his struggles with depression. From there, he and his brothers created this podcast so they could help other players. The topics don't stop at mental health and hockey, though.

"Go on," Beckett says, crossing his arms over his chest and jutting his chin, wearing a shit-eating grin. "Tell Boston about the first time you met the love of your life."

The love of my life? That has me biting back another laugh. Definitely don't think that's what I was thinking when we got into this. The bane of my existence would be more apt. The pain-in-my-ass wench I tied myself to for life. Or Vicious, maybe. But since I can't say any of that, I go with my favorite nickname for her. "Fine, I'll tell you about the first time I met my wife. It was about two years ago..."

About Two Years Ago

There is not enough caffeine in existence to rid me of the headache my stepmother's phone call just caused. No, I do not need help with my investments. If I did, the last person I'd hire to handle my retirement plans is Xander, my asshole stepbrother. The guy would probably tank my portfolio on purpose—as long as he could skim at least 10 percent off the top first.

Why the hell did my father bring him on as a partner? The kid is an unmotivated, selfish prick. The clients who aren't scared off by Xander's bad attitude will cut ties when they realize he's a thief.

With my head thrown back, I mutter a *fuck it* and stalk to the door. I need to work out. If I don't keep myself busy, I'll end up calling my dad and giving him a piece of my mind.

Outside my apartment, I take the elevator to the gym in the basement. The building and my team—the Bolts—are owned by the Langfields. In fact, two Langfields play hockey with me—Aiden, our center and the youngest of four brothers, and Brooks, our goalie and my best friend. Brooks and I met in college. Not only did we play hockey together, but we were roommates for all four years.

Brooks and Aiden and their two older brothers are the definition of brotherhood. What they have is nothing like my relationship with fucking Xander. At the thought of him, my blood, which has just begun to cool, simmers again. I clench my fists, willing myself not to punch the elevator wall. Gavin Langfield—the brother who owns the Bolts and is far more hands-on than any owner I've ever encountered —has cameras all over this building. The last thing I want is to be fined for acting up. Sure, they signed me because I'm a fighter—they like when I protect Aiden, our star center, as well as the other guys—but I don't think they'd appreciate it if I destroyed their property.

This is my first season with the team, so I've got to prove my worth and not piss off the front-office staff. My friendship with Brooks alone isn't enough to guarantee I keep my spot. The Bolts won the Stanley Cup last year, but as always, loyalty or not, the roster was shaken up after the season ended. They traded one of their best players for me and two defensemen. Guys get too expensive or too difficult, they're gone. It's not personal; it's business.

Ha, that's what I should have said to my stepmother. Even if my decision is personal. I hate Xander, so why would I hire him?

The bass thumps loud enough to vibrate through me when I step into the gym. Aiden, our team's lucky charm, is in the corner, dancing between his sets. Camden Snow, a winger like me, is shaking his head at him while doing a set of curls.

Already, the chemistry I have with these guys on the ice is incredible. Fuck, I can't wait for the season to start so we can put it to use. For now, though, I need to work out my frustration. I head to where the punching bags are set up at the back of the gym.

As the music from the front of the facility fades, I pick up on another sound. One much more melodic. I pick up my pace and head straight for the separate room in the back. Hovering in the doorway, I watch as a woman leaps across the wooden floor, long limbs spread wide. When she lands, she spins, then juts her chest forward, her arms swooping in, her movements filled with emotion, her chest heaving.

As "Scars to Your Beautiful" by Alessia Cara plays, she runs across the floor and throws herself into another jump. This time, though, when she comes down, she lands in a heap on the floor.

My pulse races as I dart for her, and the French Canadian inside me rears its head. "Merde. Are you okay?"

The woman scrambles to her feet. Hair the color of autumn, a mixture between burnt orange and red, escapes from her bun. Wary green eyes as vibrant as the leaves on the white cedar trees outside our home in Canada blink up at me. Her skin is coated in a sheen of sweat, and beneath her cream-colored leotard, her chest rises and falls heavily, causing her nipples to strain against the fabric and make my mouth water.

She's gorgeous and absolutely nothing like the women I usually date. Though I guess dating would be a gross exaggeration.

Her expression is reserved, even timid, making it obvious she didn't sneak into the building with the goal of hooking up with a hockey player. That kind of shit happens often, and even a year ago, I gladly would have fucked a woman who did. But since coming to Boston, my priorities have changed.

"I'm fine. You just scared me."

"I can see that," I say as I take another slow perusal of her body.

Her legs are bare and pale, and when she spins back toward the mirrored wall and strides to her phone, where the music is playing from, her mesh skirt sways. Beneath it, her leotard barely covers her ass.

Damn. I can't help but eat up every beautiful inch of her.

Without hesitating, I advance, coming right up behind her. Before I can get a closer look at just how perfect her curves are, though, she spins.

Lips pursed, she gives me a pointed glare. "Do you need something?"

Oh, I need so many things right now, but I'm pretty sure she wouldn't appreciate any of the ideas filtering through my mind. "Your name would be a good start."

I smile down at her. I've been told I have a bad boy smile. Apparently, it makes it nearly impossible for women to resist giving me what I want, and right now, what I want is my head between this one's thighs. Her innocent, doe-eyed expression be damned. If she's bold enough to wear a leotard that revealing, I have to believe this attitude is an act.

"See something you like?" she asks, calling me out on my obvious inspection.

I run my thumb across my bottom lip, smile still in place. "Very much so."

She blinks those big green eyes of hers in shock, like she didn't expect that answer. Like maybe she's surprised she even spoke to begin with. Like I dragged the words out of her. I like that idea a little too much. Softly, she adds, "I don't do this."

"Share your name with people you've just met?" I scratch the back of my neck. "Do you not like it? That's okay. I'm really good with nicknames. Give me a minute, and I'm sure I can come up with a good one."

She coughs out a surprised, almost derisive laugh. "Does this normally work for you?"

Smirking, I nod and take another step closer. The pull to her is impossible to resist. She smells so fucking good. Like ice cream. I'm about to lick her to see if she tastes as sweet.

Lowering my head to catch her eye, I say. "My name's Tyler. Now it's your turn." I splay a hand on the mirror beside her head, staring her down, waiting for her response. I keep my other arm at my side, giving her more than enough room to escape. But though she wears a confused frown, she doesn't look uncomfortable.

To be honest, I'm confused too. Just getting her name is proving harder than getting into most women's pants.

"Wasn't aware that I asked for it," she tosses back. Her hand goes to her lips like she's surprised that sass slipped out. I liked it though. Like that I'm getting to her. There's probably something fucked about that.

My eyes skate down her body and I take in every curve. She's so small in comparison to me. Dainty. That's what my mother would say. Pocket-sized. I think I'd like to keep her.

"Like I said," she enunciates, dragging my attention back to her face. There's a raspiness to her voice that makes my dick jump. "I don't do this." She motions between us with her finger.

I lick my lips, tempted to nip at that digit. "Don't do what?"

"One-night stands."

I arch a brow, considering my response.

"Or," she adds before I can formulate a single word, "public *sex*?"

She says the last word like the thought has just occurred to her. Like she's spewing thoughts as they flit through her mind. This time she's the one lifting a brow as she whispers, "Is that what you're after?"

There's no stopping the laugh that rips from deep inside my chest. Fuck, it feels good. When I stepped into the gym, I was angry, ready to beat the shit out of the bag. But that one laugh has tension easing in my shoulders, and I feel lighter than I have in far too long.

Dipping lower, I murmur, "Have dinner with me."

Her cranberry-colored lips tip up into a smile. "What?"

"Have dinner with me. You don't do one-night stands, and I want to get to know you."

"I'm not going to sleep with you after dinner." Eyes narrowed, she studies me like she expects this to be a deal-breaker.

Normally it would be. I don't date. Hockey is my life. I have no room for women. They normally need more attention than I'm capable of giving. But, strangely, I want to give this woman my attention. She may look like a beautiful, innocent angel, but she's a vicious little thing. I can sense it hovering just below the surface. She'll put me in my place, keep me on my toes, and make me work for every little piece of her.

Yes, I want this woman.

Nothing in my life has ever come easy. More than once, I've been told that all I'm good for is letting people down. But maybe I can prove those people wrong. Maybe I'll look back one day and realize that this was the moment everything changed. The moment I finally got it right.

"Have dinner with me anyway."

My little ballerina's eyes fall to the floor and she flexes her toes as she considers my request. Ten seconds later, she looks up and surprises the hell out of me when she says, "Ava is my name. And okay, I'll have dinner with you, Tyler."

Seven hours later, I set my cologne on the bathroom counter and head for the door, only to stop when my phone rings.

I can't help but smile at the name that flashes on the screen. "Hey, Bray," I say as I grab my keys off the counter.

"She's still not home."

My stomach plummets. Fucking Trish. She has one fucking job. Come home. Take care of her kid. Show up.

Okay, it's three jobs, really, but that's literally all the responsibility she has. I pay all her damn bills so that she can focus on Brayden. Yet she can't even bother to do that.

Paying her bills means I know Bray is taken care of, but it also means it's harder to keep track of Trish. At least when she needed money, she was working.

She didn't have the kind of job that kept her sober, but it was better than this.

"I'll be right there." Teeth gritted, I glance at the clock on the wall. Six forty-five. Dammit. I'm going to be fucking late.

I shake the thought from my head. Right now, Brayden has to be my priority. He probably hasn't eaten dinner. He's twelve, the same age I was when I lost my mom. He could make himself a sandwich, maybe even cook if he wanted, but he won't. The kid is stubborn. He'll starve himself just so he can tell her he hasn't eaten.

Trish may deserve the guilt trip, but more than that, Brayden deserves to eat. Every kid does.

As I step out into the hall and lock my door, an image of the woman I met only this morning flashes in my mind. She was mesmerizing. Looked like a fucking mystical fairy, swaying beautifully. Innocent. Pure.

I should have known I couldn't have her.

Outside of hockey, nothing has ever come easy, and I don't know why I thought it ever could.

With an aggravated growl, I stalk for the elevator. There's no way I'll make it to dinner, and I don't have Ava's damn number, so I can't warn her. Fuck. After the difficulty I had prying her name out of her, I didn't even try to get her contact info.

Feisty little thing. She probably would have made me work all night for that.

I've never met a woman who wasn't happy to give me her number when I asked. It's my blue eyes and the tattoos. The muscles don't hurt either. Neither do my dark hair and fair skin.

Normally it works to my advantage.

Today is the lone exception.

Then again, as coach always says, "Nothing worth it ever comes easy."

I have a feeling Ava is worth it.

Somehow I'll make it up to her.

Ava

"Would you like to order a drink, or do you want to wait for the rest of your party to get here?"

With a deep breath in, I make eye contact with the bartender. "I'll have a dirty martini, please."

My sister would be so proud. We talked about doing this for years. Move to a city, flirt with boys, drink dirty martinis.

Sex and the City, Emily in Paris, and my personal favorite, *Center Stage.* We watched every episode of Sex and the City and Emily and Paris, planning our next great adventure. And I've lost track of the number of times I've seen Center Stage.

"Vodka or gin?"

Mind blanking, I blink up at the woman.

Her eyes soften. "Most women prefer vodka."

"Yeah, okay, thank you." God, I feel like an idiot. No matter how many movies and books I've devoured, nothing prepared me for leaving my hometown in the middle of Nebraska.

When I moved to Boston, my parents were distraught. They

couldn't believe I'd gone behind their backs and applied for jobs so far away.

Honestly, I hadn't.

It was all my sister's doing. When I got the email asking if I could come in for an interview the following week, I blinked at the screen. Then I fell into a fit of laughter. My sister, on the other hand, squealed.

She made me promise that I'd go. And I have never in my life said no to her. From the moment I was born, my purpose was linked to her. Her needs dictated my life.

I don't mean to sound bitter, but it's the truth. My parents created me in a lab for the purpose of saving her.

I did it time and again and would do it a hundred more times if I had to.

As the bartender gets to work on my drink, I pull out my phone to text her.

> Me: Did you know martinis can be made with either vodka or gin? The waitress asked which one I wanted, and I swear a neon sign appeared above my head and flashed I've never had alcohol! LOL.

> Me: Also, my date is late. He's lucky he was so hot. Otherwise I'd pull a Samantha and throw my dirty martini at him.

I laugh to myself. My sister does the best Samantha impressions. I, of course, am more of a Charlotte.

Quiet, demure Ava. The sister who always does what's asked of her. Who never says no.

When the bartender pushes my drink toward me, I snap a picture of it and send it to my sister.

> Me: To becoming more like Samantha!

A heartbeat after I hit Send, the rush of excitement whooshes out of me, and I settle into the silence. *Alone.*

That's been the hardest part of this move. I don't know a soul. Though my new job came with a furnished apartment, I haven't met any of my neighbors yet. I'd need to step outside my little haven to do that.

It's been three days since I arrived, but the entire process has been overwhelming. Until today, I've lain in bed, ordering decorations and supplies for my new place. This morning, I finally worked up the courage to venture out.

That's how I met Tyler.

Possibly the most gorgeous man I've ever seen.

And he asked me out.

Me. Ava Erickson. The woman who's never been on a date.

Nervous energy has me tapping my toes inside my heels.

Also, I never wear heels. But if there's ever an appropriate time to wear them, it's while on a date.

I stare at the cloudy liquid in my martini glass and the two olives speared with a pick. I lift the pick and give them the tiniest taste.

Instantly, salty bitterness hits my tongue, the flavor similar to what I'd imagine the ocean would taste like. I can't hide the scowl that forms on my lips.

"Gross, right?"

The question, spoken close to me, makes me snap my head to the side. The woman seated on the stool beside me has blue eyes and long blond hair.

Unlike her, I have red hair. It's my most notable feature. Maybe my only personality trait.

Long red hair. Quiet Ava.

"It's, um, interesting."

The girl's blue eyes dance. "Okay. Cheers, then." She holds up her drink, which has an adorable yellow and pink umbrella in it.

As if on autopilot, I lift my glass, causing the liquid to slosh over the side a little, wetting my hand, and tap it against hers. Then, with a deep breath in, I take a sip.

Instantly and without my permission, my body shudders. Oh no. No. No. No. The bitterness is too much. Rubbing my tongue over the roof of my mouth, hoping to get rid of the taste, I set my glass down and push it away. What kind of person would willingly order this? It's awful.

The girl beside me covers her mouth to keep from spitting out her own drink because she's laughing so hard. "Billy, can you make my new friend here something fruity?"

I wave a hand. "Oh, that's—" My refusal dies off when my brain snags on one little word she used.

Friend.

Warmth blooms in my chest and in my cheeks.

I don't know if I've ever had a friend.

"No, it's not okay. I'm celebrating tonight, and if you don't have a drink, you can't properly get in on the toast."

I laugh at her honesty. "Okay. Billy, please make me something fruity."

With a chuckle, the bartender slides the disgusting concoction away from me, but my new friend stops her. "Wait, Hannah is on her way. She'll drink that."

Shrugging, the woman steps away and gets to work making a drink partway down the bar.

"What's your name?"

"Ava. And you're...?"

"Besides your new best friend?" She teases with a big smile. "I'm Sara."

Best friend? Giddiness bubbles up inside me. Maybe I'm too old to get this excited, but I'm relishing it, nonetheless. "And what are you celebrating?"

Billy returns, this time bringing a drink adorned with a pretty little umbrella just like Sara's. She doesn't walk away. Instead, she studies me, as if waiting for me to take a sip. So I bring the glass to my lips and savor the fruity flavor.

Sara beams like she knew I would like it. "My friend Hannah— who is perpetually late—and I got promoted today."

"That's amazing. What do you do?"

"We work in PR for Langfield Corp. She handles the Boston Revs, and I work with the hockey team."

Excitement rattles through my bones, and my spine snaps straight. "I just got hired by the Langfields."

Her eyes go wide, and she slaps a hand to the bar. "Oh my god. Shut up!"

I giggle. This girl is too much, but in the best way. I've never met someone who shows her every emotion so freely. She's loud, energetic, and kind.

She's a Carrie. I can feel it. My sister would love her.

"Yes, I'll be working in the charitable relations department."

Though I'm from halfway across the country and not very familiar with sports in general, I recognized the Langfield name when I received the email in response to the application my sister filled out for me. They're well-known all over the US, and probably in other countries, and not just because of the five gorgeous Langfield siblings—four of whom are single—or because they have more money than the royal family. No, I was familiar with them because of their charity work.

The Langfields donate an obscene amount to medicine yearly. Especially children's hospitals that specialize in cancer research.

Working for them is a dream I would never have even considered. One that, if I think too hard on, may make me burst into tears.

"Oh my gosh. Your office is on the same floor as mine." Sara squeals. "This is going to be so amazing."

"What's amazing?" A woman appears on Sara's other side, settling on a stool and plopping her clutch down on the bar. Her wavy hair is a lush chocolate brown, and her almond-shaped blue eyes are fanned by the longest lashes I've ever seen. Just above her lip is a small Cindy Crawford–type beauty mark. Her clutch is Louis Vuitton, and her shoes are Louboutin, making her quite possibly the coolest person I've ever seen. "I could just about kill Damiano right now, so I could really use good news. Oh, and please tell me that drink is mine."

She reaches over Sara and slides the dirty martini down the bar. She takes one long sip before plucking the stick of olives out of the glass and biting one off.

With a sigh, she finally turns her attention to us, smiles, and holds out her hand. "Hi, I'm Hannah."

Now *she's* a total Samantha. Immediately, I love her.

"This is Ava," Sara says, her voice infused with excitement. "And she's just accepted a job with the Langfields."

"Please tell me you're not Beckett's new nanny." The woman hits me with a glare I don't understand.

Sara rolls her eyes. "She's working in charitable relations. Besides, we all know Beckett is too much of a control freak to have a nanny."

Hannah bites off the other olive. "That man is the bane of my existence. If you don't know it yet, he's as controlling as they come." She says this directly to me. "Owning the baseball team isn't enough. He has to micromanage all of us too."

"He's a little better now that he's fallen in love with Liv." Sara turns toward me. "Liv is our boss." She waves between herself and Hannah. "She's the best. She and Beckett got married in Vegas a few months ago." She leans in closer, her eyes darting around, as if to confirm she won't be overheard. "Between you and me, I'm pretty sure it was a drunken mistake, but god, is that man gone for her."

Hannah's lips turn up, the expression a little sardonic. "Thank god for that. He's finally letting that poor woman stay home with her kids rather than travel with the Revs to every away game. Drunken mistake or not, that Vegas wedding means I'm officially the new Liv."

"And I'm the other new Liv." Sara shimmies her shoulders. "So where are you living?"

"Um," I hedge. I just met these women. Should I be giving up that kind of information? If they're my coworkers, it's okay, right? "At 2018 Langfield Way."

Sara bounces so exuberantly she almost slides off her stool. "Ah, she's our neighbor too. It's nice, right?"

"If you don't mind all the Neanderthals in the gym in the morning," Hannah drawls.

That comment instantly sends my mind whirling to my interaction several hours ago. To Tyler.

The best thing about the apartment, other than it being rent-free, is the gym. And not because I'm huge on exercise. No, the best part about it was the studio in the back. The room with mirrors and a beautiful waxed floor with the long barre along the edge.

A spot to dance.

For years, ballet was my only solace.

After two lonely days where I constantly questioned my decision to move to Boston, discovering the quiet room felt like a sign that I'm exactly where I'm meant to be.

I immediately texted my sister a picture of the space, then I found the right playlist and lost myself for over an hour. Until I looked up and saw the man with piercing blue eyes. Eyes I instantly wanted to study for hours so I could describe their shade exactly. He wore black fitted sweats and a tight black T-shirt that showcased the most defined body I'd ever seen. And tattoos. So many tattoos.

Despite being alone with a stranger, a sense of calm settled over me. It was clear he'd been watching me, yet it didn't scare me.

Maybe it was because I'd been doing the one thing I loved. Maybe it was because I had promised myself that this year would be different. That I would be different. I'd take risks. Take chances.

Whatever the motivation, I didn't sink into myself. Instead, I channeled my inner Samantha and held strong, not giving an inch even while I knew he would take a mile.

"See something you like?"

The man's lips curved up into a lascivious smirk that made my skin heat beneath my white leotard. I didn't allow myself to cower as he surveyed me. He'd already checked out my ass, that much I knew. With the way the leotard cut high on my thighs, he probably got an eyeful. And if he looked down, he'd probably see my nipples pebbling against the thin fabric.

"Very much so."

"They're not Neanderthals, they're hockey players." Sara's voice interrupts my memory.

Blinking rapidly, I lean forward. "Hockey players?"

Hannah sighs. "Yeah. They only occupy four floors, but they act like they own the building."

"Four floors is more than enough for me," Sara chirps.

My heart stutters. Oh god. Tyler couldn't be...he didn't seem...oh no. He so did seem like a hockey player. The muscles. The cockiness. The swagger.

A lump forms in my throat, making it hard to speak, but I force the words out anyway. "They live in the building with us?" I knew the deal was too good to be true.

Sara shrugs. "Yeah, but they aren't so bad."

"Says the woman who has stacks of NDAs at the ready and has to catch all the puck bunnies on their way out of the building." Hannah waves down the bartender to order another drink, totally unfazed.

Meanwhile my stomach roils with dread.

"That's why the Langfields put us up there too. To keep tabs. Not that our presence deters them. But also to fill in the apartments they might otherwise lease to people not connected to Langfield Corp. The whole non-fraternization thing keeps the guys from sleeping with their neighbors."

Sara tips her glass at Hannah. "I think that went out the window when Beckett married Liv."

Hannah snorts. "You think we play by the same rules as Beckett Langfield?"

Sara lowers her chin a fraction, focusing on her drink while she shifts in her seat. Hmm. Curious. Maybe, like me, she's found herself interested in someone in the building.

God. *Interested in someone in the building.* We flirted. He pinned me against the mirror. I may have fantasized about his lips touching mine, even while I defiantly told him I wasn't that type of girl.

Then he asked me to meet him for dinner.

Here.

He asked me to meet him for dinner, and since I didn't want to give him my number or tell him where I lived—I've watched enough *Dateline* with my sister to know better—I agreed to meet him at the bar at seven.

I glance down at my phone, and instantly, my heart sinks. The 7:45 blinks up at me innocently.

I've been stood up.

"Want to grab a table?" Sara asks, standing. "We can tell you all about the players and the guys we work with. Gotta make sure you know who to stay away from."

Hannah slides off her chair. "Tyler Warren. Remember that name.

The man is beautiful. All he has to do is look at you, and you'll be pregnant, but he's the biggest player on the team."

My stomach knots painfully in response, but I force a smile to my face. Looks like I dodged a bullet. And I made friends. So although I've been stood up for what should have been my first date ever, I suppose I can chalk tonight up to a win.

War

"Did you have a date?" Brayden surveys me over the bowl of pasta I push toward him.

This isn't the first time he's asked, but now that the clock reads 7:45, I can guarantee Ava thinks I'm a supreme dickhead.

"You trying to tell me I look pretty?" I bat my lashes. As I dig into my own pasta, I do my best to ignore the ball of lead in my stomach. It's impossible, though, as I picture Ava sitting by herself, waiting for me.

It only now occurs to me to call the bar. Fuck, why didn't I think of that to begin with?

"You even smell like you had a date."

Despite how shitty I feel, I shoot him a grin. "You really are buttering me up. I already told you that you can stay here tonight. No need to work so hard."

With a roll of his eyes, Brayden shakes his head.

He never smiles, so I do it enough for the both of us. Kids should smile. They should also have a warm place to sleep and the love of a person who cares enough to make sure they're fed.

These aren't negotiable terms, and it enrages me that this kid doesn't have any of it.

"I'll be right back." I stand, phone in hand, and stalk to my bedroom. First I text Trisha for the fifth time in the last hour, telling her I've fed her kid and that he's staying with me for the night. Then I call the restaurant and inquire about Ava. The bartender assures me that she made friends. Two women. Thank fuck. And that they're now having dinner. I tell her to put their bill on my card and please send my apologies. I order the flaming chocolate for her, since that specific dessert is the reason I picked the restaurant for tonight.

Feeling a modicum better, I head back out to finish my dinner.

Later, I'm woken by the sound of banging. I jackknife to sitting from where I fell asleep on the couch, cursing and hoping the noise doesn't wake up Brayden. He's got school in the morning. He doesn't need this shit.

When I swing the door open, Trish is there, messy hair, smudged lipstick, hazy eyes. "Where is he?"

Her voice is scratchy from smoking, yet still too loud for the still night.

I step out into the hall and shut the door so we don't wake him. "Keep it down."

Trish pushes against my bare chest, the move weak, uncoordinated. "Don't shush me. That's my kid in there. I'll wake him up if I want to."

"Yeah, that's your kid," I hiss, anger getting the best of me, and point toward the door. "Your kid who spent the whole day wondering where his mom was because you weren't there when he woke up for school and because you never came home. *Again.* We both know you weren't working, since I'm the one paying your bills. I'm not asking where you were. Don't need to. I already know the answer. But if you can't get yourself together for him, then don't show up here and go on about him being your kid."

She throws an arm out to push me again but stumbles forward this time. I grab both her arms to steady her, hit with the stench of alcohol, cigarette smoke, and Chanel No. 5. Even as my stomach twists from the vile mixture of scents, my heart aches for her. She's an adult and she needs to have her shit together so she can take care of her son, but her husband died a few years ago, and from what I've been told by the volunteers and staff at the Y, she hasn't been the same since.

That's how I met Brayden.

When I was traded to Boston, I promised myself things would be different. I spent the off season volunteering at the YMCA, and back when Trish still worked, he spent a couple of hours after school there each day.

We became friends. Or something resembling it. Friendship for a kid who has more snark than an old man on a street corner with a cigarette looks different from what most expect. Sarcasm is his love language, so when he's an ass to me, it's because, deep down, he appreciates me. Even if he didn't, I'd show up. That's what he needs. A person in his life who's there when he needs them.

The door next to mine swings open, catching my attention as well as Trisha's. The wild red hair registers before the identity of my neighbor does. It isn't until she steps into the hall, arms wrapped around her torso, that it hits me. My mood swings like a pendulum, lifting at my sheer luck. Damn, is it really possible that the woman I'm obsessed with is my neighbor? Looks like I didn't need that number after all.

As a smile spreads across my face, hers puckers in a scowl.

That's when I remember that I'm holding on to a woman who looks like she's just been fucked. Her hands are pressed against my bare chest, and I'm gripping her upper arms, holding her in place. "It's not —" I snap my mouth shut and release my hold on Trisha. "Go inside."

The way her lips turn up makes my stomach twist. She's so drunk she actually believes I'm inviting her in. She's offered herself up on a platter more than once. Says since I'm paying her, I might as well take advantage of the perks.

Bile rises in my throat at the thought, but I take a deep breath and tamp down the reaction. Once she's inside and the door is shut, I turn to Ava.

"It's not what you think." I step toward her, hands up.

She shakes her head. "Right."

"I didn't have your number, and there was an emergency."

The laugh she lets out is louder and more sardonic than seems fitting for such an angelic-looking woman. "Yeah, an emergency."

Hot anger pulses through me. This fucking night. I lower my head and run my hand through my hair, determined to start over. "There's this kid—"

"Save your breath." She holds up her hands. "I'm working for

Langfield Corp, and I heard you're a *hockey player*." The last two words leave her like they're a curse. Like my status as a hockey player damns me in her mind.

Hands fisted at my sides, I straighten. "And?"

"And I will be handling charitable relations for the company." She lifts her chin, as if that revelation should surprise me.

"Okay?"

"So we'll be working together."

I bark out a laugh. "No. I play hockey. You work for the corporation. We do not *work* together."

"We're neighbors."

Though she probably thinks it's a deterrent, that fact tugs a genuine smile from me. Yeah, we are.

"I kind of figured you lived in this building, since we met in the gym downstairs." I lick my lips and take another step forward.

She takes in a surprised breath, her chest expanding and her arms tightening around her torso. She's so fucking pretty it hurts.

"I'm sorry I missed our date," I rasp, taking another step. "I'd like to make it up to you."

The door to my apartment swings open, and Trish's drunken drawl interrupts us again. "Tyler, are you coming to bed?"

Ava winces, her eyes falling shut.

"Fuck." I squeeze the back of my neck and temper my aggravation. "It's *not* what you think."

She's already backing toward her door. "Like I said, we work together. We're neighbors—"

I follow, trying to block out her excuses. "I'm not saying it's perfect, but nothing worth it ever comes easy."

She looks past me, the move spurring me to do the same. When I glance over my shoulder, I discover Trish leaning against my doorframe wearing nothing but a bra and panties. Fucking A.

"You're not worth it." Ava's words strike me exactly as she intended. Then she's gone, leaving me standing in the hall, fists balled, heart flayed open.

She's not the first person to tell me that, and I doubt she'll be the last.

TEXT MESSAGES FROM AVA'S AND TYLER'S PHONES

THE LAST TWO YEARS...

Ava: Hi, Sis. Well, my first and only date was a complete dud. Not only did the guy stand me up, but I found out he's my next-door neighbor, and then I caught him sneaking another woman into his apartment when I got home. On the plus side, I made friends. I start work today. Wish me luck!

Sara: Hi, this is Sara, your new best friend! Save my number.

Ava: Haha. Hi, Sara! Saved.

Sara: Great. Good luck on your first day. I'll try to stop by your office before lunch. If you're free, we should grab something.

Ava: That would be amazing.

A few months later

Brooks: War, we're supposed to be at the charity event in five minutes. You picking me up still?

Aiden: War, where you at?

Hall: No worries, War. I told the sweet new redhead I'd take your spot.

Bray: Thanks for picking me up from practice. I'm sorry you had to miss your thing.

Tyler: You never have to apologize. Glad I got to spend time with you.

Several months later

Ava: Hi, Sis. Can you believe I've been at Langfield Corp for a full year already? We have an event at the Y today. Ten bucks says Tyler Warren is a no-show. God, that man drives me nuts. He rarely shows up for any of the things he's assigned to, and when he does, he's late.

Unknown number: Hello, Vicious. I'm going to be late.

Ava: Who is this?

Unknown number: Your favorite hockey player.

Ava: I don't have a favorite hockey player.

Unknown number: Aw, don't hurt my feelings. I can admit you're my favorite Langfield Corp. employee.

Unknown number: And if I'm not your favorite, then why do I catch you staring at me every time we go out with our friends?

Ava: No idea who you are or what you're talking about, but I have a job to do.

Ava: Also, how did you get my number?

Unknown number: Your bestie Sara gave it to me.

Ava: I'll kill her.

War: So you do know who I am. Don't worry, Vicious, I won't call you unless I need you. But feel free to use this number whenever you want.

Ava: Why would I ever want to call you?

A week later

Brooks: That was the worst game of truth or dare I've ever played.

War: LOL

Brooks: I can't laugh. My dick hurts too much

Aiden: I still can't believe you chose to get your dick pierced over admitting why you missed the charity event at the Y.

War: You chose to get your dick pierced rather than admit why you hate shamrocks.

Brooks: I think we can all agree, since we now have bars through our dicks, that we won't speak of what we didn't admit to.

War: Like how you're a virgin saving yourself for Sara?

Aiden: Do your dicks look bigger now, or do you think mine's just swollen?

A few months later

War: You're staring at me again.

Ava: I am not staring at you.

War: I'm not going home with her.

Ava: Go home with whomever you want. And stop texting me. You're sitting right across from me, and your date looks bored.

War: She's not my date.

Bray: Hey Ty, my mom still isn't home.

Tyler: I'll be right there.

Ava: You and your not-date sure did disappear quickly last night.

A few months later

Tyler: Want to come with me to see Josie tonight?

Bray: Yeah, practice ends at six.

Tyler: I'll pick you up.

This Past Summer

Tyler: I bought a house.

Fitz: What?

Tyler: I'll call you when I drop off Bray. I think I figured out how to get everything I want.

Ava: Hi, Sis. I met someone! You were right. When you stop looking, it just happens. I'm so glad you pushed me to move to Boston. I can't believe it's been two years. I miss you so much. But I truly think this is where I'm supposed to be.

CHAPTER 2
TYLER

Brooks: You're late, and your favorite redhead is pissed.

Aiden: It amazes me how you bring out this side of her. To the rest of us, it doesn't exist.

Hall: If you tell me it's because you're finally getting laid, I'll tell Ava it's my fault.

Brooks: LOL

Aiden: You're sick, Hall.

Aiden: By the way, Lex screens my texts, so she's def going to read this.

Brooks: LOL. Lennox just up and smacked Aiden on the back of the head.

WITH A HUFF, I slip my phone into my pocket. I love my teammates, and I'm fortunate enough to consider them friends. Brooks Langfield, our goalie, specifically. The guy has stuck with me since college. He's quiet and levelheaded most of the time, and up until he met his fiancée, Sara, he didn't so much as look at women. His focus was fixed solely on hockey.

His younger brother Aiden is our center and one of the greatest players the NHL has ever seen. He recently reconnected with his ex-girlfriend, Lennox Kennedy—*yes, of the Boston Kennedys. Known for Kennedy Records, Kennedy Diamonds, Kennedy Properties*—and they didn't waste any time getting married. She may be American royalty, but she's down-to-earth and a blast to be around. Best of all, she keeps Aiden truly smiling. He's one of the best guys I know, and he's always building up the people around him, but behind his happy-go-lucky personality, he battles bouts of depression. It makes me happy to know he's got an amazing wife in his corner.

Then there's Daniel Hall. He's a winger like me. He, Aiden, and I—the first line—spend a lot of time together. Outside of team practice, we put in extra time on the ice, working on our own plays. And if we're not at Bolts Arena, we're texting. Since Hall came to the NHL, he's been my go-to guy when I want to go out. The boy is never not down for a good time. But my priorities have changed over the last few months, and he's been nagging me about not being around as much.

Hence the comment about getting laid. That's another thing I haven't done in a long-ass time.

I don't miss it nearly as much as I thought I would.

I'm going to need to tell them the real reason I've been avoiding going out. I can't even imagine their reaction—how I've managed to keep it a secret this long is mind-*fucking*-boggling. Not a single person besides our assistant coach Fitz knows—well other than my attorney and the people involved. I haven't wanted to jinx it. Haven't wanted to get my hopes up. But this meeting could change everything.

Leg bouncing, I watch the clock, itching to get out of this office. I really am going to be late today. Not that I have a choice in the matter. This appointment is the most important thing I've got going on. Even more important than hockey. Not that Ava will understand.

Since we got off on the wrong foot two years ago, she's made it crystal clear what she thinks of me, and honestly, it's easier to let her believe it than to try to prove her wrong.

Brooks: Just a heads-up, your brother is here.

Jaw clenched, I stare at the text that comes through from my best friend. This one is in a thread between the two of us only.

That word, *brother*, rankles me. Stepbrother? Brother? In any other scenario, the distinction is insignificant to me. Family is family.

Except when Xander Warren is involved.

Yes, the dipshit took *my* father's last name. He and his mother probably cooked that up together. The list of people I genuinely hate is short, but Xander tops it.

It hasn't always been this way. When my father married his mother, we were young. Both six.

Even then, though, Dory made it clear that I was not welcome in my father's home.

So I lived in Canada with my mother and only visited Boston in the summers. Unlike most kids, I dreaded the last day of school. It meant having to leave my mother for eight weeks. It meant being stuck in a place where I knew I wasn't wanted.

My father made a killing in the stock market, but he worked long hours, and when he wasn't working, he was networking. Always out. Always traveling. Barely around, despite how little time the two of us had together.

But despite all of that, I loved him. *Love him.*

He's oblivious of the way his wife treats me and ambivalent to the way Xander does.

Maybe I should hate him too, but he's the only family I have. So in honor of that, I've worked to maintain some semblance of a relationship with Xander and Dory. Even if they couldn't care less about me.

Or I should say I tried. Nowadays, I don't make any effort at all. Unfortunately, Xander has become a fixture in my circle as of late. In a cruel twist of fate, he's dating Ava. And since she's best friends with Brooks's fiancée and Aiden's wife, it's a real mindfuck.

If I didn't despise her just as much as she despises me, I'd consider warning her. But fuck it. They deserve each other.

As the door to the conference room swings open and my attorney appears with a smile on her face, my anxiety eases slightly. "Did she sign?"

"She did. Once she confirmed that the money had been transferred, of course."

Head hung, I punch my fist into my hand and blow out a breath. "Thank fuck."

Stepping up in front of me so I'm forced to look up, Madi narrows her dark eyes. "Don't get ahead of yourself. You have a long road ahead of you. And if you're going to be a dad, you need to watch the language."

A dad. *Fuck.* I can't believe I'm really going to be a dad.

On autopilot, I shoot her my signature smirk. "Come on, who could say no to this face?"

All she gives me in response is an arched brow. Madison Scott is not easily influenced. A few years ago, she married movie star Duncan Scott in what can only be described as the biggest scandal to ever hit Hollywood. The woman is basically immune to my charm, and that's exactly why I hired her. I don't need a yes-woman. I need the best of the best, and I need a woman to give it to me straight. Fortunately, she's both.

"You're a single thirty-two-year-old man who travels for ten months out of the year and is known for getting into fights on the ice. You aren't exactly the ideal candidate for adoptive father of not one, but *three* kids."

Her harsh words are like a slap. Damn. "I've got Maria to help, and Brayden is like a built-in babysitter." Maria is a nurse I hired because one of the children I'm trying to adopt, Josie, is a cancer survivor and spent a good chunk of her little life in the hospital. Outside of me and Bray, Maria is another stable person in Josie's life. That should count for something, right?

Madi seems unmoved by this though, continuing on in her explanation of just how difficult this adoption will be. "And Josie has spent a big chunk of her nine years on this earth in a hospital. She's been abandoned by not only her birth mother, but her foster parents. She needs stability." Madi's lips pull down in genuine sympathy. "Scarlett's only two. She'll keep you on your toes, she may be yours now, but this entire situation is an uphill battle. I don't want you getting your hopes up."

Straightening, I cross my arms over my chest. "I never get my hopes up." I don't. I'm an eternal pessimist. In my experience, if something can go wrong, it will. Not one aspect of my life has been easy. Nothing has gone according to plan. But in comparison to what Josie has been through? What I've experienced has been a walk in the park. Between the four of us—Brayden, Josie, Scarlett, and me—I figure we've earned a little good luck by now. I blow out a breath. "But Scarlett and Bray are mine now, right? A judge will want to keep all the siblings together."

It's wishful thinking. I know this. I met Josie at a charity event last Christmas. Everyone at Langfield Corp knows her. She was diagnosed with lymphoma sixteen months ago, and when her foster parents received the news, they left her at the hospital. As in, they walked away and never came back.

The thought of her spending her days and nights alone in a hospital at only eight fucking years old made me sick for weeks. I could relate in a way, though my experience was completely different. It was just me and my mom, and she was the one that was sick, but I was still alone in that hospital. And after she died...

My jaw hardens. This isn't about me. It's about Josie.

After I met her, I wanted more than anything to cheer her up, to take away some of the loneliness, but I worried that visiting a little girl on my own would look weird.

So I brought Brayden along.

And week after week, I fell more in love with her.

Despite all the hardships she's faced, Josie is filled with optimism. She radiates a goodness, a purity, so rare and special. And fuck, is she funny. The girl reminds me so much of my mom. Smiling through the pain, laughing through the hard days.

Within weeks, I was hiring an attorney and working out plans to adopt her.

But what Madi said to me today? It's the same thing she told me a year ago. I'm single, I'm a hothead and I'm a hockey player. In other words, I'm not a good bet.

I'm not worth it.

Maybe it's true, but it never sat well with me. I don't have a family.

Josie doesn't have a family. I would move heaven and earth to be the person she can rely on. To give her a warm bed, food, and whatever medical care she needs. What else could possibly matter?

After Madi gave me the hard truth about my odds, I set out to find her birth mother, hoping that she could help me get custody of Josie. I knew she was only sixteen when she relinquished her rights, so I assumed—naïvely, of course—that she'd done it because she wanted a better life for her daughter. That when she learned that her little girl was all alone in the world, she'd jump at the chance to help.

I was proven wrong by yet another woman.

Krista Sternoff is no better than Brayden's mother, Trisha.

When I first found Krista, I was sure I could convince her to help me. She was living in an almost bare studio apartment with her two-year-old daughter, Scarlett, sleeping on a mattress on the floor. That was this past summer. After that, I gave up my apartment in the hockey building and vowed to dedicate the rest of my life to these kids. I bought a house in the hopes of moving everyone in. Brayden, Trisha, Krista and her two kids. I paid for food and clothing and every other necessity. All I asked was that Krista stay sober and be a mother to Josie and Scarlett. I knew the situation wouldn't be perfect, but it was the only way I could come up with that could guarantee Josie, Brayden, and Scarlett would be safe and cared for. That's when I hired one of Josie's nurses, Maria, to move in with us. To be a support and comfort to Josie during the transition.

Krista lasted three weeks.

I was in Denver for an away game when Maria called to tell me that Krista had gone out to the grocery store and hadn't come home.

She reappeared a week later.

For a week, she didn't check in on her kids. She didn't call to let us know she was okay. No, she chose to spend that week high or drunk or god knows what.

The next day, I had Madi draw up an offer I didn't think she'd refuse.

I was right.

For fifty grand, Krista signed over her rights to Scarlett.

The process of adopting Josie is much more complicated. Krista hadn't regained her parental rights to Josie before she took off, so we're back to square one with her.

For now, I'm fostering with the hope of adopting, but because I travel so much, it's an uphill battle.

"Yes, judges typically want to keep siblings together, but Josie and Scarlett have just met, and Brayden isn't their biological sibling. He's not even yours. You're his guardian and nothing more."

A mixture of pain and relief washes through me at that last statement. I made Trisha the same offer I made Krista, but Trisha chose rehab over signing over her rights to Brayden. As much as I want to be Bray's dad, I'm impressed that she's willing to do the work to be a better mother. I'll gladly pay for the most expensive rehab facility if it means Brayden has a shot at a sober mother.

In the meantime, I'm the closest thing he has to a parent, and he and Josie have bonded over the last year. We're a family of strays, sure, but we're still a family, and I'd do anything to stay together.

"Is there anything I can do to sway the judge?"

Madi's eyes bulge, and she takes a step back. "Like bribing him?"

"Fuck no," I huff, my leg bouncing again. "Something legal."

Her shoulders sag instantly. "Oh. Well, providing more stability at home would go a long way. Another parental figure would be ideal, but since you're single, a long-term nanny could work." She hums, lips pursed. "Though I think it's a bit too late for that."

Irritation oozes through me like poison seeping into my bloodstream. "How could it be too late? I've barely had a minute to wrap my head around becoming a dad, let alone get shit set up." I'm trying hard to do the right thing, but jumping through the hoops the courts create is a fucking full-time job. One would think they'd be on board with the idea of giving Josie a home so she doesn't have to remain in the hospital. That they'd happily allow a person she knows and trusts to adopt her rather than placing her with strangers.

Even if I had to hire a nanny, Josie would still have her sister, Brayden, and Maria. And I'd be there as often as I could. It's so un-fucking-fair. I'm trying to do the right thing, and still, it isn't enough.

I shouldn't be surprised, though. That is literally the story of my life.

"You've got months until the hearing, and even then, as long as you can show the judge that Josie has a stable home life and is fed and taken care of, you will remain her foster parent while the process of adoption continues."

She clears her throat and straightens further, clearly gearing up for a come to Jesus moment. She gives me these kinds of lectures often. I appreciate them as much as I despise them. Because they always give me the push I need. So I sit silently and wait.

"But," she finally begins, the single word terse, "no fights. No bars. No random women. Stay out of the press, Tyler."

I grind my teeth, biting back the urge to say *I've been doing that for months*. More than months. Since I met Brayden, I've worked to set a good example for him. Going so far as to give up my apartment in the city and buy the house in the suburbs so the kids could attend better schools and have privacy and a place to call their own.

I don't go out. I don't fuck random women. I've settled down. *I'm boring*. I'm practically an old married man. Just don't have a wife.

With the exception of Daniel Hall—who's still a baby at only twenty-four and just beginning his hockey career—my friends have settled down too.

In a surprising twist of events, Coach named me captain this season. I can't imagine he would have done that if he couldn't see all the ways I'd made changes. It feels good, knowing that one person believes I'm worth it.

Now I have to get the court to agree.

"Got it. No bars. No booze. No fights. Now," I say, my tone turning sardonic, "if I can find a woman willing to be a mother to the kids, I'll be golden."

Shrugging, Madi says, "A wife would be ideal, but yeah, you get the point."

I laugh at the absurdity of her statement. A wife? Where the hell would I find one of those?

Chapter 3
Ava

I LOVE everything about my job as head of charity relations for Langfield Corp.

With one enormous exception: Tyler Freaking Warren. The man all of Boston calls War because of his propensity to start fights on the ice.

The guys may be a rowdy bunch, but they're all invested in making Boston a better place. They were here on time, and they're lined up on the ice, ready to start their game for the charity skate. All but one, naturally.

War is nowhere to be found. I shouldn't be surprised.

I rarely deal with the players unless it's for charity events like this one. But every time the team is set to appear, he saunters in late.

His life, his priorities, and mainly his dick take center stage.

I hate him for being such a conceited asshole, and I hate myself even more for letting him get under my skin in a way no one else ever has.

Since the night he stood me up two years ago, I've seen the person Hannah warned me about time and again. Gone was the Tyler that sweet talked me in the gym, the man who's blue eyes glittered with what I saw as hope and possibility. In his place was War, the egotistical fuckboy that makes me want to pull out my hair. Living next door to him and hearing him come in at all hours of the night, aware that he was likely out with a different woman every time, has only helped me forget the odd encounter we had when we met. And if we run into each other when we're out—which, unfortunately, happens often since we share the same group of friends—he'll smirk right before he disappears, like he wants me to know that he's about to find another woman interested in his fuckboy ways.

I don't normally curse—I barely raise my voice—but for War, even if it's only in my mind, I make an exception.

The man drives me absolutely mad.

"Have you heard from Josie?"

I practically jump out of my skin at the question. It was harmless enough, of course, but I was so in my head that I didn't see Beckett Langfield approach. The billionaire eyes me like I'm being dramatic as he waits for my answer.

"Not since you asked yesterday." I pull my phone from my pocket and check my notifications.

Still nothing from Maria.

Brow furrowed, Beckett nods. "Let me know the minute you do." With that, he buttons his suit jacket and strides away, heading toward the bench where I assume he'll watch the game with his brother Gavin, the head coach of the Boston Bolts.

"It was nice seeing you, Becks," Sara calls from beside me.

On her other side, her best friend Lennox snorts. Lennox is married to Beckett's brother Aiden, and Sara is engaged to Brooks. With Lennox now working with me in the charitable relations office, just about all of my friends work for Langfield Corp.

Beckett doesn't turn. He doesn't even slow his stride.

"Rude," Lennox grumbles.

Beckett Langfield may come across as the grumpiest of the billionaire brothers, but he holds a special place in my heart. Though the world really only sees the scowl and crossed arms, he's actually one of the most tender-hearted people I know. And he's been my favorite Langfield since the day he introduced me to Josie, a little girl who stole my heart a year ago.

Beckett is one of a very few people in Boston who know my family history. And because of that knowledge, he came to me with an idea to have an event at Boston Children's Hospital and gave me an unlimited budget.

That night, the two of us met Josie, a little girl who had just been diagnosed with lymphoma. Her foster parents had recently abandoned her at the hospital, yet she was joy personified. It took all the strength I had to leave that room that night. The idea of her being alone, having no one, gutted me.

Beckett sat with me until she fell asleep, and then he turned a blind eye while I cried in the back of his town car the whole way home.

The next day, he called me into his office, gave me a credit card, and told me to visit Josie as often as I wanted, on the clock or off it. To bring her treats, clothing, toys, books. Anything she wanted. Anything that would make her stay just a little easier. For months, I spent every free minute I had in Josie's hospital room.

Sundays were extra special, because my girlfriends would come with me after Sunday brunch. We'd play games, watch movies, order dinner, and stay until she was ready for bed.

In July, Josie was reunited with her birth mother, and although I'm hopeful that this is the best scenario for her, it has gutted me. I haven't seen her in almost six months, and each time someone asks me about her, like Beckett just did, I have to fight back tears. Because the only connection I have with her is through Maria.

She can't tell me much because of HIPAA, but apparently she's been authorized to at least let me know that Josie is happy and healthy, which is all I can truly hope for.

A round of cheers erupts, snagging my attention and pulling me from my depressing thoughts. On the ice, the kids attending the event, all from the YMCA, are pointing and screaming at none other than Tyler Freaking Warren, skating onto the ice. *Late.*

Add that to the long list of his annoying attributes.

Everyone loves him.

It baffles me. The guy can't bother to show up on time and has done nothing but cause fights on the ice for the last few years—he's more than earned the nickname War—yet Gavin named him captain this season. Not only that, but Brooks—who is one of the most down-to-earth, genuine people I've ever met—swears he's one of the best guys he knows. And the kids? They go crazy for him at every one of these events.

It makes no sense.

Aiden Langfield is the goofy nice guy who sings on the ice, and he's a god on skates. So I get why everyone loves him.

War, on the other hand, isn't even nice. He's broody and has a chip on his shoulder. Why the hell is everyone so obsessed?

I know it sounds like I'm obsessed with him too, but I'm not. I'm just perplexed.

Gavin makes a big show of dropping the puck, and War goes straight for Aiden. Rather than kids versus Bolts, the teams are made up of equal numbers of both.

I cheer a little too loudly when Aiden breaks away, leaving War in the dust, then passes the puck to a kid who heads toward Brooks at a pretty decent speed.

Aiden stays by his side the entire way, protecting him from the kids on the opposing team who are trying to catch him. The other players, including War, hang back, giving him a chance. Because of the way they play things, it's now the kid versus Brooks. Of course my money is on Brooks. He's the best goalie in the league, after all. But to my surprise, Brooks practically dives *out* of the way, allowing the puck to slide into the goal.

Beside me, Sara hums, the sound one of pride, and on the ice, the players on both teams cheer. War skates toward the kid at lightning speed and practically knocks him over with a hug like he normally gives Aiden or Daniel when they score.

Odd.

"God, I love this game," Sara says beside me as I ignore the hint of warmth blooming in my chest.

My phone buzzes in my pocket, and I jump for it, hoping it's the phone call I've been waiting for. I deflate a second later when I realize it's just my boyfriend.

> Xander: How long is this thing going to last? I'm starving.

I search the stands and spot him in the crowd before I respond. The Langfields are catering a dinner for all the kids and their families upstairs in the suites after the game. And while staff was invited, there was no mention of whether it was acceptable to bring plus-ones, so it feels wrong to invite my boyfriend along. I told him that, but he showed up anyway. He tends to do that any time the players will be in my proximity. As if he needs to be involved when his stepbrother is present. Why, I haven't quite figured out. They hate each other, and outside of these events, they don't talk. Thank god for that. If Xander had an actual relationship with Tyler Warren, I don't think I could continue my relationship with him.

How I ended up dating a man who is even tangentially related to Tyler Warren, I'll never know. The universe clearly has a sick sense of humor.

We've only been dating for about six months, but I think I can see a future with him. Honestly, his worst attribute is his relation to the bane of my existence. And his slight obsession with him.

Me: I'll be stuck here for a few hours at least. Want me to meet you at your place?

Xander: Aren't they having food at this thing?

Me: Yeah, for the kids and their families, but not until later.

"Oh my god. He's going to score again," Lennox yells.

I snap my head up just as the boy scores on Brooks a second time.

This celebration is similar to the first. All the Bolts players cheer and skate around him in celebration. But unlike the last time, War lifts the kid onto his shoulder, then he skates around the rink, hollering and grinning. The kid isn't small, either. He's got to be at least fourteen, and on skates, he's probably taller than I am, but War doesn't struggle in the slightest.

My cheeks heat at the sight. Embarrassed that Tyler Warren has any effect on me, I turn away. "I'm going to see if the families need anything," I say to my friends as I shuffle in the other direction. The farther I can get from Tyler Warren, the better.

Just as I step away from the ice, my phone buzzes in my hand. This time, it *is* Maria. I practically float out of the arena and into the hallway. It's a text notification, but I'm hopeful that she has finally gotten the okay from Josie's mother for at least a FaceTime.

Once I'm alone and in the quiet hall, I unlock my phone to read the text. But the moment I do, my stomach tumbles.

> Maria: Hey, can you stop by the hospital tonight? Josie and I are here.

Chapter 4
Ava

"TAKE A DEEP BREATH," Sara says from my side, her hand in mine, as she guides me down the hall on the pediatric floor. Hannah is on my other side, but as the nurses' station comes into view, she marches over, demanding to know which room Josie is in. She's unflappable under pressure. A true Samantha.

Lennox stayed back at the event to keep things running, but she made us promise to call her the second we find out what's going on. I barely made it back to show them the text without breaking down. There was no way I could have driven myself here.

My chest tightens painfully. God, what if the cancer is back?

Sara tugs on my hand. "Don't. We aren't thinking worst-case scenarios right now. We'll have answers shortly."

With a harsh breath in, forcing my lungs to expand, I nod. In the last two years, these women have come to mean everything to me. Though I keep much to myself, they love me anyway, and they can always sense what I need.

Hannah, still all business, strides back to us. "She's in her old room." From her dark tone, it's clear she's just as concerned about that detail as I am.

Yes, I miss Josie and ache to hold her in my arms again. But if I had to choose between seeing her or guaranteeing she never had to set foot in a hospital again, I'd somehow survive without her.

Movement at the door of her room snags my attention. Maria. Her appearance has always reminded me of Kris Jenner. Her dark pixie cut, much like the rest of her, screams that she's all business. Like she has little time to worry about things as trivial as blow-drying long hair. She's got kids with cancer to worry about. It makes everything else seem so unimportant.

I pull free of Sara's hold and rush toward my old friend as she exits Josie's room. Before I'm halfway to her, she's speaking, her tone reassuring. "It's not the cancer. She's okay." She catches me and gives my arms a comforting squeeze before I can dart past her into the room. "Take a breath."

I sag in relief at the news. "Why is she here?"

With what looks like exasperation, Maria shakes her head and pushes her glasses up. The move exposes the gray hairs at her temples. It's only been a few months, but she looks older, more tired. Rather than her typical scrubs, she's wearing a sweater and jeans. "I swear the girl lives to push my buttons. She took a tumble out on the pond while skating and needed stitches. They're monitoring her for a concussion, though it doesn't look likely."

Tipping to one side, I peer past her. I won't truly believe she's okay until I see her.

"*Ava*," she yells from her room.

A smile finds my lips at the sound of her sweet voice.

Maria gently pushes me toward the door. "Go. She missed you. We can talk after."

I have to hold back a sob when I see my favorite little girl for the first time in far too long. Her freckled face is bright and lit with a mega-watt smile. Her shoulder-length strawberry-blond hair is a mess, but her eyes are dancing. Standing at the foot of her bed, I assess her, searching for the stitches. But when she sits up from where she's been reclined on her pillow and holds her arms out, I dash to the bed and throw my arms around her, careful not to squeeze too tight.

"God, I missed you," I whisper, trying like hell not to cry.

That was my sister's number one rule when we were kids. No

crying. Focusing on the bad did no one any good. If we're breathing, we're smiling.

From day one, I've followed that rule with Josie. Breakdowns are saved for outside this hospital room.

I pull back to study her, cupping her cheeks. My heart is lighter just being in this girl's presence. Knowing she's okay after that scare only makes the moment sweeter.

She beams up at me. "I missed you too."

"But you're happy? Everything's okay?"

The bravest little girl I've ever met smiles. "I'm great. I have the best home on a lake, and I have a little sister and an older brother. And Tyler. He wants to be our dad."

Before I can process her words, there's a thundering voice in the hallway. *"Where is she?"* Then a man is rushing into the room, interrupting the peace that has settled over me. He doesn't acknowledge me, and I couldn't form a word if I tried. Instead, I watch as Tyler Warren settles on the bed beside Josie as if he is entitled to be in her proximity, making the mattress dip with his weight.

"Hey, fighter." He grasps her arms and looks her over, his brows pulled low and his jaw rigid. "I'm sorry I wasn't there. I was on the ice, but as soon as I heard, I rushed here. How are you feeling?"

Josie's smile grows. "Good. I got to see Ava. *My Ava.*"

In response to her pure joy, War's face relaxes, all those sharp features softening in a way I've never seen. Then he does the most unexpected thing. He smiles, his entire face lighting up. Like her happiness brings him happiness.

"What is happening?" I whisper, my heart lodged in my throat.

Finally, the only person I've ever truly despised turns to me, as if he's only now realizing he has an audience. His smile slips, and his face morphs into an unreadable mask.

"This is Tyler," Josie says. "Like I told ya, he wants to be my dad."

CHAPTER 2
TYLER

GREEN EYES GROW WIDE, and all the color drains from Ava's face. Knowing her, she wants to scream or lash out. Tell Josie that I'd make the absolute worst father.

By some miracle, though, she swallows that inclination and instead forces a fake smile.

How does no one else see it? The duplicitous woman has everyone fooled. Innocent Ava. Sweet Ava. Angelic Ava. Or Josie's personal favorite, *my Ava*.

She talks about her all the time. She always has.

I knew the two of them were close, but judging by Ava's reaction, she is only now discovering my relationship with her.

While a rational person may be bothered by that, for some reason I enjoy watching Ava squirm.

"Where are these stitches?" I ask, working hard to ignore the woman gaping at us.

Josie spins her head to the side, showing me the spot still matted with blood behind her ear where a line of stitches falls just outside her hair line. Thank fuck. She would not be smiling if they'd had to shave her hair. Girl has been yapping about how long it's grown since she left this hospital room last.

"You know better than to skate when I'm not home."

"I told her to wait for you," Maria chimes in from the door. "I was putting Scarlett down for a nap, and when I came back, expecting to find this one where I left her, watching *Zombies* for the sixtieth time, she was nowhere to be found."

Scarlett. My heart plummets. "Where's Scarlett?" Fuck, this day keeps getting worse.

"She's with the nurses in the playroom. She's fine." Maria waves dismissively. Of course she has everything covered. But damn, she shouldn't have to. I hired her to ensure that Josie's medical needs are taken care of. She's not a nanny, but she's the only other stable person in Josie's life, and I can't lose her. Madi's words from earlier echo like a warning through my brain.

The kids need stability. I need a person who can help me prove to the court that I can be trusted to raise them. That Josie will be safe in my care.

"You told me you'd take me to the skate with you and Bray, and then you didn't come home," Josie says softly. The girl doesn't whine. She doesn't complain. God, I almost wish she would. I wish she knew that it would be okay if she did. That she knew I wouldn't stop loving her, even if she did complain. But we've got a long way to go before she feels that safe with me.

I pull her into my chest, brushing my lips against her head. "I know. My meeting ran late, and I couldn't get back there to pick you up before I had to be at the arena. I'm sorry. But you know it isn't safe to be on the ice without me." I tap on her head. "I wear a helmet and I'm like the best skater around."

The woman hovering on the other side of the bed lets out a sarcastic huff, garnering our attention. When Josie and I look in her direction, her cheeks turn red.

It's okay, vicious one. Let everyone see you for who you really are.

"I'm sorry," Josie says, her voice barely a whisper. "Are you mad at me?"

Dipping lower, I make sure her eyes are locked with mine before I respond. "Never, fighter. Worried. Never mad."

With her tiny arms wrapped around me, she squeezes, her words muffled against my chest. "Is my mom coming?"

Dread slams into me like a freight train. Josie asks the same question every night before bed, and up until this afternoon, I held on to the tiniest sliver of hope that Krista would turn her life around and tell me to fuck myself and fuck my money. I held tight to the possibility that she would be adamantly against signing over her rights to her kids.

But I can't lie to Josie. I won't.

Lying to a child does nothing but shake their foundation. Inevitably, they find out, and any and all trust is irrevocably damaged. So even if it's like swallowing razors, I pull back and look her in the eye. "No. It's just going to be you, Scarlett, Bray, and me from here on out."

Attention lowered, she nods.

She fucking nods, her expression completely neutral.

Then she smiles and says, "Can we go home?"

It takes everything in me not to stand up and punch the wall. To not scream into the universe about how unfair this is. She doesn't cry or yell. She barely even reacts to the news that her mother isn't coming home. And that fills me with a rage so wild I worry I can't contain it. So I stand, drop one more kiss to her head, and tell her I'll go check with her doctor.

As I back away from the hospital bed, Ava moves in and wraps her arms around Josie. The way the little girl settles there, the comfort she finds as they speak in hushed tones, is beyond maddening. Because in that moment, I know exactly what she needs. And I know that I'll never deny her.

Chapter 6
Ava

JOSIE PEERS up at me as we wait for the elevator. "Do you promise to come visit me?"

From her other side, Maria nods. "I'm sure we can arrange a time to visit with Ava in the next week or so."

Relief washes over me. God, I hate that Maria is setting boundaries regarding my visits with Josie, that she has to act as a buffer between War and me. That if I want to see my girl, I'll have to do it at *Tyler Warren's* home.

How in god's name did this happen? Did I hit my head and wake up in an alternate universe? One where War almost seemed *nice*. Caring. Not toward me, of course, but toward Josie.

And the strangest part of the night? Discovering that he's trying to *adopt* her. I still can't wrap my head around the news. Maybe I really did hit my head. I must have fallen on the ice at the arena. Maybe I'm still lying there, unconscious. That's the only reasonable explanation.

Josie tugs on my hand. "I want to show you my room. It's so pretty. We have our own pond. That's where the ice-skating rink is. And we have a movie theater. It's like the one you and your sister always wanted."

Warmth rushes through me at Josie's words, at the knowledge that she remembers such a small detail about me. I've been to the house. This past summer with Xander. The home is beautiful, I remember that. After discovering that War and Xander were related that day, I was in shock and remember little else. "We'll set something up, okay?"

She throws her arms around my waist and hugs me tight. "Thank you, Ava. I love you."

Maria meets my eyes as I hold Josie close.

"I love you too." To Maria I mouth, "We need to talk."

In response, all I get is a frown and a simple nod.

I'm trying to decode her reaction when War reappears. "You ready to head home, fighter?"

At the sound of his voice, I turn, and as I do, I'm metaphorically knocked on my ass at the sight. Cuddled against Tyler's chest is a chubby little girl with the lightest of blond hair pulled back in a pony-tail. She's got her thumb in her mouth, and her blue eyes are saucers as she studies me just like I do her.

"Sissy," Josie coos, reaching for the little girl's toes. "This is my sister, Scarlett," she says, peering back at me.

War shifts, the movement making it impossible not to take him in. He obviously rushed here from the charity event. He's dressed in a button-down shirt and suit pants—the standard pregame-slash-charity event uniform—but he has no jacket, and his sleeves have been rolled up his forearms. Between the little girl he's cradling and the ink peeking out—

No, Ava. No way am I looking at Tyler Freaking Warren and thinking he's hot. He's a thorn in my side. A genuinely bad guy.

Who is adopting two little girls...

"See something you like?" That cocky son of a B taunts, his blue eyes glittering with mischief.

God, I hate him.

"She's beautiful." I pull my shoulders back, unwilling to let him rattle me. "How old is she?"

"Two," he says, just as Maria chimes in with the same response.

I use that excuse to turn toward Maria. "Could you call me once you get home and settled?"

"Yes. Thank you for coming." She pulls me into her arms and whispers, "I'll explain everything soon."

Sighing, I pull back and give her a nod. I can't imagine any kind of explanation that will make this make sense, but I'll gladly let her try.

"Wait, so you're telling me War—as in the Bolts bad boy captain and instigator—is adopting Josie?" Lennox blinks rapidly, bright eyes full of shock.

Hannah and Sara dragged me back to my apartment once War and his...family?...went their way and we went ours. Since the elevator, I've been basically catatonic. I don't remember the car ride or entering my apartment. I'm pretty sure Hannah dug my keys out of my purse, but I can't be sure.

Sara settles beside me on the couch, holding a mug out in front of me. "Made you tea."

I offer her a weak smile and pull the mug to my chest, soaking in the warmth of it.

"It was the strangest thing I've ever seen," Sara adds.

"And the hottest," Hannah says, her voice a little too loud in my small, quiet apartment. "Learned something new about myself today— I find dads *hot*. War was already the hottest guy on the team, but with his reputation, I've always sworn that I wouldn't touch him with a ten-foot pole. Now, though?" She fans her face. "After witnessing him holding a little girl in his arms? The way he was so worried about our Josie? Girls, what the hell?"

"First of all." Lennox snaps up straight. "War is *not* the hottest guy on the team."

Snorting, Sara sinks into the couch, clutching a throw pillow to her chest. "And who, pray tell, is, bestie?"

Lennox crosses one leg over the other with a huff. "Daniel Hall is the prettiest. Camden Snow has that all-American boy thing going for him. Brooks"—she rolls her eyes—"has the whole 'touch her and die' vibe down to a science, and *my husband*"—she grins at that last word— "has the star power. He flashes those pearly whites, and everyone melts—"

Hannah folds her arms across her chest. "And like I said, War is the hot one. He's got fuckboy written across his forehead. Or inked on his arms, I guess." She narrows her brown eyes on me. "Don't tell me you weren't drooling over those damn forearms."

When I stare back at her, still unable to form a coherent sentence, she smirks.

"He's hot," she continues. "Dark windswept hair, glacier-blue eyes, strong cheekbones, and don't even get me started on that mouth. His lips are biteable."

"Spoken like an author," Sara teases.

Hannah shrugs, using a hand to flip her dark hair over her shoulder.

"You interested?" Lennox tosses out.

Head dropped back, Hannah barks out a throaty laugh. "God, no. The man is a walking, talking red flag. The baseball team is full of problematic men, so I spend my days babysitting more than enough of them. I have no interest in adding another to that list. Besides, that bad boy only has eyes for our doe-eyed redhead here."

When no one so much as bats an eye in response to her statement, I gape and sputter. "Th-the man hates me."

Hannah arches a brow. "I don't see you arguing about how hot he is, though."

Heart thumping loudly in my ears, I snap, "Can we focus on how the man I hate is adopting my Josie?"

Sara drapes an arm around me and squeezes, enveloping me in her sugary scent. "She seems really happy."

Guilt and shame swamp me. She's right, and yet here I am, upset about it. "God, am I an awful person for being annoyed that he gets to adopt her?" She seemed happy, and he acted as if he legitimately cares about her. She's not in the hospital anymore. She's living with a sister I didn't even know existed and has her own bedroom. War's house is gorgeous, and he can give her anything she'd ever want.

I look around my tiny apartment, deflating. If not for the Langfields' generous compensation package, I couldn't even afford to live in a place this nice. If adopting Josie had been at all possible, I would have already been pursuing it. But I spoke to her social worker. There's no way a single woman who lives in a one-bedroom apartment with a bunch of athletes for neighbors would be approved.

Sara's grip on me tightens. "You aren't awful for loving Josie. Or missing her. Of course you wish you could be the one to adopt her, but there's no denying that you're relieved that your girl has someone in her corner, fighting as hard for her as War apparently is."

Lennox leans forward, her pink hair falling over one shoulder. "Remember when War had us all over after he moved in? God, he was adorably shy when showing me the little girl's room." She breaks out in a grin. "He swore it was decorated that way before he moved in, but he was super awkward, asking if I thought a little girl would like it. Thinking back on that moment, I don't know how I didn't see that he was the one who painted it. There were little birds on the walls just like he did for Vivi's bedroom."

I remember the day they decorated Vivi's room well. Gavin's wife Millie, who also happens to be Daniel Hall's twin sister and a good friend of mine, wasn't in the picture at the time. Gavin had just found out he had a little girl, and the guys all came over to paint while the girls and I watched Vivi. That was just another in a long string of instances where it was obvious that everyone I knew loved War. And god, was it annoying. They went on and on about his artistic abilities for days. Sure, the birds he painted on the walls to match Taylor Swift's album were adorable, but that doesn't mean he isn't a selfish, cocky, womanizing jerk.

Why am I the only one who sees how much of a jerk he really is?

It's as if they view him from a completely different lens. Rose-colored glasses that make him look like a wonderful person. Honestly? Maybe I saw a little of that today too. And I don't like it. Because that means that maybe I was wrong about him.

If he's going to be Josie's dad, then despite how hard it is to comprehend, I can't help but hope I was way off in my assessment of him. I hope more than anything that he can be the guy she deserves. Good. Caring. Loving.

I blink back tears. "She really did seem happy, didn't she?"

With murmurs of agreement, the girls crowd in close, and we spend the rest of the night cuddled together, chatting and coming up with ideas for how to spend more time with Josie now that we know she'll be part of the Bolts' family. While it isn't a perfect situation, it's more than I had before. And I'll take Josie any way I can.

CHAPTER 7
TYLER

NOT SURPRISINGLY, I came home from the hospital to a couple hundred texts from the guys. Clearly their damn women can't keep their mouths shut. Every one of them knew about Josie before I had a chance to check my messages. They came over the next morning, and over a cup of coffee—spiked with Jameson, because the conversation called for it—I told them everything.

To say they were shocked that I managed to keep this entire other life hidden from them would be an understatement. But, of course, because they're the greatest guys in the world and closer to me than my own family, they assured me that they'll be here every step of the way. They'll rib me about this forever, and I can't blame them. If I was in their position, I'd be all *what the fuck* too. Because we're more than teammates. We're brothers. I could have confided in them. They would have helped me. Now that I realize that, I won't shut them out again.

It's not a lie, though, that I didn't want to get my hopes up. Telling them somehow made it all seem more real. And if it's real, then it means I have something to lose, and like I've said before, the only luck I have is bad luck, so I didn't want to risk it.

I slip my phone back into my pocket and focus on the scene around me—one they wouldn't believe unless they were here to see it. The theme song from Disney's *Zombies* blares from the television while Josie paints Maria's nails bright pink and sings along with the music at full volume. Scarlett bounces on the floor, clapping and singing along too, though she doesn't know most of the lyrics and the ones she does know come out in an adorably garbled two-year-old language.

Bray and I are in the kitchen, watching SportsCenter with closed-captioning on since we can't hear a damn word the commentators are saying.

In other words, it's a typical Wednesday night. I'm home with my favorite people and soaking in every moment of it before I have to leave for a short stretch of away games.

When the song finally comes to an end, Bray and I let out matching sighs of relief. Then he cracks a smile. With all the changes he's been through over the last year, it would be a miracle if he smiled at all, let alone more than he used to. But he does. Like me, being part of a family has buoyed him. Even if that family is loud, more colorful than we could have imagined, and has been infiltrated by Disney and girls.

"Liam says his dad can take me to practice while you're traveling."

I give Brayden a nod. This is good. The kid is making friends. I wish I could take him to every practice. Hell, I wish I could coach his hockey team. But I'm nowhere near retiring. At thirty-two, I've still got another four years in me. Maybe more. Or maybe that's wishful thinking. Since I can't always be here, I need help getting him to his five-a.m. practices and the games throughout New England that I'll miss while playing my own. At least until he can drive himself. Hockey families live life on the road from youth to adulthood.

Yes, having a partner to share the load with would be ideal, but for a guy like me—who lost all faith in women long ago and can't help but envision meeting a woman I think is the real deal, only to discover she's a puck bunny after introducing her to my kids—a nanny is my only option.

Then again, that plan has the potential to bite me in the ass too. Because, once again, women.

Maybe I should find a Manny. That's a thing, right?

Probably, but men kind of suck too.

Clearly, I don't trust people, period. Kids are the only exception to that rule. And the Langfield brothers. And Hall. And Fitz.

Okay, I guess I trust most of my teammates. And Maria. And the Langfield women are okay too.

I've been proven wrong too many times to have faith in anyone else. Take Sebastian Lukov, my former coach, for instance. After my mom died, I was forced to move to Boston, and not long after, I met Brooks. It took a little convincing, but eventually, he talked me into meeting up for a morning skate.

At that point in my life, I hated everyone. I'd just lost my mom, and my father was busy with work and had no idea how to deal with a grieving, moody teenager. Hockey wasn't his thing. Still isn't. By then, Dory had been around for several years, and Xander followed my father around like a puppy, happy to tag along with him to the club to play pickleball or golf. My dad was far too busy with work and his own hobbies to drive me to hockey practice or the games in the Boston area and surrounding states. He'd pay for it, sure, but in his words, he wasn't my personal taxi.

My mom and I had lived on a shoestring budget, and after working long hours to make ends meet, she made sure I was at every practice and had the gear I needed. Not only that, but she never missed a game. How she did it all is still a mystery to me, but she always said that when it came to the people who matter, a person makes it work.

So when Brooks introduced me to his Uncle Seb—a former hockey pro—I kept my expectations low. At first, at least. After that first skate, when he offered to pick me up for practices, I agreed, but still kept him at arm's length. Eventually he was the one who shuttled me to all my games, though he was really doing it for Brooks and Aiden, since their own father was busy like mine. Later, when Brooks and I went to college together, I could explain away Seb's presence in my life because, once again, Brooks was there.

When I went pro and Brooks and I were drafted to different teams, Brooks to the Bolts from day one, and me to Minnesota, I figured that was the end of my relationship with Seb. Since I was no longer playing with his nephew, why would he show up? But at my first professional game, he was there. He took me out to dinner afterward to celebrate. That was the moment I finally lowered my walls and put my trust in him. The moment I finally allowed myself to believe that maybe I wouldn't be disappointed by everyone in my life.

Then last year I found out Seb had been cheating on his wife and lying to everyone we knew, and my heart broke. For a while, I held on to hope that maybe he'd lost his way and could turn things around. Redeem himself. And I stupidly held on even after he got fired and never once reached out to me, never once returned a call or text I made to him. And believe me, I tried.

I'm loyal that way. I truly thought our relationship was a real one. Solid.

But only a few weeks ago, he did some shady shit and fucked with Aiden's head, knowing the kid was suffering from depression. In that moment, all my illusions were shattered again.

So here I am, back to not trusting people.

"You think you can make it to the end of the tournament in Maine on Sunday?" Bray asks, pulling me out of my inner turmoil.

I dig my phone back out of my pocket and hold it between us so he can take a look at it with me. "I'm in Philadelphia tomorrow, then Chicago after that. But it looks like we'll be back Sunday morning, so long as we're not delayed, I should be able to get up there."

Brayden breaks into a smile but quickly squashes the expression. "Cool, cool. I mean, it's no big deal if you can't."

Fuck, it makes my chest ache, watching him gear himself up for disappointment. I work hard to be transparent in hopes of not crushing him when plans have to change. There are times, unfortunately, when I can't help it. My job is extremely demanding, especially now that I'm captain. But like my mom, I make an effort for the people who matter. So for him, I'll always try my best.

I wrap an arm around him and squeeze his shoulder. "I want to be there, Bray."

He's begrudgingly accepting the affection when my phone buzzes and Madi's name flashes on the screen.

"I gotta grab this." Standing, I swipe the device from the counter, then head for the back deck. Whether she's calling with good news, bad news, or no news, it'll be far easier to hear her without Josie and Scarlett randomly bursting into song.

I round the butcher-block island that divides the kitchen space from the living area. It's massive, with enough barstools to seat twelve. The floors are dark wood and match the beams cut across the high ceilings in the oversized living room. The whole floor is bright and open, thanks in part to the floor-to-ceiling windows with a killer view of our own private lake. There's a small pond too, perfect for skating in the winter, and the lot is surrounded by tall spruce trees, reminding me of the landscape in Canada, though my mother and I could never have afforded a house like this.

As I step onto the deck and close the glass door, the cold bites at my skin. It's a welcome sensation—my body is most comfortable in the cold. On the ice at the rink, on a frozen pond back home in Canada, here on my deck. I breathe in a deep lungful of frigid air as I survey the scene inside. My home is warm and comfortable and filled with the people I love the most. I never intended to have a family of my own, but that was another one of my mother's sayings: *The best things in life aren't planned.*

"Ready for Christmas?" Madi asks when I answer.

There's no stopping the smile that forms on my lips as I imagine Brayden's reaction to his Christmas gifts.

"Yeah, I've got three days off in a row so I won't have to travel until the twenty-ninth. It'll be nice. How about you? Where do the famous Duncan Scott and his family spend Christmas?"

Madi laughs. "We'll be in Bristol. The kids are thrilled about it, since Duncan doesn't have to be on set again until summer. His next movie is being filmed in Italy, so we're all going."

"That's great, Madi. I'm really happy for you."

"Thanks." Halfway through that single syllable, her cheery disposition fades, and she sighs. "Tyler, I'm calling because the state has been in touch. You should expect a visit from Josie's social worker in the next week or so."

My stomach twists, the sensation urging me to look away from the joyful scene in the living room. As if I don't want Madi's next words to touch my family. To sully their happiness. They're in this perfect bubble—Josie is smiling as she paints Maria's nails, and Scarlett claps along with the music coming from the TV. Even Brayden has joined in on the fun. He's sitting on the floor beside Scarlett now, tickling her belly.

Instead, I focus on the darkness over the lake, the almost black water, the color of which bleeds into the trees. If not for the light dusting of snow, they'd be nothing but a dark wall enveloping us. "Should I be worried?"

"The hospital was required to notify them of Josie's injury. It's typical for them to visit after an incident like that. But this is what I was talking about. If they come while you're away, who will they find taking care of Josie?"

"Maria is here." The words are sharp with aggravation. "I have a job, Madi. Just like the majority of parents. I can't watch her every move, but she's happy, she's cared for, and she's loved. What more do they want from me?"

"A stable home where Josie's best interests are put at the forefront. And that's what you are giving her. We just need them to see it." Madi's tone is filled with sincerity and empathy.

She sees how hard I'm trying, and she'll fight for our family. Of that I have no doubt. That's all I can hope for, I suppose.

"Just live your life like you have been. And enjoy the holiday with the kids. There's nothing like that first Christmas," she says wistfully. "I guess I never asked; do you have siblings? My sisters spoil the crap out of our kids."

Unease churns in my stomach. "I have a stepbrother. We're not close. But his girlfriend is actually very close with Josie. They're all coming here for Christmas."

She hums. "Kids tend to make underlying issues seem less important. Hopefully that's the case for you and your brother."

Stepbrother. I have to bite back the urge to correct her. And yeah, that's never going to happen. I'd like Xander to spend as little time with my kids as possible.

"But how nice for Josie to have found a friend with your family. Having a positive, stable female presence in her life should be good for her after all she's been through with Krista."

The unease ramps up to something akin to dread. It swirls and grows and threatens to consume me, even as Madi makes small talk. Finally, when I make an excuse to end the call, I turn back and watch Josie. She's happy here. Happy with us. We're all she needs.

Even as I repeat those thoughts like a mantra, I know in my heart that's not true. Suddenly, I'm regretting my decision to host Christmas with my family—and Ava—because I know exactly what Josie needs, and it's the one thing I can't give her.

Chapter 8
Ava

WHY IS it that when a woman harps on something, she's labeled as difficult or whiney, but when a man does it, the woman in his life is expected to put up with it without complaint?

"How do you forget to tell your boyfriend you're leaving an event we attended together? It's like you don't care about me at all."

I consider my words for what feels like the seven hundredth time this week. It's not that I forgot about Xander, per se... Okay, maybe I did. But admitting that won't do me any favors. It's that Josie took precedence over everything else in that moment. Then the shock of her adoption—and the identity of the person doing the adopting—threw me for a loop.

I didn't check my phone until the next morning, so I understand why Xander was mad. What confuses me, maybe even irritates me, is that an hour after the first *where are you?* text, he messaged that he was headed home, and I didn't hear from him again. He didn't seem all that concerned about my well-being. In fact, I heard through the grapevine that he went out with a few of the younger Bolts players. Unlike Brooks and Aiden, the younger guys go out pretty regularly, and when they do, they're surrounded by puck bunnies. I'd like to think Xander doesn't notice the women, but I'm not naïve.

But since I'm the one who forgot about him, I can't really say anything about his whereabouts that night.

I reach across the car and squeeze his thigh. "I'm really sorry. It was selfish of me, but truly, I care about you. I hope you know that. When I heard Josie was in the hospital, I shut down. You know how that stuff affects me."

Xander links his fingers with mine. The move instantly reminds me of why I'm with him. He really is a kind, caring guy. And I'm a jerk for having forgotten all about him.

Because he's right, I 1,000 percent did.

"Try not to forget about me tonight, yeah?" He pulls my fingers to his lips and kisses them. As the light ahead turns red, he stops and eyes me. "You look beautiful."

Heat creeps into my cheeks. "Thank you. You look pretty good yourself."

He's dressed in a deep green sweater and a pair of corduroy pants, and as always, his dark hair is trimmed short, and it's gelled and professional. His brown eyes are warm as they rove over me, and his face is smooth. He spends quite a bit of time and money on his skin-care routine, and it's paying off.

When the light turns green, Xander blows out a breath. "I just wish we were celebrating anywhere but his house tonight. Maybe next year we can spend the holidays with your family."

Humming, I focus my gaze out the window. Christmas at War's house will surely be different from how my family celebrates.

My mother always went all out, with decorations and magic galore. I don't see Tyler Warren going that route, even if his house is as far as it can get from the bachelor pad one would expect him to have. I actually can't see him hosting Christmas, period.

His father suggested we all spend the evening at the lakeside home so that Tyler wouldn't have to travel with the kids. The entire family was just as shocked as me to learn that Tyler was raising three children. Apparently there's an older boy named Brayden, along with Josie and Scarlett. Obviously I'm ecstatic about seeing Josie. We've been Face-Timing daily since I saw her at the hospital, but we haven't had that playdate yet. She's off school for the next two weeks, so with any luck, we can see each other at least once more during the holiday break. Despite my eagerness to see my sweet girl, I never could have imagined spending my first holiday with Xander at the home of my sworn enemy.

The two men couldn't be more different.

Xander is sweet, and despite the night out he had with the Bolts players, I've never known his eyes to wander. He hasn't ever stood me up. If anything, he's always around. Sometimes even when I don't necessarily want him there. Hell, he comes to more of the Bolts charity things than War.

Not to be cheeky, but War just skates by on his talent and good looks. He shows up—late—and charms everyone around him with ease. He never gives his full attention to any conversation or topic, always scrolling through his phone when we're out at bars—because yes, my best friends are with his best friends so we're often together— zoning in and out of conversation, unless one of the guys is talking to him. They're about the only people in existence he deems worthy of his sole focus. The girls he hangs out with? Never. He's a playboy interested in only one thing, and he somehow manages to find women who are clueless enough, or maybe desperate enough, to give him what he wants despite the minimal effort he puts in.

"Excited to see Josie?" Xander asks, pulling me from my musings.

My chest tightens. "I really am. I've never wanted kids, but I'd do just about anything for her."

Xander's warm eyes find mine again. "I know, baby. Because you're an angel."

As we turn onto War's street, darkness settles around us, bringing with it a sense of dread.

"And," Xander says, oblivious to the shift, "I'm so glad you're mine."

CHAPTER 9
TYLER

"WHAT ABOUT THIS ONE?" Josie says from her room.

With Scarlett in my arms, I stride down the hall, headed downstairs, since my family should be here soon.

Everything about this holiday is strange. I'm pretty sure I shocked the hell out of my father when I called to tell him that I'm now a father with three kids in my care.

But it's going to be fine. Everything is fine.

I stop outside Josie's open door and peek into the pink room, finding her standing in front of Maria. She's wearing a green dress, but she's tugging on it, as if she's uncomfortable. Maria tuts gently and grasps her arms to stop her from fussing with the skirt. It's made of some type of mesh material and juts out and away from her body, kind of like a tutu.

Honestly, it looks like it belongs on a younger girl. Like Scarlett. I look down at the two-year-old and realize she's wearing the same green dress. Where they got these matching outfits, I haven't a clue. All I know is the girl who's always smiling does not look the least bit happy.

With a quick knock, I push the door open farther. "Hey, fighter, you almost ready?"

Josie swallows down her frown, takes a deep breath, and offers me a smile. "Yeah. I was just finishing up. Do you think your parents will like the dress?"

Her words stop me in my tracks, and suddenly, I feel like I'm six again. Or seven, eight, nine. Somewhere around there, and even years after. Pick an age, and I have a story about a time I tried to change myself in hopes that I'd be what Dory or my father wanted.

It never worked, by the way. Dory wouldn't have liked me even if I'd been a carbon copy of her own precious son. My dad? I can see now that I wasn't ever a disappointment to him. He just wasn't emotionally available, nor was he always physically there. But I craved that connection. Especially after my mother passed.

Changing myself, searching for the secret that would lead them to care about me, took up far more mental capacity than I'd like to admit.

Thank fuck I've had enough therapy to handle this moment right here. Failing Josie isn't an option, and I won't allow her to fall into the same insecurities I spent years working through.

As I settle Scarlett on the floor, she happily plucks at the tutu on her own dress, oblivious to the heaviness that's settled in the room.

"First off," I say to Josie, "you look absolutely beautiful."

Her tentative smile blooms into the full one that hits me straight in the heart.

"Second, you don't have to dress a certain way—or act a certain way—in hopes that people will like you. Be yourself. You're awesome."

She glances away from me shyly, but I tug on her hand to force her to hear me.

"Most importantly, Jos, if anyone makes you feel less than awesome, remember this: I'll do just about anything to remind you of what an incredible human you are. Now you tell me, do you want to wear this dress, or would you be more comfortable in something else?"

Worrying her lip, she surveys her sister. Then she turns back to me and shrugs. "I kind of like that we match. Ya know, since it's our first Christmas together."

I tug her into my chest and hug her. "It's our first Christmas together too. All four of us. You, me, Scarlett, and Bray. The first of many, right?"

She loops her arms around my neck and squeezes, her body relaxing against mine. My chest is so tight it's hard to breathe. Knowing that I can be that soft place for her to land is overwhelming, but I'll continue to work every day to make her feel safe. I've been doing it for a year now, showing up and visiting even when it felt awkward. Spending afternoons with her, working to find common ground, a way to relate, when our connection consisted of nothing more than her needing someone and me wanting to be that person.

In truth, being needed like this is a gift I never considered before meeting her, and I'd be lying if I said I didn't need her even more than she needs me.

Against my chest, she sighs. "Do you think your parents will like me?"

Over her head, I meet Maria's eyes. She's been watching our interaction silently. She does that often. She gives us our space to find each other, to work things out, but she stays close, in case we need her. "I've told you this before, and it's the truth, so believe it. It's impossible for people not to love you, fighter. You're the coolest kid around." I lean back so I can look her in the eye. "Want to help me set the table? I asked Bray to do it, but we both know he probably got distracted and is watching hockey downstairs."

With a nod, she giggles.

We're halfway down the stairs when the doorbell rings. Surprisingly, Brayden is finishing up with the table. Though SportsCenter is blasting over the Christmas music I put on to get us into a festive mood.

I went all-out this year. A huge Christmas tree. Elves and reindeer on every shelf. Even a freaky Santa toy that dances and sings. It's as tall as Scarlett, yet she isn't bothered by its animatronic creepiness like the rest of us. No, every time he shakes, she breaks into belly laughs, which leaves the rest of us laughing because Scarlett has the most obnoxiously loud cackle.

There's even tinsel, and not just on the tree. Somehow, it's clinging to couch cushions and even the wall. It looks like Clark Griswold threw up in here.

Grinning—because it's impossible not to be happy when

surrounded by all this holiday cheer—I stride for the front door. Josie peels off and heads toward Brayden to help him finish.

With Scarlett on my hip, I swing the door open. Immediately, my smile dies. "Oh," I huff out as I survey Xander. "I thought you were my father."

"Merry Christmas to you too." His tone is sarcastic and his expression is pinched as he steps inside. At the sound of gravel crunching behind him, the look smooths out. The only other people attending tonight are our parents. Looks like they've arrived just in time to be our buffer. "What's this one's name?" he asks in an obnoxious tone, wearing a fake-ass smile as he takes in the little girl in my arms.

"It's Scarlett."

The words have barely left me when Ava steps out from behind Xander.

I swear the air is ripped from my lungs at the sight of her. Her dress is green, a color I've never seen on her. Hell, I've never seen her wear anything but white or cream or, yeah, white. The hue matches her eyes almost perfectly, making it impossible to look away.

"Hello, Scarlett." Xander steps in too close and pinches my daughter's cheek.

She scrunches her face, then buries it in the crook of my neck.

"I'm your Uncle Xander, and this is your Auntie Ava."

I step back and pivot to put extra distance between him and Scarlett. "You're not married. She's not family."

Scowling, he looks at Ava as if he's looking for backup. "She's two. I don't think she understands the difference."

"Maybe so, but Josie does," I hiss. "If she hears, she'll latch on to the idea of Ava being family, and if you two don't work out, she'll be crushed, and that girl doesn't need any more disappointments in her life."

Ava tilts her head as she studies me with a frown. It's a look of concentration rather than hate, which is what I usually get from her. A loud screech sounds from behind me, startling her, and her eyes go wide.

"*Ava,*" Josie sings as she runs past me and barrels into the woman who's still standing on the front steps.

Without hesitating, Ava picks her up, and the two of them hug long and hard.

Eventually, Josie pulls back, her eyes full of wonder. "What are you doing here?"

The smile that spreads across Ava's face isn't one I'm familiar with. It's soft and pure and genuine. "It's Christmas. Where else would I be than with my girl?"

For the first time since the day we met, I feel myself relax around Ava. She gets it. All that matters is Josie, and if she's what Josie needs, then somehow, some way, I'll make this work.

Chapter 10
Ava

"WHERE'S THE GOOD WHISKEY?" Chandler Warren booms from where he's inspecting the liquor cabinet.

For probably the fifth time tonight, I assess War, dissecting his reaction. This kinship I feel with him came out of nowhere, and it's freaking me out. Kind of like the warmth that seeps through me when I watch him squeeze Brayden's shoulder as he gets up from the table and heads in his father's direction.

I recognized Brayden immediately. He was the boy playing hockey at the YMCA charity event last week. The one War hefted onto his shoulder after he scored a goal. I've seen him at several other events since I started working at Langfield Corp, though I can't remember War being at a single one of them. What the heck? I've been thrown for a loop, but I can't just come out and ask why he's here—without his own family—or how they know one another.

Maria headed out to be with her family shortly after we arrived. Her kids are home from college, and since the Bolts have a few days off, she's spending the holidays with them. I'm relieved that she gets the time away, but at the same time, I'm desperate to ask her all the questions that are swirling in my mind.

Questions like why is War adopting Josie? What happened to her mother? And when did the man across the table become this person?

This good guy, this perfect parent? Because the War I know is the antithesis of those traits.

Brayden pushes his shaggy dark brown hockey hair out of his face as he hands Scarlett a crayon. I'm almost positive he's not Tyler's biological son. I'd know if he was, right? It would be public information. Sara and Hannah would definitely know. So would the guys. Even though the two don't share DNA, they share so many traits. Brayden's eyes are almost the same striking blue as Tyler's, and though his face isn't covered in a day-old scruff, he has a similar bone structure. Strong cheekbones, narrow face, lips that pout all on their own. He'll be a heartbreaker one day, just like the man beside him.

The little girl on his lap has her tongue peeking out of her mouth, totally focused as she scribbles all over the Santa picture Josie plopped in front of her when she started to fuss as we cleared the table.

Josie's incredibly good with her little sister. Patient, loving, and attentive. Not that I'd expect anything less. The only thing Josie has ever wanted was a family, so witnessing these interactions warms me in a way I can't explain.

"Can we play Go Fish?" Josie appears at the table, already holding a deck of cards and scanning the group expectantly.

"I would," Bray replies, nodding at the little girl in his lap. "But she'll probably steal the cards from me."

With a laugh, I scoop her up. "I can balance her and play with my other hand. Deal the cards, love bug."

Grinning wide, she rounds the table, dealing out cards to each person. When she gets to Xander, she pauses, her expression turning cautious. "Do you want to play?"

He nods. "Sure. Deal me in. I'll grab a drink, then be back to play." He stands and presses a kiss to my forehead.

I suck in a breath, hoping Josie didn't see. I don't typically shy away from public displays of affection, and the way Xander offers it freely is one of the things I love most about him. But War's words when we arrived have been playing on repeat in my mind all night. We aren't married. I'm not Josie's aunt, and I don't want her to get her hopes up that I will be one day. Though that wouldn't be terrible. Even if I can't be her mom, I'll take any position in her life.

Fortunately, Josie is busy dealing and doesn't notice. But Brayden does. His blue eyes are piercing as he assesses me. It's uncanny, how similar the expression is to War's. I give him a smile, doing my best not to squirm under his scrutiny. Rather than return the expression, he lowers his focus to his cards.

Before I can overthink the interaction, a chubby hand grasps my face. "Mama," Scarlett murmurs.

My heart skips, and heat creeps up my cheeks. With a shake of my head, I huff out a breath. "She probably calls everyone that, huh?"

Josie giggles, her face lit up as brightly as the lights on the tree. "Nope. I'm sissy, Brayden is Bray and Maria is MiMi."

With a long breath out, I kiss the top of the little girl's head. "Aren't you a little love."

I don't ask what she calls War. It's better that I don't know. If she calls him Daddy in my presence, I'll probably turn as red as the suit the creepy dancing Santa is wearing. It's the only ridiculous decoration. Every other piece is tasteful and festive. It's unnerving how warm and welcoming his house is. How comfortable I feel in it.

I should be uncomfortable. I should be staring at the door, ready to run. Instead, I don't want the evening to end. And I'm wishing I could wake up here in the morning and watch the kids light up as they open their gifts. Though I despise War more often than not, after seeing him in dad mode tonight, I have a feeling he's gone over the top as Santa.

And I don't know how I feel about that.

"You're good with her." Dory returns from the kitchen, a glass of wine in her hand. There's not a strand of gray in her hair, nor a wrinkle on her face. She's the opposite of my mother, who never had the time or money to focus on how she was aging, let alone the interest. The only thing my mother has going for her is her red hair. Red often doesn't go gray, and my mother's hasn't. Dory's long blond hair is curled into loose waves, and her hands glitter with diamonds. Her necklace sparkles just as brightly in contrast to the burgundy sweater set it's settled on. She's as beautiful as she is kind. Xander is fortunate to have such a close relationship with his parents. In the last several months, we've had dinner with them weekly, meaning I've had the opportunity to spend time with both his mother and his stepfather, and I've come to treasure my relationship with her.

"She's sweet." I give the little girl on my lap a squeeze.

With her hand wrapped around a crayon, she practically murders the image in front of her, covering it in slashes of red.

Chuckling, I drop a kiss on the top of her head and savor the soothing scent of her baby shampoo. Then I pat the seat beside me. "Want to play with us?"

With a wave of her hand, she rounds the table. "I'll let Josie sit by you." The smile she wears is knowing as she eases into a chair across from me.

Of course she's noticed our bond. All night, my girl has been by my side, and that's right where I want her. Josie plops into the empty chair, immediately resting her head on my shoulder, and I nuzzle mine against hers, relishing the precious time I've been given with both girls.

"You're a natural mother," Chandler booms as he approaches.

Behind him, both War and Xander are watching me. War's gaze is intense, making my stomach do an odd little flip. Is he angry? I blink and avert my attention, not liking the way his scrutiny weighs on me. Instead, I focus on Xander. Instantly, I realize that was a mistake, because he's radiating a warmth I've never seen.

"She is, isn't she?" he says, his tone brimming with pride. He settles beside Chandler, always seeking his approval. "You want to have one of our own, sweetheart?"

My stomach bottoms out, and there's no stopping the scowl that overtakes my face. Because I'm a glutton for punishment, I peer over at War, only to find his eyes lit up like he's delighted by my reaction.

That only makes my frown deepen.

Xander knows I don't want children of my own, and he knows why.

If heartbreak were a living, breathing thing, it would be beating wildly beside me. Always. He knows that.

Truly the only time I feel even remotely whole, remotely alive, like I can walk and breathe at the same time, is when I'm with Josie. So I turn my focus on her, willing my racing heart to settle. As I drink her in, my fractured nerves realign and my breathing evens out. "My love bug right here is enough for me."

Josie tips her head back, beaming, completely unaware of the tension building inside me. The little one on my lap throws her head back, walloping me in the chest and forcing a surprised laugh from me.

I kiss her nose. "And you, my little love. Don't worry, I didn't forget about you."

These two are perfect. What I would create would never be perfect, because broken people don't create beautiful things.

"Of course," Dory prods, picking up her glass of wine. "She's still so young, Xander. You both are."

Chandler huffs, as if this is a topic he has any say in, smoothing a hand over the front of his sweater. "Xander and Tyler are the same age, and Tyler is raising three kids." With a long sip of whiskey, he arches a brow at his stepson. "A beautiful wife, a baby. They're the next steps. Xander knows this. Our clients love that our company is family-owned. That my son works with me."

Jaw rigid and eyes icy, War pulls out the chair beside Brayden, the move making its legs scrape harshly on the hardwood floor. "Are we going to play?"

Tension thrums at the table, even as we all turn our focus to the children's game. In my periphery, I catch Xander staring at War. His expression almost a sneer. It's unsettling, that action. I've never seen this side of him.

Chandler often challenges Xander, but it's always related to work. As if he's pushing him to strive for more. This is the first time I've ever seen him interact with both of his sons, and I swear it felt like he was pitting them against one another just now. Telling Xander to get in line, using War's new status as a father to do so while simultaneously touting Xander's position in the family business.

Did he ever hope War would go into finance too? Did he encourage his passion for hockey, or did he try to push him in a different direction?

Silently, I survey one man, then the next, assessing all three of them, trying to read between the lines. Though it seems that not a single adult at this table is an open book.

Dory smiles dotingly at her son, then focuses on her cards again. Does she notice that Chandler is pitting the boys against one another? Does she even care? I haven't so much as seen her address War, and it's...troubling.

Chandler is wearing a self-satisfied smirk as he sips his whiskey and scrolls on his phone. Even Xander is hard to read right now. He put me in this terrible position, bringing up a topic he knows is traumatic for me. It's a subject I've been honest about since day one, yet now, he's acting as though I haven't made my intentions clear. And what the heck is with the way he's got his chest practically puffed out, like he's peacocking for his father?

Then there is Tyler Warren. He might be the easiest to read. He may be wearing a blank expression, but the anger rolling off him is palpable. I'm still staring when Brayden nudges him and holds his phone out, showing him something that's probably sports related, based on the topics the kid has brought up tonight. Only then does War's body slump and his face soften. It's clear he cares.

How is it possible that in this room filled with people I once thought so highly of, Tyler Warren is the one I feel most connected to in this moment?

"Can we play already?" Josie whines.

War chuckles. "Okay, fighter. Can I be on your team? I'm not very good."

I roll my eyes and look down at my cards.

"Got something to say, Ava?" War's tone has my eyes flying up, and my stupid cheeks go warm when I see the amusement in his eyes. I need to stop being so easy to read. It's clear the jerk loves to goad me.

Josie scoots closer to him. "'Kay, but no telling everyone what cards I have." She pulls hers close to her chest and peers up at him with the same knowing look he wears when he stares at everyone else. It's so strange seeing the two of them together. It's like they fit. I'm equally annoyed and intrigued by it. How does a tattooed bad boy *fit* with the sweetest little girl to ever live?

"Have I ever steered ya wrong, kid?" he says, wearing the same expression.

She shrugs. "There was that time you promised to let me paint your nails and then you refused to let me pick the color."

"I told you I'd do any color but pink."

Brayden hides behind his cards, shaking with laughter, and I find myself doing the same. When I look at War again, he smiles. Then he does this thing that has me all out of sorts.

He winks. Yup. Tyler freaking Warren winks at me.

My body betrays me as a sizzle of heat rushes through me. What was that? I'm pretty sure the man hasn't smiled at me since the day we met, and I know for a fact that I've never seen him wink. It's dangerous. Deadly. Seriously, a wink from this gorgeous man should come with a warning. He shouldn't be allowed to do it. The gods, or whoever is out there determining who gets winking abilities, shouldn't allow people who have that kind of swagger to wink. It's *unfair*.

"Do you have a four?" I ask Brayden.

"Go fish," he says with a smile.

I pick up a card, which is not a four, and sigh.

Tyler knocks shoulders with Josie, and when it's her turn, she giggles. "Do you have a four, Ava?"

"Tyler Warren, are you helping her beat me?" I say, affronted, as I hand Josie my card. She sets it down next to hers with a big smile.

War is still sporting that same smile, only this time, his eyes dance as he watches me with a focus that rivals how he acts when he's on the ice. Determined. Cocky. Sure of whatever plan he's hatched. "What can I say, Vicious? I play to win."

The way he's looking at me should make me uncomfortable. It should make me annoyed. Instead, it only makes my heart beat wildly in my chest. An experience I don't want to even try to understand. Flustered, I look away, only to find both Dory and Xander with their eyes on me. And neither of them appears happy.

After two rounds of go fish, Chandler stretches and says it's time to go.

My stomach sinks. Though I'm still confused and frustrated by the way he acted earlier, I don't want him to leave. Once he and Dory are gone, Xander will want to go too, and I'm not ready to say good night. This is the first holiday I've enjoyed in years. Despite that bout of tension, it's been magical. Spending time with Josie is always a joy, but tonight, witnessing how happy and carefree she is in her home, surrounded by the people she considers family, it's nothing short of beautiful.

For a little while, it made me forget how much I miss my own family. How much I miss the years where the laughter outweighed the tears.

Before guilt can seep in—along with the pressure of knowing my mother is not enjoying this night in the same way I am—Josie grabs my hand. "Will you help me get ready for bed and read me a story before you go?"

My heart melts into a puddle at the request. As if I'd ever say no. "Of course, love bug. What about Scarlett?"

Tyler pushes back from the table. "I'll take her up. Come here, mon chou." He holds his arms out to his little girl.

Arching a brow, I hold Scarlett closer.

He chuckles. "I'm French Canadian, remember."

"So she's your little shoe?"

"Means cabbage, actually." Brayden coughs out a laugh. "He tried to use it with me, but I pushed him into the boards."

Scarlett launches herself at War and snuggles into his neck, already rubbing her eyes.

With a hum, he kisses her head, then smirks at Brayden. "As if I'd ever let you push me into the boards." With that, he's sauntering away, tossing an "I'll be back" over his shoulder.

Watching him walk away while murmuring unintelligible words to Scarlett has my stomach doing that silly little flip again. What the heck? I can't blame the reaction on his forearms today, since he's wearing a black sweater. Will he give her a bath before bed? If so, surely, he'd have to pull those sleeves up—

"You okay over there?" Brayden mutters.

Blinking, I drag the back of my hand over my mouth and swipe at the liquid pooling there.

Crap. I was definitely drooling.

God, this is bad.

Since when do I find War hot?

I do not find him attractive. No, I hate him.

Only, that's not entirely true. When I met him, I thought he was hot, but since then, nope, I haven't given him a second thought.

If only that were the truth. Gah. I'm losing it. It's the baby thing. Or the dad thing. It's definitely not a *him* thing.

"Ready to bring me up?" Josie asks, clambering out of her chair and saving me from my thoughts.

"Yup." Standing, I push my chair in gently. Then I check in with Xander, even though I'm still irritated with him. I promised I wouldn't forget him, and I meant it. "You okay with hanging out for a bit while I tuck her in?"

He pushes back from the table and nods toward the door to the deck. "Can we talk for a minute?"

Josie's gaze bounces between us. So does Brayden's.

Dory, bless her, calls Josie over. "What did you ask Santa to bring you?"

I smile at her, appreciating her willingness to buy us a few minutes, even if she's only doing it for her son, and then slip away with Xander. The icy wind whips around us, blowing my hair into my face and instantly making me shiver. "Everything okay?"

"Why are you acting weird?"

Arms crossed, I tip my head back and glare at him. "What are you talking about?"

"What the hell was that with Tyler? Why did he call you vicious?"

Frowning, I sigh. "I have no idea why Tyler does anything he does. Why don't you ask him?"

"Oh, believe me, I would love to ask him why he's flirting with my girlfriend right in front of me, but the better question is, why were you flirting back?"

I swallow. I have no good argument. Though I wasn't exactly flirting, I certainly wasn't able to keep my eyes off him.

Fortunately Xander doesn't seem to expect a response. He just launches into his next rant. "And what was that whole *these kids are enough for me* comment? They aren't your kids, Ava. Josie isn't your daughter."

The words slice through me, cutting so deep I expect to find blood pooling at my feet. The worst part is that I'm not even prepared for them. Normally, I'm ready for the inevitable bad things. I expect them. It's a defense mechanism built up over years and years. But I truly didn't see his harsh words coming.

"W-what?"

"My dad's right, Ave." He softens his tone, though it does nothing to soothe me. "It's time we take the next step. Moving in together, marriage, kids. It's what's expected of me."

What's expected of him? He wants me to have children with him because it's *what's expected of him*? I'm so dumbfounded by his audacity that all I can do is blink as a wave of rage overwhelms me.

He's mad because I'm close with Josie. He thinks that because I love her, I'll eventually want my own kids. But if so, he hasn't been listening to a thing I've said since we met. I couldn't stop loving Josie if I tried, the moment I met her I was a goner, wanting to be close to her isn't a choice, but it is a choice not to get pregnant and allow another child into my heart only to suffer another unimaginable loss.

"Go say good night to Josie, and let's get out of here. It's getting late, and the guys are meeting up for a drink tonight."

He just lectured me about settling down, having kids, doing what's expected, and yet he plans to go out for a drink *with the guys* on Christmas Eve? Make it make sense. I may be too passive in almost every respect, but when it comes to the little girl waiting for me upstairs, I'm surprisingly assertive. "I promised Josie a story. We can go after that."

With that, I suck in a breath and shuffle inside.

CHAPTER 11
TYLER

Brooks: Merry Christmas Eve, guys. Love you all.

Aiden: Aw, duck. You're making me emotional. I love you too, big bro.

Aiden: And you, Tyler Warren, my favorite captain.

Aiden: And you, Daniel Hall, my good boy.

Me: Why am I not your good boy?

Brooks: LOL

Hall: Because you're a daddy.

Aiden: Heyoooo, didn't see it going that way, but ya know, now that he says it, can we call you Daddy War?

Me: Fuck you all.

Brooks: Hey, I didn't say anything.

Me: Fine. Brooks, you're exempt.

Brooks: How are the kids? All set for Christmas morning?

Me: They're good. Just waiting for my dad and his family to leave and hoping the social worker doesn't pick tomorrow to show up and check on us.

Brooks: That a thing?

Me: Yeah, after Josie's fall, they think I need supervision. Apparently being a single dad without a steady nanny gives them reason to worry.

Brooks: That sucks. You're the best thing that's ever happened to those kids.

Aiden: You know what you need?

Hall: A hot nanny for me to bang?

Me: Dude, the last nanny around the arena was your sister. Do you really want to talk about who is currently banging her?

Me: Here's a hint, it's our coach.

Hall: That was low! Even for you.

Me: Play stupid games...

Aiden: No, he needs a wife.

Brooks: Aiden, you're an idiot.

Me: Lol, the lawyer suggested the same thing.

Hall: Did you know that mail-order brides are really a thing? There are a ton of hot ones. Check out this contract! <link to website>

Brooks: I'm out. My fiancée just told me I have to undress her to find my present.

Aiden: Oh, if my wife isn't wearing candy I can eat off her, this will be a very unmerry Christmas.

Me: Merry Christmas, guys. Thanks for checking in.

AS I CLOSE out of our text thread, I swallow a laugh. The last thing I want to do is wake Scarlett. I'm lying beside her in her toddler bed, my body curled around her in a way that'll make it extra hard to move tomorrow. But it's the only way I can get her to sleep, and I am in no rush to get downstairs and deal with Xander and Dory again.

Tonight hasn't been nearly as terrible as I thought it would be. I have my kids to thank for that. They held my focus pretty steadily, making it easier to let Xander's comments roll off my back.

Their joy, especially Josie's, was worth any discomfort, and as much as I hate to admit it, Ava is mostly to thank for that.

My little girl really does deserve someone like that in her life. A woman who loves her. Who puts her first. Madi isn't wrong. A wife would be one hell of a solution. If only I could find someone who would put these kids first. But is that even a possibility? Their mothers won't even do it. How can I expect another woman to?

Honestly, a contractual marriage is probably the only kind I'd ever enter. With all the obligations and expectations spelled out ahead of time, leaving no room for getting attached or getting hurt.

Wouldn't hurt if the woman was as attractive as Ava.

My phone buzzes in my hand, so I unlock it, being sure to keep the light from the screen from flashing Scarlett.

Hall: Seriously, check out this chick!

As I'm reading, a picture of a woman pops up.

I snort at the image. Sure, she's gorgeous, but this can't be real, can it? Mail-order brides? God, people are nuts.

Me: Where do you find this shit?

> Hall: It came up as an advertisement when I
> was reading Calliope's column.

This kid and his damn mythical Calliope. I swear he's used her name in every conversation we've had since he discovered her column this year. It's a sex column, though he gets all ass-hurt if we refer to it as that, saying it's a column about life. Yeah, Calliope's sex life. Not the least bit interested but curious about these apparent contracts, I scan the terms.

Wife agrees that husband is the owner of her body. All orgasms, if any, will be given only with his consent. This includes self-induced pleasure and usage of toys.

Disgust rolls through me. What man in their right mind thinks like this? I can think of nothing hotter than walking in and finding a woman using a toy. Why the hell would a guy want to restrict that? And *owner of her body*? This was obviously written by a man with a small dick. I don't need to agree to some ridiculous contract to have my wife begging for me to touch her.

My wife. My stomach knots at those words. Where the fuck did that come from?

I scrub a hand down my face. Fucking Hall and his contract are getting to me.

Irritated, I focus on my phone again, ready to text him and let him know what an idiot he is. Before I can close out of the contract, another line catches my attention.

Wife will only speak when spoken to.

I'm still blinking in shock when giggles float in on the air and my curiosity is suddenly shifted. After pressing a kiss to Scarlett's head, I ninja myself out of her hold without waking her—and hopefully without straining my back even more than I already have—and fall to the fucking floor.

Silently laughing, I roll my head back and stare up at the ceiling.

What the hell am I doing with my life? Sometimes, I don't recognize the man I am now. But when another giggle rings out, my heart thumps against my chest, and a warmth I never felt until a year ago flows through me. Anxious to see the smile that goes along with that sound, I stand and sneak out of Scarlett's room, then head across the hall.

Josie is dressed in Christmas pajamas and snuggled under a pink comforter one shade brighter than her pink walls. Lyrics from Taylor Swift, Lake Paige, and Melina Rodriguez are stenciled on the walls, along with purple birds I drew freehand to match the *1989* Album. Ava, who is stretched out on top of the covers with her back to me, is giving Josie her full attention. She's always giving Josie her full attention.

"Melina and Lake sang together?" Josie's face is lit up like she can't believe it.

"Yup. It was a really magical night. There were Christmas carolers decked out in these old-fashioned dresses, and there was even a reindeer hanging out in front of the fire station with three kittens on its back."

Josie giggles. "Now I know you're making this up."

Sucking in an exaggerated breath, Ava props herself up on an elbow. "You believe that Lake and Melina sang for a Christmas event in a tiny town, but you don't believe there was a reindeer? I left my phone downstairs, but I'll show you pictures the next time I see you."

Josie snuggles against her, giggling, and Ava rests her head on the pillow again, threading her fingers through the little girl's strawberry locks.

"Were there a lot of kids?"

Ava hums. "Yup."

"Sounds magical." The longing in her tone makes my heart crack. "Bet there were a lot of families too."

I hold my breath, waiting for what she'll say next. Ava stiffens, as if she, too, is concerned about the way this conversation might turn.

"Do you think my mom is okay?"

Eyes closed, I take a deep breath, assuming Ava may need my help to navigate a response.

Before I can announce myself, she responds with an answer more perfect than any I would have come up with. "I hope so."

"Me too. She didn't really feel like my mom," Josie says almost matter-of-factly.

"What do you mean?"

Every second has become a balancing act, not only for Ava, but for me, as I consider how to join the conversation. I hope like hell Ava says the right thing, but at the same time, I don't have the first clue what that would even be.

Josie's lips twist as she considers her response. She's always considering her words. She's never rash, and she never yells. "It's just a feeling, I guess. Have you ever had a really comfortable pillow or stuffed animal you loved? I had both in the hospital, and they made me feel better when I was sad. You too. You always cheered me up when I was lonely." She beams at Ava like she is her entire moon and stars. "She didn't feel like you. I wish you could be my mom."

Ava pulls Josie to her chest, and in a strangled whisper, says, "Me too, love. Me too."

I step out into the hall, my heart in my throat and at a complete fucking loss.

Josie needs Ava. Yet here I am, selfishly trying to adopt this little girl. Maybe I want her, but she certainly doesn't need me.

Pulling on my hair, I tiptoe out of the room and head downstairs.

Chapter 12
Ava

I LIE in bed beside Josie until long after her breathing evens out. I don't know when I'll see her again, when I'll get to comfort her again, and that knowledge is like a knife to the chest. When I finally force myself to roll out of her bed, I know I've been in here for far too long.

I can only imagine how livid Xander is, but I can't get myself to care about his feelings right now.

Josie wishes I could be her mom. The feeling is 100 percent mutual, and I don't think I've wished for something so hard since I was sitting in a hospital bed beside my sister all those years ago.

Determined to make a plan to see her again—even if it means sucking up to War and playing nice—I head down the steps.

It's eerily quiet downstairs. The only sound is the low Christmas music still playing.

"Hello?" I stand in the middle of the empty living room and turn in a slow circle. The main floor is one big, open space, so there's nowhere for Xander and his family to hide, yet all I find as I scan the house are the dinner dishes drying on the counter and the Christmas tree glowing in the dark living room.

I spot my purse on the table and scurry toward it, in search of my phone. As I reach it, the door to the deck opens. Relief floods me as a figure steps inside. Though the feeling is quickly crushed when the man comes into focus. Rather than Xander, War is the one who pads through the room, his head down and a hand raking through his dark and unruly hair.

"Is everyone outside?" I frown because it's clear the deck is empty.

With snowflakes melting in his hair, Tyler stiffens, and his blue eyes go wide with surprise. He's changed into red-and-green flannel pants in the same pattern as the pajamas I helped Josie into not long ago. With a blink, his eyes go back to their normal cool blue, and he lowers his brow, studying me. "Did you forget something?"

"Uh…" I look around the room. "Apparently my ride?" The words come out harsher than I mean for them to, so I force myself to take a deep breath in and let it back out. "Xander's not outside on the deck by chance, is he?" Humiliation has my cheeks heating, but I work to keep my voice steady. I will not cry in front of Tyler Warren. He'd never let me live that down.

He stalks closer, though his movements are easy, comfortable. "Everyone left."

My stomach sinks. "This has to be a mistake. I'm calling Xander."

With a dismissive shrug, he wanders toward the fireplace.

Hands shaking, I dig my phone from my purse. Once I lift it and the screen illuminates, my unease turns to annoyance. There isn't a single text or missed call notification waiting for me. Xander really left without a word. I hit his name in my contact list. Rather than ring, the call goes to voicemail. I pull the device away from my face and stare at it, dumbfounded. As I'm blinking, at a loss, a text pops up.

> Xander: Out with the guys. Hope you enjoyed playing house with my stepbrother's kids tonight.

A jolt of shock courses through me. Is he—did he—is this for real?

"He coming back for you?" Tyler asks over his shoulder as he pulls the metal curtain of the fireplace closed.

With a hand to my throat, I zero in on the flames licking up the logs and growing in strength and size. "No—he's, uh—" I clear my throat and force myself to look at the man across the room. "No, I think we're over."

That's probably putting it mildly. We're definitely over. There's no coming back from him *leaving me* at his freaking brother's house on Christmas Eve to go out to a bar with his friends. I could ignore the rumors I've heard in the past about him going out, but there's no writing this off as a bad night.

War's blue eyes widen and practically glow in the firelight. "He left you here?" With a low groan, he pushes to stand, as if the move is painful. He shakes it off quickly and strides across the room, his attention now fixed on my phone. "Did he just break up with you? In a text?" His focus returns to my face, his expression knowing, as if he can read every thought in my head.

Maybe? I don't know. But we're done either way.

Can I even blame him? He's right. I was playing house, longing to be part of Josie's family. I'd happily do it for the rest of my life. But when the subject of having a family with Xander came up after dinner, I practically recoiled. I thought he understood why I felt that way, though. Thought I'd sufficiently explained why having kids of my own is not in the cards.

War hovers close, his scent assaulting me. It's not bad. Not at all. And that's a problem. Because I want to sink into him. I want to bury my face in his soft white T-shirt and inhale the smell. Hold it in my lungs. Cling to the comfort it's created.

"I'll, uh—" I lift the phone. "Call an Uber and be out of your way shortly. Sorry."

Jaw locked tight, War grasps my wrist. "It's Christmas Eve."

I lower my head and bite down on my lip. "I know. I'm sorry. I'm sure I'm the last person you want here right now."

He slides his thumb across the inside of my wrist. "Ava." His voice is soft, soothing.

I don't dare look up. Not with the way my eyes are filling with tears.

"Ava, look at me."

I steal all the courage I have, blink back the moisture in my eyes, and force my chin up.

"You'll stay here. You'll wake up tomorrow and have Christmas morning with us." He smiles. "Josie will be thrilled."

I give him a single nod. I can't form words right now. I'm humili-
ated. Angry. And maybe the tiniest bit relieved.

Maybe more than a tiny bit.

Because Xander did me a favor by leaving me here. If I don't have
to leave yet, then I don't have to say goodbye to Josie yet.

My heart lifts at the thought of her waking up and finding me here.
"Yeah?"

I hate how hope teases my tone. Our history makes trusting War to
not laugh and say "no, obviously I don't want you to stay here" nearly
impossible.

"Yeah." He releases my hand. "Let me grab you something to sleep
in." Without waiting for a response, he turns and jogs up the stairs.

The second he's out of sight, I wrap my hand around my wrist and
rub at the spot he just stroked. I've always been particularly careful
about the clothes I wear, making sure to keep my arms covered. Bulky
sweaters, long sleeves even on the hottest days of summer. No one
touches the bare skin on my arms. Not even Xander.

When my phone buzzes in my hand, I almost drop it. My mind is
all over the place. It takes a couple of heartbeats for the name on the
screen to register, but when it does, I immediately answer.

"Hey," Hannah says before I can greet her. "Did something happen
between you and Xander?" This woman. She has no trouble getting to
the point. But how the heck does she know about tonight?

"Um…yeah, pretty sure we broke up. Why?"

"Ass," she hisses, though it's barely audible over the voices in the
background. The sounds fade quickly, like maybe she's walking away
from a group. "I just got a text from a reporter who spotted Jasper at a
strip club. Seriously, is it too much to ask to go a single night without
having to clean up his messes? It's Christmas Eve, for god's sake."

Jasper Quinn is the first baseman for the Boston Revs and the bane
of Hannah's existence. He's constantly being caught in compromising
positions, which means she spends more time than she should spinning stories for the jerk. If he doesn't clean up his act soon, I wouldn't
be surprised to hear that Beckett Langfield has traded him. If—or
maybe when?—that happens, Hannah will probably go on a shopping
spree to celebrate.

"I hate that you have to deal with him when you should be relaxing and celebrating." It's all I can think to say. I'm at a loss for how Jasper's escapades are connected to Xander. Seeking comfort, I head toward the fire. I settle beside the large brick hearth, soaking in the warmth. "Are you with your family?"

"Yeah, the dads are all in town for the holidays and a few of my brothers too." It sounds like she's covered her mouth when she adds, "But I think she's already tired of husband number five. He didn't make the trip."

I bite my lip to hold in my laugh. Hannah talks about all of her mother's ex-husbands in such a funny way. There are four of them, and she's remained close with all of them as well as their many sons. I'm not surprised at all. Anyone who meets Hannah would want to keep her around.

She clears her throat. "The reporter sent me a picture. Xander was in it too."

Of course. Any time he meets a guy who plays for one of the Langfield teams, he cozies up to them in hopes that they'll hire him to do their financial planning. He's done a decent job with the rookies who don't have ties to the area, Jasper being one of them.

My stomach twists at the idea of my boyfriend leaving me here to go to a strip club. At the idea that he planned to drop me off at home alone on Christmas Eve to go to said strip club. "Do I want to see the picture?"

"Probably not, but if I were you, I'd make myself look at it anyway. It'll help you remember to never get back together with the ass. Oh! Now we can go on a *have a day* vacation!"

Despite the circumstances I find myself in, I can't help the laugh that escapes me. Hannah doesn't put up with bullshit. She doesn't date, either, so it'd be hard for her to get back together with an ex. But she does have a fund she sets aside for friends who are stupid enough to date and then suffer a break up. She calls them '*have a day*' vacations. Knowing Hannah, it involves lots of booze and lots of shopping. Sounds like a perfect day. "Fine. Send it over." With a sigh, I take in the Christmas tree, examining the ornaments. I get caught on the tiny ballerina hung beside a hockey player. Rather than twisting, my stomach is back to flipping. Crap. I'm not sure which is worse. "Merry Christmas," I say, ready to end the call and the night.

"Wait. You're clearly not with Xander, so where are you?"

"With Josie," I say, instantly imbued with some of the strength that disappeared when I discovered Xander had left.

"Aw, say Merry Christmas to our favorite girl for me. Brunch Sunday?"

"You know it."

And if I'm lucky, maybe War will let me bring Josie along. Maybe I won't be her aunt. And obviously I'm not her mom. But if I can find a way to be friends with War, there's a chance I can still be someone she can depend on.

CHAPTER 13
TYLER

I SHOULDN'T BE EVEN MILDLY surprised that Xander would break up with a woman on Christmas Eve. Through *text*. Yet here I am, stumbling down the hall in shock, carrying a T-shirt and the smallest pair of sweats I could find.

He broke up with Ava.

Ava's single.

Neither of those facts should cause this kind of tightening in my chest. Her relationship status has no bearing on my life. *She* has no bearing on my life.

Except she's Josie's favorite person, and my kids' happiness is all that matters to me.

The three of them are the center of my universe.

That truth is why I'm in a rush to get back to her.

"Where are you going?" Brayden calls from his bedroom at the top of the stairs.

I stop in my tracks and peer over my shoulder. For a breath or two, I consider concocting some story, playing off why Ava is here. But I quickly think better of it. The first night Brayden's mom chose a bar over coming home, I promised him the truth. Swore he could trust me to tell him where she was, where I was. Guaranteed that he could trust my word. That I wouldn't sugarcoat the difficult stuff. So I turn on my heel, clothes still in my hand, and stop in his doorway.

"Xander left without telling Ava while she was tucking Josie in. I'm not really sure what's going on with them, but I told her she could stay tonight, so I'm bringing her clothes."

"Dick," Bray mutters, his focus split between me and his phone, where he's been watching game highlights all night.

I glare at him. "Language."

"You know you're thinking the same thing."

It takes more strength than I'd like to admit to fight back a smile and force seriousness into my tone. "You okay with her joining us for Christmas morning?"

Lowering his focus to his phone completely, he shrugs. "It's your house. Invite whoever you want."

"It's your house too." I step into the room and duck, forcing him to look at me. "This will always be your room. I will always be here for you, and I'll always take your feelings into consideration. So if you're uncomfortable with something, tell me."

Bray runs his tongue over his lips, his eyes fixed on the wall behind me. There are a few Bolts posters on it and a jersey from last season signed by all the players. It was his birthday present. I've never seen the kid so excited.

It's the opposite of how he's trying to appear right now. Though I know it's all an act. "Cool," he says simply.

I raise a brow and tilt my head so I'm in his field of vision. "So? Is it okay if she stays?"

Going for nonchalant but not quite hitting the mark, he replies, "Yeah, she's nice. And she makes Josie happy."

I hook him around the neck and pull him into my chest, not letting go until he wraps his arms around me and gives me a real hug. "You're a good big brother."

When he pulls back, his lips are lifted in a genuine smile. Like me, Bray fell hard for Josie. It's impossible not to love that little girl. Just like it's impossible not to love this kid. "Thanks, Tyler."

I squeeze his shoulder and back toward the doorway. "Always. Get some sleep. Tomorrow's gonna be a busy day, and the girls will have us up early, I'm sure."

With a laugh, he shakes his head. "Yeah, don't stay up too late with your pretty friend."

I roll my eyes. "She's not my friend."

"Yeah, yeah. We all know you love collecting strays. Someone left her behind, so you'll find a place for her. You always do."

A little stunned by his assessment, I head down the steps.

Collecting strays? Is that what he thinks? Is that really what I do?

Downstairs, Ava is sitting on the hearth, inspecting the Christmas tree. She glows in the light of the fire, her hair looking almost golden. For a second, I study her, take her in as she is, rather than as the woman I call *Vicious*. Rather than the quiet woman she has the world believing she is. In this moment, I think I'm seeing the real her for the first time since the day I found her dancing in the studio off the gym. I'm getting a glimpse of the warmth. The depth. Even as she smiles while perusing the ornaments, she emanates sadness. And fuck if I don't ache to know what's caused it.

Not because I want to use it against her.

But because I hate seeing her struggle.

And because I recognize that bone-deep sadness that comes from loneliness after loss.

Clutching the pile of clothes to my chest, I shake the ridiculous thoughts from my mind. She's not a stray. She doesn't need my help. She doesn't need fixing.

Tomorrow she'll go back to her life, and the girls will circle her like they always do. They'll lift her up, and eventually, she'll find a man worthy of her. Xander definitely wasn't, and I'm not foolish enough to believe I ever could be.

"Got clothes for you."

She swivels, slapping a hand to her chest, as if I've startled her.

I hold the clothes out, rooted to the spot, chastising myself for the thoughts I allowed to float through my mind. For pretending I have any clue who this woman really is.

She lets out a slow breath and a quiet "thank you," but makes no move to stand. Instead, she straightens, her body stiffening and her eyes roving the room, like maybe she doesn't know what to do with me here. Like maybe she's uncomfortable.

Why wouldn't she be? I have done everything in my power for the last two years to make her life miserable. Showing up late, ignoring her, taunting her.

Since I'm to blame for her discomfort, I make the first move. "You up for a drink before bed?"

"Um." She remains focused on her hands in her lap for a moment, but when she lifts her head, she gives it a nod. "Yeah, I could have a drink."

"Wine?"

"You got any good bourbon?"

I bite back a grin. It's not the first time she's surprised me tonight. I'm about to make a list of all the things I've gotten wrong. "Yeah, I think I've got something you'll like."

In my office, I set the sweats and T-shirt on my desk, then pick up two tumblers and the bottle of James Whiskey I picked up the day I came across this house.

I put an offer in on a whim after I discovered it on my way home from one of Bray's hockey games. It was dark, and I got lost in the area. Or maybe I was found. Though I'm not sure I believe in that shit. Either way, I ended up in front of this house, and the moment I saw the for-sale sign, I knew it would be where I could give Brayden and Josie a better life.

Maybe make a better life for myself too.

And god did I want that.

I went to the liquor store, bought this bottle, and told myself I could open it once the house was officially mine.

That's the only time I've had a drink from it. But tonight feels like the right time to have another. And no, I don't want to dig into the reason behind it or why I'm sharing it with Ava.

I settle on the bricks beside her and hold out the glasses for her to take. Once I've poured two fingers into each, I set the bottle on the floor and take one glass from her. "Merry Christmas."

With a coy smile, she taps her glass to mine. "Merry Christmas."

I watch her take a small sip, expecting her to cough. Instead, she hums appreciatively. Damn. That small sound only adds to the many layers of Ava.

"Can I ask you something?"

I nod.

"What made you want to adopt Josie?"

I rough a hand over my face. "How could I not want to? She deserves the world. How her mother could walk away, her foster parents too, blows my mind. It hurts, knowing they did it, but honestly?" I worry she'll use this next part against me if I don't get the wording right, but I go for it anyway. "I'm not even angry that they abandoned her."

Like I expected, she scoffs, but I don't let her get a word in before I continue.

"You know why? Because she deserves better than anyone who would leave. But I do feel bad for them. They're missing out on one hell of a little girl." I look around the room, cataloging all the shit I never had as a kid. "And I have the resources to take care of her. What's the point of having all this, of working so hard, if I can't use what I've got to help other people? If I don't have someone to share it all with?" With my forearms on my thighs, I swirl my glass between my knees. "Maybe it's not enough, but I love her. So yeah, maybe it's selfish, but I want to adopt her because I want to be the one who does it all for her. I want to be her dad."

When I finally turn to look at her, I'm not sure what I expect, but it's not this. In the light of the Christmas tree, her green eyes are deep and full of understanding. She takes another sip of her drink as if she's really considering my words, then gives me a soft smile. "That's a really good answer." She shakes her head, and then her eyes seem to dance around the living room again. "And you're giving her all of it. I've got to admit, I couldn't wrap my head around you being the one to adopt her."

I smirk. "Admit it, you still can't."

She giggles as she brings her lowball glass to her lips. After another long sip, she lets out a slow breath. "Only because I wish it could be me." The admission is so quiet I almost miss it, and a heartbeat later, she blinks away the look of longing that's come over her. "Sorry, I think the alcohol is going to my head."

"Don't do that." I straighten. "I like when you're honest with me. When you're a little vicious, even."

Her smile grows. "I swear it only happens around you."

Glass just hitting my lip, I chuckle. "Yeah, sure." It's a tease, but damn if I don't know it's the truth. And damn if I don't enjoy that truth a little too much. It's heady, knowing that I affect her in any sort of way. I bump my knee against hers. "Don't sweat it. You may still have a shot if the judge turns me down."

Shifting so she's facing me, Ava blinks. "They can do that?"

"Sure." I blow out a breath. "I have to prove that I'm fit to be her father, and if what my lawyer says is true, I'm fighting an uphill battle."

"That's ridiculous. Look at everything you've done for her. I love Josie with my whole heart, and I don't even like you, yet I'd pick you for her father any day of the week." Her voice cracks, and she blinks back emotion.

The righteous indignation that fills her on my behalf, the way she cares so deeply for my little girl, has me leaning forward and swiping a thumb below her eye, catching the falling tear. "Thanks." It's humbling to know that she'd pick me. That she believes I'm worthy of filling the role of Josie's dad.

We're closer now, my face and hers only a breath apart. My hand on her. My thumb now stroking her cheek. Her lips part, and her eyes move back and forth, taking me in. I find myself doing the same, cataloging her every feature. The way her body is inching closer and how her watery mossy-colored eyes are blown wide.

I'd only have to clear an inch of space to know what those lips taste like. To swallow her breath. Maybe get to the heart of her sadness.

"What does your lawyer say you should do?"

Her words have me pulling back, instantly awash in the knowledge of what a grave mistake I almost made.

Ava is heartbroken and maybe a little drunk. God, she must be to say I should be Josie's father. She hates me.

I run my hand through my hair and watch the flames flicker in the fireplace. "Prove that I'm stable. That I have a system in place to support Josie. It's not as easy as it sounds, since I'm a single parent who travels for a living."

"But you have Maria."

With a nod, I take another sip, relishing the way the whiskey burns. "She's a Band-Aid for the situation. Maria could up and quit while I'm out of town, and then what?"

Affronted, Ava rears back. "She would never."

I hold my glass out like I'm making a toast. "Maria is a saint. That's for sure. And while you and I know that, the judge doesn't. I'd never admit it outside this room, but he isn't wrong. Josie deserves a mom and a dad. I'd be hoping another amazing family would come along and snatch her up if it weren't for Scarlett and Brayden. But they need her." I take another sip of my whiskey, licking a drop off my bottom lip. "We all need her."

"Did your lawyer have any suggestions? I mean she has to have a plan, right?" Distress laces Ava's tone. Like this is her problem and not mine. It's nice to have someone care as much as I do. And it's always been clear to me that when it comes to Josie, Ava cares.

Maybe that's why I continue to open up, to spill all the overwhelming thoughts that have been swirling and keeping me up late into the nights as I search for any possible way to keep all the kids together. "She said Josie needs a mother figure. Another parent who can be here when I'm not."

"So you need a wife." The declaration is so simple, so flippant.

I choke on my drink, coughing and pounding my chest with my fist. "*Now* you sound like my lawyer."

Ava straightens, her eyes as big as saucers. "She said that would help?"

I kick at an invisible speck of lint on the hardwood floor in front of me. "Yeah, it would show stability. It'd be good for all the kids, really. I'm never gone for more than a few days, and I rush home as quickly as I can, but I do travel a lot."

"I'll do it," she whispers.

I snap straight with so much force I almost topple off the brick hearth. "You'll do what?"

"Marry you. I'll do it."

I cough out a laugh, even as a wild mix of emotions swirls through me. "Wasn't aware I proposed."

She glares in the way she reserves for me only. "Come on, it's a good idea. You want to be Josie's dad, and I want Josie to be happy. Tonight was proof enough that she's happy here, so I'll do what I can to make sure she stays with you."

"And you want to be her mom," I point out.

She shrugs, the move unapologetic. "Well, yeah."

"But you wouldn't just be her mom." I set my now empty glass beside me. "Scarlett and Bray are part of this family too. Bray may not be mine yet, and maybe he never will be legally, but he needs people who care about him just as much as the girls do. This isn't about you living out some fantasy you have of being Josie's mom."

Her glare darkens. "I'm not an asshole, War."

I blow out a breath. Once again when it comes to her, I'm getting it wrong. "All I mean is that this isn't the kind of decision you should make on a whim. This is life-changing. You're not talking about a farce of a marriage to get one over on the judge, are you? Because I can't put the kids through that. We can't get married, only to get divorced after a year or whatever. And living separately wouldn't work. There'll be more home visits and inspections coming up."

"No." She places her hand on my knee. With that simple touch, the heat of her hand against the flannel fabric of my pajama pants, it's as if she's put a spell on me. One that makes it impossible to look away. "I get that you need full-time help. That they need full-time parents."

"Until Scarlett turns eighteen," I rasp.

She doesn't even blink. "Okay."

"This is fucking crazy." Finally shaking free of her glamour, I pick up the whiskey bottle and pour two more fingers for myself. Pointing my glass at her, I say, "You know that, right? This is nuts. You don't even like me. And you were dating my stepbrother. Is this some sort of revenge?"

She scoffs. "God no. Do I seem like the type of person who would use kids for revenge?" She shakes her head. "Don't answer that."

She doesn't. I may give her shit about a lot of things but one thing I think we both can agree on is that both of us care about Josie. She would never use her for any sort of revenge. I almost feel bad for saying it. Swallowing down my guilt, I bump my knee against hers again. "You're not. But still, this is crazy. We could never pull it off."

Realizing that I'm not saying no, Ava lights up. She's more animated in this moment than I've ever seen her. "No. It's brilliant. We both get what we want. We know exactly what the arrangement is and isn't. And we agree that the kids are what's important here. Their happiness. Their safety. *Their lives.* Because after her time here with you and Scarlett and Brayden, there's no way Josie will be truly happy anywhere else."

Just the thought of her being taken from me creates a pain in my chest so acute I have to rub at it with my free hand. "Of course not."

"And do you think there's another woman out there who could be a better mother to Josie?" She blinks and scoots back. "Oh shit," she breathes, clutching at her neck like she did earlier. "Are you seeing someone?"

I laugh at the absurd turn this conversation has taken. "No, I'm not seeing anyone. And just tonight, I was thinking that I should find a mother for the kids, and that if it weren't for our mutual dislike of one another, you'd be perfect for that role."

She grins almost like she enjoys my response.

"So we agree—outside of our obvious distaste for one another—that we're the best option for Josie."

I dip my chin. "I suppose."

"And we're both single." She arches a brow, as if she's waiting for me to confirm.

Once again I give her a tiny nod. "But Scarlett's only two. We're talking about a long-term commitment."

Ava nods. "Sixteen years until she turns eighteen. I can do the math."

"Don't you want a happily ever after with someone like Xander? A man who will give you the white picket fence, kids of your own, a love story?"

She scrunches her nose and then coughs out a humorless laugh. "A man like Xander?" She snags her phone off the floor by her feet and taps at the screen. Then she's holding it up. The image on the screen is grainy and dark, but I can clearly see the nearly naked woman with her bare ass grinding in Xander's lap and the huge smile on his face.

"Is that from tonight?" I grit out as I take the phone from her to inspect it. Rage fills me and bubbles over. How could he leave her here on Christmas Eve to go do that?

"I don't need a man to give me a love story." Her voice is soft but determined. "And I definitely don't want one with anyone like Xander. I'll write my own. Josie *and* Bray and Scarlett"—she holds eye contact, her expression serious—"can be my love story."

"So you're not looking for anything from me?" I ask the question, even though I'm not sure what kind of answer I'd prefer from her.

"I'd like us to be friends," she says evenly.

The words hit like a knife to the gut. I've never hated a sentence more, and I don't want to dig into the reasoning there.

Clearly reading my reaction wrong, she adds, "I'd prefer it if my husband didn't hate me."

"I don't hate you," I say softly.

Her eyes light up, full of mirth. "Say it again like you mean it."

I chuckle. "I don't hate you, Ava. I just—" I groan, sifting through my thoughts, hoping to put them in order in a way that makes sense. "I want you to be sure. Take the night to think about it. Hell, take a week. By morning, you'll probably change your mind."

Me? I'll be left dreaming of what could have been. And kicking myself for pushing back rather than dragging her to a justice of the peace right now.

"I don't need a night. I don't need any time at all. This is how it's supposed to be, War. Can't you see that?"

Yes. "I don't know. Fuck, this is crazy."

She grins. "You said that already."

I swallow past the lump in my throat and ask her one more time. "You really want to do this?"

"Yes." Her smile only expands, just like my damn heart. She's so goddamn beautiful. There's no way this won't hurt. She'll fall for my kids, she'll live in my house, and she'll be my damn wife, but she'll never truly be mine. This isn't my love story, but it is theirs, and there isn't a chance in hell I'll keep my kids from living it. She lifts her pinky and holds it up between us. "Pinky promise."

Jesus Christ, this woman is so rare. My swallow is hard as I stare at that finger. Never have I ever longed for a goddamn pinky in my life, but right now, I want to reach for it. It's a lifeline. A solution.

Blame it on old habits dying hard, but I can't help but push a little more. Standing, I ignore the gesture and instead hold out my hand to her. "Then I guess we should head to bed, wifey."

She blinks at my hand. "What?"

"We're going to be married. For a long time."

"I-I'm not sleeping with you," she stutters.

A sharp laugh escapes me. "You are. But yeah, I'm not fucking you."

She winces in response to my brash declaration and finally drops the damn pinky.

I blow out a breath. Jeez, some moments I forget how fucking innocent she is. I'm an asshole. I should have grabbed her pinky. But I wouldn't have wanted to let go. I'd have wanted to tug her closer. She'd have fallen into me, not expecting it. And then...

No, Tyler. And then *nothing*. "It's just sleeping," I say gruffly. "If we can't share the bed for a night, how the hell are we going to live together for years?"

That word—years—echoes between us, resonating, soaking in. That's what this is. A true commitment. Though it won't be a real marriage, it will be a partnership, and if we're going to make this work —and god, for some reason, I really want to—she needs to be comfortable around me. And I need to get over whatever this fucking obsession is with her.

I offer her my hand again. "I'll be a perfect gentleman, I promise."

She swallows thickly, scrutinizing my hand. Like she's worried it'll morph into a bear trap the moment she touches it. I hold my breath, certain she'll tell me to get lost. That she had a momentary lapse in judgment, but she's come to her senses. That she can't possibly put up with me for years. I don't want her to do that, though. So I lift my little finger and waggle it. "Pinky promise."

Instead of recoiling, she surprises me for the hundredth time today. Looping her finger with mine, she meets my gaze. "Okay, let's go to bed."

Chapter 14
Ava

I KNOW what you're thinking. I couldn't possibly have just offered to marry Tyler Warren. I hate him. I've spent the last two years lamenting how he's a narcissist who cares about no one but himself. Agreeing—*no, proposing*—to be his wife for the next year, let alone sixteen, is insane.

But hear me out.

I might have been a teeny bit wrong about him. Not completely, because I still think he's a womanizer who stood me up two years ago in favor of a one-night stand. Something I made clear I wasn't interested in.

But he's not *only* a womanizer. Is any person really *only* anything?

God, I hope not. If so, then I have no idea who I am. For so long, I was nothing more than the girl who provided blood and body parts to keep her sister alive. If that's all I was, that would be pretty pathetic.

Although I don't regret a single donation, I've got to be more than that. Right?

Maybe this is my shot. My chance to be someone else.

It's clearly the most out of character thing I've ever done. Or it's the most in character. Dedicating my life to someone else's happiness. I suppose maybe I am still the same person I always was.

But it's for three kids who need me. War isn't at risk of losing Brayden and Scarlett. They're safe here. But Josie? Without War proving that she has a stable, loving home—that it is in her best interest to stay with him—she'll be at risk of losing the first family she's ever had.

I refuse to let that girl lose anything else.

I may be the best chance she has of staying in this house. I'm not saying I'm perfect, and if anyone found out my secret, I'd probably be the last person they'd deem worthy of raising a kid. Still, I truly believe this is the right thing to do. I'll always put those kids first. They'll be safe and happy and loved. That should be enough, right?

Assessing myself in War's bathroom mirror, I make peace with my decision and glance at the clothes I dropped onto the counter.

Putting them on will make it more real. His clothes. His house. His bed.

And I'll be his wife.

Not in the biblical way, of course. Just in the *we're going to raise kids together and build a beautiful life for them and*...holy shit, I'm going to be *married* to Tyler Warren.

Spiraling, I pick up my phone and text my sister.

> Me: It's late, I know. I should have texted earlier. It's after midnight here, though, so Merry Christmas. I have some pretty unexpected news and I'm not even sure how I feel about it, but...

> Me: I'm getting married!

> Me: Okay, deep breaths. It's not how you think. We're doing it for Josie. Remember that guy I told you about a couple of years ago? The one who stood me up and

Having no interest in reliving all the turmoil that's festered between us, I delete the message.

Let's try this again.

Me: I'm marrying Tyler Warren. He's a hockey player. I've told you about him before, remember? He's adopting Josie. It's not love in the traditional sense, but I love Josie and he does too. And I really think this is my purpose. Why I found myself in Boston. For her. And her sister. I just met Scarlett, and I'm already in love with her. Tyler is also the guardian of a teenager, Brayden. He seems like a good kid. It will take time for them to be comfortable with me, but I'm going all-in. You always said nothing worth doing is worth doing halfway. I wish you were here. I wish we could wake up together tomorrow, and I wish you could meet all of them. Even Tyler.

Me: I'll text you tomorrow. I love you.

The weight of the night hits now that I've texted her. I always work out my feelings through our conversations. My messages are as therapeutic as diary entries.

A gentle knock sounds on the door, startling me. "You okay?"

"Yup." I set my phone down and scan the room, garnering the last of my energy. "Be right out."

No more dilly-dallying. Morning will come soon, and with a house filled with kids on Christmas, I can only imagine the energy I'll need.

I pick up the T-shirt and immediately roll my eyes. Of course he picked a Bolts shirt emblazoned with *Warren* and a big 7 on the back. Despite my better judgment, I slip it on. I can't sleep in my dress, and I'm too tired to argue with him, which is exactly what would happen if I asked for a different shirt. With a quick glance at my reflection, I stalk out of the bathroom. "Is it a hockey player thing only, or do all guys like seeing their name on a woman's back?"

Tyler is already beneath the covers—thank god; I couldn't handle another minute of awkwardly staring at one another before getting into bed—and as I shuffle to the empty side, he blinks at me, looking shell-shocked. Though he opens and closes his mouth a couple of times, no words come out.

"Okay," I say, frowning at his lack of response. "Guess it wasn't intentional." Slipping into bed, I adjust the sheet and comforter and swallow back a moan at how comfortable the mattress is. "I can't imagine you'd be eager to see me, of all people, wearing your last name. It's just that Sara and Lennox are always going on about how much the guys love seeing the girls in their jerseys. It's a whole thing for them. But then again, they're all kind of…kinky?" I shrug.

Yeah, that's how I'd categorize them. They're also oversharers, which is apparently what I am when I'm nervous, because did I really just say the word *kinky* while climbing into bed beside Tyler Warren?

Also, how come every time I say his name in my head it's a whole thing. Tyler Warren? He's like a god in my mind. Untouchable. I'm so embarrassing.

"Sorry, I'm being awkward. Just go to sleep. I swear I'll be more normal in the morning."

Pulling the comforter all the way up to my chin, I turn toward the door, my back to him, and pray for sleep to take me. Or a black hole. Either would be acceptable right about now.

War shifts, causing the bed to dip, and then he's closer. Too close, since the air that escapes him when he lets out a heavy sigh tickles the back of my neck. "I didn't actually get to see the back of the shirt on you. May I?"

I peer over my shoulder and find him motioning to the covers. Without a word, I nod. If I speak now, I'll blurt out something else ridiculous.

He gently pulls the covers down, the move far too charged. I hold my breath, certain that if I don't, the tension in the room will drown me.

Every syllable he speaks in that gravelly tone vibrates through me. "I can't speak for all men, but yeah, I really like seeing you wearing my number." He tugs the covers up again and shifts back, taking his heat with him. "I just didn't expect you to wear it without pants."

My heart all but stops when realization dawns. Crap. I walked out of the bathroom without putting on the sweats he gave me. "Uh, I—"

War chuckles. "Go to bed, wifey. We've got a big day tomorrow."

I wake to the sound of giggles and a loud, drawn-out *"Tyler!"*

"You know the rules. Knock before entering." This voice is deeper, groggy.

"But it's Christmas, Bray. Our first Christmas as a family. We need to wake him up. Let's jump on the bed."

I'm still fighting to open my eyes, confused about where I am, when the door swings open and the voices grow louder. "It's Ava! Brayden, it's Ava."

"I can see that," he grumbles.

Finally, I force my eyes open and blink into the dim light until the voices become people in front of me.

Brayden is holding Scarlett, who is wiggling against his chest, anxious to get down. Josie is bounding toward me, wearing the biggest smile.

Finally, memories from last night return, and it hits me. I slept over. I'm in Tyler Warren's bed.

Holy shit, I'm in War's bed.

"Merry Christmas," he murmurs in my ear, hugging me to his chest.

My heart thumps wildly now that I notice the way he's wrapped around me, his arms cradling me, his face buried in my hair, his head on my freaking pillow.

"Santa granted my wish. Ava is still here," Josie squeals as she jumps onto the bed.

Lungs seizing, I roll out of War's arms.

This is not good.

Once I've put a little distance between us, I dart a look at Brayden again. While Josie may think this is just a fun sleepover, it's clear from the teenager's amused face that he knows what adults normally do during overnight visits.

"Merry Christmas, love bug," I say to Josie, breathing through my panic. I open my arms wide and catch her as she catapults into them. I inhale the fragrance of her shampoo and kiss her head, finally beginning to find my bearings. This is just the reminder I need. I'm here for her. For them. The kids, that is.

"What am I? Yesterday's news?" War shifts, wearing a pout.

Josie launches herself into his arms next. "You told me you got me the best present ever, and you weren't lying. Is she staying all day?"

War chuckles now, his smile wide. "Yeah, I think so." He nods to Brayden. "How'd you sleep?"

Brayden settles a still squirming Scarlett on the floor. She's barely touched the ground before she's running toward the bed and fisting the covers, trying to pull herself up. I reach down for the little blondie and help her up. Once she's got her knees on the mattress, she crawls right up my body and sits on my chest, her full diaper making a plopping sound.

"Pwetty." She smacks her warm, slightly sticky palms against my cheeks. Her rosy cheeks, the crusties in her eyes, and the blond wisps falling into her face do nothing to hide just how perfect this little girl is.

Brayden cringes. "Sorry, I didn't change her diaper."

With a smile at him, I shake my head. "No worries. I can do it. Good morning, Scarlett." I rub a hand over her head, relishing the feel of her silky baby hair. "And yes, you are very pretty."

She pats her chest and smiles. "Pwetty."

Giggling, I shift her so I can get out of bed and change her. Only the moment I swing my legs over the side of the mattress and the cool air hits them, I realize that I'm still not wearing pants.

And any preconceived—and wrong—notions Brayden may have are seemingly confirmed.

"I'll, uh, take care of it." War hops out of bed and scoops Scarlett up. Once she's settled in the crook of his arm, he meets my eye, his lips folded in. Clearly, he's holding in a laugh at my expense. "Come on, Bray. Once we get this one's diaper changed, we can get breakfast started, and then it's present time."

I slip back under the covers, hiding my bare legs before Josie notices.

Beside me, she shouts, "Presents!" But rather than barrel out of here, she turns her attention back to me, snuggling into War's pillow. She looks so cozy in the plaid nightgown that matches his pants. Now that I'm seeing them again, I realize that Scarlett's jammies were the same plaid. Brayden's too.

My heart trips over itself. Did Tyler Warren buy matching Christmas pajamas for all of them? And if so, why is that so freaking adorably hot?

I bat away thoughts surrounding War's attractiveness. But the pajamas only solidify my decision to marry him. Not for me, but because these kids deserve the kind of love and devotion he is clearly lavishing them with.

"This really is my best present," Josie says in that soft, whispery voice she always used when we'd snuggle in her hospital room and watch movies. She'd share little thoughts with me. Not true secrets, but thoughts that were important to her. Every time she trusts me to keep one, my heart grows another size.

I run a hand through her hair and cup her face. "What is, love?"

"You are. Christmas morning wouldn't have been the same without you."

Warmth creeps up my neck and into my cheeks. With fair skin like mine, there's no way to hide the blush. I so badly want to tell her that I'll always be here. But before I do, I need to check in with War. If he's changed his mind, I can't really blame him, since I accepted a proposal he hadn't made and all but forced myself on the man.

A man who dislikes me greatly.

A man I dislike as well. Obviously.

At least, I *did*. I'm not sure I can continue to hate a man who isn't at all what I thought. I'm beginning to realize that I made a lot of assumptions and based my opinion on what I think may have been misconceptions. How could they not be? A narcissistic playboy doesn't choose to move away from his friends and purchase a large family home so he can adopt three lonely kids.

"Waking up to your beautiful face has definitely made this the best Christmas," I admit.

"We should have had a sleepover in my room. Boys smell, and my room is prettier than this one."

I laugh at the matter-of-fact way she lays it all out.

"You think Tyler smells?" I tease.

She shrugs. "No. He actually smells really good." She snuggles deeper into his pillow. "For a boy."

Joy bubbles up inside me. God, it feels good to be here with her. I never could have imagined Christmas going this way. Just the thought of how I could have woken up by myself this morning, how instead of giggling with Josie, I'd be lying in the dark, lost in the past, has me rolling closer to her and sniffing War's pillow.

Pulling back, I let my mouth drop open and widen my eyes in an exaggerated way. "His pillow does smell." I give her head a sniff next, tickling her while I inhale her sweetness. It's a tease, though in reality, I'm soaking her in. "You're right. I should have slept in your room. You smell so much better."

We stay like that a little longer, laughing and cuddling, until I send her downstairs, promising I'll follow once I get dressed.

Once she's gone and I'm left in the quiet room lit only by the morning sun peeking through the blinds, I realize I'll either have to stay in War's clothes or put my dress back on. The memory of his whispered words about how he liked seeing his number on my back has my body heating even as I get out of bed, pantsless, and my bare feet hit the cold wooden planks.

If I'm really moving in with him, then I'll definitely request he add a plush area rug.

Or will I have my own bedroom?

If he had an extra room, wouldn't he have offered it to me last night? It's not like he wanted me to sleep in his bed.

Or did he?

God, I could go round and round in my head all day if I'm not careful. Overthinking and overanalyzing every interaction we've had over the last twenty-four hours won't do me any good. So I head to the bathroom and slip on the far too large sweats he pulled out for me last night. I have to roll them four times to keep them from slipping down my hips. Then I squeeze a small glob of toothpaste onto my finger and run it over my teeth and give my hair a quick finger combing, working to make the mess look a little tamer. When I'm finished, I look a little less like Anna from *Frozen* when she wakes up and more like myself— albeit a happier version. Because even though I don't have my own clothes or a toothbrush, I woke up to three smiling kids, and honestly, I can't think of anything better.

CHAPTER 15
TYLER

"GRAB THE BERRIES, MON CHOU." I open the oven a crack and peek in. Every Christmas morning, my mom would make the same French toast casserole, and when it came out of the oven, she'd set the oversized baking dish on the table between us and hand me a fork. The two of us would sit like that and eat straight from the dish. Mom saved all year for gifts, but I couldn't list more than a handful I received in the twelve years we had together. But this casserole? I remember the way each one tasted, the things we talked about, the laughs we shared. My mother made everything magical, and Christmas morning was no exception.

There were only two of us then. This morning, with five of us here, we can't exactly eat out of the pan, so I pull a stack of plates from the cabinet.

If my mother were here, she would have figured it out, and the tradition would have continued. Then again, if my mother were here, so many things would probably be different. Me, for one.

"Bacon should be ready," Bray calls from the living room. He's got Scarlett on his hip, keeping her away from the Christmas tree and all the presents I stashed under it last night. The two of them are wearing matching pajamas. Josie and me too. The kid rolled his eyes when I gave them their early Christmas present before my family showed up last night, but he donned them without complaint, and if I had to guess by the way he keeps smiling at the girls, he doesn't mind matching too much.

I open the door of the second oven, and sure enough, the bacon is crispy perfection. "Can you put Scar in her highchair and set the table?"

"I'll get Scarlett's milk," Josie offers as she drops the container of berries onto the counter.

Meals are always a little chaotic, but the kids love helping out, and I want to encourage that, even if it means cleaning up extra messes. Usually Maria is here with us too. She'll pour the milk into the sippy cup, then Josie will carry it to her sister and act like she did all the work.

Worried I'll have a big mess on my hands if I let her pour herself, I pull the bacon out quickly and set it on the stovetop, then hustle to where she's already holding the milk carton, her little arms straining. I get to her just as one hand slips and gently take it. "I've got it. Can you go entertain Scar before she starts throwing things?"

With an exaggerated nod, she wiggles her butt and makes a beeline for Scarlett.

"Alexa, play Bing Crosby Christmas tunes," I say, recreating another one of my mother's Christmas traditions.

When "Mele Kalikimaka" plays loudly through the speaker, Brayden eyes me from where he's setting the table. I wink at him, and in response, he lowers his head and gives it a shake, his typical smirk the only indication that he's enjoying himself.

"Hey, Bray," I motion toward the kitchen, calling him closer. Before we sit down, I need to check in with him about what he saw this morning—a woman in my bed.

Brayden leans against the counter, staring at me. "What's up?"

"About this morning." I grip the back of my neck, trying to figure out what to say.

He shakes his shaggy hair. "It's no big deal. You can do what you want. It's your house."

I glare at him. As much as I lament telling him the truth, I'm not sure how much I should share. But letting him believe it was a casual fuck isn't going to fly either. I've never brought a woman around him. It's been a long time since I've even considered spending the night with someone. I don't like how he thinks that I'd do that so casually. But he's too old to not question what Ava and I are doing when she arrived here last night with Xander. So I decide to give him a shortened and diluted version of the truth. "She needed a place to stay. You know that."

He scrutinizes me, eyes narrowing, as if he's thinking about the perfectly good pull-out couch in my office as well as the super comfortable one in the living room.

With a deep breath in, I give him more truths than I intended. "I've always liked Ava. I'd like it if you'd give her a chance. If she's willing, she may become a more permanent fixture in this house."

He lifts one shoulder and eyes me through his shaggy hair. "That will make Josie happy."

I take a step closer and place a hand on his shoulder, squeezing. "I think she could make us all pretty happy if we're open to it. I'm trying here, Bray. Really trying to give us a family."

Brayden seems to relax beneath my grip. "You're doing a good job." He nods over to the table where the girls are giggling as Scarlett whips strawberries at Josie, who's pretending to catch them in her mouth but missing every single one. That's going to be fun to clean up. "They're laughing. And honestly," he shrugs again, "this is the nicest Christmas I've had since my dad died. So, if I haven't said it lately, thanks."

I pull Brayden against my chest and hug him. We don't do this enough—clearly—because for a second, he freezes, but when I squeeze him tighter, he relaxes and hugs me back. Then he pulls away. "Okay, don't get all emo on me."

Laughing, I throw him a bone and act like the cocky hockey player he's used to, pointing toward the scene before us. "I did good, didn't I?"

The first thing I did when I came downstairs was plug the tree lights in and start a fire. It's now crackling and keeping the oversized room warm while big white flakes flutter from the sky on the other side of the floor-to-ceiling windows. It's one of my favorite things about this house—the view of the backyard filled with oversized trees and the lake. Reminds me of Canada.

The scene only gets better when the woman dressed in my long-sleeve Bolts shirt and sweats enters the room. The clothes hang from her tiny frame, and her wavy red hair falls loosely past her shoulders. Her cheeks are rosy and her eyes are bright as her mouth drops open.

"It's like a Christmas dream," she says in raspy wonder. With a hand to her mouth, she surveys each one of us. "You all look so perfectly Christmasy in your matching pj's. I don't fit in."

It takes effort to remain where I am rather than stride over to her. "These pants came with a matching flannel shirt," I tease. I went for a white long-sleeve T-shirt instead, knowing I'd overheat in the flannel top. "I could get it for you."

With a light laugh I've never heard directed my way, she shakes her head. "I'm okay. Thank you, though."

"Might give you more coverage than that T-shirt alone," I call, turning around and closing my eyes to banish the image of her that threatens to haunt me. Damn, did she look good in nothing but my shirt last night. Fresh-faced and bare-legged, with a sassy attitude she reserves only for me.

I like that last part a bit too much.

Makes me want to push her buttons.

"Come sit next to me," Josie calls from her spot beside Scarlett.

When I finally make it over to the table with Scarlett's sippy cup, everyone is sitting, leaving one open spot, the place between Ava and Brayden. The instant the cup is in her hands, Scarlett pulls back, ready to throw it, but Josie grabs it before it can clatter to the floor.

"Come on, sissy. No milk on the floor."

Heading back into the kitchen to grab the plate of bacon and the French toast casserole, I blow out a relieved breath. Looks like I won't be mopping the floors just yet. Though after breakfast, I'll have no choice in the matter.

"I can help," Ava offers, following me. "Holy crap, this looks delicious."

"Tastes even better," I promise.

She arches a brow. "Did Maria make it?"

With my head tossed back, I cough out a laugh. "Think I can't cook?"

A saucy shoulder lift is all I get in response.

Huffing, I snag a fork from the drawer and scoop a bite of casserole, being sure to get a berry in the mix to give her the full effect. Fork held aloft, I stalk up to her. "Open."

She sucks in a surprised breath. "You're going to feed me?"

"*Open.*"

The woman loves to push back, but she gives up pretty easily this time. The moment she opens her mouth, though, I'm rethinking my actions. Shit. I should have known that the sight of her closing her lips around the fork would affect me. What I couldn't have imagined, though, was the delicious moan that escapes her. At that simple sound, all the blood in my body rushes to the one place it has no business being right now.

"Holy crap," she mutters. "That's delicious."

"Lucky for you, your future husband's more than just a pretty face." I toss the fork into the sink, then don oven mitts and pick up the casserole. With a nod, I gesture to the bacon. "Can you grab that?"

"So we're still doing this?" she murmurs as she steps up beside me and picks up the platter.

"Serving breakfast?" I tease.

What she really wants to know is whether, in the light of day, I've changed my mind about her proposal. Up until thirty seconds ago? Fuck yeah, I was questioning it. Concerned we couldn't really pull this off. Unsure that I could commit to spending the next however many years in this woman's presence without pulling my hair out.

Then I heard her moan, and it changed everything.

"*War,*" she grits out.

It's perplexing, the way her anger makes me giddy. I thrive on pissing her off. It's probably something I should discuss with my therapist.

Later. Like after we're married and he can't talk me out of it. Because yeah, I want to marry Ava. I want to marry the shit out of her, and then I want to find out whether she'll make that sound when it's not her mouth doing the work. When my lips are doing the tasting instead.

"Yeah, wifey, we're still doing it. You should probably call me by my real name now, though. Or husband. Your choice. Now, let's serve breakfast before the minions revolt and start throwing things."

Her laughter follows me to the table. It's new to me. I've heard it directed at Lennox, Hannah, and Sara, but now that it's because of me? I won't lie; it's a sound I wouldn't mind hearing for the rest of my life.

When Josie notices the bite missing from the casserole, she picks up her fork, begging to try a scoop right from the dish too. As if it's meant to be, I dive into the story of how my mom and I always ate it that way.

"Did your mom leave like mine did?" Josie asks as Ava takes the fork from her to dig out a bite.

Wordlessly, Ava hands it over, then drops a small serving onto her plate, cuts it up, and slides it onto Scarlett's tray. Instantly, my little girl fists a bite, shoves it into her mouth, and squeals.

With a smile on my face, I turn my attention back to Josie. "No, my mom died when I was twelve. But I have lots of great memories of her like this one, and I can't wait to share them all with you."

The whole group grows somber in response to my sad confession, but the spell is broken a moment later when Scarlett throws a strawberry at Josie.

"What other traditions did you have?" Josie asks.

"The pajamas are another of my favorites. My mom and I always had matching pj's, and she always gave them to me on Christmas Eve."

Ava's green eyes meet mine. "My mom did that too. It was always my favorite gift. My sister's too."

"My mom and I used to go outside and look for reindeer tracks after we opened presents," Brayden offers.

My chest tightens at the sadness shining in his eyes. Fuck, I didn't even consider how hard today would be for him since his mom hasn't called. I really hope she makes an effort this afternoon. "We should do that today, then."

That, thankfully, has his lips quirking. "Yeah, that'd be cool."

"Oh, I want to see a reindeer," Josie hollers. The girl is always excited. "Ava saw one a few weeks ago. Do you think it's the same one?"

With a tinkling laugh, Ava digs her fork into the casserole. Even though we all have plates, we eat straight from the casserole dish. One by one, we pull it close, then pass it along, though Josie and Brayden make sure to help Scarlett when she's finished with what Ava set out for her and gesturing for more. It isn't lost on me, the way they wordlessly continue my tradition. There were no words of apology or a *sorry for your loss.*

It's a relief. My mom has been gone for decades, yet it never gets easier. Rather than doling out empty platitudes, my family is honoring her and our memories in a way that means more than I can explain.

"No, love bug, I don't think it's the same reindeer. That one lives on a farm in Bristol." An uncertain smile curves her lips. "But if *Tyler* says it's okay, maybe I can call his owner and see if we can come by his farm one day and meet the reindeer."

I like the sound of my name on her lips, even if she says it in that soft voice, her eyes meeting mine as if she's unsure how she feels about it. I'm guessing that's how a lot of this will play out. Testing things. Toeing the line. Figuring out just how far each of us will go.

My lips curl at just the thought of it. Yeah, I'm going to like that a lot.

Josie practically climbs onto the table and grasps my outstretched arm, almost causing me to drop my fork into the baking dish. "Can we, Tyler? Pretty please? I'll do the dishes and make all the beds."

Laughing, I press a kiss to her head. "How about you eat your breakfast, and Ava and I will see what we can make happen?"

Josie launches herself off her chair, scurries around Ava, and wraps her arms around my middle. "You're the bestest ever."

I set my fork down and hold her to me, dropping my head against hers. "Merci, mon chou." When I pull back, Ava is watching me, her green eyes full of curiosity and wonder, like she's seeing the real me for the first time.

"You bought her a drum set?" Brayden groans as Scarlett bangs on the last of her gifts.

Already, I'm second-guessing the choice. It's a plastic toy that lights up and makes premade sounds. It's not like she'll be making her own percussion sounds. Or maybe she will, since she's already walloping on it. In theory, it's great. It plays fun little tunes that aren't too terribly loud. In practice, it does sound an awful lot like she's beating on a drum.

"Couldn't exactly give her a hockey stick." I cock a brow at the pile of gear at Brayden's feet. He unwrapped every piece of hockey equipment he could need this morning. *Every* piece. I know that because I went to the store myself and told them I wanted one of everything. When he started playing, he wouldn't let me buy his equipment. He was adamant that I didn't spend my money on him. Now that it's Christmas, he can't really complain, and he can see that I spoiled the girls just as much.

We're all spread out on the floor. I stationed myself by the tree, making it easier to pass out presents. Josie is on Ava's lap. No surprise there. Scarlett is beside them with her drum in front of her, and Brayden is on her left, his legs spread wide to keep Scarlett relatively contained.

"Let me grab a trash bag to clean up all this paper," Ava offers.

Josie gets up off her lap, but when Ava pushes off the floor, I haul myself up on my knees and hold out a hand to stop her.

"Wait, we have one more present."

"Is it mine?" Josie says, bouncing on her toes.

I laugh. The girl is surrounded by a mountain of gifts. She never acts spoiled, but she does like pretty things, so I'm not surprised by her question. "No, this one is for Ava."

Ava's eyes jump to mine. "I didn't—" She shakes her head. "I didn't get you anything."

I smile. "No worries. This is a gift for both of us, really."

Frowning, she scrutinizes me as I reach into my pocket and pinch the band of the gold ring I've kept locked up for far too long. When I pull it out and hold it between us, the emerald sparkles in the glow of the fire. Just like Ava's eyes did last night.

As suspected, it's the exact shade of green.

"Holy shit," Brayden mutters.

"Oh my god," Josie squeals.

Their comments sound distant. My focus is fixed firmly on the woman I'm about to ask to be my wife. I tilt my head, brow furrowed, silently saying *are you sure about this?*

Her eyes go wide in a way that says *what the hell did you do?*

That expression, the one of sheer panic and maybe a little fury—probably because I'm doing this in front of the kids—only eggs me on. There's no resisting the opportunity to push her. This moment, if she allows it, is like magic, and that's exactly what every one of us in this room needs. A little magic, as well as a bond, a tether to keep us together forever. To keep us safe from the outside world. Our family full of strays.

Maybe Brayden has a point.

"The last few months with these kids have been nothing short of magic. But until now, something has been missing. *Someone* has been missing. And in the last twelve hours, it's become abundantly clear that you are that person. Honestly, this gift is probably more for me than it is for you because, you see, I'd like to extend the magic. And I'd really like to keep you." With a long exhale, I survey each kid. "*We'd* like to keep you. Right, guys?"

Josie nods so emphatically I worry she'll give herself whiplash.

Scarlett is already nuzzling into Ava's side.

Brayden just laughs. "Yeah, you'll fit right in."

With my heart in my throat, I meet those emerald eyes. It's a dangerous thing because they really do break through every wall I've ever erected. "So what do you say? Will you be ours?"

Either she's the most talented actress I've ever seen, or my spiel was even better than I hoped it could be. In slow motion, her eyes fill with tears. Then I swear her lip wobbles as she breaks into a wide grin, as if she's truly surprised by the question. As if she didn't concoct this scenario herself in this exact spot beside the fire last night.

Either way, I don't expect her to lunge toward me and wrap her arms around my neck. The whispered *thank you* makes my chest tight, and when she lets go, the loss of contact hits harder than it should.

She sits back on her knees and holds out her hand, waiting for me to slide the ring onto her finger.

For a moment, the world falls away. The kids' chatter, the sound of that damn drum toy, the crackle of the fire, none of it exists as I slide the ring that used to belong to my mother onto Ava's finger, my hands trembling.

With her pinky, she grabs a hold of mine and stops the shaking. That little squeeze is all I need to center myself. "Where did you—" Her eyes meet mine, and she shakes her head, like she just knows it's my mother's ring. Her expression softens, and once again, I get the feeling that Ava and I are much more alike than I ever could have imagined. "It's perfect."

It hits me in this moment that I might really be in trouble. That remaining detached may be more difficult than I anticipated. Because I really want to kiss my future wife.

"Traditionally, the bride says yes," I taunt.

With a roll of her eyes, she settles between the girls, and just like that, the rest of the world returns. She wraps an arm around Josie before looking back at me, her expression carefully neutral. "Of course I want to be your—all of yours. Yes. Yes, I'll stay."

The way she answers, making it about them, is exactly what I needed. Letting out a long breath, I look away from her. So what if this is the first meaningful gift I've received since that last Christmas with my mother? This is about the kids. What we're doing is about them, not about me finding some long-forgotten happiness. Focusing instead on how Brayden lights up as he scrambles over to hug her and how tightly Josie is clinging to her, already yammering about moving Ava in and begging for her to sleep in her room and not mine, I push to a stand.

"Husbands and wives share a room," I grumble as I walk past them, headed for the trash bag Ava originally offered to get.

"Jealous of a nine-year-old girl?" Ava mumbles, following me toward the kitchen.

Out of earshot of the kids, who are already distracted by their gifts, I whirl around and put my hands on my hips. "What are you doing?" My tone is harsher than I mean for it to be, but I could really use a moment away from her. Otherwise I'm at risk of letting wild ideas like happily ever afters and shit like that take over.

Guys like me don't get happily ever afters. Arranged marriages? That's more like it. A partnership? That's something I can control.

Feelings, though? Not a chance.

"Doing the dishes, you grump." She saunters over to the sink, where the empty casserole dish is soaking. "And I thought maybe we could have a moment away from the kids to discuss what just happened."

Working to keep my breathing even and deep, I take her in, but I don't respond.

She sighs. "Or not." Standing in front of the sink, she rinses the dish and gets to work scrubbing it. "Has anyone ever told you that you're very hot and cold? One minute, you sweep me off my feet, and the next, you drive me nuts."

She doesn't look at me as she speaks, which is a relief. Feeling a little less out of sorts, I pull a trash bag from the box on the pantry floor. When I turn around and see her bent over the sink, her red hair cascading down her back, my name and number front and center, that relief evaporates.

In the space of two heartbeats, I'm pressed up against her, my chest flush with her back. "Remember that comment you made about my name on your back?"

She nods against my chest, still focused on the dishes. She hasn't pulled away, but she's trying hard to ignore me. To ignore this moment. Probably because I've once again gone from cold to hot. But I won't be ignored. Not when there's no escaping the pull between us.

I slip my arms around her waist and find her hands in the soapy water. When I lace our fingers, I relish the bite of the emerald digging into mine.

Lowering my mouth to her ear, I can't help but let out a possessive growl. "Now it will be your last name too."

TEXT MESSAGES FROM AVA'S AND TYLER'S PHONES

Hannah: Merry Christmas, girls. Hope Santa was good to you even though you were very naughty this year.

Sara: The naughtiest! And yes. Santa got me a projector for the roof so Brookie and I can watch movies while in the hot tub.

Lennox: Aiden and I will be over soon to check that out.

Sara: You have your own hot tub. Stay out of this one, you freak!

Sara: And merry Christmas, girls. Don't know what I'd do without you. Love you all!

Lennox: Aw, love you too, soon-to-be sister. And the rest of you. This has been the best year of my life. Marrying Aiden is obviously part of that, but you girls are too.

Ava: Merry Christmas, girls. Love you! Brunch Sunday?

Brooks: Merry Christmas, boys.

Aiden: Merry Christmas. Heard you've got a new toy for me to check out.

Brooks: Stay out of the team hot tub.

Hall: Merry Christmas to me! As soon as I get back from my dad's house, I'm checking out whatever this new present is.

War: You sure you want to play with Brooks's toys? Sara is kinky AF.

Hall: *shudders* Okay, yeah, rethinking that. I'll just hang in my dad's hot tub.

Brooks: LOL and you think your dad and Lake are any less kinky?

Hall: Fuck you. Why do I even talk to you guys?

War: Because you love us. Merry Christmas, boys.

Brooks: Kids like their presents?

War: Not as much as I liked mine.

Aiden: Yeah? What'd you get?

War: A family. And a real fucking happy one, at that. You shoulda seen their smiles when they opened their presents. Best day ever.

Dad: Merry Christmas, son. Thank you for having us last night. You have a beautiful family.

Tyler: Thanks Dad. Merry Christmas.

Xander: What time are you coming over, angel? We have Christmas dinner at my mom's at three.

Xander: Hello?

Xander: Pick up the fucking phone.

Xander: I'm at your apartment. Where the fuck are you? If you ghost me on Christmas and make me go to my family dinner alone, we're done.

Xander: You're going to regret this.

Chapter 16
Ava

"THEN HE SAID he was his boyfriend and she was his girlfriend. It was literally the cutest thing I've ever seen," Lennox is saying as Josie, Scarlett, and I approach the table. War and Brayden dropped us off on the way to the rink, and out front, War hopped out to pull Scarlett's stroller from the trunk and show me how to open it up.

The past two days have been a whirlwind. After cleaning up Christmas brunch, we bundled up and went outside in search of reindeer tracks. That turned into a snowball fight.

The kids and I ganged up on War and won, though I suspect he threw the game, which is annoyingly adorable.

After we were all sufficiently frozen, we went inside, where War gave me one of his comfy sweaters and another pair of enormous sweats. When he came out in a short-sleeve tee, his tattoos on display, I practically choked on my tongue.

Somehow, I'd forgotten all about the panty-melting tattooed arms, but as I watched him carry sweet Scarlett around, the image was burned into my memory. And when she fell asleep on his chest during *Elf* and one of those arms was the only thing keeping her in place, I knew I was screwed.

Because I'm extremely attracted to my future husband.

While she napped, War arranged for a car to pick me up so I could get some things from my apartment. Josie was adamant that she come with me. It was more of a blessing than I would have imagined, because it kept me from sitting alone in the silence and overthinking what I'd done over the previous twenty-four hours.

It tempered thoughts of how I had moved into that apartment two years ago on the heels of one of the worst days of my life, how it had been my escape and my salvation. How I was up and leaving this haven now, when I wasn't sure I was making the right decision.

Rather than dwell on any of that, I quickly packed enough to last a week. Because taking this one week at a time was far more palatable than preparing for a sixteen-year stretch.

I didn't see the messages from Xander until I got back to War's house. I'm not sure how the jerk could think I'd still plan to go to Christmas dinner with him after he left me at War's house. In what world—even if I didn't know about the strippers and have photographic proof to remind me of what an ass he is—would any woman welcome her boyfriend back into her arms after being left on Christmas?

Nope. Instead, I went and got engaged to his stepbrother. Because that's way more normal. I'm just thankful that Maria will be back tomorrow and Tyler will leave for an away game the following day. That will give me time to slowly adjust to all these changes.

"I still can't believe Fitz has two people to fuck, and I've got none," Hannah whines.

I cup my hands over Josie's ears, although it's probably too late, and gasp.

The sound garners Hannah's attention, and when she locks eyes with me, she blanches and mouths an "oh my fuck, I'm so sorry."

Sara whacks her in the arm. *"Duck.* God, it's like this is your first time."

Hannah shoots daggers at our blond friend. "Is that a dig at my lack of sex life?"

"Little ears," Josie pipes up.

Hannah throws her arms out wide. "Come to me, my favorite nine-year-old, and tell me all about your magical Christmas."

Josie peers up at me and whispers, "Your friends are weird."

Despite the observation, she happily skips to the table and launches herself into Hannah's arms.

"I need a hug," Lennox whines.

Josie, eating up the attention, makes her way around the table, doling out hugs before settling in the seat between Sara and me.

"Where are Millie and Vivi?" I ask as I pull Scarlett from her stroller and study it, looking for a way to fold it up. Sara hops up and does it for me—how the hell did she figure that out?—then puts it in the corner.

"Paris. Gavin swept them away on Christmas morning. Pretty sure he's trying to knock her up. Give Vivi a sibling," Lennox says.

Sara coughs out a laugh. "Uh, I doubt it. Millie's got big plans, and they don't include any more babies. At least not for a while."

"When she gets back, we'll invite her and Vivi over," I say to Josie. "I bet Vivi and Scarlett would love to play together."

"How was your Christmas?" Hannah asks, eyes dancing. She called on Christmas Day to remind me not to go back to Xander.

I promised I wouldn't and then told her who I was marrying instead. She did a proper scream and then told me how she'd always known War was obsessed with me. I let her in on the real reason we were getting married since what we have is far from a whirlwind romance that occurred in only ten hours' time. She is still convinced it's more than that. The other girls remain completely in the dark, though.

"I had the best Christmas ever," Josie says, her sweet voice a soothing balm, as always.

Lennox pushes a mimosa in my direction, eyeing Scarlett to make sure she won't swipe it.

As I reach for the glass, Josie leans forward, eyes wide, and whispers, "But I think Ava"—she thumbs over at me—"had an even better day. When I woke up, I found her having a sleepover in Tyler's bed."

"*Josie.*" I set my glass on the table with a little too much force. Thank god I haven't taken a sip yet. If I had, Scarlett would be wearing it.

"*Shut up,*" Lennox shouts, her voice echoing off the walls.

"Yup." Josie nods, chin lifted with pride. "Then he asked her to marry him, and now she's going to be my mom, right?" She peers over at me, a hint of wariness in her expression, despite her confident tone. It guts me, the caution there. The poor thing is worried that I'll change my mind.

"Yeah, love bug." I stroke her hair and frame her face with my free hand. "That's the hope. But no matter what, I'll always be here for you, okay?"

The way the tension drains from her body pinches my heart. "Okay."

Sara eyes me over Josie's head, silently making it clear that I can't get away with not telling them the full story. Her eyes go from serious slits to wide with shock, though, when she catches sight of the ring on my finger. "Oh my god, look at that rock."

Blushing, I can't help but study the beautiful emerald. And I can't help but be reminded that this is the exact ring I would have chosen if asked to design my own. A simple gold band with filigree designs and a round emerald. It's obviously an heirloom, and I know he didn't have time to go shopping sometime between midnight and seven a.m. on Christmas morning.

The look in his eyes as he slid it on my finger told me everything I needed to know. Whoever this ring belonged to, and I have a feeling it was his mother, was very special to him. It made me think that, just maybe, I'm special to him. Or I could be.

Flexing my fingers, I shake the thought from my mind. This isn't a real marriage. Believing this is a fairy tale is a bad idea. That's how people get hurt. How hearts get broken.

We're doing this for Josie and Scarlett and Brayden.

My entire life has been in service of other people. It's what I'm made for. I can absolutely do this.

"Tyler Warren, you sweet boy, you," Sara says as my husband-to-be appears with Brayden in tow. We've just finished brunch, where we drank way too many mimosas and I had to cover Josie's ears three more times because these women don't know how to censor themselves. It's official—girls' brunch is not meant for kids. I'll have to find a sitter next time.

Wow, look at me thinking of babysitters and maternal things like that.

War only gives her a *who me?* look in response.

I pull my little love bug into my side and hold her tight. "Josie here told the girls our news."

A slow grin spreads across his face. "Ah, so they know that it was all an act."

A hint of dread worms its way through me in response to the clear calculation in his tone. What the hell is he doing? This is not the place to tell our friends the truth about our agreement. And I can't believe he thinks it's okay to bring it up in front of the kids.

"What was an act?" Lennox asks, squinting.

My cheeks heat, and my heart is thumping against my breastbone. I get it if he doesn't want the girls to think he actually has feelings for me, but this is mortifying.

He doesn't turn away from me as he replies. "The hatred my future wife has always harbored for me. Apparently she just wanted my attention."

Instantly, the unease dissipates, but it's quickly replaced with irritation. That shouldn't be surprising. When it comes to Tyler Warren, I'm always irritated.

Hannah lets out a dry laugh. "*Right*. Because *she's* the one who was putting on the act."

"Oh, I don't deny that I wanted her attention and that I acted like a jerk to get it," he says, his voice and expression filled with far too much glee. He faces me again, mischief in his eyes. "But now she's all mine. Right, Vicious?"

"Why did I say yes again?" I ponder aloud, sarcasm dripping from my tone.

Though the question is rhetorical, Josie answers anyway. "Because you wanted to be my mom."

Everyone at the table laughs, and I smile down at her, even if it hits too close to the truth. If War is bothered by the comment, he doesn't let it show, though.

"I should probably tell the boys asap, since none of you know how to keep a secret," he says, his attention drifting between Lennox and Sara specifically.

Lennox grins. "Oh, honey. When was the last time you checked your notifications? I can't imagine the group chat isn't already blowing up."

Brayden must have been a pickpocket in a previous life, because before War can reach for the device, he's got it out and is holding it in front of War's face to unlock the screen. "Dude," he shouts. "You have ninety-eight notifications."

"Let me see that." Grumbling, War reaches for it.

Before he can take it from Brayden, Hannah swipes it out of the teenager's hand. "The first message is from Aiden. Looks like Lennox has the biggest mouth." Hannah waggles her brows. "'Holy shh'—look at me censoring; see? I'm getting better at this—'you finally got your dream girl to give you a chance.'"

My heart stutters, and my attention flies to War, who just shoves his hands into his pockets and rolls his eyes.

"This one is from Brooks. 'Congrats, man. Ava is the best. Glad you finally got the girl.'" Hannah's devious smile grows wider with every word she reads, mirth filling her tone. "Hall chimed in next. 'Duck'— he didn't actually say that, but I remembered the rules—another one bites the dust.' Hall again: 'But I'm happy for you, man. We all knew it was only a matter of time.'"

"All right, I think we've heard enough." War stretches out one long arm, but before he can grab the phone, Hannah is passing it to Lennox.

"No, I don't think we have," my pink-haired friend says. "Exactly how long have you been pining for our precious Ava?"

War scoffs. "I don't—I didn't." He huffs and meets my gaze. "Can you make them stop?"

I should, but I'm too bewildered to form a coherent sentence.

"Since he first met her," Josie says, popping up on her knees on the chair beside me, her hands splayed on the white tablecloth. "Right,

Bray? He told us all about the beautiful ballerina he met and how it was love at first sight."

Brayden only side-eyes War and shrugs.

With a gasp, Hannah zeroes in on Josie. "When was this?"

I'm also wondering when this happened.

"Brayden and Tyler were visiting me in the hospital, and we were playing Pretty Pretty Princess. I asked if he had his own pretty pretty princess, but he just laughed and said I was the only pretty pretty princess in his life. Then I asked him if he'd ever been in love." Josie glances at War, not the least bit ashamed of herself for giving him up, despite his frown. "He said no, but that he once thought he could fall in love. It was when he watched the prettiest ballerina dance. When I asked what happened to her, he said he never saw her again." She eyes me. "But later, when Tyler was in the bathroom, Brayden told me that he saw Tyler's pretty ballerina all those years ago. He said she had long red hair and green eyes, just like you. And you're a ballerina, right?"

It takes everything in me not to look at War. To tamp down on the hope that threatens to bubble up in me when I consider what she's saying. It's in my best interest not to let myself believe that he's felt anything but animosity for me since that day he found me in the studio.

Because the way she describes it, her retelling of how *he* described it, was exactly how I felt. The closest thing to love I've ever experienced was in the moment he had me backed up against the mirror and asked me out on a date. That man was Tyler. He's been War ever since. He's asked me to call him Tyler again, but I think doing that will screw with me. All of this is screwing with me.

Love at first sight? That's absurd, right?

"That's why I asked Tyler to sign me up for ballet," Josie continues, like her confession hasn't completely upended this conversation as well as my understanding of Tyler Warren.

I still haven't looked at him. I can't.

I can't look at anyone. Head down, I study the tablecloth, my empty glass. Every eye is fixed on me. I can feel it. And I want to turn and run, rush back to my apartment and hide while I consider what this all means.

If it means anything at all.

"I always wanted to take ballet," Sara says, drawing attention to herself.

Relief floods me. I could kiss her for taking the pressure off me.

"But I'm way too much of a klutz for that."

"Oh my gosh, do you remember when we did that talent show in college?" Lennox asks, full-on laughing.

From there, the conversation shifts, and I ease back into my body and out of my mind.

Until I'm daring enough to glance at War. I don't know what I expect to find. I'm not even sure what I want to find.

What I'm met with is a pair of cool blue eyes searching mine, as if he's trying to read my mind, trying to determine what I think of Josie's statement. It's simple, but it feels like a revelation.

The man I thought was War might just have been Tyler all along. Is it possible I got it all wrong?

Chapter 17
Ava

THE CAR RIDE home is anything but quiet. Josie babbles on about every topic that pops into her head. Scarlett sings nonsensically to what sounds like the tune of a song from *Zombies*. Brayden sits in the back seat behind Tyler, smirking every time he catches him so much as shifting in my direction.

But my thoughts are louder than it all. The what-ifs, the could-it-possibly-bes, and the maybes swirl inside my head. It takes a great deal of effort to shut it all down and remind myself that I have a job to do. I'm here to be the emotional support for these kids. A parental figure to care for them while Tyler travels.

I'm basically the help.

Regardless of what Tyler and I felt for that blip in time two years ago, back before we actually *knew* one another, we aren't living that happily ever after now. Those feelings don't factor into this scenario.

I may recognize that he's not who I thought he was, but that doesn't change what we need to do now. We'll be friends. We'll be partners that raise his kids because that's what's best for everyone.

All the self-preservation I've been working on goes out the window when Tyler pulls into the driveway and squeezes my hand once. "Can we talk after the kids get settled?"

I nod, certain my voice wouldn't work if I tried to speak. Behind me, Josie throws her door open, calling for me, and with a sigh, Tyler releases my hand. Then he straightens, switching into dad mode in front of me, and climbs out, heading for Scarlett.

"Did you know I start ballet this week?" Josie tells me as we follow the boys and Scarlett to the door.

"You may have mentioned it a few times," I tease, smiling down at her. She hasn't stopped talking about ballet since Tyler confirmed that he signed her up for classes on Christmas.

"Will you take me?" I can sense the nervousness in her voice. Like she's still not 100 percent sure I'm staying. I wish she knew just how much everyone loves her. All the things we're doing just so we can keep her. I never want her to worry that I'll disappear.

"Of course. I'll go over the schedule with Tyler tonight and make sure I know where you need to be and when."

"Do I hear two of my favorite girls?"

Josie darts into the house at the sound of the voice, and when I step into the kitchen, catching a whiff of fresh-baked cookies, I find her wrapped up in Maria's arms. Before I can shuck my coat, she's got a cookie in her mouth and she's telling Maria all about brunch and how Hannah has a potty mouth.

I choke on a laugh. "She did get better by the end."

Josie peers up at the ceiling like she's considering my words, then gives a nod. "True. It's all about progress."

Maria holds back a snort as she shuffles over to me. "Merry Christmas."

I sink into her embrace, happy that she's finally home. I've been nervous about how she'll react to all of this, but so far, she doesn't seem surprised.

"Did you have a good time with your family?"

She pulls back, one brow arched high. "From what I've been told, I doubt I had as good a time as you had here."

Across the kitchen, Josie watches on, still chomping on a cookie, without an inkling of remorse on her face. "What? I tell Maria everything."

I fold my arms across my chest. "And what exactly did you tell her?"

Josie shrugs, her expression serious. "The truth."

I can't hold back my laugh. "Well, then, guess there's nothing left for me to tell."

Maria rolls her eyes. "Yeah, wishful thinking there, missy. Tyler took Scarlett up for a nap, so that gives the two of us plenty of time to have a cup of tea and catch up."

"What am I going to do?" Josie asks, her hands on her hips and her bottom lip stuck out.

Already settled on the couch, Brayden calls, "You can pick a movie to watch with me."

Josie brightens comically. "Oh, let's watch *Zom*—"

"Anything but *Zombies*," he shouts.

Always expressive, she's back to pouting, now with her arms crossed over her chest. "You said I can pick."

Brayden drops his head back against the sofa. "Isn't there anything else you want to watch?"

"*Zombies 2*?" She scurries into the living room, her voice hopeful.

He palms his face and groans. "Okay." Then, with a glare in our direction, he adds, "Don't go far."

"You're the best, Bray." Maria links her arm with mine and drags me toward the kitchen island. "I'll make the tea while you spill it. How's that?"

"Ha ha," I deadpan. But as she asks, I dive into the story. There's no way she'll believe a lovesick-puppy tale like the girls do. Honestly, I'm not sure why I even allowed myself to get swept away like that. I was the one who proposed this insanity to Tyler, not the other way around. If he had been interested all this time, wouldn't he have come to me with the idea?

"Truly, it's for the kids," I tell her, hands clasped around my warm mug. "I love them. He loves them. He needs help, and I'm happy to give it."

"But marriage?" Maria gives me a concerned frown as she brings her tea to her lips. "Why not just say you'll be the live-in nanny?"

I shrug. "They need something more permanent. And I've always loved Josie. I can't imagine anyone else filling this role."

Her expression shifts into a small smile. "Me neither. And I've never seen Tyler look at a woman the way he looks at you."

I snort, even as my cheeks heat. "Like he wants to murder me?"

She shakes her head. "The man just agreed to spend the next two decades living with you. And he didn't offer to move the girls into one room so you'd have your own space, did he?"

Gaping like a fish, I blink at her. "I—" I snap my mouth shut. I don't have a clue how to respond to that. Because honestly, moving the girls in together would make sense. Scarlett sleeps through the night, so she wouldn't disturb Josie, and either of their rooms is big enough to share.

But he never considered the idea.

Would it be weird for me to mention it to him?

Do I want to?

Strangely, the thought of having my own room here doesn't bring me comfort. Maybe because it would make our status as *co-parents only* official. Partners in this strange endeavor, raising kids together and nothing more.

I don't exactly love that.

But there's no way we could be more. Right?

Maria smirks. "That's what I thought."

We spend the rest of the afternoon talking about the kids' schedules. Maria gives me a rundown on what their lives look like from day to day, and eventually, Tyler joins us, and we settle in with the kids and watch a movie. When he chooses the seat next to mine on the smaller couch, rather than near Brayden on the larger one, Maria cocks a brow at me.

While I settle in, I allow myself to imagine that she's right. And I give myself permission to picture what a real marriage might look like.

And you know what? The image isn't half bad.

CHAPTER 18
TYLER

Aiden: Should I start putting together my speech?

Brooks: What the hell are you giving a speech for?

Aiden: My best man speech, obviously.

Hall: Wait, who's getting married?

Hall: I kid, I kid. All of you motherfuckers are. Even Fitz had to go and get coupled up.

Aiden: Is it called coupled up when there are three of them?

Hall: He's got a couple to himself. Pretty fucking impressive.

Fitz: I'm right here, guys. I'm not sure how I ended up in this text chain, but I'm right fucking here.

Hall: My bad!

Brooks: LOL. See you on the plane tomorrow, Coach.

Aiden: Okay, back to my question. War?

WITH A SIGH, I drop my phone onto the mattress beside me. After the slew of messages that Hannah fucking read out loud in front of Ava and the girls, I could use a break from my so-called friends.

Why the fuck does everyone think I've been pining for Ava? For two years, I literally lived to taunt her. To ignore her. To piss her off.

Sure, things have changed over the last couple of days. I know she isn't the person I thought she was. Or maybe she is, but I can see now that she's so much more than that.

One thing that hasn't changed? She's still quick to judge me. If not for the kids, I guarantee she'd be repulsed by the idea of marrying me.

Doesn't mean I don't like her. Or think about her far too damn often. Doesn't mean that her presence beside me every night doesn't keep me up for half of it. Wondering if we'll ever share the intimacy of a real marriage. Wondering what she'd do if I made a move on her. Would she kiss me back? Would her body come alive for me? Would she pant out my name when she came?

I scrub a hand down my face, irritated by this train of thought. I'm fucking hard beneath the covers just thinking of the possibility of a moment with her. Meanwhile, she's been in Josie's room for over an hour. Wouldn't be surprised if she stays in there all night to avoid me and the conversation we need to have.

Maybe it's better this way. I could set up a separate room for her. The girls could share a room. Hell, they'd probably love it. Ava and I don't *have* to sleep together.

It's better to keep things the way they are. Making a move will probably only scare her off. And I need her to do this with me. Even if she sticks around, there's no way our marriage will ever be real.

Staying the course is a more realistic long-term approach.

Not thirty seconds after I've convinced myself of this, the door opens and the redhead who is the star of all of my fantasies lately appears in nothing but sleep shorts and another one of my long-sleeve shirts, her hair a mess and her eyes tired. "Hey, sorry. I fell asleep in Josie's room."

I shake my head. Hopefully she takes the gesture as a silent way of saying it's no big deal, when in reality, I'm working hard not to say *come lie with me. I'll hold you while you fall asleep.*

"You still want to talk?" Ava asks as she disappears into the bathroom. She's looking for a hair tie so she can braid her hair like she does every night. It's always a loose one and done to the side. She reappears, stepping into the bedroom, her fingers already forming the braid as she watches me expectantly.

It's just another thing that throws me. Reminds me of the past. Confuses me just enough to have me questioning it all again.

I shake the confusion off and focus on her question. "Sure. It was just about the wedding."

Ava gives me a full once-over, smirking. "No shirt? Getting awfully comfortable there."

My blood heats as I get lost in her expression. In the way her green eyes challenge me. I love this version of her. The one she saves just for me. This is the ballerina I fell for in the gym.

"You keep stealing 'em, so I figured you needed them more."

Cheeks pink, she ducks her head and loops the elastic around her hair. Then, grasping the bottom of my T-shirt, she pulls it up a smidge, giving me a peek of her freckled skin. "I could take it off if you need it."

That flirtatious tone of hers is new. And I really fucking like it.

My swallow is heavy. So is the sensation low in my gut. "Maybe we should talk first?"

The fabric drops just as quickly as her smile. "Right. About the wedding. Do you think it's weird that our friends didn't even question our engagement?"

I sigh, annoyed with myself for shutting down her flirtation. "Yeah, it was strange."

"I was dating your brother last week. You'd think that would make them at least a little suspicious," she says as she walks toward the bed.

I grind my teeth, though I shrug off that word. *Brother.* "Has he contacted you?"

At the edge of the mattress, she lowers her head and fidgets with the comforter. "He's sent a few texts, but I haven't responded."

Straightening, I fist my hands on either side of me. "Wait, he left you here on Christmas Eve and you still haven't talked?"

She shrugs, gaze averted. "Nope."

"So he doesn't know we're getting married?"

Finally, she looks at me, her lips pressed into a flat line, and blinks. "No idea what he does or doesn't know. You saw the picture. He was too busy with strippers on Christmas Eve to care. Maybe he knocked one of them up, since he was all about breeding that night."

I frown as I study her. "You don't sound that upset."

Pulling the covers back, she raises a brow. "Ya know, I'm really not. Turns out, I cared a lot less about that relationship than I thought."

Anger bubbles to life inside me. I hate that she dated him. Hate that he got any pieces of her when all I get is a façade.

Maybe it's better that he doesn't know. As soon as he does, my father will, and then it's only a matter of time until Dory has one of her infamous fits. I'm not exactly looking forward to dealing with that, but since my father and I don't talk often, I can probably put it off for a bit.

"Want me to talk to Lennox? See if she can quickly put together a nice event like she did for Gavin and Millie?" Ava continues, clearly having moved past Xander completely. As she slips between the sheets, I try not to focus on how much closer she is now. Or the coconut scent of the product she runs through her hair before she braids it.

That product combined with her natural scent makes her smell like the most delicious dessert. Reminds me of the coconut cake my mom bought for my birthday each year.

I clear my throat, because thinking about my mom when we're discussing our wedding isn't doing me any favors. "I took care of it already. That's what I wanted to talk to you about. My lawyer got the license expedited so we can go to town hall tomorrow morning before my flight."

Ava has barely settled in beside me before she shoots up, her jaw falling open. "Oh."

I study her, gauging her reaction. "Is that okay?"

Blinking, she shakes her head. "Yeah, of course. I didn't realize it would happen so fast, but a quickie wedding at town hall makes sense. No need for a big thing."

I frown, wishing I could read her mind. This woman is always guarding her thoughts like they're sacred. Or, sometimes, like they're ideas she's ashamed of.

Is that what this is? Was she looking forward to a real wedding? I try to explain why town hall makes sense. Try to make her see that I care. Too fucking much, if we're being honest. "I figured this was our best option. Once we're married, Madi can file the amended adoption paperwork, which lists you as a petitioner as well."

With her teeth pressed into her bottom lip, she nods. "Yeah, that's good. Really."

"You tell your family about it?" Maybe that's what this is about. Maybe they want to come to the wedding?

She looks away, tangling her fingers in her lap. "Yeah, I told my sister. Are the kids coming with us tomorrow or...?"

I shrug. "It's just a few minutes at town hall. No need to drag them out into the cold."

"Right." She dips her chin, her mouth set in a firm line. "Makes sense. Anything else I should know while you're gone? I went over the kids' schedules with Maria, so the two of us should have everything covered."

A sigh escapes me. Looks like that's all I'll get from her regarding the wedding.

I should be happy that she agreed to marry me so quickly. That her focus has turned to the kids so quickly.

But I'm not.

Chapter 19
Ava

Me: I'm trying not to freak out right now, but I'm getting married today.

Me: In like five minutes, actually.

Me: And I haven't told Mom or Dad.

Me: Currently sitting on a bench in town hall waiting for the clerk. Tyler has barely looked at me all morning. I can't help but feel like I'm letting you down. When I moved to Boston, I promised I would live for me. No more putting other people first. But I swear, Andrea, this is what I want. Even if Tyler ignores me for the next two decades. Even if we only interact when it comes to the kids. Because I want to be their mom more than anything. Is that pathetic? Maybe. Yes, I love my job and I have amazing friends. But after today, I'll still have all of that. I'll keep them, and now I'll also get to keep Josie. So I'm sure you're thinking that I'm back to doing things for others instead of myself, but I swear I'm more selfish than that. I'm doing it for me. I do want this. And also, I secretly want

"WE'RE READY FOR YOU."

I jolt in my seat and manage to hit Send without finishing my message. Oh well, I'll text my sister again when we're done.

Tyler is already standing, and god, does he look good. Over and over this morning, I've had to remind myself that he's not wearing the perfectly tailored suit for me. He's going straight from here to the airport, and travel suits are a must.

But each time I look at him, I find it hard to breathe. He's always gorgeous, but he's never looked better than he does now.

Except on Christmas morning, when he and the kids wore matching pajamas, and he sat crisscross on the floor with Scarlett in his lap, face lit up as he watched her and Josie and Brayden open presents.

God, Ava. And you're trying to convince yourself that you aren't attracted to your groom? Good luck there.

In my defense, anyone would be attracted to my groom. The blue of his tie brings out the color of his eyes, making them sparkle. Though his dark hair is styled, it's still a little wild, since he's been running his hands through it, and the damn tattoos I still haven't gotten to explore properly peek out from the collar of his shirt.

He holds out his hand to me. "Come on, wifey. You have the rest of your life to ogle me. Better not make the clerk wait."

I roll my eyes and let out a heavy sigh. "Just when I was thinking about how pretty you are, you had to go and open your mouth."

Tyler barks out a laugh and shakes his head as he wraps his hand around mine. Once I'm standing, he leads me toward the open door.

I never could have pictured my wedding looking like this. Not that I've ever been the kind of girl to picture a perfect wedding day. My sister and I were more concerned about making it to prom. Then college. A wedding seemed like too much to hope for, and a wedding without my sister at my side was something I refused to picture at all.

But if I were the type of girl to picture her wedding, I can't say I would have conjured up the image before me. A small, tidy room with no windows and a middle-aged man wearing a taupe suit and a toupee? Nope. Never.

"Do you have your own witnesses?" he asks without looking up.

The woman who led us in replies before we have the chance. "His attorney arranged for Janice and me to stand in."

"Great," he says, focus still fixed on the paperwork in his hands.

Tyler pulls out a beige plastic chair for me. It's a bucket seat, the kind that moves when a person sinks into it, kind of boomeranging back and forth. I lace my fingers and cross my ankles, suddenly feeling incredibly foolish for having stressed about what to wear today. It's not even white. And I almost always wear white. It's a cream-colored sweater dress and the only thing I brought with me to Tyler's that seemed suitable for my freaking wedding.

If that's what this is. It feels more like a boring meeting.

"All right, Mr. Warren, if you could just sign right here," he says, his voice monotone.

Tyler angles forward and drags the pen across the white paper with practiced ease. Makes sense. He probably signs lots of autographs. Though there's no way he actually read the document.

"And Miss..." The man trails off, having no idea what my name is now that the form is no longer in front of him.

"Mrs. Warren works just fine," Tyler says gruffly. "It's the only name that matters now. Right, wifey?"

With a heavy sigh, I slide the paper closer. Is it possible to kill a man with a pen? Looks like it'd make a semi-decent weapon.

Beside me, Tyler chuckles. "Just sign the paper, Vicious. You can plan my demise later."

Huffing—and irritated that he can read me so well—I sign the damn marriage certificate, then I slide back into my chair. "Are the vows next?"

The man puts his fingers on the paper and spins it, then signs it himself and pulls out a rubber stamp. "You're all set. Congrats"—he looks at the paper, stamp held aloft—"Mr. and Mrs. Warren." With a *thunk*, he marks our marriage certificate with his seal.

My heart sinks. Pathetic. The man couldn't be bothered to remember the name he spoke aloud only a moment ago.

Tyler's chair makes a squeak as he pushes it back, and then once again, he's holding his hand out to me. "Ready?"

That's it? We're just...done?

While heat builds behind my eyes, I follow him out of the room and to the exit. I realize he's got a plane to catch, but it all feels so impersonal.

He feels impersonal. Like the man I've known him to be for the last few years. War. *Not Tyler.*

God, how could I have been foolish enough to think things had changed? That *he* had changed. Maybe he's that man for the kids, but when it's just us, it's better if I remember that this is who he is.

As Tyler pulls the door open, the winter breeze rushes in, bringing with it a few flurries.

I tighten my cream coat, only now realizing that I never even took it off for the "ceremony." So much for worrying about what I was wearing today. Tyler will never even see the dress.

"They didn't even say *you can now kiss the bride*," I mutter as we shuffle out of the building without so much as a picture to commemorate the occasion.

"Yeah, he seemed a little preoccupied," Tyler says as he pulls out his phone and buries his face in it.

The justice of the peace isn't the only one who's preoccupied, it seems.

"Well, I guess that's it." Swallowing past the emotion lodged in my throat, I dig my phone out of my coat pocket and navigate to the Uber app. Might as well go to work from here. I took the day off since I was getting freaking married, but it looks as though I was wrong to think the occasion would be worth any kind of celebration.

"Wait, sorry." He slips his phone into his pocket and fixes his attention on me. Finally. "Just wanted to confirm that your ride was here."

"Oh, I was just setting up an Uber." I hold up my phone and give it a little shake. "I hope you have a great trip, though. I'll make sure to have the kids call, or you can just call whenever you want to talk to them, I guess," I stammer as awkwardness seeps in.

Tyler steps closer, ducking a little. "Bray has a phone. They normally use that to call." He smiles. "Or Josie calls using Alexa."

"Right." I nod twice, unease still swirling inside me. "And...um. I-I know you normally go out after games"—I blow out a harsh breath as nerves skitter up my spine—"but if you could just be discreet about it." With a breathy laugh, I shrug, my face hot with embarrassment and my gaze lowered to my hands. "Don't want the judge to see pictures of you with other women and figure out this was all for show."

"What?" Tyler grits out.

At his stern tone, my eyes snap up to his of their own accord. "I'm just saying. I—"

He steps in so close I have to tip my head back to maintain eye contact. He's breathing heavy, his jaw tight and his eyes murderous. "That may not have been the wedding you deserve, but make no mistake about it—you are very much my wife, and I take my vows seriously."

"We didn't make any vows," I scoff, even as I'm still stuck on those two little words—*my wife*—and the possessive way they rolled off his tongue.

"*Merde.*" Breathing heavily, nostrils flaring, he slips a hand up the back of my neck. Then, tangling his fingers in my hair, he tugs so I'm forced to meet his eye again. "How about these, then?" He licks his lips. "I vow to be faithful to you and only you. For as long as we're married, I won't so much as look at another woman. I vow to put our family first, and that includes you, Vicious. You're a Warren now. You're *my wife*."

My heart trips over itself, then takes off at breakneck speed in my chest. Did he really just—

"Your turn," he murmurs, his mouth inches from mine.

"My turn?"

"Yeah, Vicious. Cut me with your words. I dare you."

"I thought "

"You thought wrong," he all but growls. "Now do your little thing with your pinky. Hold it up and pinky promise me that you'll be faithful. Promise me that I can get on that plane today, leave you with our kids for a week, and know that I'm the only one you'll think about when you're in our bed at night."

His words almost knock me over right here on the courthouse steps. Where is this coming from? This feverish behavior. This possessiveness. And the pinky promise. It's almost cute how he's craving that from me.

Is he...? Could he be...? No, there's no way my husband actually likes me, right?

Brows lowered, he shakes his head. "Is it really that hard to promise me fidelity?"

"I didn't know that was part of this agreement—" At a loss for words, I duck my head and wring my hands. I never considered that he'd be celibate for the entirety of our marriage, but he seems so affronted by the idea that he'd be with another woman. With a deep breath in for courage, I add, "We've never even kissed."

He brushes his lips against mine. "Seulement dans mes rêves." Then his mouth is on mine, stealing my breath. I may not know what those words mean, but god, he could have told me I'm the devil, and I wouldn't care.

He devours me with his kiss. Obliterates every preconceived notion I had about this marriage. Groaning, he grasps my hair a little more firmly and tugs me closer. "That's it, Vicious. Give me every last piece of you," he murmurs against my lips. Then he's diving in again, tangling our tongues and absolutely ruining me.

I claw at him, finally free to touch him, pulling him closer, wishing more than anything that we didn't have layers of clothes between us and winter weather swirling around us.

This, I realize now, is what a kiss is supposed to feel like. This is what my sister and I dreamed about, what I never imagined I'd have.

At the sound of a car horn, I startle and pull back, panting.

Wearing a delicious grin, Tyler clutches me to his chest and holds me tight. "It was everything I dreamed of and more," he whispers. Before I can wrap my head around his words, he spins me in his arms and rests his chin on my shoulder. "Your wedding gift, wifey."

A gorgeous burgundy SUV is parked in front of me, decorated with an obnoxiously large bow on the top of it.

"It's a seven-seat Rolls Royce with all the bells and whistles. I wish I could stay and spend the day driving around with you, but maybe you could drop me off at the airport?"

My breath stutters as I take it in. "You bought a car for me?"

Without replying, Tyler grasps my wrist and guides me down the steps. Like a kid showing off a new toy, he points out each feature, his face bright and his tone giddy. "Wait, I forgot to show you my favorite part." Encircling my wrist once again, he drags me around the back.

When the license plate comes into view, I let out a loud laugh and peer up at him. "Mrs. War?"

He grins. "Now everyone will know you're mine."

I shake my head, stupefied by this eager, sweet side of him I've never seen. "I didn't know—"

Cupping my cheek and leaning in close, he smiles. "Now you do. So promise me, wifey. Promise me you're mine."

It's impossible not to smile as I make that promise. Then I kiss him again.

In a daze, I navigate through Boston traffic to the airport, then to the Langfield Corp building. It isn't until I'm sitting in my office, rereading the text I just received from Hannah, that I realize this wasn't all a fever dream.

Because on the device in my hand is a screenshot of Tyler Warren's Instagram page. The first image is of the two of us on Christmas morning. It's a photo Josie forced us to take. In it, we're sitting side by side in front of the tree, looking tired but happy, my hand held up to show off my gorgeous ring.

The caption below the picture reads *Our forever starts today. Mr. & Mrs. Warren.*

Tyler_WARren_7

♡ 903k ◯ 54k ⟋

liked by **pumpkinspice_13** and **others**

Tyler_WARren_7 Our forever starts today.

TEXT MESSAGES FROM AVA'S AND TYLER'S PHONE

Dad: Could you give me a call, son? Dory told me about your news, and we're a bit confused.

Sara: OH MY GOD! Did you just see War's Instagram? Ava! We need a FaceTime chat immediately! Why do we have to be on a road trip for two weeks!?

Lennox: You're complaining? I get no sex for two weeks.

Lennox: Also, congrats, Ava! Though I already told you in person at work.

Hannah: Our girl is all different shades of red.

Hannah: <pic of Ava hiding her face>

Hannah: The number of comments on that Instagram post is insane! Our little Ava is a star!

Ava: You guys are crazy. It's all because it's Tyler.

Hannah: No, it's because you're the gorgeous woman wearing no makeup and Tyler's Bolts T-shirt in the photo he decided to go official with. #mostwholesomepictureever #mybestieishot

🔊

Xander: What the fuck is this about you marrying my asshole stepbrother? Is this some kind of ploy to get me to apologize? Okay, fine. I'm sorry I left you there. But how the fuck are we supposed to get married and have kids if the guys my father works with think you play stupid games like this?

Xander: Ava, pick up your phone.

Xander. Call me.

Xander: The marriage is REAL?

Xander: You cunt. My mother says you really married the asshole. This is fucking insane.

Xander: Okay, you've made your point. Now pick up the goddamn phone so we can work this out.

Xander: Did you move in with him? I just stopped by your place, and the doorman says you don't live there anymore.

Xander: WHAT THE FUCK, AVA?

Xander: CALL ME.

Xander: Slut.

🔊

Tyler: I landed, wifey. Heard we may have broken the internet.

Ava: ...I don't even know what to say to you.

Tyler: LOL. Told you I'd make sure everyone knew you were mine. I'll call you and the kids later.

Tyler: P.S. Thanks for marrying me today. You really were the most beautiful bride I've ever seen.

CHAPTER 20
TYLER

"A WHOLE WEEK away from the family, huh?" Fitz appears beside me on his surfboard. "You enjoying the break from the chaos?"

Game three of this away stretch is here in California, and like we do any time we find an ocean, we're surfing. Before this week, Fitz was the only one who knew about my adoption plans and the three kids that are living with me. I'm not any closer with Fitz than I am with the other guys, but until recently, the two of us and Hall were the only single guys left in our group. When I stopped going out as much, it was hard not to tell him the truth. Besides, I needed someone to talk to about how I went from being the single guy who cares about nothing but hockey and sex to a guy who would do anything to be a father.

Even marry a woman who hates him.

After that announcement though, everyone knows that Ava and I are married and trying to adopt Josie—they just don't know we're married *because* we're trying to adopt Josie.

I sit up on my board, catching my breath from the ride out. There are only a few other surfers out this early, just as the sun is coming up over the horizon, turning the water a shade of pink that reminds me of a certain nine-year-old back in Boston.

"I miss them like fucking crazy." I laugh.

Fitz's smile is thoughtful. "I get that. I can't wait to get home."

Dropping my head forward, I give it a shake. *Finally.* Fitz has finally admitted to being in love with Declan, his best friend since they were kids. On top of that big change, the two of them are also dating Melina Rodriguez. She's a mega popstar, and Declan is a firefighter in a small New England town. Their differences seem vast, but already, it's clear they're solid.

"How are things with Ava?"

"You mean my wife?" I try to wipe the smile from my face, but it's no use. I'm dying to get home and figure out where we go from here. Anxious to see whether that kiss was a prelude to more or nothing more than a tease.

Knowing Ava, she'll play coy and make me work for it. I don't mind a bit. I love the games we play. Keeps me on my toes. So long as I'm the only one in the game with her, I'm happy.

The woman has me all twisted up inside. When she egged me on by saying we'd never even kissed? God, I couldn't help but tell her the truth. *Only in my dreams.* Pretty sure she doesn't speak French, so the meaning went right over her head. Even so, I took what I wanted, and now I'm fucked. Because that kiss, *that fucking kiss,* will be replaying in my mind for eternity.

I need to kiss her again.

Fitz chuckles. "She does have a name. You don't have to remind us that she's *your wife* every time we mention her."

All I can do is lift my hands and drop them with a splash. I can't help it. I'm fucking happy. But it's all still surreal. We've talked via FaceTime every night, but always with the kids.

Heart thumping, I consider Fitz. Consider telling him everything. Other than Maria, everyone we know thinks that I swept in when she was heartbroken over Xander and went for it.

One would think our friends would be shocked by how quickly we tied the knot. But not one of them has balked. Hell, none even seem the least bit surprised. Hall is the only one who was a little prickly when he found out. But that's only because he's now the only guy in our lineup who's single.

He's got the rookies and Camden, though. He'll be fine.

"It isn't real." The words are barely audible. "I want it to be," I say a little louder. "But it isn't real. Not yet, at least. That's why I keep calling her my wife. Why I can't stop smiling. Why I'm antsy as fuck to get back to Boston when you and I both know that until now, when I was off the ice, I was always happiest on this board."

Fitz assesses me, hands on his thighs, as we float over another rolling wave. "Shit. I had my suspicions, but you played it so real on the plane the day you got married."

I shrug. "We'd just kissed for the first time. And by some miracle, she'd just fucking married me. That's gotta mean something, right?" I rough a hand down my face, the morning air cool on my damp skin.

"Is this because of the kids? I know you were worried the judge wouldn't approve a single guy adopting three kids."

"Yeah. My dickhead stepbrother left her at my place on Christmas Eve so he could, get this"—I pause for dramatics—"go to a strip club."

Fitz rolls his eyes. "How original."

Anger sizzles, but I don't let it win out. Because if he hadn't done that, she wouldn't be my wife right now. "We got to talking, and yeah, I admitted that I was nervous that the adoption won't go through, Then she went and proposed."

Fitz lets out a surprised laugh. "No shit?"

I shrug. "The woman can be so damn selfless. Without much thought, she just said *I'll do it.*" I shake my head, still surprised it was all so easy. Nothing is ever easy for me. "But she loves Josie as much as I do. And you should see her with Scarlett and Bray. She's really trying. I can tell she wants to make this work."

"And then she kissed you." Fitz says it with this knowing smirk.

"Well, *I* kissed her. But she didn't stop it." Just the thought of the surprised little moan that escaped her has me smiling again. "I know she agreed to be my wife because she loves Josie, but it feels like maybe there's more there too." I scratch my head. "There always has been."

He points at me, blue eyes piercing in the brightening sun. "Talk to her. Tell her what you're feeling. Be honest. Seriously." He runs a palm over his board, sloshing water from it as he does. "Brooks gave me this advice when I was in my head over Mel and Dec. Have an honest conversation. That's the only way to make a relationship really work. Especially when there are more than two people involved in it."

I flick water at him. "We're not bringing anyone else into our relationship." Just the idea has my stomach twisting. The thought of anyone else touching my wife has the fighter in me ready to throw punches.

"Hate to break it to ya, War, but there are already three other people involved in your relationship." He stares me down.

Tilting my head back, I sigh up at the sky. He's not wrong. It's not just my feelings at stake, it's theirs too. "So I talk to her," I grumble.

With a laugh, Fitz drops down and paddles for a wave. "Yeah, you talk to her."

> Me: How was work today?

Ava: Work has been interesting. Today was the first day Beckett has been in the office since someone blasted on social media that we got married.

> Me: 😊 You must have loved that.

Ava: He sat me down and spent thirty minutes lecturing me about all the ways married life is superior. I assure you, I didn't love it.

> Me: The man is a bit unhinged.

Ava: You think?

Ava: Honestly, it's kind of adorable. He's so in love with his wife. How was your day?

> Me: <sends picture of sunrise on surfboard>

Ava: Holy crap, you surf? And wait, how do you have a phone in the water?

Me: Let's circle back to your enthusiasm over my ability to surf. 😊

Ava: Your obsession with yourself is showing.

Me: <sends selfie with the surfboard in the frame, along with glistening eight-pack abs>

Ava: That's a really pretty sunrise.

Me: ...

Ava: Fine. You're hot. Happy now?

Me: Yes, wifey. Considering all I do is dream about you, I'd be thrilled if you at least found me attractive.

Me: Wifey?

Ava: Sorry, was stuck on your dream comment.

Me: Want me to tell you about them?

Ava: Are you flirting with me?

Me: Have been for two years. Glad you're finally noticing.

Me: Send me a picture.

Ava: <picture of one hand holding a steaming cup of tea in front of fireplace>

Me: Why aren't you wearing your ring?

Ava: Possessive much?

Me: Yes. Put it back on.

Ava: 😊 I was washing the dishes. Didn't want to lose it.

Ava: <pic of ring on finger>

Ava: Happy?

Me: Yes. Keep it there.

Ava: You expect me to wear it at all times when you don't even have a ring?

Me: Maybe you should buy me a present, if you're so worried that people won't know I'm married.

Ava: Just saying that if you want people to know I'm yours, it's only fair that you wear my ring too.

Me: You are mine, Vicious. And I'm yours.

Ava: Promises, promises.

Ava: I'm being summoned for bath time. Have a good night.

Me: Night, wifey.

"Can you please tell Playboy to get pierced already?" Camden is bent over, groaning as he laces up his skates.

Eyeing Hall, I shake my head. "You're a grown man. If you want to get a piercing, then get a damn piercing."

My winger throws out his arms. "I don't understand why you can't call another team activity. You did it for Brooks."

He's referring to how Aiden, Brooks, and I got our dicks pierced a few years ago during a game of truth or dare gone wrong. So very fucking wrong.

My best friend laughs from where he's putting on his gear. "That is not at all what happened."

Aiden smirks. "Doesn't matter how it happened. All that matters is that we've got the glitter." He cups his junk over his boxer briefs like a fucking teenager, then hops up onto the bench and launches into his own version of Taylor Swift's "Bejeweled."

"Best believe we're all bedazzled,
When we skate on the ice,
We can make the arena glitter.
Well, except for you, Hall,
Girls think they're getting it all,
But you don't got glitter."

"Oh my god. Someone stop him." Brooks drops his head into his hands.

With my hands covering my ears, I nod at Hall. "You, stop talking about our dicks." Then Aiden. "And you, stop singing about them."

Aiden jumps down with a shrug. "Whatever. I can't imagine your wife is complaining about the jewels."

Glowering, I step up to him. "Don't mention my wife and anyone's jewels in the same sentence again." Spinning, I stalk back to my locker and add, "I can't believe I'm the captain of you fools."

While they all go on entertaining themselves behind me, I pluck my phone off the shelf. The assholes annoy the shit out of me sometimes, but I'm biting back a smile as the stupid lyrics Aiden just belted out play in my head. Can't wait to tell Ava. I'm sure she'll get a kick out of it.

I unlock my phone so I can tell her to ask me about it later, but before I can navigate to the messages app, a notification pops up, alerting me to an email from Madi. Quickly, I click over and read through it. The smile I was tempering slips free now. Because the paperwork is ready. I respond, telling her that I'll send it over to Ava. Then I mentally make plans to fly home to sign it tomorrow. We aren't scheduled to return to Boston for a week, but I'm eager to get this done.

I click the link to have it sent to the printer in my home office and type a quick message to Ava, asking her if she'd be willing to stay up tonight so we can talk.

Because I don't just want to tell her about Aiden's dumb song.

I hold my left hand out, assessing my fourth finger, and a thought springs to life.

"Hey, Hall. Want to take a ride to the tattoo parlor after the game? I'll find one that does piercings."

Chapter 21
Ava

"DID YOU ORDER THE PIZZA?" Brayden stands in the kitchen, inhaling a bag of Doritos as I come down the stairs after putting Scarlett down.

I swipe the bag from his hand as I pass. "You won't even be hungry by the time it's delivered." On my way to the pantry to put it away, I snag one for myself and pop it into my mouth.

Brayden chuckles in a way that sounds so much like Tyler. The sound is far too cocksure for such a young kid. It's uncanny how alike they are despite not actually being related. "I'm a growing boy, Ava. Believe me, I'll house an entire pizza myself."

"Hope you ordered a few, then. I'm starving," Hannah calls from the couch.

Brayden eyes her, probably thinking that such a petite woman could never eat that much. He'd be wrong. Despite how tiny she is, Hannah lives life large. Her laugh, her style, her drinking, and yes, her appetite.

The Bolts are playing tonight, so Hannah and Lennox came over to watch with us. Maria is seated beside Lennox, laughing at some over-the-top story my pink-haired friend is telling her. Josie is practicing her dance moves in front of the fireplace. She finally starts dance this weekend, and to say she's excited would be an understatement.

Me? I'm more anxious to see Tyler. It's been a long week, and we've got another to go, but already, I'm on pins and needles, wondering what happens next.

I've replayed our kiss a thousand times, along with every word spoken in those few short minutes we had together after our little wedding ceremony. Every breath, every swipe of his tongue, the way he stepped in closer, and closer again, as if he couldn't stand leaving even a millimeter of space between us. The way he groaned when his lips made contact. The way he tasted, minty and mine. It makes no sense, that description, but he overloaded my senses, so it's the best I can come up with.

My phone buzzes with a text, which I regret looking at the moment I see it.

> Xander: Slut.

God, I'm so over his messages. I should block him. That would be the reasonable reaction. Then again, I wonder if that will just make him escalate and actually show up at Tyler's house. That's something I'd like to avoid. Besides, there is a degree to which I get that he's hurt. He probably thinks I was cheating on him with Tyler. Why else would we get married just days after our breakup? At best, it had to seem like there were feelings between Tyler and me while Xander and I were dating. I obviously can't tell him that our marriage is one of convenience. Even if I could, is that really still true? I'm not so sure.

The one thing I do know? The slew of berating texts doesn't make me want to set aside a time to apologize.

I close out of the app and slide the phone back into my pocket, determined to focus on the good in my life. "Don't worry, I over-ordered."

"No, I over-ordered." Lennox grins.

I laugh. "She's right. She made a list, and I ordered them all, not realizing she was writing down choices for us to pick from."

"Options," Lennox sings. "Always good to have options."

As the pregame commentary begins on screen, excitement flits through me. It's almost game time. I've never enjoyed watching either of the Langfield teams nearly as much as I do now. The sight of my husband on the ice sends electricity through my body every time. Two nights ago, when one of the players from Seattle checked him into the boards, I screamed, and the whole room went silent.

I swipe my phone from the island so I can send Tyler a quick good-luck message. For a moment, I consider admitting that I can't wait to see him, but since I don't know where we stand, I decide against it. Once I've clicked on our text thread, I realize he sent me two while I was upstairs putting Scar to bed.

> Tyler: My attorney has the paperwork ready. I'm going to send it to the printer in my office so you can read it over. If it looks good, I'll fly home tomorrow so we can both sign it and get it filed immediately. Also, if you're still up when I'm finished tonight, I'd like to talk to you. Just you. If that's okay.

> Tyler: I'm really excited to get home to you and the kids.

That admission makes warmth bloom in my chest.

Not just the kids. He's anxious to see me too. Giddiness has me folding my lips in and tossing my head back to hold in a squeal. I may actually get to see him tomorrow. Then maybe we'll see where we really stand.

Not wanting to forget the contract but knowing I want to focus on the game for now, I set a reminder in my phone so that I can look it over later on. Then I grab my glass of wine and head to the couches. It's incredible, the sensation that washes over me at the thought that I'm spending a cozy night with some of my favorite people, cheering on the man I'm starting to think could be included in that group too.

"Good night, love bug." I release my hold on Josie and nod at Maria, who's standing behind her, waiting to take her up to bed. It's nice having Maria around to help, though now that I'm here permanently, she's started talking about going back to work at the hospital. I'll miss her when she does, so I'm soaking up all the extra help now.

Brayden has already disappeared for the night. I can't blame him. The guys' loss put a damper on the evening.

"You'll still be here tomorrow?" Josie asks, just like she does every night.

As much as it kills me to know she still doesn't feel secure in her place here, I give her a reassuring smile, and like I've been telling her for weeks, I promise, "I'll be the one waking you up with kisses on your nose, sweet girl."

With a giggle, she nuzzles her nose against mine. It's become our thing. Then she hugs all the girls before following Maria up to bed.

"That girl," Hannah says as she watches her disappear.

"Tell me about it," I mutter, heading for the kitchen to grab the bottle of wine. It's almost empty, and it's our second one. "I can't wait until the adoption goes through and she doesn't have to worry that she'll be taken from her home."

Lennox follows me, empty glass in hand and expression aghast. "They can do that?"

Hannah's right behind her. "Until the judge approves the adoption."

"Speaking of," I say, remembering the contract in Tyler's office. "Tyler said the attorney sent the paperwork. Let me grab it."

Without waiting for a reply, I take my wineglass with me to the home office.

Against one wall of the masculine room is a row of dark wood bookshelves that are shockingly full. A large oak desk sits in front of the window with a black leather chair situated behind it. Then there's the sports memorabilia. Everywhere. When I spot the printer, I make a beeline for it. My friends are here, so I'll have to snoop the shelves later. I snag the stack of papers from the printer tray and settle in the desk chair, reading the top quickly as I shift, making sure I've got the right document.

Marriage Contract

Hmm. Not exactly what I was expecting.

I scan the page, my eyes narrowing further with each ridiculous word I read. "What the hell?"

The door swings open, and my friends appear. "What's taking you so long?" Hannah asks. "Oh, shit. Look what War has been hiding in here. He's a secret romance lover. I told you he was the hottest guy on the team."

"Oh, let me see, let me see. Does he have any stalker romances?" Lennox darts to the shelves in a pink flash.

"Who knows, but he definitely has a death wish," I grit out as blood rushes in my ears. "Listen to this. 'Wife agrees that husband is the owner of her body. All orgasms, *if any*, will be given only with his consent. This includes self-induced pleasure and usage of toys.'"

Hannah snaps up straight. "What the fuck?"

"Exactly. But wait. It gets better." I scan the document and pick out another clause that has me ready to rip the pages to shreds. "Wife will only speak when spoken to."

"He didn't," Lennox hisses.

With a grunt, Hannah yanks the stack of papers from my hand. "Oh, he so did," she mutters as she reads over the contract herself. "Wait, it says you'll agree to be a good wife, and he'll agree to be a good husband."

"Finally, something for him to do," Lennox tuts. "Although if he's giving you orgasms, at least you're getting something."

"He's not giving me orgasms," I seethe. Tyler has another thing coming to him if he thinks this is how our marriage will go.

"Oh, this motherfucker." Hannah tosses the papers onto the desk but keeps reading. She stumbles forward, the wine in her glass sloshing, and screeches, jabbing at the paper with one finger. "Look at the definitions section. That motherfucker."

Tyler has irritated me for years, but this is the first time anyone has so overwhelmingly agreed with me. I pick up the paper she gestured to and find what has her fired up. Beside the term *good wife* is a description. *A woman who knows her place.* In parentheses, it reads *for further instruction, see* The Good Wife's Guide from Housekeeping Monthly *May 1955.*

Above me, Hannah laughs like a maniac. "Oh my god, this is outrageous. I can't believe women actually lived by this at one time."

"Have dinner ready," Lennox reads aloud. "That's not terrible. I don't mind cooking for Aiden."

Hannah glowers at her. "Every night?"

She grimaces. "No. He cooks almost as much as I do."

"Read the next one," Hannah demands.

"Prepare yourself," Lennox reads, using an exaggeratedly proper tone. "Take fifteen minutes to rest so you'll be refreshed when he arrives. Touch up your makeup, put a ribbon in your hair." She throws her head back and cackles. "Okay, yeah. I see what you're saying."

"Strike up a conversation about one of his interests during dinner. After a long day at work, he may need a lift, and one of your duties is to provide it," Hannah grits out, her eyes slits. "Clear clutter, light a fire, and encourage him to sit and relax. Minimize noise from the washer, dryer, or vacuum." She huffs. "Which is it, *Housekeeping Monthly*, do you want a clean house or a quiet one?"

I peer over at Lennox, and when her lips twitch, I have to bite back a laugh. Because this is all so ridiculous. And my husband actually sent this to me to sign?

"Encourage the children to be quiet." Hannah's on a roll now. "Let him carry the conversation." Each word is louder than the last. "Remember, the topics he chooses are more important than yours. Oh no, this motherfucker didn't."

Lennox snags the paper from the desktop in front of Hannah. "You're going to have an aneurysm if you keep reading this."

Hannah grunts and tips back the last of her wine. "Where's the vodka?"

I frown. "You want a dirty martini?"

"No, I want to pour it all over his office and light the place on fire," she seethes.

Lennox wraps her up in a hug and squeezes her tight. "Breathe, little pyro." She hands me the page she took from Hannah. "Take those away from her before she loses it."

"Me, lose it?" Hannah hisses, pointing at me. "We should be worried about this one. She married a psychopath."

I snort. "She's not wrong."

"What are you going to do about it?" Her eyes are crazed now, scaring me a little.

Head tipped back against the office chair, I study the ceiling. I still can't wrap my head around this damn thing, and yet I feel helpless to even react. I never intended to tell my best friends the truth about our marriage, but in this moment, I don't know how else to explain it. "I married him so I could be Josie's mother. So those kids would have a family. And even if he's a terrible husband, he's a good dad, and the kids deserve this family." I blink back tears and press a hand over the ache that's formed in my chest. *"I promised Josie."*

Hannah shrugs out of Lennox's hold and paces to the opposite end of the room and back. "You're going to stay married to this misogynist? And you're going to sign this contract?"

I lift my shoulders in defeat. "What choice do I have?"

"Ava," Lennox says softly. It's such a pitiful sound.

I close my eyes and try to come to terms with all of this. "It's fine. We don't have what you and Aiden have, but these kids are my world. They deserve all the good, and without a wife, the chance of a judge approving Tyler's adoption of Josie goes down considerably. It's what's best for her. I can do anything if I know it'll help her."

Hannah roars. She legit throws out her fists and roars at the ceiling. "Fine. You'll follow his stupid rules. You'll follow these rules so well he won't know what hit him."

"She will?" Lennox's face scrunches up in confusion.

I feel the same way.

Hannah stares me down, her expression even more crazed. "Yes." She steps forward and lets out a maniacal laugh. "He'll never know what hit him."

The good wife's guide

- Prepare yourself. Take fifteen minutes to rest so you'll be refreshed when he arrives. Touch up your makeup, put a ribbon in your hair.
- Strike up a conversation about one of his interests during dinner.
- After a long day at work, he may need a lift, and one of your duties is to provide it.
- Clear away the clutter. Make one last trip through the house just before your husband arrives.
- Run a dustcloth over the tables.
- During the cooler months, light a fire and encourage him to sit and relax. Your husband will feel as though he's stepped into a haven of rest and order, and it will give you a lift too. After all, catering to his comfort will provide you with immense personal satisfaction.
- Minimize all noise. At the time of his arrival, eliminate all noise from the washer, dryer, or vacuum. Encourage the children to be quiet.
- Greet him with a warm smile and show sincerity in your desire to please him.
- Listen to what he has to say. You may have a dozen important things to tell him, but the moment of his arrival is not the time.
- Let him carry the conversation. Remember, the topics he chooses are more important than yours.
- Don't greet him with complaints or problems.
- Don't complain if he's late for dinner or even if he stays out all night. The inconvenience to you is likely minor in comparison to what he's faced at work.
- Make him comfortable. Insist he sit in the most comfortable chair and bring him a fresh drink.
- Offer to take off his shoes. Speak in a soothing and pleasant voice. Don't ask him questions about his actions or question his judgment or integrity. Remember, he is the master of the house, and as such, will always exercise his will with fairness and truthfulness. You have no right to question him.
- A good wife always knows her place.

TEXT MESSAGES FROM AVA'S AND TYLER'S PHONE

Tyler: You awake?

Tyler: Guess you fell asleep. I'll be home tomorrow night. Looking forward to seeing you.

Sara: Oh my god, Ave. Wait until you see your husband. I've never seen a man more smitten. He practically tripped over himself, rushing to leave for the airport.

Lennox: This didn't age well.

Sara: What did I miss?

Hannah: He's a dead man. But you're not allowed to say anything. Tits before dicks.

Sara: I'll cut off his dick before I ever choose one over you girls.

Ava: Thanks, Sara.

Lennox: You okay, Ave?

Hannah: Of course she's okay. She's Ava Fucking War. She's going to teach that slimy excuse for a man what happens when you F with one of us.

Sara: Damn. War really did a number on you, huh?

Ava: you have no idea.

Madi: Hi, Tyler. Need any edits done on the adoption petition, or does it look okay?

Chapter 22
Ava

"HOW'S DINNER COMING ALONG?" Hannah's tinny voice bounces off the walls in the kitchen.

I peek into the oven where I've dumped the fully prepared roast that was delivered twenty minutes ago into a Dutch oven I found in one of the cabinets. "Looks good." I don't cook, and I don't intend to learn for Tyler's sake, but I do intend to overcook this meal and teach him that a woman's place—especially this woman's place—is *not* in the kitchen.

"Your hair?"

I close the oven door and peer at my reflection. "A rat's nest on top of my head."

She giggles.

"And the kids?"

"Having pizza with Maria's family downtown." I wouldn't dream of forcing them to endure this awful dinner. Let them have pizza and dessert so they're loud and sugared up when they get home.

They'll be back in an hour, which gives me just enough time for what I have planned. Then, once they're in bed, I'll spend the rest of the night as far away from Tyler Warren as I can get and do my best to avoid him until he gets back on a plane.

"Good girl," Hannah hums. "Now remember, tease, tease, tease, but don't let him near the goods."

"Ha," I cough out a sarcastic laugh. "As if I'll let him anywhere near me."

"You say that now." She sighs, like she expects me to break. "But he'll walk in there being all *War*, flaunting those tattoos. Then you'll get a whiff of him, and before you know it, you'll be on your back, and he'll be eating you for dinner."

I blink down at the phone. "Did you just make his name an adjective?"

"Did you just skirt past the whole tattoo thing?"

Scoffing, I roll my eyes. "He's not that irresistible. I resisted him for a whole two years."

"Exactly. You had to actively resist him. And that was before you were married. Before he was being all hot dad. If you don't put your foot down now, you'll never get the upper hand in this marriage."

"Oh, don't you worry. I know what's at stake, and I know precisely what I need to do." The sound of a car door slamming has my heart skittering. "Oh, he's here."

"You've got this. Remember, he wanted to restrict your orgasms, and *nobody* restricts Baby's orgasms."

"I think the line is nobody puts Baby in a corner—"

"Work with me here."

"Right. Okay." With a tap on my phone screen to end the call, I spin toward the door, ready for action. "No one restricts my orgasms."

Tyler

"I'm home!" I slam the door and hold my breath, waiting for the sound of squeals, for the feet padding across the floor, for the little humans hurtling their bodies against mine so they can squeeze the life out of me.

But I'm met with nothing but silence. "Hello?"

I drop my suitcase by the door and tug on my tie. Where is everyone?

"Coming," Ava calls from deeper inside the house.

Chin lifted, I search the main floor for her. The tree is still up and twinkling in the corner, there's a fire roaring in the hearth, and the smell of garlic and rosemary fills the air.

At the sound of footsteps on the hardwoods, I turn and spot Ava. Her red hair is a mess on her head, and she's wearing a cozy-looking sweatshirt set without a stitch of makeup on her face.

She's never looked more gorgeous.

"You're a sight for sore eyes." On instinct, I pull her into my chest, cradling her head with one hand and wrapping my other arm around her waist. Then I tug gently on her hair, tipping her head back so I can drink her in up close. "I missed you."

Her lashes flutter, and her cheeks pinken, like maybe my reaction has surprised her. Like she didn't expect me to be so affectionate, so honest.

Good. I like to keep my wife on her toes.

She blows out an unsteady breath, and though I'm dying to taste her, I want to give her time to adjust, so I restrain myself. For now. "Where are the kids?"

Ava shifts in my arms, like maybe she wants some space, so I release her. Then she straightens and looks up at me, wearing a smile that seems forced.

"They went to dinner with Maria. After so much travel, I assumed you'd like to decompress in a quiet house with a drink before they came home."

Disappointment washes over me. "Decompress? Fuck no. I miss them."

Her lips part, her eyes widening, like once again, she's thrown off by my answer. But she quickly pulls her shoulders back and dons a neutral expression. "Well, we probably need to discuss some things before they get home. Dinner should be ready shortly." With that, she spins on her heel and heads back to the kitchen.

With a frown, I watch her go. Something is off.

Even so, she's right. We do have things to discuss. She didn't answer when I FaceTimed her last night. It was late, so I wasn't surprised that she'd fallen asleep waiting. But it means we didn't get to have the conversation that Fitz and I discussed.

"Feel free to get yourself a drink while I finish up," she calls.

"Would you like something?" I ask as I head toward the bar. I wasn't planning on having a drink, but with the strange tension swirling between us, I think we both might need one.

"I'm fine."

With a shrug, I pull out a single wine glass. We have a game tomorrow, so I only allow myself a small amount. "Did you get the documents I sent to you?"

When she doesn't respond, I carry my wine to the kitchen, where she's holding a bulky Dutch oven and wearing a scowl. *Okay.* Something is definitely off.

"Need help?"

I set my glass on the table, but when I turn to take the Dutch oven from her, she skirts around me and plops it down with a loud thud.

"Smells delicious." It really does, and I'm hoping the compliment will soften her strange mood.

She shrugs and pulls the lid off the baking dish to reveal a seriously charred piece of meat. I think it's supposed to be a roast, but it's shriveled and dry. "Hope it's good. I don't eat meat, but I wanted to make something special for you."

"Didn't you eat bacon on Christmas morning?"

Her eyes widen. "Oh, I only eat pig."

"That's—" I frown. "An odd distinction." Shaking off the strangeness of the moment, I pick up the serving fork and a steak knife and stab at the roast, but when I try to cut into it, the fork won't come back out. Wiggling it back and forth, I stare down at the hunk of meat, my tongue in my cheek.

"Something wrong?" she asks in a syrupy-sweet voice.

I shake my head. "Nope, just starving. I think I'll take the entire thing." With the serving fork, I heft the roast up out of the dish and drop it onto my plate. As it lands with a splat, I stare at it, trying to figure out what to do next.

Should I try a bigger knife? Would a bigger knife even do me any good?

Ava sits across from me with a plate of vegetables and digs in. When she takes her second bite and I'm still staring at my food, I realize I need to do something, so I pick up the entire piece of meat, and like a caveman, I take a bite right off the top.

I chew...and I chew some more. My teeth have nothing on this steak, though. It's *terrible.* I keep my face neutral as I reach for my wine and take a long swig to wash it down. "So the paperwork?" I rasp, my throat dry.

Ava smiles. "It's on your desk. All signed."

Relief floods me. "Excellent. I really wanted to get that part out of the way. I know the way we started this was awkward, but I'm glad we agree that this is what's right for our family."

Her jaw hardens as she chews. Then, with her eyes narrowed on me, she picks up my glass and downs the rest of the wine.

I cough out a laugh. "Thirsty? I can get you a glass of your own."

"Oh, but why would we do that when what's mine is yours and what's yours is mine?"

A huff of a laugh escapes me. "Very true." I stand and shuffle to the bar for the bottle and another glass. Looks like I'll need a bit more to get through that roast.

"So you had your attorney draft that?" she asks as I return to the table.

I fill both wine glasses halfway and set the bottle down. "Yeah. Figured we should get it taken care of as soon as possible. This way our roles are laid out clearly."

She picks up her glass and drains it quickly. Then she holds it out, silently signaling that I should fill 'er up. When I don't move quick enough, she stands, reaches across the table, and snatches the bottle.

"So you read it?" She drops back into her seat.

Anxiety rushes through me as I study her. "Yes?"

She holds the bottle close to her lips, scrutinizing me with narrowed eyes. "*All* of it?"

I'm not sure what she's getting at or why she's so unhinged, so I answer slowly. "I think so?"

An angry, closed-mouth *humph* is her only response. Then she pushes the chair back, causing it to screech against the hardwood floor. When she stands, she sways a bit but quickly rights herself. "Well," she slurs, cheeks red and eyes glassy, "you can take your contract and go fuck yourself. How about this for my *purpose*? I'll be in our bedroom *purposefully* giving myself all the orgasms, whether you like it or not."

Orgasms? Like it or not? What the hell?

I'm still blinking, frozen in shock, when the bedroom door upstairs slams. What the fuck just happened? And is this all because of the petition to adopt Josie?

So maybe I didn't actually read every word, but Madi and I discussed it in detail. There isn't a single line in it that should have upset Ava like that.

I bolt out of my seat and stride for my office, determined to get to the bottom of this. But as I cross the threshold, the front door swings open, and Josie screams "Tyler, we're home!"

And just like that, my night is consumed by the three kids I missed more than I ever could have imagined possible before I met them. Hugs and bath time take priority, followed by three stories too many. It's after ten when I finally sit at my desk and leaf through the stack of papers on top.

Contract for Marriage

What the…?

I flip through page after page, my jaw dropping farther as I scan each one. *Shit.* I've seen this before. It's the damn contract Hall sent to me over Christmas. I must have accidentally sent this to the printer, rather than Madi's petition. *Fuck.*

My stomach sinks, and my heart goes with it when I get to the last page and see Ava's signature scrawled below the line that reads *wife*.

In that moment, I know I'm fucked. Looks like I'll be sleeping on the couch tonight.

CHAPTER 23
TYLER

Me: I had an early flight this morning, but we need to talk.

Ava: Don't worry, master. The kids are taken care of, dishes are washed, and I locked all my toys away. I promise to behave the next time you're home.

I GRIT MY TEETH. This fucking woman.

Me: Ava, cut the shit. I'm serious. We need to talk.

Ava: Oh, do you not like the term master? Is sir better?

Me: Bray has a game today. I know you aren't talking to me, but if you could show up, it would mean a lot to him.

> Ava: <pic of Josie and Scarlett from behind with the ice rink in the background> We're already here.

> Ava: <video of Brayden scoring a goal>

> Me: I'd love a picture of you too. Maybe at home. In our bed.

> Ava: <pic of Ava giving me the middle finger in our bed>

> Me: There's my vicious girl. Missed you.

> Me: Maria mentioned that Scarlett needs a new jacket. There's a credit card in the top drawer of my desk. Feel free to buy yourself something pretty too.

FreeMSG American Express Fraud Center: Reply YES or NO if you used card ending in 7777 at Bass Pro Shop, $125,769.88.

"Bass pro shop?" And over a hundred grand? Dread forms like a lead ball in my gut as I reread the text.

I'm still gaping at it when I receive another notification. This message is from my favorite redheaded villain.

> Ava: Got a new jacket for Scarlett and a little something for myself too. <pic of Brayden holding a smiling Scarlett in front of a hot tub at Bass Pro Shop>

> Me: You spent 125K on a hot tub and a jacket?

> Ava: A boat too. And life jackets, of course. Safety first. Did you know they sell adult toys here too? Thanks for buying me something pretty.

Holy fuck, this woman is driving me insane. We haven't talked in three days other than when she updates me on the kids. She's not a monster, just stubborn. Honestly? I kind of enjoy the little tantrums she throws.

Though I wouldn't classify this one as little. The charge she just made to my Amex officially puts it in the epic category. I type *yes* and hit Send, and instantly, I'm notified that the sale went through.

> Ava: Thanks, Daddy. I'll make sure to put your gifts to good use tonight.

> Me: Great. Send me a video when you do.

This fucking girl. There's no way Bass Pro Shop sells vibrators, but I play along. It's too fucking fun to resist. I can't even be mad about the boat. We have a damn lake, and I only have a jet ski. It'll be a blast to spend our days on the water together during the offseason. And a hot tub? I can think of a few ways I could make that enjoyable for both me and my stubborn wife.

"Aw, are you texting with the wifey?" Hall leans over the armrest and zeroes in on my phone.

Pressing the device to my chest, I glare at him. "Boundaries, Playboy."

The kid laughs like I can't possibly be serious. "Not going to lie. I figured you were pulling the fake relationship scheme." He thumbs over his shoulder. "You know, like Brooks and Aiden did. But you seem pretty smitten."

Brooks leans around the seat, his big body taking me by surprise. "And we weren't?"

Sara pops up behind us, looming over me like she's kneeling on her seat. "Yeah, who says we aren't just excellent at faking?"

I shake my head. "That's not a compliment."

"Oh, please. We all know I never have to fake it with my man. His big dick energy keeps me screaming all night—"

Brooks slaps a hand over her mouth. "Not in front of my team-mates, crazy girl."

She shrugs, and when he releases her, she huffs. "He started it."

"Actually, I didn't. I'm just here, minding my own business, trying to text with my wife about the hot tub she bought."

"Oh, that's so adorable," Sara coos. "Mills," she shouts, her voice far too loud for the cramped interior of the plane. "Did you hear that? He just called Ava his wife. I'm guessing that means you guys made up? And hot tub?" She zeroes in on me again. "Tell me more. Brookie and I love a good hot tub night."

Aiden pipes up. "Lex and I used to enjoy the hell out of the one on the roof at the apartment."

A shudder racks through me. "That's definitely something you shouldn't say out loud when you're surrounded by people who use that hot tub regularly."

From her seat beside Gavin at the front of the plane, Millie gives us a thumbs-up. "Happy for you," she mouths, patting a sleeping Vivi's back.

Hall nudges my arm. "I was happy for you first."

"Oh my god, it's not a competition," Brooks grumbles as he drops back into his seat.

"If it was, I'd win. You're always busy with Sara, but I make sure I'm available for my friend here so I can help him out when he needs it." He nudges me again. "Like the marriage contract. Bet ya put that to good use."

Irritation coursing through me, I yank my arm away. "Stop fucking touching me." His goddamn contract is what caused my current predicament, but I can't talk about it here, because then everyone will know the marriage is fake.

"Come on, the mail-order bride one was gold." He barks out a laugh, completely oblivious to my anger.

Grunting, I shoot daggers at him. "Are we talking about the same contract? The one about orgasms and control? I can't believe something like that even exists."

Sara appears over my head again, blue eyes bright. "Oh, tell me more about the orgasm contract."

She disappears quickly, then Brooks is muttering, "Stop saying orgasms."

In response, she whisper-yells, "Only if you give me one in the bathroom right now."

"We can hear you," Hall sings, head tipped back.

"You'll hear me from the bathroom too if Brookie does his job."

I cough out a laugh, and behind me, my best friend groans.

"Ya know, Calliope says—"

Before Hall can start in on another Calliope column colloquy, I slip my AirPods into my ears, scroll to my Hozier playlist, and close my eyes, wondering what my wife will text me next.

Chapter 24
Ava

BEAMING, Josie darts across the room and skitters to a stop in front of me. "Did you see my plié?"

The past week hasn't been so terrible, despite my irritation with my husband. I'm not proud of how I've handled communication with him. We're supposed to be raising kids together, creating a safe, comforting unit for them. Instead, it feels as though I've been leading them toward an unstable environment.

After that kiss on our wedding day, I got swept up in a fairy tale. I let myself believe that this could be my happily ever after. But the contract was like a bucket of ice water dumped over my head. A reminder that I'm here to serve a purpose. And it has nothing to do with my own wants.

It triggered old hurts. Reminded me of the reason I was brought into this world in the first place—for the benefit of someone else—and I reacted badly.

But I won't lie and say that some of my payback hasn't been fun. The hot tub that was delivered two nights ago is definitely included in that fun. I had a grand old time sending Tyler a picture of me beneath the bubbles last night, making sure he couldn't tell whether I was wearing a suit.

Of course I was. The kids were asleep, but I'm not *that* unhinged.

Yet.

My week hasn't totally revolved around torturing Tyler. Without him here, I've had the chance to get to know Brayden better. He showed me the gym in the basement and taught me how to use the punching bag. It's done wonders for my aggression.

And I left work early today so I could pick Josie up from school and take her to ballet.

After a long drink from her water bottle, she pops up on the toes of her pastel pink ballet slippers to hug me. Since we arrived, I've been swamped with memory after memory. Each one hits me like a movie reel, as if I'm watching footage of someone else's life.

Chasing after my sister, mimicking her every ballet move, wanting to be her more than anything.

"I did see your plié, love. It was amazing." I crouch in front of her and tie the string that's come loose into a bow.

"Josie tells me you're a dancer as well." The voice is deep and smooth.

Head tipped back, I peer up at her dance instructor. I was a bit surprised to find that she had a male teacher. In all the years I danced, I never had one.

I push my hair out of my face and stand with a laugh. "I haven't really danced in years."

The man has dark hair and blue eyes like Tyler, but that is where the similarities end. His eyes are warm rather than piercing, and he's only a few inches taller than me. Dressed in a tight T-shirt, he's clearly a work of art.

When I force my attention to his face, chastising myself for checking him out, I realize he's doing a similar appraisal of me.

"You know what they say: it's never too late to start over."

I shake my head even as the idea of it, the atmosphere in this room alone, sends flutters through my belly.

With a single step closer, he gives me an encouraging smile. "We have adult classes."

"I'd make a fool of myself." I chuckle uncomfortably.

Head dipped, he lowers his voice. "I offer one-on-one instruction too. May help you feel more comfortable until you're ready to join a class."

Finally, I let myself honestly consider the idea, and my heart stutters. Dancing again, taking back one of my true passions, feels like a step forward. Like maybe it's exactly what I need to feel like myself again. "Yeah, maybe," I breathe, unable to hide my smile.

He brightens and takes a step back. "I've got to get in there before the little girls start pulling hair."

"Right."

"But check our website. My schedule is posted there. And you can sign up that way too." His gaze volleys between me and the group of girls who are now running in circles in his studio.

"Great, I'll look for that."

He focuses on me again. "Or I could text it to you, *Mrs.*?"

"A-Ava," I stammer. "Just Ava."

His lips curl in a satisfied smirk. "Okay, Ava. I'm Benoir."

"Benoir," I repeat slowly with a nod and a smile, hoping the flush creeping up my neck isn't visible. "It's nice to meet you. How about you put your number in my phone, and I'll text you so you have mine?" I hold the device out like I have the first clue what I'm doing. It kind of feels like he's flirting, but honestly, before Xander, I barely talked to men, let alone flirted. I don't even understand how Xander and I ended up together. He just appeared while I was out with the girls one night, and after that, he seemed to be everywhere I went. At the coffee shop and even the grocery store. We ran into each other so often it began to feel like a joke. Though he swore it was fate stepping in and asked if I'd run into him at dinner.

There was no need to try to flirt. It just happened. But *this*? It definitely feels like flirting.

And maybe it's wrong, but I kind of like it.

"Can we get ice cream after ballet?" Josie asks as Benoir passes my phone back to me and strides back into class.

Ducking my head, I cup her cheek and smile. "Maybe after dinner."

"Aw, man, I'll never have room for ice cream in my belly after Maria's lasagna."

With a laugh, I press a kiss to her forehead. "Then how would you have room for Maria's lasagna in your belly after ice cream?"

She shrugs. "Priorities, Ava. We eat the ice cream, but we don't tell Maria."

I arch a brow at her. We both know we won't lie to the woman who does so much for us.

"Is Tyler going to be home tonight?"

Speak of the devil. The moment she says his name, a text from him appears. I lock my phone screen before I get dragged into something I don't have time for.

"Tomorrow. But I think he has a game," I tell her. "Now go. The break is over."

"You'll stay?"

I point to a bench behind the glass wall. "I'll be right there watching you the whole time."

With a grin, she skips back into class. And as I shuffle back to the bench, I take out my phone, preparing myself for whatever he has to say.

> Tyler: Come to the game tomorrow night.

I stare at it for a few seconds, my stomach in knots, before hastily typing a reply.

> Me: Are you summoning me?

> Tyler: It's been a week. We need to talk, and I'd rather not do it with the kids around. Come to my game. We'll talk after.

> Tyler: You signed the contract.

> Me: And I told you what you could do with it.

> Tyler: I signed it too. Now it's binding. Come to my game tomorrow, Vicious. We need to talk.

> Me: You're an ass.

> Tyler: I'm aware. For the record, the contract was a joke. Hall sent it. And if you'd pick up your damn phone when I call, you would know that.

> Me: I'll be sure to thank Hall for all the orgasms last night, then.

> Tyler: Ava.

> Me: No, this is good. We needed this reminder. You do you, and I'll do me. Or maybe other people. We'll stick with focusing on the kids. That's our marriage contract going forward. Got it?

> Tyler: No. You signed the document, so now we have to follow it. Don't test me.

I let out a derisive snort, garnering the attention of a few of the mothers sharing the bench.

> Me: What are you going to do, spank me???

> Tyler: There's a list of punishments for me to choose from in the contract. Take a look. Better yet, don't test me and we won't have to worry about it.

Fuming, I scroll back up to his first text and take screenshots to send to Hannah and Lennox.

> Me: My husband has lost his damn mind. I may just kill him.

Immediately, my phone rings, and Hannah's name flashes on the screen. "Hey," I whisper. "I can't talk. I'm at Josie's dance class."

"Okay, I'll make it quick, then. Don't kill him. That's a far too easy punishment. We're going to drag this death sentence out a bit."

Okay, I'll bite. Straightening, I ask, "What are you thinking?"

She launches into a frighteningly well thought-out plan, making me giggle. The moms are all staring again, but I can't hold it in. And I can't temper the excitement that races through me at the thought of Tyler's face when he finds out what we're up to.

"Okay, I'm in."

CHAPTER 25
TYLER

Ava: No, this is good. We needed this
reminder. You do you, and I'll do me. Or maybe
other people. We'll stick with focusing on the
kids. That's our marriage contract going
forward. Got it?

OH, my wife is really looking to push my limits. I gave her one last night to pout, but I'm done with the distance. We are going to talk today, whether she likes it or not.

And to be honest, I'm a bit pissed off. Ava's a reasonable person. And although her anger over the ridiculous contract was justified, if she'd answered her damn phone, I could have explained Hall's stupid joke and smoothed things over.

But she obviously believes I'm not worth the effort of working through our issues. What pisses me off the most is that she really thinks I would have a contract like that one drawn up and sent to her. That I believe a woman should be treated like that.

When have I ever given her any reason to believe that's the kind of guy I am?

Should I have signed the contract and held it over her head?

Maybe not.

But I do love fighting with her. Especially if the option of kissing her is off the table. And I think it's safe to assume that if I tried to kiss my wife right now, she'd punch me in the face.

"Hey, Cap," Hall drawls, leaning over my shoulder. "You excited to be reunited with the wife tonight? She gonna take the hardware for a ride?"

I stand from the bench and give Hall a hard shove. When he lands on his ass, he grimaces up at me. "What the fuck is wrong with you?"

Anger simmering just beneath my skin, I grit out, "What's wrong with me is that my wife found the damn contract you sent to me."

From across the locker room, Brooks looks up, brow furrowed. "What contract?"

My stomach knots. Fuck, so much for the guys not knowing the marriage is fake.

Still on the ground, Hall guffaws. "No way."

"Yes way." I have to fight the urge not to kick him while he's still on the floor. "And she fucking signed it."

Hall gapes, then sputters, "I-I'm sorry. I don't even know what to say to that."

"Yeah, now you get why I'm so fucking pissed."

"I don't," Brooks grumbles, "and I'd rather be focusing on my pregame visualizations than playing twenty questions, so spell it out for me."

We all have pregame rituals. Brooks puts on headphones, closes his eyes, and visualizes every play an opponent could use to get past him and into his goal. Aiden follows along with whatever spicy book his wife is reading—this is a new routine and one I'm still not sure I'm on board with, considering he cloned her phone in order to do it. Hall and Camden play cards with a few of the rookies.

I bounce between the guys with AirPods in place in case I want to listen to music and a deck of cards at the ready if the mood strikes. It usually becomes clear to me pretty quickly where I'm needed. Sometimes guys just need help getting out of their heads. Other times they need to be amped up so they're ready to fight for a win on the ice. Helping my teammates is what keeps me focused. Tonight, though, I don't have it in me to be of any help to them. Not when I'm so livid. Not after the text my wife sent, implying that she thinks she's going to screw other people.

One way or another, I'll make it clear that the only person she'll be going near is me, whether it's by wooing her or pissing her off by enforcing the damn contract.

I think she secretly likes the idea of being bound by me. Of being controlled by me. And god, what I would do to see her as she hurtles over the edge. Witness the way her cheeks flush, how her teeth sink into her lip, how pretty she sounds crying out my name.

It will happen.

Maybe not tonight, but eventually, her orgasms will belong to me. Just like she does.

"Forget it. Go back to your visualizations. I'm fixing it," I grit out.

With a shake of his head, Brooks turns away from me, likely thinking I'm an idiot.

Queen's "We Will Rock You," the Bolts song for this season, blares as we take the ice for warm-ups. Every year Aiden picks a new one, and this one might be my favorite so far.

Normally I keep my focus centered around the game during warm-ups. The adrenaline buzz kicks in, giving me a high that I've never been able to replicate. I love this game in a way that most wouldn't understand. It gave me a purpose during a time when I had none. A family when I'd lost my own. Nothing in my life has ever come close to competing.

Until now.

Tonight, another kind of excitement courses through me. The impending battle off the ice keeps my heart pumping. Finding my wife in this arena is my first priority. I have to confirm that she's here—even if I had to strong-arm her into coming. Then I can put 100 percent of myself into the game. Later, we can figure our shit out for good.

Pushing off the ice, I propel myself forward. The bite of the cold within the rink only strengthens my resolve. Out here, I'm the captain, the king. And right now, all I want is to find my queen.

If Sara isn't down in the box with us, then she sits in the stands. Always in the same place. She doesn't like to be in the owner's suite with the Langfields because she wants Brooks to hear her screaming like a freaking lunatic. Now that Lennox joins her for home games, their shouts are ridiculously easy to pick out. If I know my girl, she's with her girls. So Sara's regular spot is where I look first.

The flash of red catches my attention quickly. Waves of autumn that frame her pretty freckled face. She's laughing, happy. I dig my feet into the ice and slow to a stop, mesmerized by her.

Though I'm stunned by her, my teammates are still flying across the ice, and Hall barrels into me from the side before he can stop.

"Fuck." I grunt and catch my balance before I fall, which, for the record, never happens.

As I straighten, catcalls from the stands echo around me.

"Focus, number seven," Sara calls with a maniacal laugh.

Beside her, Hannah grips my wife by the upper arms and spins her, joining in on the laughter as she points at Ava's back.

When the sight registers, my blood runs cold.

I push Hall off me with more force than necessary. "What the fuck is my wife doing wearing your jersey?"

All logic leaves me as I glower at the 18 on my wife's back and those four letters, H-A-L-L, above it. I skate to the edge of the ice and pound on the plexiglass barrier with my stick. "Ava Warren, get over here right now."

Even with the music blasting, the words carry. I can tell by the way she zeroes in on me.

Tilting to one side a fraction so she can see me beyond the fans filing in and finding their seats, she looks one way, then the other, then points at herself in a teasing *who me?* way.

"Go play your game, War," Lennox yells.

Aiden appears at my side. "Come on, dude. She's just riling you up."

Hall grins from my other side. "Just a little foreplay, Cap. She's teasing you. Thought you liked it."

Teeth gritted, I shake my head. "She's pushed too far." With a whistle, I drop my stick. "Mrs. Warren!"

"What the fuck are you doing?" Gavin yells from our box.

My gloves get tossed to the ice next. Then I rip off my helmet and shove it into Aiden's chest. "Remember when I kept your stupid fucking stalking to myself?"

He nods.

"You can't say shit."

"Fuck, you're really crazy about this girl," he mutters.

There's no denying it.

"Homicidal."

"What do you need?"

"Just hold that." Without waiting for him to agree, I skate to the gate and launch myself over the boards.

Skates still on, I march in front of the stands, headed straight for my wife. The adrenaline fueling me now is because of this game she and I are once again playing. When I reach the girls, I stop and yank my jersey off. Ava's green eyes flare as she stands stock-still.

People in the row in front of her look up at me with their mouths hanging open.

"Could you give me a moment alone with my wife?" I ask as politely as I can.

They skitter over to empty seats down the row, mumbling unintelligibly.

In front of me, my wife's eyes are blazing and her jaw is locked tight. She's furious, but I don't give a fuck.

Welcome to my perpetual state, wife. Play stupid games, win unhinged prizes.

I hold up my left hand and point to my fourth ring finger. Her eyes widen as she takes in the wedding date inked onto my skin in a green that matches her eyes.

"My wife. My jersey." Angling in close, I force the oversized garment over her head.

"Tyler Warren," Sara hisses. "I'll be cleaning up this mess for the next week."

I ignore her. I ignore everyone but Ava. "Remember the contract, Ava. *I own you.* Now lift your arms and show everyone what a good wife you are."

"Fuck you," she whisper-hisses.

I'm pretty sure that's the first time I've ever heard my girl curse. That fact shouldn't have me smirking like this. "Yeah, Vicious. You can do that too. But right now, I have a game to play."

I don't push my luck by stealing a kiss. I simply spin and head down the steps.

There's already a jersey waiting for me. One of the coaches probably sent a minion to the locker room for it. I throw it on as Gavin yells at me. He's pissed, and rightfully so. Keeping my mouth shut, I lower my chin in acknowledgment. Because yeah, I am a fucking idiot, and I'm sure I'll pay for it by doing suicides all week.

As I get back on the ice, Hall skates up next to me, wearing another fucking cocky grin. "Guess the glitter wasn't enough to keep your wife satisfied, huh?"

I can put up with a lot of shit, but tonight, I've reached my limit. So I let my fist do the talking.

Chapter 26
Ava

IT ALL HAPPENS SO QUICKLY, and it knocks the air from my lungs. One moment, I'm teasing Tyler and laughing with the girls, showing off the *Hall* jersey Hannah brought for me to wear. The next, I'm being swallowed up by my husband's legit hockey jersey—not a replica like fans purchase—still stupidly stunned by his tattoo.

A tattoo of *our freaking wedding date* on his ring finger.

Then, in front of the entire arena, he slams his fist into Daniel Hall's face.

"Holy shit." Hannah claps a hand over her mouth.

Sara instantly jumps over the seats and heads for the ice. Crap. She wasn't wrong about having to clean up this mess.

"What the hell did Hall say?" Lennox is still beside me, fanning herself.

Hannah thumbs over at me. "Probably something about this one."

I'm not focused on their words, though. All my attention is fixed on the ice, where Aiden and Brooks are holding Tyler back while Gavin and the training staff check in with Daniel.

The hit came out of nowhere, so the minute Tyler's fist connected with his jaw, he crumpled to the ice.

"Stand up," Hannah hisses. She's biting her thumb and chanting those words over and over.

When Daniel finally stands, with the help of Gavin, the crowd around us erupts in cheers, and I finally take a breath.

Tyler is fighting against Brooks's hold, distress written all over his face. He knows he fucked up, but by the way he watches Hall, I think he's more worried about his friend than he is about the consequences of his actions.

Despite the bitterness between us and how irritating he can be, my heart splinters at the devastation plastered on his face. He's distraught and wants to apologize, but the second time he tries to break free of Brooks, Gavin points to him and yells.

That's all it takes for Tyler to simply nod and head for the bench.

"This is bad," Lennox whispers.

"No shit. Fuck, I feel bad." Hannah turns to me, her lips downturned. "I think we pushed too far this time."

"Me too," I whisper, feeling small beneath my husband's jersey. And oddly protective of him. This is all my fault.

"This is a really bad idea," I mutter as I tug on the fabric of the jersey. My legs are bare, and I'm not wearing anything other than the giant article of clothing my husband forced over my head earlier.

When the garage opens, my nerves riot. "Such a bad idea," I whisper to the empty bedroom, but I don't move. I stand beside the bed, waiting for Tyler to appear.

The Bolts barely won tonight, and Gavin benched Tyler for the first period. Camden Snow did a decent job in his place, but the entire team was off. Teammates don't fight, and captains are supposed to lead by example.

And Tyler never would have punched Hall if not for my stupid decision to wear the guy's jersey. So here I am, prepared to apologize.

As enraged as I was at how he acted like he could control what I wore to the game, it was hot, the way he lost his cool. How the idea of me in another man's jersey riled him up. Sometime tonight, my thoughts drifted to what it would be like to do other things with my husband, and that's where they've stayed.

Sex with my husband. Would it really be so bad? We could channel all that rage into something we'd both enjoy.

Like I said, this is a really bad idea.

The bedroom door swings open, and Tyler, clad in a bespoke suit, appears in the doorway, head down, tie loosened like he was working at removing it as he came up the steps. That War swagger is still there, but along with it, palpable anger emanates from him.

"Hi." My voice is small, but it halts him in his tracks.

Glacier blue eyes spark as they widen and take me in. Just as quickly, they narrow again. With a scoff, he pulls at the tie around his neck and tosses it to the floor. "You're playing with fire, Vicious. I'm not in the mood." He slams the door, keeping his attention averted.

I blow out a breath and fist my hands to keep my fingers from trembling. With my chin lifted, I will my voice to remain steady as well. "You tell me you want something real. Kiss me like you'd give me your last breath. Then send me a marriage contract obliterating it all. Then you fight with one of your friends, *your teammate*, over me in front of thousands of people, and now you're here telling me you don't want me again? The hot and cold is getting old, Tyler. Make up your mind."

His chest expands as he takes in a long, loud breath. After he's let it out, he gives me a sideways look, his jaw rigid. "Once again, you've got it all wrong. I told you I didn't send you that damn contract. Hall sent it to me as a joke, and somehow, I printed it, thinking it was the document Madi sent over. I'm tired of hoping you'll listen to a word I say, and I'm sick of trying to convince you that I'm a good guy."

He roughs a hand down his face, looking more haggard than I've ever seen. Crap. My heart cracks even further, knowing I'm the cause of it.

"I've got a split lip," he goes on, holding my gaze. "As does one of my best friends, and my coach is pissed at me. Now, I come home and find you still wearing someone else's jersey, as if you haven't taunted me enough." He stands tall, chin jutted, and throws his arms out wide. "You win. You wanted to punish me, I'm punished."

I spin on my heel and stalk toward the bed, making sure he sees the letters emblazoned on my back. "I'm wearing *our* last name, asshole." Grasping the hem of the jersey, I whip it over my head. Then I toss it at his feet. Some type of spirit must have taken over my body, because gone is the woman who hides behind layers of clothing. I'm completely naked, but I don't cower. Instead, I stand tall, whip my head over my shoulder and glare at him. "I'll never make *that* mistake again. But you want to punish me?" I press my chest to the mattress, my head tilted and my cheek flush against the bedding. Arms flung out. Ass up. Taunting him. "So punish me."

CHAPTER 27
TYLER

MY MOUTH WATERS and heat rushes through me. *Punish me.* I've never heard anything as hot as those two simple words.

I'm glued to the spot, gaping at my literal dream girl—who's bent over and naked—unable to formulate a fucking response.

Her long red hair cascades down her back. It's so long that it falls to the place where her waist curves. She's on her tiptoes, and her small, toned, freckle-covered legs have my heart tripping. And that goddamn ass. I fist my hands and focus on my breathing. If I don't, I'll lose control. Because her ass is unreal. It's exactly what I expected the first time I saw her, when she was in nothing but that leotard. She hides it beneath leggings and oversized sweaters. Tonight, though, nothing is hidden. She's bare for me. Begging for me. Teasing me as she wiggles it and eyes me over her shoulder, waiting to see how I'll react.

"Not exactly a punishment, if you're begging for it."

Humming, she gives her ass another shake. "No one's ever spanked me before. Punish me, Ty. Remind me that I'm yours."

"Oh, you are so fucking mine."

Her words land exactly how she intended. They taunt me into moving. In three steps, I'm standing above her, taking in every inch of her creamy skin, right down to the puckered hole that I'd bet anything no one has ever touched. "You're so fucking perfect I don't even know where to start."

"Anywhere," she whimpers, grinding her hips against the bed.

"Does it hurt, Vicious?"

"Does what hurt?"

"The ache to come. That's what you want, right? You want me to control each orgasm, don't you?" I press my palms to her ass cheeks and hold them there, giving her nothing else.

"Yes," she whines.

I give her no warning before I lift one hand and swiftly bring it down on her left cheek. Her skin blooms a beautiful shade of red as she cries out. Before she can recover, I repeat the action on the right side.

This time, she moans.

With my hands splayed on the mattress at her sides, I loom over her but don't touch her. "The last time you came, what did you use?"

"A toy." The words come out breathy.

"Where is it?"

"Top drawer next to my side of the bed."

Her eagerness gives me a thrill. I can't help but chuckle at the thought of it as I leave her there waiting and go for a little show-and-tell of her sex drawer. "Well, well, well. Looks like I was right about sweet little Ava."

Green eyes watch me as I take in one toy after another, lifting them up and inspecting them. Hitting buttons to make them vibrate, rolling my thumb across the smooth surfaces, until I select the one I want for the time being.

When I hold it up and show her, she licks her lips.

"I take it you approve?"

She sucks in a heady breath and nods.

Humming, I glance into the drawer again. "Do you think I'll need lube to get this in?"

"Maybe."

I chuckle. "If I do, then I haven't done my job."

Without any more delay, I return to my spot behind her and gently tap the insides of her feet with my own. "Wider, Vicious. I need room to play." With both hands, I spread her ass cheeks.

She fights me, trying to wiggle her legs closed, likely embarrassed.

I'll have none of it. "This ass is mine, just like the rest of your body." With that, I spit on her hole.

She hisses. "Ty—"

Her words are cut off sharply as I press my thumb to her hole and use the wetness I created to push inside, past that ring of muscle.

"You're so fucking tight, baby. I think this should be your punishment. Me fucking this tight hole until you come all over my bed. Won't even touch your pussy, and still, it'll be the best orgasm of your life."

"Tyler, please." Clutching the comforter with both hands, she begs, though I'm not sure she knows what she's begging for.

I slide my thumb out and grind my hips against her ass. "Or would you prefer the toy in your pussy while you suck my cock?" It's only fair to give her options. Either works for me.

"Please let me suck your cock," she whines.

Holy fuck. I wasn't aware I had a corruption kink, but getting this sweet, innocent girl to beg for my cock—to say the fucking word in that raspy tone—yeah, I've never been so hard in my life.

I circle the tight muscle again, taunting her. "Because you don't want me to fuck this ass?"

With her cheek still pressed to the bed, she watches me. Then she licks her lips. "Because I've never wanted someone more."

"Good fucking answer." I crouch behind her so I can get a good look at how wet she's made the bed. "You're already staining my bed."

She lifts her hips, forcing her pussy closer to my face. "Our bed."

"Fuck, I love when you talk married to me."

She giggles. "You're ridiculous."

"Absolutely, when it comes to you. Now let's see just how wet you get when you suck me off." With the bulbous toy equipped with a clit stimulator in one hand, I use the other to spread her pink lips and slide it inside her.

She cries out at the intrusion, the sound dripping with need.

Then I press on the button, and the toy starts vibrating inside her. "Feel good, baby?"

"Yes." Her moan is muffled by the comforter as she buries her face in it.

I slide the clit suction into place, my fingers gingerly swiping over the wetness that coats every inch of her. "You feel like heaven. I'll let you suck me off tonight, but eventually I'm going to fuck this pretty pussy and this perfect ass. And when I do, you'll beg me to never stop."

As she pants and grinds against the bed, I can't help but stare at her. This perfect angel of a woman. Sweet, innocent Ava. My vicious wife. I'm going to destroy her.

Chapter 28
Ava

I BARELY RECOGNIZE MYSELF. This woman only exists when I'm with Tyler. He has never allowed me to sit quietly like the rest of the world does. He doesn't let me blend in. He forces me to step out of the shadows and claim what I want. And I want to be the vicious woman he claims I am. So much so that I truly believe I'm becoming her.

How else can I explain what I just did?

Stripped naked, begged him to punish me, and taunted him into pleasuring me. There is not a single other person in this world I'd even consider doing this with.

With anyone else, I'd be hiding behind layers of clothes. Though in this position, he still can't see the insides of my arms, I've never allowed anyone even a chance at seeing my scars.

Now I'm going to willingly beg for his cock. "Please, *Ty*."

He lowers himself until his body heat soaks into me. "I love when you call me that." His voice is like honey drizzling over my aching nerves. "Now, do me a favor baby and remember how crazy I am about you because I'm about to do some very bad things to this perfect body."

His warmth disappears an instant before a smack lands on my ass with a loud *thwack*. The burn only electrifies the vibrations from the toy. It's like a live current racking through me.

I whimper incoherently, unable to even string together a sentence.

"Don't whine. Tell your husband what you want. I'll always give it to you."

A rush flows through me at his words, at the sharp tenor and the promise it brings. And I 100 percent believe him. "I want—" I peek back at him again. "No, I need your cock. Show it to me."

Tyler's lips curl, as if he's impressed with the way I phrased the statement. Like I've pleased him. "Eyes on me," he commands as he slides his belt free of its buckle. He undoes his pants, and they drop to the floor with a dull thud. His shirt goes next. I practically orgasm on the spot when he grabs it by the center and rips the sides apart, sending buttons clattering to the floor. He's been frustratingly patient in his torture so far, but not anymore. Good, let him be as desperate as I am.

"Turn around. Head down here," he commands.

I obey quickly, spinning awkwardly with the vibrating toy still working me over. Lying on my stomach like this, the toy should remain in place, with the suction on my clit for maximum pleasure while he fucks my mouth.

And now that I'm fully facing him, I get a peek at his bare, tattooed chest, the ripples of his muscles covered in beautiful ink that I could spend hours studying.

We haven't talked about the one on his finger. I'll deal with whatever that means later.

In nothing but a pair of tight black boxer briefs, Tyler steps forward and grabs a fistful of my hair. "This drives me fucking wild, Vicious. I can't put into words what color it is, but fuck, do I love it. Means I get to spend the rest of my life coming up with the perfect name for it."

With my teeth pressed against my bottom lip, I peer up at him through my lashes. "Are you going to finish getting undressed?"

"Eager to see your cock?"

My heart thumps against my breastbone. "My cock?"

Nodding, Tyler slips his thumbs beneath his waistband and drags his underwear down his legs. "Your husband. Your cock."

"Kinda like my wife, my jersey."

He chuckles. "See? I knew you were a quick learner."

I'm all-in when it comes to banter, but the moment his—no, *my*—cock comes into view, any clever comeback I could formulate evaporates from my mind. "You're..."

"Tattooed," he finishes for me. "And pierced."

"Does that say *Vicious*?" With my heart in my throat, I study the word scrawled in black script at the base of his dick.

War runs his thumbs over the word and cups himself. "You've got me by the balls, baby. No sense in denying it."

"Holy shit. That had to hurt. When did you get that?"

He strokes himself once, the movement making the black lettering inked onto the underside of his dick disappear. "The week we got married. And I like the pain."

"Somehow that fits."

He thumbs the set of barbells that form a cross of sorts below the head.

I meet his eye. "Can I...?"

"Vicious," he grinds out. "You can do whatever the fuck you want to me. Suck it, lick it, tug it, bite it. Just please, put your mouth on my cock right now and take your damn punishment like the dirty girl we both know you are."

A bolt of lust so powerful I almost orgasm on the spot floods me. I'm not that girl. Not outside this room. But here and now, staring up at this god of a man, filled with more need than I thought humanly possible, I feel powerful. In control of him.

My husband.

I open my mouth, tongue out. He steps closer, gliding his fingers through my hair with one hand, and tugs me up a fraction. Then, with his other hand, he guides his decorated dick into my mouth. The metal is cool against my tongue. It's unexpected, and for a second, I worry I'll gag. But he goes slow, allowing me to adjust to the feel of him. I roll my tongue across the beads, the movement pulling a grunt from him.

"Fuck, baby. Look at you, already so good at this."

With a moan, I try to take more of him, but he tugs on my hair, stopping me.

"Slow, baby. I've been dreaming about this for way too fucking long. Want to last."

I can't go slow, though. My body is buzzing with the need to come, and with the vibrator sending waves of pleasure through me, I can't help but slurp and suck faster, torturing him as I chase my own orgasm.

"Oh, my dirty girl can't slow down, huh? You going to come with your husband's fat cock in your mouth? Going to squirt all over the comforter like a dirty little slut?"

I cry out, the sound muffled as he thrusts deeper.

"Okay, Vicious." He thrusts again and again in a smooth rhythm. "I'll give it to you your way this time. Fast and hard." His movements get more unsteady, the grip on my hair tighter. As he fucks my mouth, I imagine how I must look. Completely naked, humping the bed, being used to bring him pleasure. I'm pulled from that thought, my mind splintering from my body, as pleasure floods my system, and I come on a long, garbled moan.

"Yes, wife. Take what you've earned. Show me how beautiful you are as you break apart for me."

And I do. I moan and gyrate, undulating my hips in time with my release until he swells in my mouth. When he comes on a curse, saying my name as he does, followed by a French expletive, I swear I'm the one who sees stars.

I've barely come down from my orgasm, and he's still pulsing in my mouth when he pulls back and rounds the bed. "Get up here, Vicious," he says, lying on his side of the bed. "Put that dripping pussy on my face and let me see how much you enjoyed that."

The mouth on my husband.

Licking my lips, I blink up at him, willing my shaky limbs to obey.

But before I can, Scarlett cries out from her room.

"Fuck," he hisses.

I close my eyes and take in a steadying breath. This is good. We got carried away. I almost—god. "I'll take care of her. You had a long night."

Tyler jackknifes up and grabs my wrist before I can slip off the mattress. "Go get cleaned up," he murmurs into my neck. "I've missed the kids. Let me put Scar back to sleep. Let me take care of her, and then I'll take care of you."

With a gentle kiss, he's gone.

I stay in that position, seated on the bed, naked and wondering what the hell just happened between us, for far too long.

TEXT MESSAGES FROM AVA'S AND TYLER'S PHONE

Gavin: My office, 7 a.m. We're figuring this shit out before we get on the plane to Philly.

Tyler: Yes, Coach. Sorry about tonight.

Gavin: Don't say sorry. Fix it. Sara handled the video. You're lucky. You won't be so lucky next time.

Madi: Tyler, I'm hearing rumblings about a fight that occurred on the ice. Remember what I said—no fights. Call me.

Tyler: The Langfields handled it. I'll call when I land in Philly.

Tyler: I'm sorry. I'll do better. I promise.

Dad: Tyler, your stepmother is still very upset, and we don't understand what's going on. Xander is hurting. We need to fix this.

Tyler: Why don't you ask Xander where he was on Christmas Eve when he abandoned Ava at my house. That might help with the confusion. She's my wife. He can either get on board or get over it. I'm not apologizing for taking care of the woman he threw away.

Ava: Hi, sis. Sorry it's been a few days since I texted. I can't seem to get my head on straight. I'm so scared that I'm making a million mistakes. He's probably going to break my heart, but I think maybe I'm falling for my husband...

CHAPTER 29
TYLER

"SO, uh, you want to play cards?" I sit next to Hall, wishing I was in Boston rather than Philly right about now. Leaving yesterday morning, after everything that has happened, was less than ideal.

Gavin lectured me first thing. Not only is Hall my teammate, he's also Gavin's brother-in-law. He barely mentioned him in our conversation, though. Our coach is too smart for that. No, he focused on the adoption. He knows where my priorities lie. He also knows what it takes to keep a kid with no blood relation. How each step has to be followed in just the right way, and how even then, nothing is guaranteed. And at our last game, I did everything wrong.

Madi was equally pissed. We were lucky that the fight occurred during the pregame, which wasn't being televised. And that it happened so quickly that fans didn't have time to start recording on their phones before it was over. The Langfields destroyed all footage from the arena, and Sara has spent the last twenty-four hours spinning it as nothing more than a slight disagreement between teammates rather than an unhinged captain sucker punching his friend.

To say this team is a family is an understatement. It's the family I haven't had since I lost my mother. The family I'm not quite sure I deserve.

Hall eyes me but doesn't even turn his head.

I sigh, ready to grovel—I've been informed by Lennox and Sara that it includes wooing and flowers and oral; I told them I'd handle groveling when it came to my teammates, thank you very much— when my phone lights up with a FaceTime request from Brayden. I hold out a finger to Hall and swipe the screen to answer.

Rather than Brayden, I'm met with Josie's bright smile. "Hey, Tyler."

At the sound of her voice, all my teammates perk up. Everyone in the Bolts universe loves Josie.

I lean back on the couch in the open area of the locker room and focus on my girl. "Hey, fighter. You steal Bray's phone?"

She looks adorable with her hair in a bun on top of her head. "Yeah," she chirps. "After I told him my story about dance, he said I could call you."

Bray is hovering behind her now, wearing a shit-eating grin, his eyes practically glowing with delight.

My stomach knots. What the hell happened at dance?

Hall leans closer, and his face appears in the little box in the corner of my screen. "What happened at dance, Jos?"

"My instructor invited Ava to class, and she danced with me."

At the sound of her name, my heart thumps a little wildly. She was fast asleep when I finally got Scarlett down the other night, and she was already gone when I woke up. She's avoiding me after what happened, I know that, but she can't do it forever. Not that I have a clue what I'll say when we see each other again.

"That's fun—"

"Yup, Monsieur Benoir even asked her to dance with him after class."

"Wait." Hall reels back, then tilts the phone in his direction. "Your dance instructor is a man?"

I grip the phone harder and pull it back toward me. "What else did he say?"

Brayden's lips are pressed into a tight line, but he's chuckling behind Josie, who is completely oblivious to my internal meltdown. "He told her how pretty her plié was and said he can't wait to work on her tech"—nose scrunched, she looks off to one side—"What's the word?"

"Technique," Brayden mumbles. "He said he couldn't wait to work on her technique tomorrow during her one-on-one class."

Heated fury sparks to life inside me. "Her *what*?"

Josie pouts. "She said I can't come because I have school."

"We'll see about that," I grumble.

Josie's green eyes fly wide. "I don't have to go to school?"

Beside me, Hall shakes with silent laughter.

I swallow back my anger and affect a neutral tone. "You have to go to school. I just—" Flustered, I blow out a breath. "Is Ava around?"

"She's making dinner with Hannah." This from Brayden. "They're having girl talk. Pretty sure it revolves around the ballet instructor. Lots of giggling going on over there."

Brayden is enjoying this far too much. The damn grin on his face is just as big as Hall's. *Assholes.*

"Good luck tonight." Josie interrupts my train of thought, reminding me that we have an actual game in a few hours and I need to focus. "Will you be home tomorrow?"

My heart momentarily melts for this little girl. "Yeah, mon chou." I sigh. "Be good for Ava and Maria, yeah?"

"Okay, bye."

The screen goes black before I can get any more information out of Brayden, and a lead ball settles in my stomach.

Hall shifts over now that the show is done. "Still want to play cards?"

Arms crossed over my chest, I glare at him.

"I'm sure the instructor is old. He probably stinks too," he says with a smile.

Rather than respond, I just continue to stare him down.

Scratching at the back of his neck, he lets out an uncomfortable laugh. "Didn't you come over here to apologize?" Deck of cards in hand, he splits it in half and shuffles. "It's fine. Your wife is flirting with someone else. Seems like you need a friend more than I do right now."

Flirting with someone else. My chest tightens, making it hard to breathe. "Shut up."

"See that, boys? War is getting possessive of his wife," he sings like the ass he is. "Calliope says women do this when they aren't satisfied at home. Maybe the glitter isn't helping as much as you thought it would."

"Better be careful," Brooks warns, though his tone is light. "He might punch you."

I roll my eyes. "Fine. I was an asshole. I'm sorry."

Hall starts dealing the cards. "It's that wife of yours you should be sucking up to, not me. You're already forgiven, Cap."

Around the locker room, the guys laugh. Even though it's at my expense, I can't help but relax. Hall isn't holding a grudge. Now I only have to worry about my wife and the game she's playing.

Wifey: Congrats on a great game. The kids wouldn't go to sleep until the buzzer sounded. They were super proud.

Me: Was my wife super proud too?

Wifey: <eye roll emoji> <Fanning face emoji> Yes, so hot.

Me: You probably say that to all the guys. Like your dance instructor. <side-eye emoji>

Wifey: I was wondering how long it would take you to bring that up.

Me: ???

Wifey: It's nothing.

Me: Didn't sound like nothing. Sounds like the guy was hitting on my wife.

Wifey: And what if he was?

Me: Ava.

Wifey: Oh, sounds like you'll punish me if I see him again.

Me: Don't test me.

Wifey: But you know how much I like your punishments. <devil emoji>

Me: I'll be home by twelve tomorrow. Will you be around?

Wifey: Should be.

Me: Good. I'd like to grab a drink with my wife and talk.

Wifey: I'll see if I can pencil you in.

Me: Madi got me the actual petition for Josie's adoption. We need to get it signed asap and get Scarlett's adoption paperwork finalized too, if you're still open to that.

Wifey: Of course. Whatever I can do to keep our family together, you know I will.

Me: I'll see you tomorrow, wifey.

Wifey: Good night, Tyler.

CHAPTER 30
TYLER

"WHAT EXACTLY ARE WE LOOKING FOR?" Aiden asks as he holds a vibrator at eye level and turns it one way, then the other, inspecting it.

Sara takes it out of his hand and puts it back. "Not a lipstick vibrator, that's for sure." She eyes me, one brow arched to confirm.

I offer her a nod. Definitely not a lipstick vibrator.

Why am I willingly walking around a sex toy store with Aiden and Daniel and Sara? It's Brooks's fault. I should know by now that he shares everything with Sara, and she can't let anything go. Worried that the dance instructor might be a real threat, I turned to my best friend for his opinion and advice. Somehow that turned into Sara dragging us to this store, demanding I find a gift for Ava that would ensure she's thinking about me only.

"What type of toy do you think would mimic the sensation of a piercing?" Daniel ponders aloud.

Sara's lips curl into a teasing grin. "Nothing, you sweet playboy, you. Nothing I've ever played with can compare to Brooks's glitter dick."

Brooks lets out a heavy sigh.

"You should be proud," Aiden mutters. "If Lennox said I was better than any of her toys, I'd be proud."

Hall whirls on him. "She hasn't told you that?"

Immediately, Aiden is on his phone and calling his wife. As he disappears down an aisle, he tells Lennox she owes him for not complimenting his dick enough. Only seconds later, he's apologizing for being in a sex store without her, and then he's returning to us with his phone held out. "Sar, Lex says I have to give you the phone. I'm in trouble, and now you get to pick out toys, and I have to pay for them as my punishment."

Sara cackles and taps the speaker button on the phone. "Do you want to *punish* punish him, or do you want fun things for you as his punishment?"

"I want you to get the biggest vibrating dick you can find so I can use it in his—"

Brooks hits the mute button, silencing Lennox's words. "Please god, don't talk about what you do to my brother, Lennox."

Sara glares at him. "You're such a prude."

"Why am I here again?" I mutter, walking away from the shit show that is my group of friends.

Daniel follows after me. "Because you want to satisfy your wife so she doesn't flirt with the dancer. Calliope says if you're worried your man is cheating, then he probably is. Go with your instinct."

I blink. Then I blink again. "My man?"

Daniel scoffs. "You know what I mean. Here, let me pull up the article. She has a whole thing on trusting your instincts. Girl is fucking brilliant." He's already got his phone out, which means he'll be distracted for a bit. The minute the kid starts reading his sweet Callie's words—his description, not mine—we lose him.

I clap him on the back and squeeze. "I'm not actually worried about him."

It's the truth. Though our marriage started as nothing but a contract, I know Ava will always remain true to her word. She'd never be unfaithful. And I'm happy she's dancing again. Watching her dance that first day changed me, all the way down to my DNA. It made me see her in a way I'd never seen anyone else. And I'm aching to see it again.

As that thought occurs to me, a plan forms in my head. Quickly, I circle the store, buy what I know my wife will enjoy, and head for the door.

"Where you going?" Sara yells as she holds up an oversized dildo that has Aiden shaking in his literal boots.

"To play with my wife."

"Thatta boy," she hollers as I head out into the cold Boston day. "Give her that sparkly D!"

> Me: I'm in Boston. Be home soon. Where are you?

> Wifey: At the dance studio. I'll be done here in an hour or so. Let me know where you want to go to talk, and I'll meet you there.

> Me: I've got the address. I'll pick you up.

> Wifey: Tyler Warren, you better not intimidate my dance instructor.

> Me: I wouldn't dream of it.

My wife loves to taunt me. It took a little time to find the right room, but when I did, all my effort was rewarded.

Ava is stretching on a barre, her long leg extended against it, her back rounded in a way that highlights the curves of her ass and hips. Her smooth, pale skin is covered by a long-sleeve black leotard and absolutely nothing else. Maybe it's the contrast between the black fabric covering her arms and her bare legs, but today, the look is even hotter.

When she spots my reflection, I have to bite my fist to hide my smile. I'm still in the suit I donned for traveling, and my hair is a mess —I'll blame it on the agitation that ate at me while I was searching for her—but we look exquisite together. Just like we did that first day. Me fully clothed and prowling toward her like a predator, her my innocent prey.

"Are you ready to begin, mon chérie?"

At the sound of the masculine voice, we both startle.

Instantly, I spin, my eyes skewering the man talking to *my darling wife* in his fake French accent with his fake French name.

When he sees me, he straightens. "Can I help you? This is a private class, but you can browse the list of available classes in the front hallway."

Before I can speak, Ava pipes up. "He was just leaving."

"Oh, do you know him?" He assesses me now, eyeing me as if he stands a chance to earn Ava's favor. Not that it matters. There's no choice. She's mine. Contract or not, it's all in her glare. My wife is just as obsessed with our games as I am.

"Just my husband having a little temper tantrum," she says to him, though she keeps her green eyes locked on me. "I told him I was busy for the afternoon, and he doesn't know how to take no for an answer."

"I don't." With a slow, devious grin, I take a step closer. My blood heats as her scent—vanilla and coconut—grows stronger.

"I didn't realize she was married," he says behind me. "You don't wear a wedding band."

I grasp her left hand and inspect it in an exaggerated manner. The emerald I slid onto her finger is right where it should be. I hold up her hand to him and ask whether he's the type of man who goes after women who look as though they're engaged. "Alors tu es le genre d'homme qui s'en prend aux femmes fiancées?"

He blinks at me, clearly not understanding a word of the language from the country he feigns relation to.

I demand an answer. "Réponds-moi, oui ou non?"

I can't hold back the chuckle when the man nods aggressively. What a fucking idiot. But the man is right about one thing. My wife doesn't have a wedding band. I'll need to rectify that soon.

Focusing my attention back on her, I wrap my arm around her waist and pull her close, locking her hand between our bodies, and press my lips to the space where a band should be, marking her.

"Hello, Vicious," I whisper.

"Hello, husband," she says, lips quirking.

She spins her hand, but I tug it closer and kiss her wrist, my eyes on her the entire time. "Enjoy your dancing."

"Enjoy the show," she murmurs, knowing I'll never leave her here. No, for the next hour, she's going to torture me. Make me watch her sway those hips and smile at the man still watching us. And I'm going to love every minute of it.

"Are you proud of yourself?" I hold the door to the dance studio open for my wife.

"Actually, yes." She brushes by me, her fingers sliding against my chest.

Fuck, this woman drives me mad.

I grab her hand and pull her back before she can get away. "Really?"

Ava presses both hands to my chest and looks up at me from beneath long lashes, her green eyes alight and her lips wet from rolling her tongue across them. "Yup. It's ridiculous, I know, but I love seeing you all jealous over me."

"I'm not jealous," I lie as I guide her toward her car. I pluck her keys out of her hand and open the passenger door.

She's silent, studying me as I lean over her and buckle her seat belt. It's something Brooks does with Sara. I always found it absurd, but I get it now. My instincts kick in and my body takes over when it comes to her. And I'm not the least bit upset about it. "So if I told you I was wet right now, you wouldn't be upset?" She grasps my wrist, her breaths coming faster.

Still hovering over her, I drink her in. Even beneath the white sweater she threw over her leotard, the swell of her breasts taunts me. "Why would I be upset?"

She licks her lips again. "Because he made me wet."

I nip at her bottom lip, biting down just hard enough to pull a whine from her. "Is that the story you're going with, Vicious?" I pull back a smidge so I can see her completely. "Or are you ready to combust because you liked that I was watching you with him?"

"What if it's both?" She whispers the admission, worrying her bottom lip as she watches me, like she's concerned about how I'll react.

I pull back and shut her door, then slowly round the hood of the SUV. When I climb into the driver's seat, I put the gift I picked up for her on the center console between us. "Then I'd say I need to punish you to remind you of who you belong to."

"I don't belong to you," she says, her fire returning and her chin lifted in challenge.

"State of Massachusetts would say otherwise." I start the car and turn my attention to the road, knowing I need to get far away from this place before my jealousy really does take over and I bring her back into the dance studio to show her precisely who she belongs to right in front of her instructor and the million and one mirrors she teased me with during her class.

"I'm married to you. I don't *belong* to you."

I reach for her hand as a peace offering. "Well, I belong to you, Vicious, so either way, you're stuck with me."

"For sixteen years," she says softly.

"It's humorous you think I'm ever letting you go," I mutter, rolling my neck to ease the tension that forms whenever she reminds me of her damn timeline. With a glance her way, I lower my voice and grit out, "How about you show me just how wet you are?"

Ava sucks in a breath and whips her head in my direction. "Right here?"

"Yes. Spread those legs, dip your finger in, and show me." When she still hesitates, I grip her thigh and pull it toward me.

She walked out of the studio without pants, just the leotard and her sweater. If I hadn't been there, I can guarantee she'd have put them on.

It's freezing out, but the woman does stupid things to taunt me, and now that she's taken it this far, I'm not letting her pull back.

"Come on, Vicious. Don't get shy on me now. Tease me like we both know you want to. Torture me. Don't shut down on me." It's a plea for so much more than just another intimate moment with her. These games we play are my salvation. They give me hope that the two of us can have more than just the stipulations we first agreed to. It's in these moments that I feel most at ease. I like the pain. It means I can still feel. That I'm not as dead inside as I once was.

When we come to a light, I shift and study her. She's got her lip caught between her teeth, and she's watching me just as intently. Like she's reading my every thought. Good. Let her figure it all out. I'm not hiding anything from her. I lick my lips and rev the engine, growing impatient. The instant the light turns green, I hit the gas, making the tires squeal and Ava's head snap back against the headrest.

With a throaty laugh, she teases the edge of her leotard with a finger.

Cursing, I glance from her to the road.

"Pull that little strip of fabric over and show me how you glisten for me."

"And Benoir," she purrs.

"Fuck Benoir and his fake French name," I growl as jealousy burns in my gut. "It kills me, hearing his name on your lips, baby. Makes me want to fill that mouth so you can never speak it again."

Her throaty moan has me whipping my head in her direction again. I'm just in time to watch as she stuffs two fingers into her cunt.

"Oh, fuck. That's my dirty wife. Yes, soak those fingers. Get ready to taste yourself."

The desperate noises she makes as she fucks herself with her fingers has me swelling until my dick is threatening to split my zipper. I'm racing against the clock, trying to get us out of the city and to the back roads before I come in my pants, and I haven't even touched her. Her whimpers, the wet sound her body makes as it suctions her fingers, her every sound ramp up my heart rate until my blood whooshes in my ears.

"Get the toy out of the bag next to you," I beg her.

She's too enthralled, too far gone, riding her fingers, knowing the torture she's doling out, to obey.

I dip my hand into the bag and pull out the toy I've already removed from its box. When I flip the switch, her eyes fly open, and, chest heaving, she studies it.

"Come on, baby. Put this inside your tight cunt. Let me watch you ride my present."

Pupils blown wide, she whines. "No, show me how much you want me, Tyler. Set it against your balls and come with me."

A bolt of electricity arcs through me. This woman wears a demure disguise so well, but she's fucking filthy.

"That what you need, baby? Need me to make a mess to show you just how much I want you? How I've been dreaming of you?"

As I press the vibrator to my already aching balls, I jolt. Knowing there's no way I can focus on the road like this, I take the next exit. I don't care where the fuck we are, but in two seconds, she's going to be riding me, and I refuse to let a single person see my wife as the dirty whore I need her to be. We've barely made it into a wooded area when I throw the car into park, unbuckle her seat belt, and drag her over the center console and onto my lap.

"Shit," she pants. "What are you doing?"

"Fuck me, Vicious. I need you." While I move the seat back, I take her mouth in a rough kiss and drag her over my cock so she can feel just how fucking gone for her I am.

She bites my lip, and with a mumbled *no*, she pushes back and rolls her hips in the most intoxicatingly beautiful way. Between the sight of her, the way she slides over my dick, and the vibrator still pressed to my balls, I'm hit with a wave of dizziness. But I refuse to blink. I refuse to look away from her. Instead, I focus on her hips and the way they dance against me like they did less than an hour ago when she was with fucking Benoir.

"Look at you, baby, just as desperate as I am. Did he do that to you? You think he's got a piercing that will make you scream?"

Eyes closed, she moans, lost in the pleasure.

"He got your name tattooed above his balls? Did he mark himself for you?" I taunt, gripping her hips and rolling her over me. "No, it's your husband's cock that keeps you wet. Your husband who branded himself yours. Forever, wifey. That's what I'm telling everyone. I'm forever yours and you're forever mine. Now admit it, Vicious. Tell me how much you need me, and I'll fill you so good you won't be able to walk tomorrow, let alone dance."

"Shh, keep taunting me, and I'll have to figure out a way to shut you up," she teases, sliding her fingers into my mouth, feeding me the taste of her pleasure.

I'm sucking them clean when she detonates, pulsating on top of me. In this moment, I know I'm done for. Because like a teenage boy, I come in my pants with her taste on my lips and a smile on my face.

Chapter 31
Ava

"I DON'T EVEN RECOGNIZE MYSELF," I mutter as I pull up the skirt I borrowed from Hannah.

She snorts as I duck and grimace at my reflection in the little mirror she keeps in her office. Shit. My hair is a mess.

"I'll say." She presses a finger against my neck and lets out a laugh. "Is that a hickey, or were you bitten by a vampire?"

Huffing, I back away and pick up the mirror so I can inspect the mark Tyler must have left on me while he came. God, this is embarrassing.

"He didn't tell me we were meeting *with* the attorney this afternoon."

"Probably because he expected his wife to be wearing clothes when he picked her up from dance class." She arches a brow. "Not that I'm not loving this side of my sweet Ava."

"Don't let my wife fool you. There's nothing sweet about her."

We spin in unison and find Tyler standing in the doorway, completely put together, his hands in the pockets of his suit pants as he leans casually on the frame.

"Then why'd you take a bite out of her?" Hannah digs through her purse and pulls out a bottle of concealer, then tosses it to me. "Might be a little dark for you, but it's the best I can do."

After I finished riding Tyler like he was my personal carousel, he informed me that we were scheduled to meet with his attorney, so we'd have to stop by the locker room so he could get a change of clothes. The man came in his pants and didn't even blush about it. Nope, I'm pretty sure he walked into Langfield Corp with a grin on his face.

I, on the other hand, am mortified and oh so thankful that my best friend keeps multiple changes of clothes in her office. According to her, one never knows when they'll need a wardrobe change for a date or a game. Or to go undercover to fix one of the players' problems. She's my idol, and I love her always, but today, I love her the most. Even while she continues to tease me for being such a disaster.

"Give her a minute, War. The girl needs to put herself back together before her panties get wet all over again, and from the way you're looking at her, that can't happen while you're in the room."

War throws his head back and laughs. Also, it's too late. All it took was one look at the way his Adam's apple bobs to make my panties damp. Every inch of him exudes strength and power and sex. It's a deadly combination, and one that clearly has the ability to fry my brain cells into riding him in his freaking car. Oh, excuse me, my freaking car. The one with the *Mrs. War* license plate, as if I need to be reminded that I'm his personal property.

But god, I don't even get mad about it anymore. I try to. I tell myself that I'm my own person, that the only person who controls me is me. Then he goes and looks like that, and those mantras go out the window, and I melt at his feet, begging him to pull out that monster cock of his and let me revel in the beauty of it. It's one seriously beautiful penis. Though it's probably wasted on me. I can't possibly appreciate just how perfect it is when I have practically nothing to compare it to.

Not that I'll allow anyone else to see it. I'll scratch a girl's eyes out for merely glancing in his direction.

Who am I, and what the heck has happened to me? It's like Tyler's dick has altered my brain chemistry.

"That was supposed to be an inside thought," Hannah mutters.

Blue eyes locked on me, Tyler saunters in my direction, and the rest of the world fades away. I'm pretty sure Hannah is squawking, but when Tyler is near, he's all I can focus on.

He runs his fingers through my hair and tugs until my chin is forced up and I'm staring at that mouth of his as the most beautiful words fall from them.

"Tout ce à quoi je pense. C'est te faire l'amour à chaque instant de chaque jour. Comment tu goûtes. Comment tu parles. Je suis obsédé et te voir obsédé, C'est me foutre la tête. Ne me brise pas le cœur visqueux. Je ne m'en remettrai jamais."

Before I can ask him to translate, his mouth is on mine, capturing me in the most indecent kiss I've ever experienced. I don't need to know the meaning of his words to understand what he's telling me. This isn't a contractual relationship anymore. Though our initial reason is still important, it's not all that binds us. This is so much more. It's an obsession I can't imagine waning.

Arms looped around his neck, I pull myself closer, giving in to my desires. This man. This freaking man may destroy me, and I may just let him.

"Holy shit, I need a cigarette," Hannah mutters.

Even as I giggle and pull back, Tyler cradles my head and eases us apart. All the while, he presses kiss after drugging kiss to my lips, then my cheek, then my chin. Then he smiles that cocky smile that pisses me off so much. "Come on, wifey. We're going to be late."

"It's so nice to finally meet you." Madi shakes my hand, and I'm immediately put at ease by her demeanor. She's well-known around the country—she's married to a famous actor, after all—so I wasn't sure what to expect. But the petite brunette has a kind face, and I immediately like her.

"It's nice to meet you too. Thank you for getting all the paperwork together so quickly."

She points to the chairs across from her desk, signaling for us to sit.

"Of course. I think it's wonderful that Josie helped bring her two favorite people together and that they fell in love."

Keeping my expression neutral, I eye Tyler. Is that what he told her? That we fell in love and decided to get married on a whim after Josie introduced us? Honestly, it's more far fetched than the already ridiculous truth—that we both love Josie and so we decided to get married in hopes that we can keep her.

Wouldn't the court question our sanity if they believed that story? It's not rational to fall in love that quickly. Then again, nothing we've been doing is rational.

"Also, I'm impressed by your willingness to put an agreement in place that establishes what happens should you separate. It shows just how important the well-being of the children is to you."

Once again my eyes skirt to Tyler's. This time, though, my stomach sinks. We did? Is he already planning our end?

Tyler grips my hand and squeezes. "What she means is the agreement that we'll live together until Scarlett turns eighteen, no matter what. That we'll put the kids first and raise them together because that's what they need—both a mother and father who are dedicated to them. Not that there's any kind of language in the contract regarding divorce."

But maybe there should be. Maybe if we lay out what happens when we divorce, it'll help me remember that this is all temporary. Then again, after years together, of being touched like this and aching for him like I already do, how will I ever recover when he walks away?

And he will walk away. Keeping the people who matter has never worked out well for me.

I clear my throat. "Yes, well, the kids come first. Always."

Madi smiles. "Exactly. I can see why Tyler fell so hard so quickly. Finding someone with such similar values—especially when it comes to kids—is not easy, but it really is the foundation for a strong and long-lasting marriage. Now let's go over everything so you two can get out of here."

Hours later I'm still walking around in a fog. Tyler thought of everything. Every term in the contract protects the kids. Every question he asked was to ensure that we will do all we need to over the next few months so that when social services interviews us and the court evaluates us, we'll not only meet their expectations, but exceed them. He's willing to do anything to become Josie's father. That doesn't take away from the attraction we're navigating now. If anything, it makes me want him more. But it hit me hard. The realization that I'm not only incredibly attracted to him, but I've become incredibly invested in a future together.

I'd be smart to pull back. To give myself space to remember why we're doing this. Maybe I should be scared, but how can I be, when I know that even if this part of our relationship comes to an end, Tyler will protect everyone—even me—so that we can make it as a family.

If anything, that frees me to explore the connection between us. We're married. We're attracted to one another. We have a contract in place to protect the kids should we decide we want nothing more than to be co-parents. If I keep my heart unattached, then I'll be okay no matter how life plays out. It shouldn't be too hard. The man drives me nuts 98 percent of the time. So this works. We'll be married, we'll raise our kids, and fool around.

How very Samantha of me. I slip my phone out of my pocket to text my sister. That thought would make her smile.

As I start down the hallway on the second floor, Josie's little voice catches my attention, and my feet falter. Holding my breath, I pause outside her door.

"But what if it hurts?"

"Come on, fighter. You're the strongest person I know."

I peer into the bedroom, only to find Tyler sitting behind her on her purple and pink comforter, braiding her hair. He's dressed in blue Bolts sweats and a white T-shirt, and she's in her pajamas. The way he gently twists her hair and the way the tattoos on his arm flex as he does have a tightness growing in my chest.

"But what if it does? Everyone told me the needles wouldn't hurt, but they did. It hurts, Tyler. They all lied."

My heart breaks for our sweet girl. I know the pain of being jabbed with needles day in and day out. Of being aggravated when the nurses swear it won't be that bad, yet don't offer their arms instead.

I will my breathing to steady, but it's nearly impossible. With every memory, my anxiety ratchets up. The scratchy sheets on hospital beds. The loud noises. Whispered discussions of *what if?* and *we can't tell her.* Surgeries. So many surgeries. Flowers. I still hate the smell of them.

"How about this? I'll come with you and have my teeth cleaned first. Then, if you're comfortable with it, you'll get yours done too."

Josie flips her head so quickly, the braid Tyler is working on falls free. "You'd do that?"

His expression goes soft, his blue eyes full of more warmth than I've ever seen. "Of course I would. You are one of the most important people in the world to me. Don't ever be afraid to tell me when something scares you. I'll always do everything I can to help make it better."

Josie studies him, her brow furrowed, as if she's trying to make sense of his words. I get it. I'm right there with her. I feel the same way Tyler does, but even so, to hear those words so earnestly from him? To know he cares about her, that she's that important, is everything for a girl like Josie. A girl like me. "You'd do the same for Scarlett?"

Tyler nods. "And Bray and Ava. The four of you are my world."

With tears welling in my eyes and a lancing pain in my chest, I fall back against the wall. Any chance I had of protecting my heart just went out the window. This man owns me. And I have a feeling he always will.

CHAPTER 32
TYLER

BY THE GLOW of the night light, I check in on Scarlett. She's sleeping soundly, her favorite pink bear smooshed against her face. I move the bear a little and brush my fingers through her silky blond hair. With a scrunch of her nose, she shifts, turning so her other cheek is pressed to the mattress, but she doesn't wake. I watch her for a few more minutes, wishing I had unlimited time with each of my kids.

It took a while to get Josie down since she's nervous about the dentist tomorrow, but she's finally asleep, so when I leave Scarlett's room, I knock on Bray's door to say good night.

"Come in," he calls from his bed. He's on his phone, which is pretty typical lately, but he drops it when I step inside.

"Ready for your game this weekend?"

"You mean games," he teases. He likes to point out that he plays a lot of back-to-back games, whereas we professionals need longer breaks between them. He's not wrong. The older I get, the harder it is to push myself the way I did when I was his age.

"Yeah. That's what I meant."

He laughs, his dark shaggy hair brushing his forehead. "Kyle's dad said I could sleep over Friday night so Ava doesn't have to wake up early on Saturday to drive me to the arena."

It's hard not to smile at that. It's taken a little while for Brayden to settle in at his new school, but he's finally making friends. It helps that one of his teammates is in class with him. It's just what he needs and exactly why I begged Trish to let me keep him in this school even after she gets out of rehab. Which should be any day now, actually. Fuck, I've got to follow up on that. Things are going so well here. The last thing we need is an unpredictable Trisha to rock the boat. If only I could control every aspect of these kids' lives.

It's exhausting, waiting for the court to decide whether I'm a suitable choice. Waiting for Trish to decide whether she wants to be a parent. Hell, even waiting for my wife to finally look at me like she trusts me. Because today in Madi's office, she appeared ready to run. Ready to distance herself again, even while we both knew she could still feel my touch between her thighs.

It's going to take more than a few orgasms to prove to her that I'm not going anywhere. Lucky for both of us, I'm up for the fight.

"Awesome, Bray. I'll call Kyle's dad tomorrow and make sure everything is set for the weekend. Everything else good? You all caught up on your homework?"

With an easy smile, he leans back against his headboard and picks up his phone, practically dismissing me. "Yup, Daddy War. All my work is done. You can relax now. You've done your fatherly duties for the night."

"Cut the shit," I warn him. "You know I don't consider any of this a duty. I like having you here, and if you're happy here and want to stay, we can talk to your mom."

His attitude softens, along with his posture. "I know. And I didn't mean any disrespect."

"I don't feel disrespected. Just want you to know I love having you here. You aren't an obligation. You're *why* I like coming home. Why I have this home in the first place."

"Pretty sure you love coming home now because of the redhead in your bed," he taunts.

All I can do is laugh. "Yeah, I definitely like coming home to my wife. But she's not the only one I look forward to seeing after traveling." I tap on the doorframe as I walk out. "Night, Bray."

"Night, Daddy War," he hollers.

I temper my responding laugh as I shuffle down the quiet hallway. With everyone tucked in and Maria's door shut, I allow myself to relax. In our bedroom, I find Ava sitting on my side of the bed in nothing but a towel, facing the window, her hair wet and her hands gripping the edge of the mattress. All that easiness drains from me instantly and is replaced with a heavy unease. "Everything okay?"

She doesn't startle. She doesn't even move. For a moment I think maybe she didn't hear me. But then her raspy admission almost takes me out at the knees.

"No one has ever braided my hair." She turns to face me, tears cascading down her face. They're flowing freely, like she isn't even aware of them. "I don't know if anyone ever really loved me. Not the way you love Josie. Unconditionally. Without effort."

I kneel at her feet and rest my palms on her thighs. She presses her fingers against my cheek. The move causes the towel to slip, but my attention doesn't lower to her breasts, which are now barely covered. No, my eyes find the tiny, jagged scars that line the insides of her arms.

An intense rage slams into me as I grasp one wrist to get a better look. "What the fuck is this? Who did this to you?"

Her lids flutter closed as she shakes her head. Then she takes in a long, unsteady breath. When she opens her eyes again, there's nothing but defeat there. "My sister was like Josie. She was sick." She swallows thickly, focusing on a spot somewhere near my throat rather than my face. "I was created to save her."

My anger dips, along with my gaze. I survey her scars again and press my lips to her wrist, willing her to feel at least a little of the comfort I want to give her. Fuck, I feel helpless crouched here, knowing I can't make these marks disappear.

"Is this why you always wear long sleeves?" I whisper between kisses to the jagged lines that mark her pale skin.

"It's easier to cover them up. I hate having to explain it," she rasps. "I have bad veins, but my sister needed a lot of blood during her treatment. It's just scar tissue."

"You said you were created to save her?" I ask with a frown.

"Savior sibling. That's one term people use. I'm a hashtag. A controversy, really. But my parents would have done anything to save my sister, and the doctors told them that the umbilical cord blood of a sibling with the right genetic makeup was her best chance of survival. They made me in a test tube, and here I am." She offers me a sad smile and a gentle shrug.

"*Ava.*" There's a knife in my chest, and fuck if it doesn't feel like I'm bleeding out in front of her. I don't know what the fuck to say. But as I process her words, so much makes sense.

She makes sense.

Her quiet demeanor. The need to care for others. Her dedication to Josie.

"My whole life, I was told my purpose was greater because I was created to save my sister. *She* was my purpose." She lets out a long sigh. "Now your kids are my purpose. I'm here because you need me." A sob catches in her throat. "I'm so happy to be needed, because I love them. I love them all so much, and I don't want you to lose them. I've never been loved like you love them. And they deserve that." She sniffles and wipes at her cheek with one hand. "I'm sorry. I don't mean to cry. I'm not sad about any of this. I'm happy. I'm happy I get to play a part in their lives and watch them be loved in the way they deserve. I'm happy they have you. I just—"

Hauling myself to my feet, I lift her, then spin and settle on the bed, positioning her on my lap. With my arms around her, I rock from side to side, my head on her shoulder, kissing her tear-soaked cheek. "You aren't giving yourself enough credit. Josie has known a love like that since the day she met you. We're all incredibly lucky to have you here, not just because of a so-called purpose, but because of who you are."

Ava shakes as she sobs in my arms. With every tear that falls, my heart shatters further. It guts me, watching the woman who is always fighting break before my eyes. I'm at a loss for what to do or what to say, so I hold her tight and stroke her hair until her sobs turn to shuddering breaths. Then I shift back and slide her off my lap and onto the mattress in front of me so I can braid her hair.

Her voice is rough when she speaks again. "Where did you learn to braid?"

"My mother would get these awful nauseous spells when I was growing up. It was just the two of us, and she never complained, but on the days she felt especially lousy, when she couldn't shake the migraines, she'd braid her hair before bed. She said it soothed the headaches. So I watched her and learned to do it myself. She'd close her eyes and listen as I told her about my day. It became our thing. Even when she didn't have headaches."

Ava looks at me over her shoulder, her green eyes vibrant from tears.

Dammit. Despite how they glimmer like jewels, I never want to see them like that again.

"You were twelve when you lost her?"

"Yeah. Moved in with my father that summer. I knew no one. Hell, I barely knew my dad. And Dory—" I sigh. "She wasn't like you. She couldn't care less about her husband's son. I was an inconvenience. She wanted my dad to give all his attention to Xander." I came to terms with it all years ago. For a long time, I did everything I could to get her to like me. To get her to love me. But there wasn't a thing I could do to make that woman accept me the way I needed. "That's why it was so important to me that you wanted Brayden and Scarlett too, not just Josie. I know what it's like to be the unwanted kid."

Ava leans her head back against my chest, her eyes locking with mine. "I'm really sorry about your mom."

I press a kiss to her forehead. "Me too."

She shifts and settles beside me on the bed, her head on her pillow, still watching me. "There's a charity event next weekend."

"Yeah, I know."

"Will you come?"

"I told coach I would." I sigh. "I know I haven't shown up like I should have in the past, but—"

She grasps my hand and pulls it to her lips. The gentle kiss surprises me and quiets my defenses.

"I meant will you come with me?"

My eyes widen. "Like as your date?"

Her lips lift in the smallest of smiles. "Yeah, you are my husband, aren't you?"

A soft breath escapes me at that word. *Husband.* Damn, I like the way it sounds coming from her. "Yeah, I am."

"So you'll come with me? *On time?*" Her eyes are narrowed a bit now. There's that vicious woman that I'm falling too hard for.

"You worried I won't actually show up, wifey?"

By the way she bites down on her lip and the smile that spreads across her cheeks, she's enjoying the teasing as much as I am. Makes me wonder if her chest feels as light as mine. If, like me, she feels capable of anything right now. Including confessing my real feelings to my wife.

"No. I'd just really like to go together. As a couple."

I push the hair back from her face and stroke her cheek. "I'd like that."

And despite the way I want to pull her to me and tell her that she is loved, that I love her as much as I love Josie, *that I'm falling in love with her*, I just hold her until her breathing evens out and she finally finds rest.

Chapter 33
Ava

SOFT LIPS PRESS against my neck, then drag down my back, and I feel the light peppering of kisses continue until I'm blinking awake, wondering if I'm dreaming. When I finally focus, I find Tyler, eyes on me, lips pressed to my wrist—or more precisely, to the scars that mar my skin there.

"What are you doing?" My voice comes out raspy with sleep, but somehow I find myself smiling.

Even after the heavy conversation of last night, I feel lighter than I have in a long time. Maybe it's because Tyler seems to get it. He gets me. We both suffered some awful things at young ages, and he's a more empathetic person because of it.

He also may just be the kindest, most warm-hearted man I've ever met, because right now it feels like he's trying to kiss every hurt better. Obviously, the scars have more than healed, but the emotional toll they left on me—the hiding I've done—is still there, and he's altering those ugly memories and the scars with his lips. Changing the meaning behind them. Making me feel beautiful and strong and *loved*.

"Kissing my wife good morning." His answer is lazy and slow, but his lips curve up in the corners, letting me know he's once again in a teasing mood. I love that about him. That he's not going to force me to talk about it. He opens the door for me to give him more but also gives me an out if I'm not ready.

I'm not ready. I hope one day I will be. It feels less daunting—life, the scars, the memories—now that I have him and our kids.

Our kids. That part really makes me smile.

I never thought I'd have this. A family. I was always too scared to get close to anyone else for fear of losing them, but with each of our kids it was barely a choice. I fell almost immediately. And with Tyler... well, it's clear I'm falling.

"You missed a few spots," I tell him.

Blue eyes bounce in surprise. "Oh, yeah?" He tries to wiggle down my body.

Laughing, I yank him up. "I meant up here, you goober." I purse my lips exaggeratedly, waiting for a kiss.

Of course, Tyler can never do anything simply. Just a peck of the lips isn't enough for him. He slides up my body and frames my face with those large hands. Then, once he's got complete control and I'm stuttering for breath as I literally wait for his lips to touch mine, he smirks. "I like waking up with you, Vicious. Love having you in my bed. Love holding you close all night. But mostly I love being able to kiss you whenever I want."

He doesn't wait for me to reply, not that I could come up with a single word that could express how this man makes me feel when he's so honest with me. Tyler goes all-in on the kiss. Every time our mouths meet, I swear it's like a shot of lust straight to my veins. His kisses are mind-altering. The minute his lips touch mine, I go hazy and pliable. I melt against him with each swipe of his tongue until I feel my hips undulating against his, begging for even more attention.

He pulls back, leaving me reaching for him, and with a chuckle, he presses another kiss to my chin, then my cheek, then the tip of my nose, right beside my lips.

I let out a needy growl, wanting his damn mouth back where it was and our bodies connected.

"Sorry, wifey. I have to get to morning skate."

There's no stopping the sad whine that escapes me. "You're such a tease."

"How about lunch with my bride?"

I shrug, trying to act nonchalant, even as I want to swoon over that nickname. *Bride.* I didn't feel like much of one when we got married, and yet the word still gives me butterflies. What is this man doing to me?

"I'll have to check my schedule."

Tyler hovers above me, that cocksure smirk on his face now. "It's my birthday, wifey. You can't make me eat alone."

"It's your birthday?"

His lips curve wider. "Yup."

I push against his chest, but he barely sways. "Jerk. Why didn't you tell me?"

He starts laughing. "You can't call me a jerk on my birthday."

"You can't not tell your wife it's your birthday. I need to get you a present."

Tyler's eyes dance. "I can think of a few presents you can give me later."

I roll my eyes. "How about we go out tonight? I'll make a reservation. What's your favorite restaurant?" I wince as I realize these are things I should know about my husband already.

He sighs and rolls off me, his head landing on his pillow, his focus going to the ceiling. "I told my father we'd do dinner with him and Dory. They're coming here."

"Is that what you want to do?"

Tyler rolls his head so he's looking at me again. "My father reached out. He hasn't always been the best dad, but yeah, I'd like to spend my birthday with him."

This man is incredible. Despite all the ways his father and Dory have let him down, he's still seeking out the family he's always wanted. I vow in that moment to do everything I can to give it to him. Hopefully his father is on board, but even if he's not, he'll get that same kind of devotion from me for as long as I'm around. "Okay."

"So will you meet me for lunch?" He's back to smiling again.

"Yeah, I think I can make room in my schedule for my groom."

"I can't believe this is your favorite lunch spot."

Tyler holds a giant slice of pizza in front of him and folds it in half, then takes an oversized bite. Chewing, he shrugs. "It's not so much the place. I just love pizza."

"Most people do." I knock my shoulder against his as we sit at the counter. The place is a little hole in the wall, and it's not fancy in the least, but when Tyler stepped inside, the man behind the counter set out two white paper place settings near one end, then embraced Tyler and welcomed him back.

"What else do you love?" I ask, holding up my own piece of pizza. After last night, it might seem like I'm fishing for a compliment, but I'm genuinely curious. For so long, I made assumptions about Tyler, and now that I've discovered how wrong I was, I want to know him. "Other than hockey," I tack on, infusing a bit of sauciness in my tone, hoping to convey to him that I'm not looking for an intimate conversation at the moment.

Tyler doesn't disappoint. "Surfing, boxing. Any sport that has me outside and moving my muscles, really. I also love serial killer documentaries."

A snort escapes me before I can stop it.

Tyler pokes my arm. "You asked."

"It makes sense, I guess. Why you love it when I'm mean to you."

Surveying me, he lifts a shoulder. "I do love how vicious my wife is. Female serial killers could be hot."

"Tyler," I hiss.

He chuckles. "I mean the fictional kind. I'm sure Lennox has read a book or two that revolve around a female main character with a penchant for murder."

I shrug. He's not wrong. "Do you read?"

"You're cute when you play dumb. I know you've been in my office."

The reminder of the night the girls and I snooped and I discovered the bookshelves full of all kinds of genres has me leaning in. "What types of books do you like best?"

Smirking, he wipes a little sauce from his lip. "Want me to read you a bedtime story later, wifey?"

I love this. Love bantering with him. Love sitting with him and smiling. God, I love being with him period. Even if we're just sitting in the corner of a tiny dive, eating semi-decent pizza, it's one of the best afternoons I've had in a long time.

I hold out my hand. "Pinky promise?"

That smirk turns into a full-on grin as he hooks my pinky with his and presses his lips to my finger. "Pinky promise."

Hannah taps her fingers against her phone screen with so much force I worry she'll break it.

"You okay over there?" Lennox asks, her gaze bouncing between Hannah and me.

We're seated in my office, going over last-minute details for the charity gala next week. The event will be held in the ballroom on the top of the Langfield Corp building. Since we are the venue, and we typically ask the venue to handle catering and serving, the location means even more work for us than usual.

Thank god for Lennox and her amazing attention to detail. I'm happy to rub elbows with donors and convince them to part with money they won't even miss, but picking out linens and flowers has never been my thing. Lennox is much more equipped to handle all that, along with who's who in Boston at the moment—and should be added to the guest list—and which musicians are hot right now since her family practically owns every industry in this city not already claimed by the Langfields.

Scoffing, Hannah drops her phone into her purse, then lifts her blue eyes to me. Even as she swears all is fine, I can read my best friend well. Something is very wrong. But if there's one thing I know about Hannah, it's that there is no way to pry even a single word out of her when she shuts down like this. "Outside of making sure the boys are on their best behavior, is there anything else you need from me?"

"I think we've got everything covered." Lennox's eyes light up, and she leans forward. "Did I tell you that Jake Keepers agreed to make an appearance?"

"Who's Jake Keepers?" Sara asks, appearing in the doorway. She makes herself comfortable against the wall, iPad pulled against her chest, blue hair recently redone and pulled back in a ponytail.

Lennox swings her pink hair over her shoulder with a flick of her wrist. "The next big thing."

We all laugh at her flair for the dramatics.

"Seriously. He's got an album dropping next month, but his first single comes out tomorrow. With the buzz we'll create announcing he'll be in attendance this weekend, donors will be clamoring for last-minute invites."

"So what you're saying is that you've done all the heavy lifting when it comes to your job and mine?" I tease.

She smiles. "I still need you, snookums."

"Yes," Sara agrees. "You make us look good."

My chest tightens at the sentiment, but I laugh it away. "I'm not so sure that's still true. Speaking of party planning." I straighten. "How does one plan for a party where her ex-boyfriend's parents, who are also her husband's parents, will be in attendance?"

"Awkward," Lennox sings. "We should call Millie for this one. She's good at awkward situations, considering her stepmother used to date her brother and her husband is best friends with her father."

Hannah snorts. "That family is all sorts of special. I would love to be invited for family holidays one year."

"You only want to go because you're obsessed with Daniel Hall. Is it a mommy complex thing? You want to corrupt the youth and teach him all your devious ways?" Sara teases.

Hannah rolls her eyes. "Hall is pretty, don't get me wrong, but I'm not teaching anyone anything. And I'm not attending a family function with the boy. If he were ever lucky enough to get near my pretty kitty, it'd be a one-time thing. I'm not falling in love with anyone, let alone our best friend's twin brother."

"Pretty kitty." Sara practically wheezes with laughter. "I love that."

I spin my chair and throw my body into it, trying my best not to freak out. My lunch with Tyler was good. Great really. But I'd be lying if I said I was excited about his birthday dinner tonight.

"Okay, ladies, our girl is spiraling," Hannah says, rallying the troops.

I throw a foot down to stop my spinning and let out a sigh. "Things are strained between Tyler and Xander's mother on a good day. And today will not be a good day. I'm not sure how I can make it any less awkward. And if the woman makes a single negative comment in front of our kids, I will actually lose it."

Hannah's entire demeanor softens. "Have I told you lately how proud I am of you and War? What you're doing for those kids is nothing short of amazing."

"It's really not. We just love them."

"And each other," Sara adds.

I swallow past the lump in my throat. Sara is the only person in this room who doesn't know about the marriage contract, and telling her now seems pointless. Though I'm not sure what's going on between Tyler and me, it's complicated and deep.

"Will Xander be there?" Hannah asks.

My heart stutters. Oh god, I hope not. I hadn't even thought of that. "I don't know."

Lennox sits forward in her seat. "Have you heard from him?"

Yeah, I've heard from him. He texts nonstop. But I haven't told anyone. I'm embarrassed. And if Tyler found out, he'd probably pay his stepbrother a visit. The last thing Tyler needs while we're working to adopt Josie is to end up in a fight with Xander, but if he knew what Xander was texting me, his fists would fly.

"He's texted a few times."

Hannah holds out her hand. "Give me."

"What? No." I push back my chair, as if that will stop my determined fixer.

"Ava Marie Warren, give me your damn phone, or I'll tell Beckett you're upset that he didn't throw you an engagement party. If I have to do that, we both know you'll have the entire city of Boston offering you well wishes when he puts on a parade in honor of all the love matches he likes to take credit for."

Sara dissolves into a fit of giggles. Swiping at her eyes, she sucks in a breath. "He so would."

Grumbling a few pretty curses, I take out my phone and hand it to Hannah.

With every text she reads, her face grows redder and more creative obscenities escape her. The girls pass it around, and when the device makes it back to me, I stare down at the messages, my stomach sinking.

> Xander: What the fuck is this about you marrying my asshole stepbrother? Is this some kind of ploy to get me to apologize? Okay, fine. I'm sorry I left you there. But how the fuck are we supposed to get married and have kids if the guys my father works with think you play stupid games like this?

> Xander: Ava, pick up your phone.

> Xander. Call me.

> Xander: The marriage is REAL?

> Xander: You cunt. My mother says you really married the asshole. This is fucking insane.

> Xander: Okay, you've made your point. Now pick up the goddamn phone so we can work this out.

> Xander: Did you move in with the asshole? I just stopped by your place, and the doorman says you don't live there anymore.

> Xander: WHAT THE FUCK, AVA?

> Xander: CALL ME.

> Xander: Slut.

Eyes unfocused, I ignore the rest of the chain. He hasn't stopped. The most recent came in an hour ago.

> Xander: Having dinner with my parents and your asshole husband tonight? Nice. I seriously don't know what the fuck happened to you.

He's not wrong. I don't recognize myself anymore either. But unlike him, I see the change as a positive thing. I'm so glad I'm no longer the woman I was when I thought Xander was a good guy and Tyler was the asshole. I truly had it all wrong back then.

Changing the subject, I say, "I need to get a birthday present for Tyler. What the heck do you get a guy who can buy himself anything he wants?"

Hannah's lips curve up deviously. "Oh, hunny. The only thing that man wants from you is something he can't buy."

Sara giggles. "Yup. But that doesn't mean we can't do a little shopping this afternoon to make his gift look extra pretty."

Lennox leans forward, a big smile on her face. "She means you. You're the only gift your husband needs. And we're going to make sure we give him something pretty to unwrap."

CHAPTER 34
TYLER

"HOW ARE THINGS WITH THE WIFE?"

Fitz and I have been watching film of Seattle to prepare for our next game. Brooks too, but he just stepped out to take a call. Goalies are some of the most dedicated players in hockey. They play far more than the rest of us. We're subbed out every few minutes, but Brooks typically plays an entire game, and the stress is nothing short of incredible. That's the reason I choose to do extra sessions with them when it doesn't conflict with my own training. Every moment I spend with him makes me better at what I do and who I am.

Might be an odd choice for my birthday, but knowing I have to see Dory tonight has made it impossible to relax. I swear if she so much as looks at Ava the wrong way, I'll lose it.

"She's good." I try to scrub the smile off my face, but it's no use. "She met me for lunch. I swear I could sit across from that woman day in and out and be entertained. She keeps me on my damn toes, that's for sure."

Fitz chuckles. "I hear ya. Mel is like that. I could hang with her all day, every day and never get bored."

"It's special, right? I can't help but feel like this isn't normal. But then I think of you and Brooks and Aiden. We've all found women who are truly fantastic. Fuck, are we lucky assholes."

"You're not wrong."

I lean back on the couch in his office, legs spread wide. "How are things with Declan?"

Fitz's already happy expression grows giddy. He's so gone for his best friend. Probably always has been. "Grumpy as ever, but he smiles a fuck ton more now that Mel has moved in."

"Does it bother you? That you have to be in Boston so often and the two of them are there?" I don't think I could handle it. It's bad enough that I have to travel as much as I do. I'd hate to be away from Ava or the kids even more.

Fitz shakes his head. "It would definitely be easier for me to stay in my apartment in Boston when we have early practices, but fuck easy. I drive home to them every night. I don't remember the last time I stayed overnight at my apartment." He chuckles. "That's a lie. We had a sleepover here when Dec and Mel came to the game last month."

Head tipped back on the couch, I huff. "Don't want to know what the fuck you three do for your sleepovers."

He laughs. "Right, because you're such a saint."

"Am now."

He shrugs. "Guess we're all changed men."

"Speak for yourself," Hall calls from the hallway. Folding his arms, he leans against the door. "Happy birthday, Cap."

With a chin dip, I reply. "Thanks."

"What are we doing to celebrate?"

Fitz's chair squeaks as he falls back against it and barks out a laugh. "It's funny you think you're invited."

"The fuck?" Hall groans.

"Don't get him all worked up." I rough a hand through my hair and grimace at Hall. "I'm having dinner with my family. We can celebrate in Seattle."

Between one blink and the next, Hall's sour attitude disappears. "Fuck yes. You're actually going to come out for once?"

I side-eye Fitz. "If he does."

Our coach rolls his eyes. "Fine."

Hall is pumping a fist as Brooks returns, looking at him like the kid has lost his mind.

"He's excited about having a boys' night in Seattle."

Brooks grunts. "Good luck with keeping Sara from showing up."

"Sara can come. She's more fun than you."

My comment earns me the middle finger. See? This is why I came here rather than going home to relax alone. These guys are my family. Even if things go to shit tonight, I know I've got my kids, my guys, and the only woman I'll ever need by my side.

"This isn't awkward at all," Brayden hisses out of the side of his mouth.

Ava is pacing around the kitchen, pretending to fluff the dish towels while Dory and my father sit in the living room watching Josie, who's showing off what she learned at ballet this week.

"I think I'll go check on Scarlett," he says as he points to the stairs that lead up to where Scarlett, who is teething and whimpered through dinner, is already asleep.

I grab his arm so he can't leave me alone in this purgatory. This was a bad idea. Dory has all-out ignored Ava since they walked in. She hasn't said a negative word to her, though, so there's that, I guess. If not for Josie's nonstop chatter about ballet during dinner, I'm not sure we would have made it through the meal. If we can get them out of here without incident, I'll count the evening as a success. Especially if it ends with me between Ava's thighs.

The music playing in the living room comes to an end, and Dory and my father clap. "Okay, fighter. It's time for bed."

Brayden checks the time on his phone—eight p.m.—then eyes me. "Real smooth, man. It isn't obvious at all that you're trying to get them out of here."

Before I can rough my knuckles over his head and give him shit for his snark, my father stands.

Instantly, a little of the tension drains out of me. Almost there. Just have to get them to the door, and then we're home free. Josie doles out hugs, and then she turns to Ava. "Can you tuck me in?"

Ava runs a hand over her head. "Sure can, love bug."

"Actually," Dory says. "Brayden, can you take Josie up? I'd like to talk to Ava before we leave."

My stomach plummets. Shit. We were so close.

For all his shit talk, Brayden looks at me for permission. With a small nod, I give him the okay. It's better that we don't put him or Josie through this. I can only imagine what Dory has to say.

Instinctively, I reach for Ava, motivated by the need to protect her. Her hand is shaking as I tighten mine around it. Dammit. Why the fuck did I put her in this situation?

"Xander says you won't return his phone calls," Dory starts.

My blood pressure spikes. Xander has been calling my wife? Why hasn't Ava told me that he's been bothering her?

My father nods toward the front door. "Son, why don't we let them talk alone?"

Shoulders back, I lift my chin and eye him, then his wife. "I'm fine right where I am."

Dory's lip curls in a sneer. "You never could figure out when you were unwanted."

My wife sucks in a breath so harsh, it sounds like a hiss, and suddenly, rather than cowering, she's standing tall too. "What did you just say?"

Dory rolls her eyes. "This doesn't involve you, Tyler. Go with your father. We both know that's what this is about, after all."

"What *what's* about?" I take a step forward.

With an arm extended, Ava pushes me back slightly, kind of like my mom used to when she'd have to hit her brakes a little too hard. It's protective. Loving. For a moment, I'm unable to move. My heart pounds out a warning that I need to protect her, but the pressure of her hand on my chest tells me she's got this.

"You're so worried about what I did or didn't do to your son," Ava says, her tone fierce. "But what about what you did to your husband's son?"

Wearing a snide smile, Dory tilts her head. "And what did he tell you I did?" She looks down her nose at me—a feat, seeing as how I'm close to a foot taller than she is—like I'm worthless. It's how she's always looked at me. "I took care of him when no one else would have put up with him. Tyler was a difficult child, and his hobby was ridiculously expensive. Do you have any idea the sacrifices we had to make so he could become *this*?" She waves at me like I'm still nothing but a disappointment. "Meanwhile, my son is the one helping Chandler run his business."

"I think we should say good night and talk about this another time, when we've had time to cool down," my father says, grabbing Dory by the elbow.

My father may disappoint me, but I've never been angry at my father for his shortcomings. Tonight, though? Tonight I'm pissed. His wife came into my house and talked down to my wife, and all he has to say is *let's talk about this another time*?

"What you did," Ava says, her attention returning to the original question Dory posed, "was nothing." She lifts her shoulders and lets them fall. "You did *nothing* for your husband's *son*. A boy who lost his mother." Her voice cracks. "A boy who just wanted a family. You're a disgrace. So don't speak to my husband unless you can show him some damn respect. *And love*. Because that's what a family does. They love one another." Ava looks at me, her eyes full of emotion. I swear I can see it there. How she truly feels. My vicious wife is fighting my battles for me instead of fighting against me. It's one more version of her I adore. The list of things I love about her just keeps growing. It's a problem. I'll likely get my heart broken because I'm not good enough for her, but god, I can't force myself to protect my heart.

I grasp her hand, which is still flat against my chest, and squeeze it. Then I look at my father. "I think you should leave."

With a screech, Dory smacks his arm. "Say something."

My father blinks like he's not sure how the hell things turned out like this. Then he sighs. "I'll call you tomorrow, Tyler."

Still gripping his wife's elbow, he leads her toward the door. All the way, she argues with him. It hurts watching him leave with her. It hurts even more that he didn't stick up for me or even try to understand. But I'm used to his indifference.

"I'm so sorry," Ava whispers a heartbeat after the door shuts.

"Why are you apologizing?"

"I should have let her come at me, kept the fallout there. She's not wrong. From the outside, it looks awful, how I jumped from Xander to you."

Cupping her cheeks, I rest my forehead against hers. "No one has ever stood up for me. That was beautiful, Ave."

"What?" She rears back, frowning.

I press my lips to hers. "It was hot, you being vicious *for me* like that."

Lips curling, she huffs a breath. "Really?"

"Yeah. You're unbelievably attractive when you yell at me. But fuck, yelling at others for me? That's a whole new level of sexy."

She giggles. "You're a little insane. You know that, right?"

Lips pressed together, I nod. "Stupidly so when it comes to you."

She brushes her mouth over mine, the kiss soft and far too short. "I know we started in a strange way, but I'm really glad I'm your wife. Proud, even."

Warmth floods me as I drink her in. Damn, I think I believe her. "Good, because you aren't getting rid of me."

With a grin, she pushes her pinky between us. "Pinky promise?"

TEXT MESSAGES FROM AVA'S AND TYLER'S PHONE

War: Hall, you going to chicken out again or are you ready?

Brooks: Is there a reason I need to be on this chat?

Aiden: I want to come.

Brooks: That's so weird, bro. Like so ducking weird.

War: there's no kids around. You can say duck.

War: Duck.

War: FUCK.

Aiden: Dammit! One more, and I coulda said goose!

War: Hall?

Aiden: <GIF of a chicken crying>

Dad: Can we set aside some time to talk?

Tyler: Unless you want to apologize to my wife for what happened on my birthday, I've got nothing to say.

Dad: Like I said, I think we should talk.

Ava: Hi. Sis. Sorry I've been so distant lately. Life has been ridiculously busy. I don't remember if I told you, but I'm dancing again. It's bringing back all sorts of memories. Especially seeing Josie in her leotard with her friends. Remember the year our recital was mermaid themed? I'm pretty sure that was my favorite. Scarlett is too little, but next year, I'm totally signing her up so I can get pictures of them dancing together like we did. I miss you. Love you always.

Hannah: Did you know that a man can have an orgasm without coming?

Ava: I feel I missed the first part of this conversation.

Sara: Or dinner. Buy a girl a drink before you talk sex.

Lennox: Not me, pookie. I'll talk dirty with you any time.

Millie: Hey! I think I was accidentally added to this chat.

Hannah: I added you, and it wasn't an accident. I need you to test out a theory with hockey daddy.

Chapter 35
Ava

"PRETTY PLEASE, can we go ice skating?" Josie asks, her nose pressed to the window as Brayden and his friend glide across the iced-over pond. They've got their hockey sticks and a puck, though with the sun setting so quickly, I can't imagine they can see well enough to accomplish anything.

"Maybe another day, love. You'll have to ask Tyler to go with you. I don't know how to skate."

The door to the garage opens and closes, drawing our attention.

"Daddy," Scarlett cries as the man himself walks into the house wearing a pair of joggers and a long-sleeve Bolts shirt. I swear everyone I know lives in Bolts attire. Thank god there's such a good selection to choose from around Boston. Today's shirt is black, and god, does it look good on my husband.

Josie watches longingly as he drops his gym bag to the floor and scoops up our daughter. I only recently noticed this. The way she goes quiet when Scarlett says Daddy or Mama. I can't blame her. We're all trying not to get our hopes up. While Scarlett may be ours, Josie is not yet. And god, do I ache to tell her she can call us whatever she wants.

When Tyler spots Josie where she's sitting by the window, he sticks out his bottom lip and holds out his other arm. "No hi from my other favorite girl?"

Josie glances at me, then Tyler again. "What about Ava?"

He strides across the room and scoops her up before she can protest. "Ava is my wife. You and Scar are my girls. So you going to say hi to me now?"

She rolls her eyes but snuggles into him. "Ava doesn't know how to skate."

With both girls in his arms, he rounds on me. "You *what?*"

Not able to hide my smile, I shrug. "No one ever taught me."

Tyler's eyes soften as he studies me. He's probably thinking of my confession the other night. How alone I was growing up. It's sweet, the way he holds me now until we both fall asleep. How every morning since then, I've woken to him pressing kisses to my skin. I swear he must search my body while I sleep, looking for every scar. I have quite a few, but he hasn't said another word about it. He's giving me space. Leaving the ball in my court. He'll listen if I want to talk, but he won't pressure me to do so. It's the same for me, though. Since the night when I told Dory what a shitty person she was, I feel like things have shifted between us. He knows I have his back, and I know he has mine. We're settling into a new partnership, a new normal. I'm not sure where that will lead us, but for once, I'm not going to focus on the past or the future. I'd much rather focus on the man who's holding two perfect little girls in his arms, a man I am not so slowly falling for.

"We'll have to rectify that tonight."

My stomach twists as I glance out the window. "It's dark out."

He arches a brow. "You scared of the dark, Vicious?"

I sigh. "I'm making dinner." That's not a lie. Maria helped me make meatballs before she left for the night. She's slowly reducing her hours, and although I'll miss spending so much time with her, it's what we need.

"Okay. Jos, why don't we set the table for dinner? Then you and I can work on convincing Ava to let me teach her how to skate."

Josie is all smiles as he lowers her to her feet. While Tyler sets Scarlett up in front of the television, I head back to the kitchen to check on the sauce. A moment later, he steps up behind me and grasps the oven handle on either side of my hips. With his face buried in my hair, he kisses my neck. "Hi, wifey."

A shiver works its way down my spine, and heat pools in my belly. Enveloped in the scent of him, I lean my head against his. If we could stay like this, in this little bubble, I could be happy forever. "How was your day?"

"It's always a good day when I wake up next to my wife and come home to find her with a smile on her face."

Head tipped back, I give him a small smile. "You keep saying these things, and you're going to get lucky, Mr. Warren."

He kisses my cheek. "I'm already lucky; I married you, didn't I?"

"Tyler, you're supposed to be helping," Josie whines as she holds up the forks.

Chuckling, he backs away and pads to the table.

After Brayden's friend leaves, he comes in and gets cleaned up for dinner. While we wait for him, Josie asks Tyler a zillion and one questions. We're just settling down at the table when she narrows her eyes and points at Tyler's hand. "Did you get hurt at practice?"

I follow her line of sight and find a bandage wrapped around the base of his pinky and ring finger. "What happened?"

"Just had to finish a little something," he says with a wink.

Brayden chuckles. "Another tattoo?"

"I want a tattoo," Josie whines.

I pat her on the back. "Nothing permanent until you're at least twenty-five."

Tyler cocks his head. "Why's that?"

I shrug. I'm new at this mom thing, so the number just came to me, but it sounds about right. Isn't that when a person's frontal lobe is fully developed? Something like that. "What did you get?"

When Tyler smirks, eyes twinkling, I regret asking. He looks at me like he wants to eat me alive. And he'd enjoy it. Slowly, he unravels the bandage. Then he turns to show us the back of his hand and the three letters inked on his ring finger in the same green as the band just below them. "So everyone knows who my heart belongs to."

"A-V-A," Josie says.

"You tattooed my name on your finger," I whisper, my heart pounding wildly and my gaze bouncing from the fresh tattoo to his blue eyes. Blue eyes that are beginning to feel like home.

The man didn't use words to tell me he loved me the other night. He didn't offer me platitudes when I broke down. He kissed every scar and then tattooed my name on his ring finger. He doesn't just say things, he does them.

My heart doesn't stand a chance.

"Do you have a tattoo for me?" Josie asks.

Tyler watches me as I swipe at my eyes, then turns to our inquisitive girl. "I have a few, actually." He pulls the hem of his shirt up. There's another bandage, but he points at another set of not so new tattoos. "Right here I've got your birthday. And Brayden's and Scarlett's are right below it."

"That's not my birthday," Josie argues, her little brows pulled low. "That's a bunch of lines."

"It's roman numerals." The words are hard to get out and filled with emotion. Because our wedding date is listed there too. God, this man has been busy.

"That's cool," Brayden says, his voice coming out hoarse.

Clearly, Tyler's affection still surprises us all. It shouldn't. He doesn't hide it. He's continuously telling us. Continuously showing us. I imagine it's what he would have wanted all those years ago from his father and Dory. Another bolt of rage flows through me as I imagine a boy just shy of Brayden's age, with the same insecurities, without a man like Tyler to put him first.

I hate that he didn't have that. That he ever went to bed at night feeling unloved. That won't be Brayden's story. I'll make sure of it.

"Do you have more for Ava?" Josie says.

Tyler's smirk is back. "Sure do."

My heart lurches. He cannot be talking about the Vicious tattoo. I'll melt into a puddle of mortification right here if he even hints to it.

"Where?" Josie is up on her knees, practically leaning across the table to see.

Tyler removes the bandage above his ribs. It's a few intricate designs all twined together with a red ribbon. "There's a hockey stick for Bray, a boxing glove because you're my fighter, and a ballet shoe for my ballerina, Ava. They're all wrapped in a red bow for Scarlett. I got it over my lung because I need you to breathe." His eyes lift to mine and he holds my gaze as he adds, "Each and every one of you."

"Can you teach me to box?" Josie asks. God, I've never been more thankful for her curiosity and that nine-year-old brain jumping from one topic to another. If I had to speak right now, I don't think I could.

Because I can't breathe. His words. This moment. That damn tattoo. It's stolen my breath.

"Yup, I want to show you something when we're done with dinner anyway."

"Better not be ice skates," I murmur, emotion still making it difficult to speak.

Brayden's eyes go wide. "You don't like to skate?"

"She doesn't know *how* to skate," Tyler says, his gaze remaining on me.

I roll my eyes, finally feeling a bit more like myself. Tyler's taunting normally does that. "Anyway—"

"No, we won't let that slide in this house," Brayden says.

Jaw dropping, I scoff. "Excuse you?"

"Tyler, tell her. Your mom taught you to skate. You taught me, and we taught Josie, just like we'll teach Scarlett when she's old enough."

Tyler's grin is so big it's blinding. He has the most beautiful smile. Especially when he's the one who's surprised like this. Bray tries to play it cool, but for a moment, he stepped out from behind that façade and showed just how much he loves Tyler by including himself in this family.

He's making traditions. *We're making traditions.* There's no stopping my smile. "So you trying to tell me you guys need to teach me?"

"Definitely," Brayden and Tyler say in unison.

"Fine," I grumble in fake annoyance. "But you better not let me fall."

Tyler's lips curl as he holds out that damn pinky finger. "I'd never let you fall, wifey. Pinky promise."

Rather than head out into the cold, dark night to skate after dinner, Tyler herds us all down to the gym in the basement for another surprise.

"No one's peeking, right?"

Brayden's got his hands over Josie's eyes, and Tyler's covering mine. "Unless I can somehow see through your massive fingers, I think it's safe to say we can't see."

Tyler's lips brush against the shell of my ear. "We both know you love my fingers, wifey."

There goes that shiver again.

"Come on, come on. I want to see," Josie cajoles. A moment later, her high-pitched squeals echo off the walls.

"Ah, crap," Brayden grumbles. "Sorry. She was bouncing too much, and I didn't want to hurt her."

"A ballet barre," Josie screeches as Tyler pulls his hand away from my face. She darts over to the wall of mirrors and the beautiful barre that was not here last week when Brayden showed me the room. There's also a beautiful section of brand-new flooring.

Holding my breath, I whip around and survey my husband. "When did you do this?"

With a casual shrug, Tyler slips his hands into the pockets of his joggers. "Wanted you and Josie to have a place to practice. Ya know, so you don't have to go into the city so much."

I purse my lips to hold back my laughter. "You built a ballet studio because you're jealous."

Tyler cocks a brow. "Do I look like the jealous type?"

"You tattooed my name on your finger. You threw a temper tantrum when I wore your friend's jersey, then knocked him on his butt. Hmm, am I missing anything?"

"I built a ballet studio so no other man can see you in a leotard," he mutters as he walks past me. Then, schooling his expression, he drops down to Josie's height. "What do you think? Did I do okay?"

She throws her arms around his neck. "You did the best."

He did. And I'm starting to realize he always does.

Chapter 36
Ava

"YOU LOOK BEAUTIFUL. Doesn't she look beautiful?" Josie picks up my blush brush and swipes at her own cheek as we sit side by side in my room while I do my makeup.

Tyler sidles over while he straightens his bow tie. He's devastatingly handsome in a black tuxedo. Just the sight of him has warmth gathering low in my belly and my cheeks heating. This last week has been quiet. His game schedule has been intense, and I've been busy working on this event. In the evenings, the kids keep me busy. After Tyler gets home and we put the kids to bed, where I expected there to be loads of ravaging going on, there's been none. He's been gentler since I opened up about my sister's illness. He's using kid gloves with me. I both hate it and love it at the same time.

On the one hand, I appreciate the space and respect he's given me after I sobbed over not being loved. I couldn't stand it if he'd felt obligated to say he loved me because I was practically begging for it. On the other hand, god, the sight of my husband in a tuxedo is dangerous. About as dangerous as he is when he sings Scarlett to sleep or when he braids Josie's hair. The many facets of Tyler Warren are making it impossible not to fall hard. And if I'm being honest, I'm horny.

It's nearly impossible to lie beside my husband knowing he is capable of bringing me to orgasm so easily and not jump his bones.

I have a plan, though. I'm ready to move past this pause we've taken, and I'm desperate for him to finally fuck me.

"She always looks beautiful, Jos." With a wink at me, he turns and strides to where his jacket is hanging on the back of the bathroom door.

As I watch him go, zeroing in on his butt, I have to remind myself to breathe.

"The car's here," Maria calls from downstairs.

Tyler leads our little girl out of the room. "Come on, fighter. Let's let Ava finish up."

Promising that I'll be ready in five minutes, I take out my phone, snap a picture of my gold dress and matching shoes, and text it to my sister.

> Me: No Cinderella tonight. I'm keeping the shoes and the man!

When I hit the bottom step, my husband practically growls. "Fuck, Mrs. Warren. You look damn pretty tonight."

I roll my eyes, even as my heart stutters at the heat in his tone.

"Language," Brayden chides.

Grabbing my waist, Tyler pulls me into his chest and nuzzles my neck.

"Come on," Maria says, carrying Scarlett on her hip. "Let's get a picture of the two of you."

"Oh, that's okay." I shake my head and take a step away from Tyler, only to be pulled back into him and tucked under his arm.

"I want a picture with my wife," he says quietly, making it clear his words are just for me.

Butterflies flap like crazy in my chest. "Okay, fine. But let's get one with the kids too."

"Sure, but first—" He turns me to face him. "Your outfit is missing something."

It is? Frowning, I glance down at my arms, which are bare for the first time in as long as I can remember. I'm trying to be okay with it. I'm embracing who I am. The scars are faint and unlikely to be noticed unless someone is really looking, but this is still more skin than I've shown in years. With only a few words, Tyler has made me feel like it's okay to entrust others with my truth. I don't want to hide anymore.

He pulls his hand from his pocket, and there, between his thumb and forefinger, is the most beautiful infinity band. It's gold, like my engagement ring, and covered in diamonds. With the arch of one brow, he silently tells me what he wants.

I obey, holding up my left hand. First he slides off the engagement ring, then he slips the infinity band on, followed by the emerald.

"So everyone knows you're *my wife*."

The words send a shiver through me. I've never wanted to be anything more.

Maria snaps a picture of us, then we hold out our arms for the kids to join. Scarlett is the first to dash in our direction, with Josie quickly following behind. But Brayden stands to the side, hands stuffed in his pockets and hair falling over his forehead.

"What are you doing?" Tyler lifts his chin and hits the kid with his piercing gaze.

He merely nods. "Just take the picture."

"We said family picture," I remind him. "Last time I checked, you're family."

He tilts his head, squinting, like he's trying to come up with a smart-ass retort. He tries so hard to act cool, unbothered, but he idolizes Tyler. If I weren't here, would he have joined the picture without hesitating like this? Tyler told me once how much he wants Brayden to feel like he matters to me. And the kid really does. So I have to do better.

"Pretty please?" I push out my lower lip and give him puppy dog eyes.

It takes a few seconds, but finally, he breaks. With a roll of his eyes, he stomps over. "Fine. I'll take a picture with you. No need to cry over it."

When we're done, I ask Maria to text the pictures to me. "I'm getting that one framed and putting it on the mantel," I tell Brayden with a wink. "Proof that you're not too cool to hang out with your family."

He nods and pivots away, though not before I catch him smiling. "Have fun, you two." He lifts a hand. "Don't stay out too late. Wouldn't want Daddy War to fall asleep at the ball."

I snort. "Daddy War."

With a smack to my ass, Tyler leads me out the front door. "Don't egg him on."

"Sorry, it's just too good."

On the front porch, he grips my hip and pulls me to a stop. "I wouldn't mind it if you called me Daddy War while wearing this dress and riding my cock in the back of the limo."

My whole body heats as I shake my head and hustle away from my husband. The man is dangerous tonight. And I, for one, am excited about the ride.

CHAPTER 37
TYLER

TENSION VIBRATES between us as we travel down the highway. I've given my wife space for the last few days. I needed it too, while I came to terms with all the emotions overwhelming me. The last thing I want to do is scare her away with more truths I'm not sure she's ready to hear. But tonight, when she walked down the steps in that gold dress, her red hair cascading in waves over her bare shoulders, I ate up every inch of her. From her delicate collarbones to where her dress cuts dangerously low between her breasts. I've never seen Ava dressed so provocatively. The tiny glimpse of her cleavage makes my mouth water, because I know precisely what she's hiding from everyone else. The pieces of her that I want only for myself. The pieces I think may already be mine.

More than that, though, I want the organ that beats beneath that spot. I want her heart so goddamn much it makes it hard to breathe for fear of fucking it all up. Because I always fuck it up. It's what she's expecting. It's what everyone expects.

For once I want to prove the world wrong. I want to sweep the girl off her feet, carry her into our house where our children sleep at night, and make love to her for the rest of my life.

If that's where my story ended, it would be far more than I deserve.

"I have a present for you," she says, interrupting my thoughts.

I've got her hand in mine, and I've been rolling my thumb back and forth over her smooth skin.

"Oh yeah?"

She pulls away, and I begrudgingly let her. When she pulls a small black object from her clutch, I frown, confused.

"Is this a remote?"

She licks her lips, and her lashes flutter, drawing my attention to shy green eyes swimming with nervousness. "Yes."

Realization hits like a defenseman barreling straight into me. "Is this the remote I gave you the other day?"

With her teeth pressed into her bottom lip, she nods.

"Regifting the present I purchased for you?" I chuckle. "Where did you put the object that came with this remote?"

Fingers trembling, she grasps the hem of her dress and slowly slides it up her legs.

I snap my head up and confirm the driver isn't watching through the rearview mirror. Fuck. It takes everything in me to cover her hand with mine and stop her movements. "Did you put it in here?" I ask, grazing a hand over her lower belly.

"Maybe." The word is a teasing rasp that only has me growing harder.

I lean close so that my lips are at her ear. "You're telling me the toy I bought for you is sitting inside your cunt right now?"

"Turn it on and find out." She turns her head, her nose grazing mine. Our breaths mingle and we watch one another for a long moment. The tension thickens between us while I imagine the way her lips will part the moment I hit this button. The ways I can play with her.

"You're going to let me use this on you all night?"

Her eyes dance. "You said you control my orgasms. So control them."

"The contract was fake." My words are soft, serious. "You control everything. No one owns you, no one makes choices for you, not even me."

Ava's lashes flutter shut, and she exhales as if she really needed to hear those words. I'd write her a sonnet about the subject if I thought I could ever get it right. "Fine. Please, husband. Make me come."

There isn't a scenario in which I would deny my wife after that request. There also isn't a world where I'd let another man hear her when she does. "Can we get some music, Tom?"

Nodding, he clicks the radio on quickly. A second later, Ava jolts and lets out a groan.

"Look at my beautiful wife," I say, lifting my thumb off the button. "The perfect woman who's about to run a charity event while her cum drips down her thighs."

She sucks in a surprised breath and drops her head back.

Wrapping my hand around her neck, I tug her until her lips meet mine, then I devour her, likely ruining her perfect makeup and mussing her styled hair.

Once I've pulled back, I bring my mouth to her ear and talk her through what I want to do to her. "You know how hot this is, Vicious? Knowing I'll be edging you all night? While you talk to donors and my teammates, I'll be playing between those thighs. Enjoy it while you can, talking to other men while I make you come, because this is the only time I'll share your pleasure. After, when I take you home, you're going to ride my face. I'm going to suck on that clit and lap up each drop until you drip down my chin. And then we're going to do it again."

With one hand gripped tight around my forearm, Ava gasps. I take the opportunity to suck her tongue into my mouth, and as she comes in waves, I swallow all her sounds.

"Holy fuck," she pants, surprise dusting her cheeks pink.

Holy fuck is right. That was one of the most satisfying orgasms of my life, and it wasn't even mine.

"Have you heard the rumor?"

Hall made a beeline for me the moment we walked in the door. My wife, sensing that he needed me, excused herself.

I'm irritated with my friend as Ava walks away, but when I slide my hands into my pockets, finding the small remote, my mood lifts. I hit the button once and watch as she stumbles a little. She turns back and glares at me, and I can't help but chuckle. Fuck, I love when my vicious wife makes an appearance. She takes a deep, steadying breath and smooths the front of her dress, and when Beckett Langfield and his wife, Liv, wander up to her, she pastes on a smile. Back to being perfect. With a roll of my eyes, I finally give Hall my attention.

"You are so fucking gone for her," he mutters as he nods toward the bar.

Smirking, I follow him. "That's the rumor you heard?"

Hall lets out a sardonic laugh. "No. I have more important things to worry about than your marriage."

Brows raised, I simply shrug. "I don't. So if you'll excuse me—" I spin on my heel, ready to track down my wife.

Before I can make it more than a step, he grabs my jacket and pulls me back.

When I look at him, really look at him, I notice the stress etched into his features. "What's going on?"

"Have you heard anything about the trade deadline?" Chin lifted, he surveys the ballroom. This event is being held on the top floor of the Langfield Corp building. There are floor-to-ceiling windows in every direction, and the view of Boston from up here is incredible. The arena and Lang Field sit opposite one another, blue monsters against a starry backdrop along with the bridge lit up over the ocean.

Rather than taking in the scenery like I am, Daniel keeps scanning the people in the room, probably looking for Gavin Langfield, the Bolts' owner and head coach.

"No. Should I have?" I wave the bartender over and order a bourbon to share with my wife.

"I heard rumblings that the front office is bringing Noah Harrison on, and since—"

"Shit, really?" A bolt of excitement works its way through me.

Noah played with Brooks and me in college, and then the two of us played together again in Minnesota. "But he's a winger."

That's why Hall is freaking out. Noah Harrison has had a great career, and like me, he'll earn a big paycheck no matter where he goes next. Wherever that turns out to be, he'll likely play there until he retires. There's no way he'll go to any team that won't play him with their star center. Yes, both the first and second line are considered the best of the best on the team. We get equal playing time, ninety seconds on and ninety seconds off the ice, but if Gavin is seriously considering bringing Noah Harrison on, he'd play him with Aiden, the star center. Which means one winger would be dropped to second line. Either Hall or me.

Having had a long, successful career myself, and being captain, I can't imagine Gavin would move me. If Noah is coming to Boston, then Daniel is either being traded or being shifted to play with Camden Snow and Andrew Keegan.

I give Hall's arm a squeeze. He's young, but he's an excellent player. He's got a really promising career ahead of him. Gavin fought to get him here in the first place, so there's got to be a piece of this puzzle we're missing. Being not only the coach but the owner, Gavin has a vested interest in this team's future.

"I'm sure it's just a rumor. This is what happens every January. The commentators just like to hear themselves talk."

He ducks his head and clears his throat. "It wasn't them. A guy I played with in college is in Minnesota. He told me Harrison is in talks with the Bolts."

My stomach sinks. Shit. That's a bit more serious. Still, I school my expression. "I haven't heard anything, and don't you think if Gavin was considering bringing on one of my old teammates, he'd mention it to me? I can't imagine he wouldn't want my opinion, since I know the guy so well. Not to mention my position as captain."

That may not be true, and it's possible he already got the background info he needed from Brooks. Sometimes I wonder if I'm captain by default. He couldn't choose Aiden or Brooks, nepotism and all that, but Gavin has known me since I was a kid, so we still have a relationship outside this arena, which means I respect him enough to want to impress him.

"Will you let me know if you hear anything?" Worry creases Hall's brow.

"Of course." When the bartender sets my drink in front of me, I bring it to my lips and turn so I can search the crowd for my wife. "You bring a date tonight?"

He sputters. "And give some girl the impression that I have any interest in a relationship? Yeah, no."

I eye him over the rim of my glass as I take a sip. "One day," I say, savoring the burn of the bourbon, "you'll be looking forward to nights like this so you can impress her."

Hall chokes on a bark of laughter. "Who?"

"The love of your life," I say as I finally find Ava.

"Spoken like a man in love," he hums.

I take a sip of my drink and grin. Maybe I am. But when I zero in on my wife again and spot my stepbrother kissing her cheek, my smile slips and my heart lurches right out of my chest.

What the fuck?

Chapter 38
Ava

"AS ALWAYS, ANOTHER FANTASTIC EVENT." Liv tips her glass of red wine in my direction.

Her husband hasn't let go of her hip since they approached, though he's now scanning the room and nodding here and there.

Beckett and Liv have a palpable kind of love. It emanates from them when they're simply standing beside one another. God, what would that be like? To be that loved? Liv jokes that Beckett's obsession can be suffocating, but her ability to make light of it is one of the reasons the emotion is so pure. She doesn't fear that she'll upset him, that he'll tire of her, or that his attention will wander. And rightfully so. It's clear to everyone in their orbit that his obsession will not wane.

Though it's impossible not to wish for something similar, a love like that isn't in the cards for me. I've locked myself into an arranged marriage, and though I know Tyler cares for me, I won't fool myself into believing we'll ever have *that*.

Giving Josie, Scarlett, and Brayden what Liv and Beckett's kids have, though? A real family with two parents who love them with all their heart, biology aside? That, we can handle. And if I had to choose between the two, I wouldn't even stop to think before choosing them over having some fairy-tale kind of love of my own.

I've never been a lucky person, and that isn't going to change now. No, I am under no illusion that I'll ever have that once-in-a-lifetime kind of connection.

"We couldn't do it without the generous donations from the Langfields." It's the truth, and I swear I'm not kissing their asses. More generous people do not exist.

Smiling, Liv tilts her head. "I hear congratulations are in order, by the way." She searches the room until she spots Tyler.

He's propped up against the bar next to Daniel, a drink in his hand, watching me. When our eyes catch, I can't help the blush that warms my face.

"How did that happen? I didn't even know you two were dating."

"That's a good question."

The deep voice over my shoulder startles me. Internally, I cringe. Though I can't see the man, I know the voice well. Eyes closed, I take two steadying breaths. Shoot. This will not go well, and the last place I want to talk to my ex-boyfriend about how I married his stepbrother is in front of my boss.

Remember how I said I had no luck?

When I turn, Xander gives me a warm smile and presses a kiss to my cheek. "It's so good to see you, sis."

The kindness in his tone has me swallowing my tongue.

Also, sis? Ew.

Stunned, I stammer out, "X-Xander, I didn't expect to see you tonight." *I hoped I'd never see you again.*

"Wouldn't miss this event for anything. As you know, our firm donates to many of the Langfield charities." His voice is so loud that Beckett and Liv are almost forced to acknowledge it.

And they do because they don't suck like he does.

"We appreciate that so much," Liv says. "This is your brother?" She quirks her brow, studying him.

Xander attended several events with me in the six months we were together, so I'm sure she's seen him before, though she likely doesn't know why he looks familiar. And after he called me his sister, why would she put two and two together? Again, gross.

"Xander Warren." He holds out his hand to Liv.

"Tyler's brother," I explain.

"Stepbrother." Out of nowhere, my husband appears, clearly doing his best to temper the glower he wants to shoot at my ex. They have never liked one another, and I'm only starting to understand why.

"Which makes her my sister."

That sets Tyler's scowl free. Probably because he finds the idea as disgusting as I do. Fortunately, Beckett and Liv seem none the wiser to the tension.

Beckett dips his chin at Tyler. "You know, my brothers and I have a podcast."

Eyes drifting to the ceiling, Liv sighs. "You and this podcast."

Beckett pinches her side, making her giggle. "We talk to players, get their perspective on the game—"

"That's not why he's trying to get you on," Liv warns.

Based on the charming, calculating smile Beckett is wearing, I know I won't like where this is going. "We also talk about love and all the matches I'm responsible for."

While Liv snorts, Xander frowns, clearly confused.

Tyler lets out a light chuckle. "I wasn't aware you set me up with my wife." Stepping around Xander, he pulls me against his chest and rests his chin on my shoulder, then he presses a gentle kiss against my cheek. He's claiming me, and while I'd normally be annoyed that he's playing such a trivial game with his stepbrother, in this moment, I can't find it in my heart to care. I like being claimed by Tyler. Far too much.

"If not for this very charity, I doubt the two of you would be standing here right now," Beckett continues, both brows lifted.

Tyler squeezes me. "Why this one?"

"Because this is the charity that brought Ava to Boston," Beckett explains.

My chest tightens. Shoot. He has no idea that my husband knows almost nothing about my family and certainly doesn't know why I moved to Boston.

"Really?" Tyler straightens behind me, unable to hide his surprise.

Xander clears his throat. "Because of her sister. The Langfields' charity provides all sorts of things for children's hospitals. Ava and her sister loved the movie nights they hosted best."

I study Xander, surprised that he remembers. "That's true. And it was my sister who saw the job posting online. As soon as she saw the Langfield name, she said I had to apply. She said it was fate."

"So you'll come on the podcast?" Beckett asks, completely unaware of how still Tyler has gone behind me. I'm afraid to look at him. It's been easy to live in our bubble, avoiding talk of my relationship with Xander as well as my past. But with my ex standing right here, acting like he did when we started dating, like the man I thought I was falling for, it's hard to swallow.

Tyler straightens, his chin bumping the crown of my head as he nods. "Of course. Just let me know when." He steps back, and his warmth goes with him. "If you don't mind, I'd like to steal my wife for a moment." Then, without waiting for a reply, he grabs my hand and pulls me away from the group.

"What are you doing?"

"Not another word." His voice is pure gravel.

As he guides me through the ballroom and to the hallway, my stomach sinks. I know he's pissed that Xander is here, but we can't just leave.

I stop moving and tug against his hold. "*Tyler.*"

Without looking at me, he forces me forward again. This time he doesn't stop until we're in an empty back hallway and the music from the room has faded completely.

"Tyler," I say again, irritation flaring.

Shaking his head, he finally releases me, only to turn and pace back and forth in front of me, his jaw hard and his breathing erratic. Without warning, he stops and cages me in, slapping the wall on either side of me with a *thwack*. Eyes lit with pain, he looms over me. "I hate that he knows anything about you."

I'm not scared, despite the way anger radiates off him and the way his whole body trembles. He'd never hurt me. With a calming breath, I press my hand to his heart. "I can't change my past. He and I dated. I can't erase what we had."

He searches my eyes, his lips pressed in a straight line, as if he's considering his words carefully. Finally, he says, "You told him about your family." The breath he exhales causes the hair at my temples to tickle my face. "You only told me about them a few days ago, and all you gave me was a few vague details. He knows things I don't. About your childhood. About your hopes and dreams."

It's as if he's breaking in front of me. Cracking into shards. I grip his lapels to keep him close. "We were getting to know one another. You and I never did that."

"I want to know everything, Ava. I want to know everything about you. I want to be the one who knows the most. Your dreams. Your fears. I want it all."

I can't stop the smile that curves my lips. This sweet man. Even in his anger, even in his jealousy, he brightens even the darkest moments. "He has a tiny picture of my past," I assure him. "A blip in my life. You have today."

Tyler slides a hand up my neck and rakes his fingers through my hair before giving it a good tug. "I don't want just your today," he rasps. "I want your tomorrow. And the day after that. I want all of it. I'm eternally captivated by you. I'll never get enough. It guts me that he has any of it. He knows things—"

"He doesn't know the sounds I make when I come."

Tyler blinks, and his whole body goes rigid. "What?"

I rest my head against the wall with a quiet thump. "We were taking things slow. Apparently that meant only he got off."

Face lowered, he lets out a feral growl. "Bordel de merde."

Warmth blooms in my chest. "I love when you speak French to me."

Pressing his forehead to mine, he blows out a breath. "French Canadian, mon cher."

Biting my lip, I blink up at him. "You did it the other day too. In front of Hannah."

He nods, our foreheads rubbing together.

"What did you say?" I shrug. "If you remember."

Tyler straightens and chuckles, though the sound is almost pained. "Oh, Vicious, you still don't get it."

"Get what?"

"Every moment with you is imprinted on my brain." He presses a hand to his chest. "In my heart."

My pulse picks up, but I keep my voice even. "Prove it."

CHAPTER 39
TYLER

"PROVE IT."

This fucking woman. How the hell can she have me yo-yoing between emotions like this? One moment I'm ready to put my fist through the wall, and the next I'm aching to fall to my knees and worship at her feet.

Can I do what she's asking? Show her how I really feel? Tell her what I said to her that day in Hannah's office? If I do, there will be no going back.

Does she have any idea what she's asking of me? What that kind of confession will do to our carefully crafted plan to raise kids together for the next sixteen years?

Rather than baring my soul all at once, I give her my truths one at a time, slowly, watching her reaction, hoping she's really ready for them. I cup her face and stroke the curve of her cheek, relishing the softness of her skin. "Tout ce à quoi je pense c'est te faire l'amour à chaque instant de chaque jour. Comment tu goûtes. Comment tu parles. Je suis obsédé et te voir obsédé, C'est me foutre la tête. Ne me brise pas le cœur visqueux. Je ne m'en remettrai jamais."

Ava's green eyes warm and her lips curve into the most beautiful smile. She may not understand the language, but based on this reaction, it's clear she understands the meaning behind the words.

I suck in a breath before I continue. Then, with a thick swallow, I begin. "All I think about is making love to you at every moment of every day. How you taste. How you sound. I'm obsessed, and seeing you obsessed is fucking with my head. Don't break my heart, Vicious. I'll never recover."

I hold my breath, waiting for her reaction, and I startle a little when she pops up on her toes, loops her arms around my neck, and pants "so do it" against my lips.

"Do what?" I murmur between kisses.

"Make love to me." She backs away, emerald eyes full of heat. "Find out how I taste. How I sound. *Do it*." There's a challenge to her words. Of course there is. She's challenged me every day since I met her.

I search the hallway, and when I spot a door a few steps down, I drag her toward it and push her into the dark space. Unable to control myself, I press her up against the back of the door and kiss her again.

"God, Tyler, please."

"Please, what?" My cock throbs painfully against my zipper. "What does my wife need?"

"I need you. That's it. *You*."

Fuck, I love this woman. I can't get enough of her soft lips, her warm mouth. I kiss her again.

"The first time I make love to you can't be in a closet at a party with everyone we work with nearby."

She giggles. "You said we don't work together."

I arch a brow. "You remember what I said the day we met?"

She nips at my chin. "I remember everything." Her hands skate down my chest, and then she's unbuckling my belt. "I've been waiting to be fucked by *the* Tyler Warren for years. Don't get shy on me now. Besides, it's not a closet." She looks around the space, though I don't take my eyes off her. "It's too big. More like an empty office."

Chuckling, I pull her to me and tug on the fabric tied around her neck. When I release it and her tits spill free, I curse. "Fuck, you're pretty."

In a rush, she pulls down my pants and boxers. Bracing myself against the door, I tear them off, along with my shoes. My blood is rushing in my ears by the time I lift her dress, and satisfaction shudders through me when I pull on her lacy underwear until it breaks.

"Hey," she mutters as I toss them to the floor. "I liked those."

"I'll buy you a pair in every color." I ease her dress over her head and add it to the pile. My tie and jacket follow. Impatient, I leave my dress shirt on but push the sleeves up. Then I step back.

She glares at the space between us, then at me. "What are you doing?"

I snag my jacket off the floor and find the remote. "I can't fill you right now because something else is in my place."

She slips a hand down her hip, going for the toy, but I stop her with a *tsk*.

"Don't you fucking dare."

Her eyes flare in annoyance. "*Tyler*."

"Palms flat against the door."

"What?"

Head tilted, I clench my teeth and bite out my next words. "Ass and palms against the door. You asked me to make you come. Don't tell me how to do it."

"But I want you," she whines, her words breathy. God, I love her like this. The woman who's defiant only with me, who's always meek with others, is now needy and desperate. Not holding back who she is or what she wants. And fuck if I'm not the luckiest man in the world, because what she wants is *me*.

"Then be my good little wife and let me watch you fall apart. Give me a show, and then I'll give you the cock you want so damn much."

I give myself a single harsh stroke to punctuate my demands. Attention lowered to where I'm still gripping my length, she slides her tongue over her lip, then sinks her teeth into it, so fucking hungry for release.

Finally giving in, she places her hands against the door, but like the tease she always is, she cants her hips and goes up on her tiptoes like the pretty ballerina I met that first day.

I drop to my knees so I'm level with her pelvis and press the button on the remote. As the vibrations begin, her pussy spasms. My dick throbs so painfully at the sight I have to strangle it to keep myself from coming from just her scent and moans alone.

She writhes against the door, scraping her nails along the wood grain, searching for purchase. "Holy shit."

"Look at you." Mouth watering, I drag my eyes up from her throbbing pussy to her hips, then her smooth pale stomach and the swell of her tits.

Her pink nipples are so hard she'd probably come if I blew on one. Her jaw is slack and her eyes are closed. Fuck. I need her to come. I need to be inside her more than I need my next breath.

"You going to come for me, Vicious? Going to show your husband how pretty you are when you listen?"

"Fuck you," she whines, though she gives me a pitiful smile.

"What do you need to come? You want my fingers? My tongue?"

She glares at me. "I want your cock, Tyler Warren. Give me my husband's cock. Now."

I can't hold back my laughter. I love her like this. "Fine."

At my acquiescence, her eyes practically glow. I remove the vibrator and throw it without worrying about turning it off. The sound of the buzzing is drowned out by her moan as I stand and lift her into my arms.

"Are you sure about this?" I ask as I press her against the door and grind against her, sliding against her hot sex.

"I'm done holding back. Make me yours, Tyler." With her forehead pressed to mine, she watches as I line myself up.

"You've been mine since we said *I do*." I tease her clit with my piercings, pulling another moan from her.

"We never said *I do*." Despite how out of her mind with need she is, her smart-ass taunts are on point.

She's laughing at her own comment as I slam one palm against the door and plunge inside her. Instantly, the sound dies. Half a second later, I know I'm in trouble. I underestimated how it would finally feel to be this connected to her. I've never been a saint, but it's been a long time since I've touched another woman. Already, this is entirely different from anything I've experienced. The heat of her steals my breath, consuming me in a way I can't comprehend.

As she cries out, I cover her mouth with mine, greedy for every sound, every moan, every whimper. They're all mine. She belongs to me, and I feel irrationally possessive and protective over this moment.

"Fuck, we should be in a bed." Even as I say it, I pound into her fiercely. There's no taking it easy. She feels too good. Everything about this moment is *too good*.

"Who needs a bed when we have a perfectly good door?" She tightens her legs around me and circles her hips as she scrapes her nails down my neck beneath my shirt.

"Baby, you deserve so much better than this."

"No, I deserve you," she gasps, her lips brushing mine.

There's nothing left to say. I love her. I can't not tell her.

"I think maybe they went down there."

I slow my thrusts and cover my wife's mouth at the sound of a voice nearby.

"Shh," I say as she whimpers beneath my palm.

My thighs burn as I slow my movements, but I don't stop. If anything, the ache only grows more as we try to stay quiet.

"Ava, you down here?"

Her eyes bulge comically above where I've got my whole hand over her mouth.

"What the fuck is he doing following you?" I growl, my thrusts getting angrier.

"Ava," Xander says, closer now. "I know you're avoiding me, but I just want to talk."

Thrust.

"Please, Ava. My brother disappeared. Not sure when he'll be back, but while he's gone, I need to know: did he force you into this?"

The grin on my face is so wide it hurts. "Have anything to say, Vicious?"

Thrust.

I slide my hand off her mouth, and a second later, she bites her lip.

"Ava, please. I know I fucked up, but marrying my brother is ridiculous. Let me get you out of this."

I lick her lips. "You want out of this, baby?"

Thrust.

She spasms around me, and her head falls back against the door. "Oh fuck, I'm coming."

"Ava?"

"That's right, wife. Come all over your husband's cock." I pound into her harder now, unleashing all my pent-up irritation over the asshole on the other side of the door. The fucker who didn't deserve even a minute of her time. "My perfect wife, milking my cock, begging for my cum. Tell me where you want it. Or better yet, *tell him*."

"I'm not on birth control," she whimpers even as she tightens her ankles around my hips, digging her heels into my ass.

I grit my teeth. "Tell me to pull out if you aren't ready to be mine forever, Ava, because there's no chance I don't want this."

Her eyes fly open and lock on me, and I swear we have an entire conversation like that, even as she moans through the aftershocks of her orgasm. I hold her tight, unwilling to be the one to pull away. I'm in this. I want this. Her. Our family. More babies. I'll give her everything, but she has to pick me. She needs to tell me this is what she wants. I won't decide another thing for her.

The door rattles against its frame as I slam into her.

"Inside me," she screams. "Come inside me."

Heart exploding, I pick up my pace. "*Good girl*," I moan. "I'll give you what you want. But scream my name, wifey. Let everyone know which brother you belong to."

As my wife shouts just who owns her for all the world to hear, I come with a growl, filling her, positive there's no way my idiot stepbrother didn't get the message. Ava is mine. And she'll only ever be mine.

Chapter 40
Ava

"I CAN'T BELIEVE you ripped my underwear," I say as Tyler spins me on the dance floor.

"They'll make a wonderful souvenir," he murmurs in my ear.

A big part of me was desperate to leave right after he fucked me into next Sunday against a door while his brother—my ex—stood on the other side. But this is my event, and it's far too early to bow out. Also, I'm smiling and he's smiling, and I'm not sure I've ever felt this happy or relaxed in my life.

With a pinch to his chest, I give him a mock glare. "You aren't keeping them."

"Sure, I am, wifey." The dark chuckle that rumbles out of him sends a shiver down my spine. "I'm going to frame them and put them up next to that picture of you giving me the finger after our wedding."

I roll my eyes. "No one got that on camera."

"So you admit you were cursing me that day?"

"We've come so far," I say on a laugh.

With a flourish, Tyler spins me out and then back into his chest before dipping me not so gracefully. When he rights me, my cheeks hurt from smiling.

His expression is just as bright. "I love seeing you smile."

"Tyler—"

"Can I cut in?" Xander's words cut my own short.

They stop me from telling Tyler that I love a hell of a lot more than his smile.

Honestly, maybe I'm a bitch, but I kind of just want to say "you again?" to Xander, then turn my back on him. Is the situation awkward? Yes. I did marry his stepbrother, after all. But Xander didn't seem to care what I was doing until he found out about the marriage. Why, all of a sudden, is he so desperate to speak to me? I guess, in a weird way, I'm thankful for the fractured relationship between these two. It means I'll rarely have to see him. And honestly, other than when he texts, I've mostly forgotten about him.

Tyler's grip on my hip tightens, and he pulls me to his chest. "No."

"*Ava*," Xander says in that way he used to when he thought I was being ridiculous and needed to be reminded of how to behave.

I can't hate it all that much, I guess, since it's not all that different from the way I say Tyler's name, and Tyler loves when I say his name like that. It's our thing. He's an ass, and I put him in his place, and then we do this. We smile together.

When I realize that couples around us are slowing their movements, attention drifting to us and the drama unfolding, I refocus on the issue at hand. "You should go," I tell Xander.

He shakes his head and takes a step closer, his words a whispered hiss barely audible over the music. "You're embarrassing yourself. I know you always wanted to be Josie's mom, but this is pathetic."

"Watch yourself," Tyler warns.

I place a hand on his chest, silently urging him to remain calm. The last thing we need is a scene in the middle of the dance floor at a charity event I planned. The silent auction hasn't ended yet, and nothing brings an event down like a fight. "Xander, if you'd like to talk, we can go into the hall."

"No you can't," Tyler growls, his hold almost painfully tight.

"Whatever," Xander sneers. "You're not worth it anyway. He's going to leave you, ya know. The only reason he wanted you was because I had you first. The guy always wants my leftovers."

As he shakes his head, I try to ignore the way his insults hit.

"You left your phone at the table. I was just trying to give it back to you earlier." He tosses it in my direction.

Thankfully Tyler snatches it before it hits me in the chest.

I stare after my asshole of an ex as he storms off, feeling uneasy about the entire exchange. Confused too, because I'm certain I never even took my phone out of my purse. Yet somehow Xander ended up with it. Why? Was there something he wanted from it? And if so, then why did he give it back?

There's only one thing on that phone that concerns me. But even Xander wouldn't be interested in that. Doubt rushes through me as I tell myself that though. Because I've been wrong about so many things.

"Are you okay?" Tyler rasps, tucking me against his body. We didn't stay much longer after Xander's tantrum. I probably should have, but the entire thing left me uneasy, so I checked with Lennox to make sure she could take the lead, and we took off.

I lay my hand on his cheek. Tonight was many things, but the only thing I want to focus on is my husband. "He doesn't get any more of our thoughts."

Tyler's blue eyes rove over me, like he's not quite sure whether I'm hiding my true feelings.

"Tonight, I got closure. I'm glad we saw him. Now that part of my life is done with completely."

A cocky smirk pulls at his lips. "That part of your life was over the moment you spent the night in my bed."

"Not the moment we said *I do*?" I bite down on my lip as excitement whirls in my stomach. This is us. The teasing and taunting. Now that we're actually together and I'm not forcing myself to keep my distance from him, I know what it leads to—hot sex.

He scoffs. "Please, we both know you've wanted me since long before that day."

"In your dreams, Tyler Warren."

"You're the one who proposed to me. I think that was your plan all along. You saw me as a dad and couldn't get enough."

Head lolling on my pillow, I roll my eyes. "You are so full of yourself."

He squeezes my bare hip. We're naked, and I know if he moved his leg even an inch, I'd be moaning at the friction. "You're about to be full of me, wife. But first I'm going to suck on that needy cunt of yours. Clearly, you need it, with the way you're soaking my leg."

Shocked, though I shouldn't be by now, by his words, I smack his chest. "*Tyler.*"

"Please, are you trying to deny how wet you are? How turned on you get when I taunt you?"

No. "Yes," I grit out as desire pools in my belly and spills over.

Gripping my hips, he pulls me on top of him. "Sit on my face."

I rock against his length, not the least bit embarrassed by how wet I am. "I am not sitting on your face. Have you forgotten that I hate you?"

He smirks up at me, knowing not a word out of my mouth is true. "Suffocate me, then, wife. We both know I'll enjoy it." With a hand tangled in my hair, he pulls me down so we're chest to chest and kisses me.

Already, I'm panting and writhing against him, needy for everything he gives me.

Roughly, he clutches my thighs and guides me up to his face. "Grab the headboard, baby. I need to taste you." Digging his fingers into the flesh of my ass, he helps me settle my knees just above his shoulders. Then he runs his teeth gently against my sensitive skin, sending shivers cascading down my body. When his lips suction around my clit, stars dance in my vision.

I drop my head back and groan. "Ty, that's—"

"Heaven," he mumbles against me. "It's fucking heaven."

Tucking my chin, I grasp a handful of his hair and watch as he sucks and licks and laps at me, his eyes shut like he's enjoying this as much as I am. This is one of the most sensual experiences of my life. Maybe because he's my husband, maybe because what he's doing is so much more than just setting off explosions inside my nerves. The waves of pleasure he gives me aren't temporary. No, the ripples are creating lasting effects, gripping my heart just as firmly as he grips my body.

"Ty, I'm going to—"

I can't even get the word out before I explode, my entire body spasming with an intensity so fierce I'd flop to the bed if not for Tyler's firm grip on me. I'm lost in the pleasure as he drags me down his body. Rather than continuing to work me over with his mouth and savoring my orgasm, he extends it by impaling me with his cock in one sharp thrust.

"Oh god." The words are barely audible. I can't speak because he's stolen all my breath.

"That's right, baby. I'm your god. But you're my heaven, and I'm going to live inside you for the rest of my life." He fucks up into me, hips rolling, and my vision goes black. His piercing drags against my inner walls, ramping me up again instantly. He fills me so exquisitely. The scent of him and the heat in his wild blue eyes as they watch me so intently have my nerves chanting for another release. And when he slides his fingers up my body, starting from my hips, a chill sweeps through me. Those fingers find their way into my hair at the base of my skull, and he pulls me down until our mouths are fused. He swells inside me, the sensation sending me over the edge. As he pulses, filling me once again, I come with a groan.

Before Tyler, I never wanted kids. Too afraid to create a bond that deep, only to lose that person.

But since him—since he gave me a family—I realize that it was stupid of me to pretend I could hold myself back from love. I love our kids, and I love Tyler. If we have more children in the future, I'll love them too. There's no way to guarantee we won't get hurt, that we won't lose those we love, but I'm not living in fear anymore. I'm embracing it.

We hold one another, kissing and whispering words that mean absolutely nothing but amount to everything. Sweet confessions between two people who are gone for one another. Words don't come easy, but even without them, it's obvious that our world shifted tonight.

"I love when you fuck me like you hate me," he mumbles, stroking my hair.

Tired and sated, I lay my head on his chest. "I don't really hate you," I whisper as I listen to the pounding of his heart. "You're a good husband."

"I know, baby." He presses a kiss to my head.

"And you're a really good dad." I yawn as a wave of exhaustion washes over me.

"I know that too." This time, the words are tinged with the cockiness he's so well-known for.

Eyes open again, I pinch his side. "God, I hate you."

He hums, the sound vibrating through me. And just as I'm drifting to sleep, he mumbles softly, "Love you too, wifey."

TEXT MESSAGES FROM AVA'S AND TYLER'S PHONE

Hall: Okay, boys, you all agreed—tonight after the game, you're mine.

Brooks: I'm not sure Sara is down with this plan.

Brooks: I'm down with this plan.

Aiden: LOL. Hi, Sar.

War: I'm exhausted, and we haven't even played yet

Hall: You're coming. You promised.

War: Or we could go to the tattoo parlor again, someone still hasn't gotten his glitter.

Brooks: Oh, I am totally coming to that!

Aiden: Still Sara, I'm guessing?

Brooks: Do you think I want to see Hall get his dick pierced?

Aiden: Okay, Brooks has his phone back. Should we just add Sara to the chat? It'd make this easier.

Fitz: Why am I in this chat again?

Sara: Oh my god, girls! I think I'm going with the guys so that Hall can get his dick pierced! I'm so excited!

Millie: Gross.

Hannah: HAHAHAHAHA I always forget you guys are related.

Millie: Twins, Hannah. He's my freaking twin.

Hannah: Well, your twin is about to make some woman very happy.

Millie: Try half the population of Boston. Man is gross.

Sara: Should I get something pierced? I'm thinking a clit piercing would be fun.

Ava: That sounds painful.

Hannah: Oh, War would lose his motherfucking mind if you got your clit pierced. Come on, girls, pretty please, can we do it?

Ava: No.

Lennox: I'm down.

Hannah: Matching clit piercings. We'll be like the guys. Aiden can even write a song about it.

Lennox: Oh my god, he's going to lose his mind knowing you said that.

Lennox: Yup. I just told him, and he's already working on lyrics

Millie: I'm with Ava. That sounds awful.

Hannah: You guys ruin all my fun.

Sara: NOT ME. I am the fun! But Brooks said if I get a clit piercing, we could get caught on one another, and that doesn't sound like fun.

Lennox: And I'm out.

Hannah: Well, I don't have a man or a sparkly blinged out dick...

Millie: You could always get nipple piercings like me. Gavin loves them.

Hannah: Tell me more.

Tyler: Hi, wifey.

Ava: Hi, husband. Heard you boys are going to get more piercings tonight.

Tyler: There's no way Hall won't chicken out again. Besides, I'd rather FaceTime with you after the game. You're much prettier than Hall's dick.

Ava: ...

Ava: I think there's a compliment in there.

Tyler: There definitely is. Be ready for me tonight. And make sure the toys are charged. I plan on making you come at least four times before you pass out.

Ava: Demanding and making me do all the work. Typical man.

Tyler: Have a good day, Vicious.

Chapter 41
Ava

AFTER FIVE AWAY GAMES AND ten days apart, I'm running around the house like a lunatic trying to make sure everything is ready for when Tyler walks through the door.

"Mama!" Scarlett cries out from the floor as I rush past her. She's got her arms out, making grabby hands.

I stop in front of her and boop her nose. "Do you want pizza, my little love?"

"Pizza for me." She points at her chest proudly.

I laugh. "Yes, baby girl. Pizza for you." With a kiss to her head, I pick her up and head for the kitchen. "Can you sit in your seat so I can finish up?"

She frowns.

"Josie," I holler. "Can you come sit with sissy until Da—Tyler is home?" I blow out a breath. Shit. I almost referred to Tyler as Daddy. When I'm talking to Scarlett, that's not an issue. In fact, it's becoming a habit, but Josie still doesn't call him that. She doesn't call me Mom, either. And even when Scarlett does, it's obvious it's confusing and uncomfortable for Josie. She's scared to get her hopes up, so I've tried really hard to avoid the word when talking to her.

Scarlett, naturally, doesn't know the intricacies of the situation, so she finishes the word for me, then repeats it over and over. It's her favorite word because Tyler is her favorite person.

"Daddy! Daddy! Daddy!" she sings, banging her hands against the tray on her highchair.

I run my hands through her hair. "Yes, little love. Daddy's coming home."

When the sound of gravel crunching catches our attention, she kicks her feet and points to the door. "Daddy home."

Josie bolts down the stairs, her focus determined. "Tyler," she shouts as she throws the door open and runs out into the cold.

Smiling, I shake my head and move in that direction too. It's hard not to get emotional as I stand at the window and watch Tyler open his arms to our girl and carry her toward the house, wearing a big smile. The night we came up with this crazy plan, he promised he'd always come running back to these kids. And the way they run to him just as desperately is heart-wrenching. He doesn't see the love they have for him. All he wants is to give them everything. What he doesn't realize is that *he* is everything. To them. To me.

And just like he runs to us, we're always going to run to him.

"Daddy," Scarlett calls when he slips inside the house with Josie in his arms and his travel bag slung over one shoulder.

He drops the bag but keeps a tight hold on Josie as he heads toward her little sister. I wait my turn as they get their hugs in.

As soon as he spots me in the corner, he smirks. "You going to keep creeping over there like a little stalker, wifey, or you going to come give your husband a hug?"

"That all you want?" I tease as I shuffle toward him.

He kisses both girls one more time before setting them down and reaching for my hand. Roughly, he tugs, causing my sock-covered feet to slide across the hardwoods. "You know it's not all I want," he murmurs as he pulls me into his chest and rests his head on my shoulder. He breathes me in the same way I'm doing to him. "Ten days was too much," he mutters.

Nodding, I squeeze him tight. "Too long."

He straightens, towering over me and hiding me from the girls. Then he presses his lips to mine. "Fuck, I missed you."

"Same."

"Wish you and the kids could travel with me."

With a palm to his cheek, I kiss him again. "One day."

"Where's Bray?"

I nod toward the stairs. "Showering after practice. He should be down any minute for dinner."

Chin lifted, Tyler surveys the kitchen. "And what are we having for dinner?"

"Something very special." Grinning, I shimmy my shoulders.

"You cooked?"

I laugh. "Yeah, pizza."

Pulling me into his chest again, he laughs. "Fancy."

"Hey, you said pizza was your favorite. I'm trying to give you all your favorite things tonight."

Focus fixed on my face, he licks his lips. "Yeah?"

"Yeah. Pizza, and then you get to teach me how to skate."

The way his blue eyes widen in surprise makes all my nervousness over this plan worth it. Yeah, I'll probably fall down a hundred times, and it's cold out—and dark—but I want to do this with him.

"I even bought skates."

Tyler's smile is so full of pure joy it makes my chest ache. "Best night ever. Best wife ever."

Apparently I wasn't the only one with surprises. After pizza, we all bundled up and headed for the pond, where I discovered that Brayden and Tyler had strung lights overhead and also around the trees, still covered in a dusting of snow in February.

With a flick of a switch, the entire pond lights up. The snow kissing the edge of the pond is almost diamond-like, sparkling from the overhead lights. As if Tyler has the ability to control nature, the northern lights make an appearance so the sky is a mixture of purples and pinks, like the heavens are putting on a show just for us. It's a winter dream. Nothing I ever thought I'd experience. Then again, I never could have imagined skating with my husband and our kids.

Josie spins around us, and Bray is almost as good on the ice as Tyler, so he's got a helmeted Scarlett in his arms, and he's skating slowly as music plays on his phone.

"Stargazing" by Myles Smith plays as Tyler holds his hand out to me.

"Promise you won't let me fall?" I ask from the edge of the ice.

Rather than wait for me to come to him, he tugs on my arm and clutches me to his chest. "I might not always be able to stop the fall, baby, but I promise to always be there to pick you up."

My legs wobble, not only because I'm like a newborn deer on the ice, but because of his words.

With an arm looped around me, Tyler turns us. "Grab my waist and follow my steps. It's like dancing. One foot glides, then the other follows."

It's nothing like dancing, but rather than argue with him, I focus on the task at hand. Being on the ice, the space where Tyler is most comfortable, feels sacred. Especially as the kids skate around us.

As I get more comfortable, he spins Josie until she's squealing in delight. And when Brayden approaches, he reaches out for Scarlett, who's calling out for him, and Bray swoops in to guide me.

Skating backward and holding my hands, he says, "You're not bad for a first timer."

I laugh. "Thanks, Bray. I'm trying."

He squeezes my fingers. "We can tell. And it means a lot to them."

My chest pinches as I take in his sincere expression. He's not just talking about skating. He's praising me, in his teenager way, for how I'm handling being hurtled into my role as a mother.

But once again, he keeps himself set apart from our family. He says *them*, like I'm doing it for them and not him.

There's no use trying to drive home the point again. He's not hearing it, and I understand. He's been let down time and again. All I can do is keep showing him how much he matters to me.

"Big game tomorrow?"

He shrugs. "Yeah."

"Did Ty tell you we're all coming?"

Eyes widening, he fixes his attention on me. "Really? But it's an hour away." He shakes his head. "You don't have to do that. It's not like—"

"I'm really excited," I say. I won't give him the chance to tell me once again that I don't owe him anything. "And now that I'm so good on skates, maybe your team could use me. What do you think?"

Snorting, he pretends to pull away from me. "I mean, if you're so good..."

I squeeze his hands, refusing to let him go. "Don't you dare."

He chuckles. "Fine. Come to the game tomorrow. Just, stay in the stands, 'kay?"

Tyler skates up beside us and holds out a hand to me. "What are you two talking about?"

"Bray. Bray," Scarlett calls.

The guys swap me for the toddler once again. I'd be embarrassed if I wasn't still wobbling so much.

Brayden takes off a bit faster, spinning. The sound of Scarlett's giggles floats on the chilly air.

"He's a hard nut to crack," I murmur.

With an arm around me, he hums. "I appreciate how hard you try."

"Always, Ty," I peer up at him. "And not just because you want me to. I love that kid. He just needs us to keep showing up for him."

Angling in, he presses his lips to my forehead.

"When did you learn to skate?" I ask, in need of a subject change.

He chuckles. "I'm Canadian. I was born on skates."

"Right. You came right out of your mother's womb with death sticks on your feet."

Laughing, he spins slowly so we can keep an eye on the kids. On the other side of the pond, Josie is telling Brayden a story as she spins, talking with her whole body, like she always does.

"I was probably three. My parents were still married, and they used to take me out to the pond behind their house."

"When did they get divorced?"

"I think I was five. My dad met Dory through work. It was an affair. My mom never mentioned that part to me, but I put the pieces together when I was older."

I roll my eyes. "That woman is awful. I'm so sorry I didn't see it when I was with Xander."

A low grumble vibrates between us.

"Did you just growl at me?"

Pulling back, he hits me with a scowl. "I really would prefer we never mention past relationships again."

I flatten my lips to keep from laughing. "Past relationships?" I roll my eyes. "I've had a whole whopping *one*. But yeah, I'd rather not talk about all the women who have owned pieces of you either."

"There's been one." Tyler's voice is so soft, my head innately tips closer to his, my eyes searching his expression.

Is he going to tell me about the one who got away? My stomach twists in jealousy.

"We don't need to talk about it."

"She's owned me since the first moment I saw her. Knew when I looked into her pretty green eyes that she was my forever."

A soft breath escapes me as understanding sweeps through me. "Oh."

Tyler's lips lift on one side. "Yeah, oh. I remember thinking your eyes were the same color as the ring my mother used to wear on her finger. I forgot about that though until Christmas morning when I pulled the ring from my safe."

"*Ty.*"

He shakes his head. "You're the only girl outside my mother to ever own any piece of me. And now you have a piece of her. It's how it was meant to be."

I think he's right. I think all along this was our story. Our destiny.

"My dad called while I was away."

Surprise zips through me. Tyler and I talked and texted every day while he was gone, and he never mentioned it. "Oh yeah?"

"I know it makes no sense that I still want to talk to him, that I still seek his approval."

Heart aching, I squeeze his hand. "He's your father."

"Right."

"You don't ever have to explain yourself to me. Loving someone even when it hurts is natural."

Shoulders sinking, he sighs. "I told him they aren't welcome here if Dory can't treat my family the way she would treat Xander's. I won't have my kids believing they mean less than other people do. So much of my life has been shaped by my childhood. By the way I tried to squeeze myself into a box in hopes that by molding who I was, they'd love me. I won't let our kids do that."

"I'm proud of you," I whisper, emotion pricking at the backs of my eyes. "What did he say?"

"He said I have one hell of a wife and that my kids have one hell of a mother. He's sorry he didn't find a woman who cared for me the way you so obviously care for my kids."

Tears well, but I blink them back. "He did?"

Tyler pulls me into his chest, hugging me close. "And he already told Dory the same thing. She will no longer be part of his family if she can't love the people who matter to him."

"*Ty*," I whisper, so completely shocked by this turn of events.

Chin tucked, he smiles down at me. "It was the first time he ever picked me. And it's because of you. Because you stuck up for me."

"I'll always stick up for you."

Angling down, he brushes his lips against mine. "Thank you for the pizza tonight. And for letting me teach you how to skate. This is exactly what I needed. *You're* everything I've ever needed."

His words heal parts of me, and I'm not even sure he knows it. Going for lighthearted is the only way I can keep myself from tearing up. "I like when you teach me things."

He chuckles. "Oh, wifey. I'll gladly teach you something new every day for the rest of my life."

Beaming, I hold out my glove-covered little finger. "Pinky promise?"

CHAPTER 42
TYLER

"IT'S CRIMINAL, really. We've had this hot tub for almost a month, and I haven't gotten you naked in it."

I laugh at my wife's comment. Who knew Ava would be the one trying to defile me? Steam dances around us as we relax in the bubbling water. "Feel free to take off that suit and come sit on me."

Ava eyes me mischievously. "Is this going to be another one of your lessons?" Dipping under the water, she swims across the small space and resurfaces in my arms.

Squeezing her hips, I try to remind myself to breathe. This woman is so goddamn beautiful sitting in my lap, dripping wet, wearing one of those smiles that steals my breath each time I see it. For so long, they were rare, at least around me. A small tilt of her lips when one of her friends would tell a funny joke. Like she knew her mouth should make that motion, but the expression never truly hit her eyes, where sadness always reigned.

Now I see it in her every feature.

Ava's happy.

And I feel like a goddamn king for being even a small part of the reason she emanates joy.

"What kind of lesson were you thinking, wifey?"

Rolling her hips over my rock-hard cock, she moans. "There's so much I've never done. I'm sure you could figure out something to teach me." She drops her head back, exposing her neck.

Without hesitation, I find the spot that turns her into putty in my hands and suck on the soft flesh there. I nip at it, then lick, soothing the sting. All the while, she rolls her hips over me, working herself into a frenzy.

"Fuck, Ave. The things I want to do to you."

My wife moans. "And I want them. I want them all."

I slip my fingers beneath her swimsuit and grip her ass. "Careful, Vicious. You don't know the monster you're begging for."

She wiggles, egging me on. "I think I do. We both know how much I love that monster."

She's right. The two of us, we love the taunting. I slide my hands a little farther and dig my fingers into the crack of her ass, pulling her cheeks apart so the hot water teases her tight hole.

Ava thrashes above me, arching back and then slumping against me, her teeth digging into my neck. "More," she pants.

"You want me to finger this virgin ass, Ave? Want me to make you come without even touching your pussy?"

She grinds down on me. "No. I want you to suck on my clit while you finger it."

I smile down at my beautiful, dirty wife and press one finger against her tight hole. She squirms with so much ferocity I almost slide right in, but I hold myself back, determined to make this good for her. Determined to make her crave more than my finger in this forbidden spot.

"How 'bout this, baby?" I say, voice husky against her ear. Gently, I ease my finger inside her.

She lets out a soft whimper, but I don't pull back. It'll hurt for a second, but I'm going to work her up to something that will feel so fucking good for us both.

"How about I finger this ass while you ride me in here, and once you come once, I'll take you inside and lick you from front to back. Then you'll come with my tongue in your ass."

"Don't stop," she begs.

I'm not sure if she means the fingering or the dirty talk, but I don't plan to stop either.

"You think you can be quiet when I slide my cock into this tight ass? Or will I have to dig out a ball gag for you?"

Writhing on top of me, she succumbs to her first orgasm of the night. A flush works up her pale skin, and her lips fall open on a loud moan. No, my girl has no idea how to be quiet. I claim her lips as her orgasm slams down on her. She's still whimpering from the after-shocks when I pull my finger out of her ass and straighten her bathing suit.

I give her a few moments to steady herself, then climb out of the tub and hold out a towel for her.

"Do you really have a ball gag?" she asks as she steps into my arms.

"I'm not sure how to answer that."

Mouth dropping open, she pushes away from me. "Tyler Warren."

I throw my head back and let out a loud laugh. "I'm teasing." I tug her into my arms again. "I've got all sorts of toys, but I've never used them on anyone but you. I stocked up after your little show with the vibrator."

Ava's eyes glitter with interest, sending a rush of heat through me. Does she want me to gag her? Fuck, my brain is too scrambled to remember what I've got upstairs, but I'm sure I can find something that will do the trick.

"I don't think I can be quiet." Ironically, she whispers those words.

Grasping her hips, I lift her and carry her inside. "I'll find a way to shut you up."

Ava

My pulse races and anticipation overwhelms me, my body coated in a sheen of sweat as I lie on our bed, naked and relaxed. Tyler saunters around our room completely naked, pulling a bottle of lube from a drawer and a vibrator from beside the bed, and then a tie from his closet. As he spins and stalks toward me, determination and lust evident in his every step, my nerves splinter. It's hard to breathe when he looks at me like this.

He's godlike. Effervescent. *War.*

Hannah was right to make his name a damn adjective. There's not a person on this planet who has this kind of swagger.

It's the hint of softness along those jagged edges. The surprise one will find if they dare to get close.

Tyler Warren loves with his whole damn heart, but it's rare for anyone to take the time to see beneath the tattoos and the scowls.

"You're really going to gag me?"

He lifts a brow, but rather than reply, he simply places all of his treasures beside me, then cuffs my ankles and tugs until my knees rest on his shoulders. "Let's see how quiet you are with my tongue in your ass."

Before I have time to process his words, he spreads me wide and licks. The sensation is indecent, obscene. I can't help but squirm. It shouldn't feel this good. I shouldn't like it. But god, the way he slides his tongue in and out of me makes my eyes roll back in ecstasy.

A buzzing sound fills the air, catching my attention. Then, without stopping the work that magical tongue is doing, he's rolling a vibrator against my clit.

"Oh fuck," I whimper.

"Do you need something to keep you quiet?" His voice is husky, his breath hot on my skin.

"Yes," I plead.

In one swift move, he flips around and straddles me, his knees on either side of my head, his cock dangling above my lips, his mouth suctioned over my pussy. I grip his hard length and open my mouth, anxious to torture him the way he's torturing me. I've barely rolled my tongue over the piercing when he pushes the head of the vibrator inside me. Rough and fast, he fucks me with it and bucks into my mouth.

He slides a finger into my ass, and as I moan in response, I gag on his cock.

It all feels too good. The pleasure builds, my nerves breaking apart as he works me from every angle. Breathing through my nose, I try to focus on pleasing him, but the man is focused. While he pistons his hips, his fingers fuck, and his tongue, god his tongue, works indecent circles until I'm crying out again, practically begging for him to fuck me.

"I can't—I don't—" I babble incoherently.

He pulls out of my mouth, giving me a second to breathe, but doesn't stop fucking into my ass. Adding a second finger, he milks my orgasm, stretching me deliciously, hitting a place that immediately sends me to the edge again.

"You can, baby, and you will. Do you want me inside you when you come, or should I use my tongue again first?"

Still in the throes of ecstasy, all I can do is buck up off the bed, pushing my pussy toward his face, begging for it.

Humming, he latches on to my clit and sucks. "That's it, wifey, come on my tongue again. I want you to squirt all over our bed when I fuck this ass." With two fingers buried in the tight hole, he pushes the vibrator deeper into my pussy and sucks me through another violent shudder.

"Please," I cry, tears and sweat coating my face. I don't know whether I'm crying because I can't take the pleasure any longer or if it's in desperation for my final climax.

He's working me toward a sensation I've never experienced, and with every pulse my body seems to chant, *more, give me more.*

In my delirious state, I'm vaguely aware of the way he positions me, slipping a pillow beneath my hips. Then his face is hovering over mine. "Are you okay?"

As I get lost in his beautiful blue eyes, I realize I've ever been this okay. This happy. This content.

As incredible as it is, it's not the sex. It's him. It's the trust I have in him. Tyler won't hurt me. I know this with every fiber of my being. He'd do anything to *not* hurt me.

Blowing out a shaky breath, I smile. "Please, Ty. I need you."

By the surprise glittering in his eyes and the smile that lances his face, I know I haven't worked hard enough to show him that I won't hurt him. That I love him. I'm still hiding so many parts of myself. Though I can't spill all my secrets in this moment, I have to show him that I'm trying. That I want him to know me.

But words aren't enough. I want to show him.

With a hand at the back of his neck, I tug him in for a kiss. His muttered *fuck* against my lips tells me, once again, that I've surprised him.

With his lips fused to mine, he rubs his pierced dick against my clit. Needy for more, I angle my hips so he's notched at my entrance.

"Je t'aime, ma femme, j'aime ton corps parfait, et ta chatte, et ce cul, je vais le baiser jusqu'à ce que tu jouisses sur ma bite."

As he thrusts inside me, I bite down on his lip. "What does that mean?"

He thrusts slowly, his eyes locked on mine. "I love you, my wife. I love your perfect body, and your pussy, and this ass. I'm going to fuck it until you come all over my cock."

His words alone edge me closer to the orgasm that just may be the death of me.

I whimper. "Do it now, please?"

Straightening, he slides out of me and hands me the vibrator. "Hold this on your clit for me, okay? If any of this is too much, tell me. I'll go slow."

Panting, I smile up at him. "I trust you."

His chest heaves with a relieved breath. "Good. I'd never hurt you." Drinking me in, he squirts a generous amount of lube into his hand and coats his length. He presses one finger into me and works me over, prepping me. "You feel so soft, baby. My cock is going to love it."

He works me over until he feels confident I'm ready, then he grips his cock and presses it against me. "Breathe, Vicious, I need you to breathe."

I suck in a breath of air as he pushes inside me. His fingers have nothing on his cock and the feeling of him breaking through has me hissing in air. I grit my teeth to keep myself from crying out. Right when I think I can't take another second of it, he pulls back and presses forward again.

"Just push in," I beg.

With a gentle tilt of his hips, he seats himself completely. The burn lingers, though it's morphed into the kind of pain I relish. Holding himself there, he grasps my hand, the one holding the vibrator, and rolls it over my sensitive clit.

"Oh god, yes," I mumble as the pain subsides and I'm awash in sheer pleasure. Maybe it's that my nerve endings have all been frayed, but god does it feel good. He does it again and I have to bite down on my arm to keep myself quiet.

"Such a good girl," Tyler coos as he drags the vibrator lower. "Do you think we should fill this pussy? Think you can handle it?"

He pulls back a fraction and thrusts into me again.

Instantly, I'm begging him to make me come.

Unhurried and wearing a grin, he drags the vibrator back up to my clit and takes a nipple into his mouth. The pleasure that swamps me is so intense I practically black out. With my nipple between his teeth, he tugs.

It's too much. My every cell is screaming for release. I rock against him, fucking his cock with my ass, needing more.

"There's my vicious girl. Take what you need."

My pussy pulses, begging him. "I need the vibrator, Ty."

"Yes you do. You want to come, don't you?"

"Need it," I pant.

Blue eyes lit like flames, he slides the vibrator inside me. "I'll never deny you." With that, he fucks me with abandon. The feel of the vibrator and his cock working at the same time is decadent. "Oh fuck, baby, the vibrator feels too good," he mutters and then rambles in French. The words are an aphrodisiac, lighting a fire that cascades through my limbs.

He lets go of the vibrator, using his hips to keep it in place, and fucks me with both the vibrator and his magical cock. With his arms caging me, he hovers low, his tongue finding mine.

I detonate, coming so hard he has to swallow my cries.

This night. This man. I'll never get enough.

Chapter 43
Ava

TODAY IS one of those days when I can't quite get it right. First Scarlett had an appointment with the pediatrician, and there were shots, which meant tears from both of us.

Then, just as I was scooping up my purse so I could head to Brayden's hockey game, a car pulled into the driveway. When the woman stepped out, Maria informed me that she was Josie's case manager.

For the next forty-five minutes, I resisted the urge to bite my nails while the woman inspected the house and chatted with Josie, judging us the entire time.

All I can do is hope that what she saw met her standards. Josie is happy, and she's the healthiest she's been since I met her, thank god. The home Tyler provides for her is more than adequate. She has her own room and any toy she could ever want. Photos of her hang in almost every corner. Scarlett and Brayden too. And the fridge is covered with her artwork.

Most of all, she's clearly loved. Tyler has done everything in his power to ensure that Josie is happy, healthy, safe, and comfortable. His love for her is palpable in every square foot of this house.

Maria will be returning to the hospital next month. She's been an invaluable resource, helping me integrate into life here, but it's time for us to do this on our own. Brayden treats Josie better than most brothers treat their sisters, allowing her to do his nails and watching the movies of her choosing. Josie and Scarlett may have only met months ago, and Scarlett may only be two, but already, they've developed a strong sisterly bond.

As for me? I'd go so far as to marry a man I hate to give Josie the family she deserves. Fortunately for all of us, he's become the man I love. I can't wait to finally tell him that too.

I'm no longer nervous about our relationship, though I am still anxious about what the future holds for our family, and until the court signs off on the adoption, I won't feel completely at ease.

And, of course, now I'm going to be late for Bray's game.

"I see Tyler." Josie barrels for the ice, where Tyler is standing beside Brayden's coach.

He comes to as many games as he can, and when he's here, all the kids on the team go nuts.

As if he needs the ego boost.

Maria stayed home with Scarlett. Shockingly, the two-year-old isn't a huge fan of hockey, and the shots have made her fussy.

I follow Josie so that after she greets Tyler, we can sit in the stands and let Bray have time with him. Halfway there, I spot a woman watching me from the other side of the rink. I look over one shoulder, then the other, certain she must be looking at someone else, but the rest of the crowd is already seated, since the game is set to begin. When I look back, she's still watching me, and I'm hit with a sense of déjà vu.

Josie is seated close to the players' bench near Tyler now, chatting with a girl her age. Content that she's okay, I change directions and stride toward the woman who has yet to take her eyes off me. She's in a corner all the way in the back, and she's all alone. I'm only a few feet away when I realize why she looks familiar.

"Are you following my husband?" I ask. There's no point in mincing words.

She scoffs, her brow furrowed. "Excuse me?"

Hovering in front of her, I cross my arms over my chest. "I know you. You probably don't remember—"

"Oh, I remember you." She stands, her head ducked a fraction. "I just hoped you didn't remember me."

"And who are you?"

She smiles. Rather than a nasty one like she wore that night two years ago when I met her outside Tyler's apartment—the night he was supposed to be on a date with me—this smile is contrite. Sober. "I'm Brayden's mother, Trisha."

A mix of emotions pummels me. Relief and confusion and even a little shame. With my eyes closed, I inhale deeply. "You were at Tyler's that night for Brayden."

She slips her hands into the pockets of her puffy black jacket and shrugs. "I was drunk and high. I was most certainly *not* there for my son, despite what I may have thought at the time."

I wince, at a loss for how to respond as images I'd rather not picture pop into my head.

She pulls one hand out of her jacket and holds it out. "I wasn't there for Tyler. Or more like he wasn't interested in having me there." She sighs. "Tyler is a good guy. He took care of Brayden when I couldn't even take care of myself."

I nod. That much I know to be true. "So you and Tyler never...?" I can't even finish the sentence.

"No," she says with a kind laugh. "He was only ever interested in helping my boy."

I nod once, studying her. She seems sober. Healthy. Tyler told me Brayden's mom had been in treatment, and from the look of things, she's gotten it. That *should* make me happy. Obviously, that's the ideal outcome. But just like I was crushed when Josie's mom came back into the picture last summer, my heart cracks all over again. I can't imagine Brayden moving out, and I can't imagine him not being a part of our family.

She puts her hand back into her pocket and rocks on her heels, as if she's nervous. For a moment, she looks out to the ice, where the kids are warming up, then she zeroes in on me again. "Tyler says you've been good to my boy."

My chest warms at the thought of him. "He's a great kid. Wonderful with Josie and Scarlett. Always respectful. And one hell of a hockey player."

Lips pressed together, I focus on the ice. She does too. Tyler is watching us from the boards. God, I can't imagine what he must be thinking. Did he know she was here? Did she tell him she was coming to get Brayden? I feel so out of sorts.

"He says the two of you are trying to adopt Josie."

I turn my focus back to her, surprised she knows all of this and worried she'll question what seems like a relationship that cropped up out of nowhere. "Yes, I've known Josie for a few years—"

"You don't have to explain yourself." She laughs. "If anyone should be explaining, it's me. I'm sure you're wondering what kind of mother leaves her son alone at home while she's out getting drunk and high."

Pressing my lips together, I shake my head. "I don't know anything about you."

She nods. "I know. But I know a lot about you. It was important for me, since you're the woman who will be raising my son."

My heart lodges itself in my throat, making it impossible for me to do anything but gape at her.

With her focus set on the rink, she smiles a little sadly. "He's happy here. He's finally got friends, and he's doing well in school." Her eyes well, but she blinks back the tears. "A good mother puts her kid first," she says, her voice thick with emotion.

"There are a lot of ways to be a good mother," I say softly, my own eyes misty.

"You-you'll be a good mother to him?" she asks, a sob escaping her.

I take a step closer and squeeze her wrist. "Yes. And so will you."

Ducking, she shakes her head. "I don't want to interrupt his life. I just want him to be happy."

"So let him stay with us, but don't disappear. Show up for games, come over for dinner, work on having a relationship with him. Let him know he can rely on you. If he wants to stay with us, and you want him to stay with us, he will always be welcome. But if he wants to go home—"

"His home is with Tyler." Her voice is firm as she says it. "Tyler has been more of a parent to him in the last two years than I've ever been."

Willing my heart rate to slow, I take a steadying breath. "Tyler really is wonderful, but that doesn't take away your ability to be a mother."

"I don't know how to start again. I don't think Brayden will ever forgive me. My husband died, and I just—" She shrugs one shoulder and lets it drop, her whole body deflating.

"Grief changes people. It breaks people." I offer her a weak smile. "I get it."

"But Brayden shouldn't have to."

She's not wrong, but there's no changing what's already been done. "Do you like pizza?"

Her brows knit together. "Huh?"

"Pizza? Do you like it?"

Head tilted, she scrutinizes me, obviously confused. "Yeah."

"We have pizza on Friday nights. Come over and have dinner with us."

With a hum, she gives me a once-over. "He was right about you, ya know?"

"Who?"

"Tyler. He said you're special."

Heat floods my cheeks. "Yeah, he's pretty special too. So will you come?"

CHAPTER 44
TYLER

IN THE STANDS on the other side of the rink, Ava pulls Trisha into her arms. My heart stutters at the sight. Of course my fucking wife would befriend Brayden's mom. That's the person she is.

When I first spotted Trisha talking to Ava, my stomach twisted itself into painful knots. Trish mentioned that she might come today, but I didn't tell Bray, for fear of getting his hopes up, only for them to be dashed. She looks good, though. Better than I've ever seen her. I just hope she stays this way.

We had a long talk this week, and when she asked if Brayden could stay with me, I jumped at the opportunity, promising that he could stay for as long as she'll let him. I didn't expect her to suggest that he remain with me until he graduates, but I can't deny it's what's best for him. Thankfully she knows it too.

Making it through high school can be incredibly difficult for even the most well-adjusted kids. Brayden deserves to feel settled and to know that he can rely on us. One day, I hope Trish can do that for him too, but if she's offering to allow me to be that person, I won't turn it down.

I don't have to ask to know that Ava will feel the same.

Now we just need to make sure Bray's on the same page.

My wife is understandably quiet when we're finally setting the table for dinner after the game. We've yet to get to talk about her chat with Trisha since the kids have been around, but while the kids are distracted, I corner her. Pushing her up against the kitchen counter, I glide my hands through her hair, tugging like I always do, until her eyes are on me. "Hi, wifey."

She smiles. "Hi, husband."

"Did you have a good day?" I press a kiss to the spot to one side of her lips, loving the feel of her skin there as she breaks into a smile.

"Yes. Did you?"

"I got to spend the day watching my guy play hockey, and now I have my wife in my arms, so what do you think?"

She shakes her head, brushing her lips against mine. "You're a smooth talker, Daddy War."

I scoff out a laugh. "Not you too."

"It's a great nickname," Bray calls from the living room.

Ava shakes with laughter, the sensation vibrating through me.

"God, I love that sound."

Her eyes soften. "You going to tell me what's going on with Bray?"

"You going to tell me what you and Trish talked about?"

She shrugs, but that smile remains. "I want him to stay with us," she whispers.

I kiss her lips. Fuck. I love this woman so goddamn much. It's incredible, how in sync we are in so many ways. It's the best feeling in the world, knowing that I have someone on my team.

"Come on, guys. Dinner is ready," I holler. Then, with one more kiss to Ava's lips, I head for the table.

Scarlett's been crying on and off all day, so I'm not the least bit surprised when Ava sets her on her lap rather than putting her in her highchair. Our girl snuggles into her mama's chest, uninterested in eating and rubbing her eyes like she's just about ready for bed.

"So you've got a break coming up next week," I say to Brayden.

"Me too." Josie pushes closer to the table, her face lit up, demanding attention.

Her constant state of elation hits me straight in the heart. She's been through so much, yet she never stops smiling. "I know, fighter. I noticed that Brayden has four days off from hockey, and it turns out that I do too."

Ava peers at me, a furrow in her brow. "Oh yeah?"

Brayden shrugs, stabbing his fork into a too-big bite of chicken. "Since we don't have school and a lot of kids will be out of town with their families, we don't have any games scheduled."

I arch a brow at Ava in silent communication, and when she responds with a tip of her chin, I move forward. "What would you guys think of coming to my game in Orlando, then heading to Disney for a few days?"

The squeal that Josie lets loose startles Scarlett, but Ava calms her with a gentle kiss. "Shh, it's okay, my little love."

Bray eyes me, swallowing audibly. "I saw my mom at the game today. Is this like a goodbye trip? I'm going back to live with her when we get home?"

He's so skeptical. Fuck, do I get it. Time and again, he's been let down by the one person he should have been able to rely on. It makes sense that he'd think Trisha wouldn't put him first this time, and though I wish he could trust us completely, I can't blame him for worrying that maybe I didn't really mean it when I said he will always be welcome in our home.

"If you want to go back to Boston with your mom, we can talk about it and figure things out, but if you're comfortable here," I reach for Ava's hand and squeeze it, "we'd really like for you to stay."

Brayden's attention drops to our hands on the table, and without looking up, he says, "I'm comfortable here."

On the ice, he's incredible. I wouldn't be surprised if he goes pro one day. But right now he is very much a kid who is unsure of just about every aspect of his life.

He reminds me so much of myself it hurts.

"Good. Because this home wouldn't be the same without you," I tell him.

"I agree," Ava says, her smile wobbly but her eyes bright.

"Me too," Josie adds. "You're the best big brother ever."

Brayden finally looks up, giving Josie his first smile.

"What would you think about having your mother over once in a while?" Ava asks.

Brayden pushes back in his chair, those piercing blue eyes swimming with wonder. "You wouldn't mind?"

"Not at all," she promises.

With a shrug, as if it's no big deal, despite how much it means to him, he says, "Yeah, okay. That'd be cool."

I meet Ava's gaze, my heart hammering.

"Hey, Jos," Brayden says, his grin growing. "Did you know that *Zombies* is made by Disney?"

She pops up out of her chair. "Oh my gosh, can we meet them?"

And with that, Brayden manages to once again turn the focus away from himself. But I don't miss the big smile he wears for the rest of the meal.

"So Disney, huh?" Ava asks as she walks out of our bathroom, toothbrush in hand.

Damn, I'm a lucky man. My wife stands in the middle of the room in one of my T-shirts, no pants, her gorgeous red hair loose, her face bare, and her freckles—so many fucking freckles—on display.

"You disapprove?" I remove my shirt and toss it toward the laundry basket and miss.

Rather than pick it up, I shuck off my pants and stalk toward her in nothing but a pair of black boxer briefs.

"I don't—" She shakes her head, clearly having lost her train of thought. "You," she says, pointing a finger at me. "You're very good at distracting me."

I grab her by the hips and pick her up, pulling a squeal from her, then carry her into the bathroom. "I like distracting you." I kiss her neck. "And fucking you." A kiss to her chin. "I like just being near you. So yeah, Disney for a few days with my favorite people. That okay, wifey?"

At the sink, I set her on the counter. Then I pluck my toothbrush from the holder. The two of us stare at one another while brushing our teeth, big smiles on our faces. Even mundane tasks like this are fun with her. I never could have imagined a life like this one.

When we're finished, she tilts her head, studying me. "How come you didn't tell me Trisha was the woman from that night?"

With her brush and hair tie in hand, I guide my wife to our bed. Then, once she's seated in front of me, I gently drag the bristles through her hair.

"I tried. That night."

Ava peers at me over her shoulder. "You know what I mean."

I kiss her neck, then get started with the braid. "I honestly didn't think it mattered. You wrote me off after that, and I was sure nothing would change your opinion of me. I was just happy that you were willing to be their mom. That felt more important than explaining an encounter from two years ago."

"It would have mattered to me," she says softly, tilting her face down. "But also, I'm glad I know now. I always hated thinking of the night we met."

I drop my chin to her shoulder and inhale her sweet scent. "I'm sorry, baby. I really did want to be on that date with you. I'd never been so taken by anyone in my life. Still haven't. But Bray needed me."

She presses her back against my chest. "I'm glad he's staying."

"Me too. Maybe this summer we can take the kids up to Canada. I'd love to show them where I grew up. Visit my mom's grave."

Ava turns now, completely ruining the braid I've almost completed. Legs straddling me, she wraps her arms around my neck. "I'd like that."

"We could visit your family too. I'd love to see where little Ava grew up. Maybe you can introduce me to your ex-boyfriends. I can show off how much better I am than all of them."

She lets out a little laugh but looks away immediately. She does that any time someone mentions her family. It kills me, not having the ability to make it better for her. It's like she's hiding a whole life from me or maybe hiding us from that life. More than anything, I want to have every piece of my wife just like she has every piece of me.

Grasping her chin, I force her to meet my eye. "Hey, Ave."

She tries to blink away the tears, but I don't miss them.

I stroke beneath her eye, catching each one as it crests her lashes. "I love you. I'm always going to love you. And I'm always going to want to know you. So when you're ready to share whatever is going on in that pretty head of yours, I'm right here."

She blinks like she can't believe I've finally said it. I can't really either. Only because it feels like I've been saying it over and over again to her since the day we met. Telling Ava I love her is as easy as breathing.

"I love you," I whisper, pressing a kiss to her lips. "I love you." A kiss to her chin. She lifts her neck, and I run my teeth against her jaw, then nip her neck. "I love you." She falls backward, her legs falling open for me, her hips lifting, searching for comfort. I glide my hand down her hip and then press my thumb to her clit, rolling it once. She bucks up against it and moans. "I love you," I tell her over and over as I begin to fuck her with my fingers and then my tongue. Only after she's come twice do I sink inside her, kissing her slowly as I make love to her, promising that I'm her safe space. That I'll always be her safe space. And as I come apart inside her, I whisper into her mouth that I'll always love her. No pinky promises needed. She finally knows I'm a man of my word.

Chapter 45
Ava

"WHAT ARE the chances that you're pregnant?" Tyler rasps in my ear as I'm swallowing yet another bite of Josie's churro.

I glare at him. "Shut it."

Chuckling, he holds up his hands. "That's your third dessert. And don't be mad at me. I'd be ecstatic if you were."

We've spent four days in this perfect little bubble, but tonight is the last night of our vacation. While traversing Disney has been exhausting, I have loved every second of it.

"Don't you want the honeymoon phase of our marriage first?"

With a squeeze of my hip, he presses a kiss to my neck. "We already have three kids."

I eye Josie, who's skipping a few feet in front of us. I swear the girl has skipped everywhere since we arrived. She's wearing an Elsa dress while Scarlett, who's still staring in wide-eyed wonder at the sights from Brayden's arms, is dressed like Princess Anna.

"Have you heard anything?"

We have a status conference with the judge in two days, and as hard as I've tried to steer my thoughts away from it, now that vacation is coming to an end, it's all I can think about.

Tyler sighs. "No. Madi says that not much will happen at this hearing. It's the one in April we've got to worry about."

My heart lurches. "You think we should worry?"

Tyler squeezes my hip again. "No, I mean that the hearing in April is the important one. That's when they'll declare her ours."

"Don't jinx it," I mutter, a ball of dread sinking in my stomach.

"I'm not jinxing it. I'm being practical. Josie is happy. Both of her siblings are ours. She has the best mom anyone could ask for. Why the hell would they take her from us?"

There's no stopping the smile that pulls at my lips when he calls me her mother. It's all I've wanted since the moment I met her.

"Can we watch the fireworks?" Josie asks, clumsily skipping backward now and peering back at us.

Because there isn't a thing my husband wouldn't do for her, he rushes her and scoops her up. Then, balancing her on his shoulder, he turns and heads for Cinderella's castle, where the crowd is probably already gathering.

> Beckett: Hope you had the best time in Disney with the kids. Wanted to let you know the event raised double what we did last year. We're going to match it, and the wing at the children's hospital will be fully funded.

Tears fill my eyes as I reread the text from Beckett. Just as I was preparing to power my phone off for the flight home, the message notification appeared.

> Beckett: We're going to have a ceremony when it opens. You should invite your parents. The movie theater will be named after your sister, and the entire wing will be called Josie's Corner.

With a shaky hand, I cover my mouth. *This* is why Beckett is my favorite Langfield.

While Tyler is busy trying to convince Scarlett to sit still in her seat, I take a deep breath and text my sister.

> Me: I'm sorry I haven't texted in a while. Things have been so good, though. I'm really happy. Just like you said I would be. Tyler wants to meet our family. But I don't know how to come home again. I don't know how to face everything. I feel like I'm getting everything I ever wanted. Everything we ever wanted. But I also feel like my happiness is a betrayal to you. And I don't know how Mom will handle me being this happy. I wish you were here.

When the dots start to dance, my heart rate picks up. It's been years since I've gotten a response from her.

And as the text appears, I can't stop the tears from streaming down my face.

CHAPTER 46
TYLER

IT'S late by the time we make it home. And cold. "Jeez, we should buy a place in Florida. It's too freaking cold here."

"Says the man who glides around on knives in the freezing cold for a living."

A laugh rumbles out of me. Ava was quiet on the way home, so the sarcasm is a relief. Like me, she's nervous about the status hearing tomorrow, but Madi has assured me that this is routine and that the last report from the social worker was a good one.

"Bray, make sure you shower before bed," I say as he hauls his suitcase to the stairs.

"I'll bring the girls up for baths if you wouldn't mind getting the rest of the stuff from the car," Ava says as she reaches for Scarlett, who's fast asleep in my arms.

I kiss my daughter and then press her into Ava's arms before leaning in to give my wife a kiss too. "I had a really great time with you, wifey."

Lip caught between her teeth, she smiles up at me. "Me too." She turns and wraps an arm around a sleepy Josie's shoulders. "Okay, love. Let's get your sister bathed, and then you can get extra story time after your bath."

There's a good chance Josie won't hold her to that promise tonight. Our girl looks beat.

We had breakfast with the Disney characters this morning, and I swear she sang more than Aiden does before a game.

At the thought of Aiden, I realize I haven't responded to the guys' messages in the group chat since after our game in Orlando a few days ago.

When I hold my phone up to my face to unlock it and the screen remains black, I realize I forgot to turn it back on when we landed. So I power it up as I walk out into the cold.

It vibrates at least a dozen times as I hurry out to the SUV. Not surprising. That group chat goes off. Especially since I agreed to appear on the Langfield brothers' podcast. Being in a chat with them is like witnessing sheer insanity. Beckett tries for a normal conversation, Gavin taunts him, Brooks laughs, and Aiden says the most off-the-wall things.

Over and over. Day after day.

But when I tap on the messages app, my stomach sinks. The notifications weren't from the Langfield chat. The texts are all from Madi, and each one gets more serious.

> Madi: Call me.

> Madi: Seriously, pick up your phone.

> Madi: Tyler, this is serious. I need you to call me.

> Madi: The judge wants us in court first thing tomorrow morning. I need to talk to you.

> Madi: We need to get your story worked out.

> Madi: PICK UP YOUR PHONE.

Heart racing, I navigate to the phone app, but before I can hit her name to call her back, the device buzzes, and her name appears on the screen.

"Hey, what's up?"

"Oh my god, Tyler. What the hell?"

"I'm sorry. I was flying, and I just turned my phone back on. What's going on?" I lean against the car, ignoring the chill that instantly soaks through my clothing. With the way dread is quickly gathering in the pit of my stomach, I don't want to bring this conversation into our house. The beautiful home I bought when creating a family with Brayden and Josie was merely a dream. My chest aches. I can't lose Josie.

"Please tell me you didn't marry Ava so you could con the court into giving you custody of Josie. And Tyler, I'm going to preface this by saying, anything you say to me is protected—"

"I know—"

"Unless you're defrauding the court. So please think hard before you answer."

In the window upstairs, Ava's silhouette appears. She's in the girls' bathroom, getting them ready for bed while I'm down here about to unravel our entire life.

"This can't be happening," I mutter.

"Tyler, there are text messages. Transcripts were sent to the court and to my office. They were sent anonymously, but our IT guy tracked them to a computer in your father's office."

Rage ignites in my chest. "Fucking Xander."

"Is it true? The texts were to her sister. Or at least that's what we were told."

I frown. "What does that even mean?"

She sighs, the line between us crackling. "There are hundreds of messages. She's been texting her for months with no response."

Eyeing the window above me again, I rake a hand through my hair. "That doesn't make sense. Right? Why wouldn't her sister reply?"

Madi doesn't respond, as if she's weighing her words.

"Just say it." Teeth gritted, I straighten and pace the driveway. My wife has been keeping secrets from me this whole time. I've given her the space, hoping she'd eventually open up to me. But now? Fuck, now I could lose Josie.

"Her sister died over two years ago."

My heart plummets. It's as if it's landed with a bloody splat on the concrete in front of me.

Upstairs, Ava spots me and offers me a small wave. I stare at the woman I bared my soul to. The one I thought I was building a life with, and realize I barely know a thing about her.

"Send me the text messages."

"Tyler—"

"It was real, Madi. It was real for me."

Chapter 47
Ava

"I LOVE YOU, SWEET GIRL." I press a kiss to Josie's head before heading for the door.

She didn't make it past the fourth page of her story. As much as I love this time with the kids, I'm exhausted, so I'm glad she fell asleep easily. I head for our bedroom, surprised that Tyler didn't sneak in to say good night to the girls. He never misses bedtime when he's home.

When I open the door and find darkness, a niggle of worry forms. "Ty," I call, in case he's in the bathroom. When he doesn't respond, I head down the hall, passing Scarlett's room first and then Bray's. When I press my ear to each door, I'm met with nothing but silence, so I continue moving downstairs. The living room is blanketed in darkness, the glow of the moon streaming in through the windows the only light.

"Ty," I say softly as trepidation builds inside me. Something is off.

"Right here," he rasps.

Spinning, I blink into the darkness and find him sitting near the unlit fireplace.

"Is there a reason you're sitting in the dark?"

"I'm drinking." The clanking of a glass is followed by the splash of liquid.

"*Okay.*" I step farther into the living room, moving slowly while my eyes adjust to the darkness.

Tyler sits on the hearth, his forearms on his knees and a glass dangling from his hand.

"Why are you drinking in the dark?"

"Just got off the phone with Madi. I didn't like what she had to say, so I decided I'd pour myself a glass of bourbon."

Fear pulses through me, making my legs wobbly. "Ty, you're scaring me. What's going on? Is it about Josie?"

He lifts his head, and even in the darkness, I can see the strain in his eyes, the war he's waging against himself, or maybe against me. What the hell is going on?

"Xander broke into your phone. Sent copies of your messages to the judge."

"Shit," I whisper, my heart sinking.

Tyler breaks into a sardonic smile. "Yeah, shit. So the jig's up. Judge knows we fabricated this marriage. Or you did, anyway."

"What? Stop talking in riddles and just speak to me."

Straightening, he takes a sip from his drink. "Like you spoke to me all this time? How you opened up to me while I cracked myself wide open and let you in?"

Bewildered, I shake my head. "What are you talking about?"

"I knew you were hiding something, but fuck, Ava, I fell in love with you. I shared everything with you. And you hid the biggest piece of yourself from me."

My heart races as I try to make sense of what he's saying. But my thoughts are jumbled. My world is crashing down around me, and the one person I thought would stand with me through the storm is turning on me. Dropping to my knees in front of him, I grasp his legs and plead. "What happened?"

Tyler raises his head and meets my eyes, his expression stony. "Your sister is dead."

The words hit me so hard they knock all the air from my lungs and I'm hurtled back in time until I'm reliving the moment all over again. Those four words—*your sister is dead*—coming from another man's mouth. The smell of flowers. So many goddamn flowers. The casket.

My sweet sister, who looked so unlike herself, so fake, I almost laughed as I stood over her.

My limbs go numb, and my ears ring, and the next thing I know, Tyler is on the floor, clinging to me.

"Fuck. Breathe, baby."

I suck in ragged breaths, a pitiful attempt at forcing oxygen to my brain. "I'm sorry," I sob. "I'm so, so sorry."

Tyler pulls me against his chest and rocks me as I break, as I shatter into thousands of pieces. Tears pour from my eyes as memories of the days before she died assault me. The two of us had been making plans. We were going to move to Boston together. Though with the distance these last two years have given me, I see now that she knew she would never leave the hospital. She was planning a life for me so that I'd keep moving. Because if I'd stayed in our hometown, surrounded by our family and the grief, I'd become the grief.

"She gave me this life, but I couldn't save hers," I whisper.

Tyler runs his fingers through my hair. "I'm sorry, baby," he murmurs, his tone low. "I got scared about Josie. I shouldn't have said it like that. It's not your fault. We'll figure it out."

"How? How will we figure it out? They know that our marriage started out as a lie. They know I've been texting my dead sister for years." I choke on a sob. It will never be easy admitting she's dead.

But I owe him the truth. It's the bare minimum really.

"Andrea needed a new heart." I look up at him, unable to make out his features through my tears. "That was my sister's name. Andrea." My breaths stutter in and out of my lungs. "The doctor came in and told us she was in heart failure, and I swear to god, my parents looked at me. At that moment, I wasn't a person. I was a set of organs meant to keep her alive." I swipe a tear from my cheek, though it's pointless. My whole face is damp, and so is Tyler's shirt. "My mother blinked first and shook her head, then she flushed a hideous red. I know she was mortified that she'd even let the thought enter her brain, but it was too late to hide her reaction. And honestly? I didn't blame her for it. Because I thought it too. The words almost slipped out the way they always did. *I'll do it.* It's what I always said. Any time my sister needed something, I gave it to her. A water, a blanket, a kidney."

"Jesus," Tyler whispers.

"But I couldn't save her. I would have if I could, but I couldn't. And now we're going to lose our girl because of me."

Tyler's face turns fierce. "We are not going to lose Josie."

I push back from him, suddenly suffocating. On my feet, I pace the dark room. "Yes, if I stay here, you'll lose her. I won't do that to you. Tell the court you didn't know." I let out a manic laugh. "It's not even a lie. You had no idea your wife was mentally ill."

"You're not mentally ill," he grits out, grasping at my leg as I stride past him.

I shake him off. "Tyler, this is why we got married," I hiss. *"For her. She comes first. You need to put her first."*

Hauling himself to his feet, he steps in front of me, stopping my movements. "I need to put us first, baby. Our family. All of us. There is no us without you."

Knowing what I need to do, I shake my head and back away. "No. This is the right thing. Go to court tomorrow. Blame me. She needs you, Tyler. You need to put her first. Promise me, Ty. Promise me you'll fight for her."

His eyes are wild as he stalks toward me.

I can't look at him. I can't see what I've done. Can't face it.

"I'll fight for both of us. Come on, vicious girl. Now is not the time to give up. Fight for them. Fight *with me* for them."

"I can't do it." I curl in on myself and press a hand over my sternum, willing the searing pain in my chest to abate. "You're better off without me and my baggage. What's the court going to say when they find out I've been talking to my dead sister for two years? That's not something a stable person would do. Who would give me a kid?"

"*Me.*" He pounds his fist against his chest. "I would. I'd give you my child. My children. Please, Ava, don't give up now. Be vicious for me. *Fight* for me."

I cup his cheeks, and he sags in relief. "You're such a good father. They deserve you, baby." I press my lips to his, savoring one last kiss. "I love you. You deserve a partner who's amazing. Promise me you'll find someone amazing to raise those babies with you. You'll do all the things we talked about. Babies and vacations, all the good, all the fun, all the moments."

When Tyler places his hands over mine, I make the mistake of looking into those blue eyes of his. I'll be haunted by what I see for the rest of my life. The man I love, a man with a chip on his shoulder who hides his emotions so well, is crying. Tears crest his lashes and stream down his face. "Please, Ava. Don't say you love me for the first time as you're breaking my heart."

"You'll find someone. You'll be happy. Promise."

He grunts low in his throat. "It's you or no one. So if you can't do this..." He pulls me in for a kiss. It's desperate and messy and filled with emotion. All too soon, he pulls back and speaks slowly, enunciating each syllable, like he's trying to imprint his words onto my heart. I'd let him if I could. "If you can't do this, if you can't fight, that's okay. I would never keep you if it's too hard for you. But Ava, you are the only woman I've ever loved. The only woman I *will* ever love. You're not damaged. You're not broken. You're scarred, but I love every imperfection. They're what make you who you are. My vicious woman who knows her worth and fought for every ounce of my attention. You deserve a place in this world. You deserve to live the life we dreamed of."

The tears come faster again until Tyler is nothing but a blur. If I don't leave now, I never will, so I press my lips to his fingers, kissing each hand, and pull away. Then I grab my purse by the door and leave without looking back.

The problem is, I have nowhere to go.

Chapter 48
Ava

IT'S funny how when a person's life falls apart, the most minute details are what float to the surface and get stuck there. That's the only explanation I have for why, when I leave Tyler's home, I remember Beckett's text from hours ago.

So I steer the car in that direction. It's nonsensical, and I might be turned away, but if I can't be with the people I love, then it's the only place I want to be right now.

I glance back at the house and suck in a sharp lungful of air, then send up a prayer, begging whoever is listening to make this easier.

It's useless.

It's a lesson I learned when I lost Andrea.

Time may change the way the ache feels, but it never takes it away. Being apart from loved ones, regardless of the reason, if the love is true, honest, and unconditional—like the kind Tyler has given me—is the most painful form of torture.

God, it's like a knife to the chest, knowing what I'm doing to him. If I truly believe that he loves me that way, how could I put him through this pain? How could I just walk away?

Despite the thoughts swirling in my mind, I press harder on the gas.

Because as much as I love him and would avoid hurting him if I could, I'm a mother first. Josie has to come first. And she needs him more than he needs me. I won't be the reason she loses the only family she's truly ever had.

I know how devastating that kind of loss is. Andrea *was* my family.

Sure, our parents were there too, and they're good people. They did everything they could to keep our family whole. They love me. I matter to them, despite the thoughts my mind conjures up in my darkest moments. But the grief we suffered—the living, breathing kind —altered our lives forever. They grieved my sister even while she was alive, like they knew they would one day bury her.

I didn't.

Her death *shocked* me. I gave her blood, organs, bone marrow, and every dream, laugh, and moment I had.

But I failed. And I've yet to accept it. Maybe that's why I still text her. Or maybe it's because I spent my whole life sharing every moment with her until two years ago, and now, it's the only thing I have left. My side of the story. Because her story ended.

A sob racks my body, causing the car to swerve.

Headlights illuminate the road before me, snapping me out of my despair. There's nothing I can do but keep moving forward.

The blanket is scratchy, yet I pull it up to my nose. Samantha is on a date, but the rest of the girls are at a sex toy store, searching for the rabbit vibrator. My tears are never-ending, but I can't help laughing when Charlotte makes a comment about how cute the pink vibrator in Carrie's hand is. When Carrie points out that it's got a remote, though, I cry harder.

I'm so pathetic. Am I really watching *Sex and the City* and crying over memories of Tyler and his remote?

"What the fuck? Is that a—oh god, are you watching porn in the children's hospital movie theater?"

I practically jump out of my seat at the voice behind me. Fortunately, as I fumble with the TV remote, I manage to hit pause. I can't remember off the top of my head what happens next. For all I know, Charlotte could be giving a blow job, and then I'll never recover. I dart a look at the screen, where a giant pink vibrator is now illuminated and standing tall, then at Beckett Langfield, whose face is as pink as the toy.

Clearly distressed, he runs his hands through his hair. "Liv always tells me not to get involved in other people's love lives. I've never agreed until this moment. Fuck, Ava. My eyes are bleeding."

The loudest snort bursts from me, and I drop my head back, the tears I've been crying turning into laughter. For a solid minute, I giggle uncontrollably. At the absurdity of this moment. At Beckett's face. At the pink dildo on the screen.

When I finally get my breathing under control, Beckett is seated beside me, wearing a slight smile.

Silence settles between us, and I resist the urge to slide under the blanket completely to hide. "How'd you find me?"

"Your husband is very worried about you."

Hands in my lap, I pick at a piece of lint on the coarse fabric of the blanket. "He called you?"

Beckett coughs out a laugh. "No. He sent a message in the group chat, asking the guys if you'd contacted any of their women. Since I know how much the movie theater meant to you as a kid, I had a feeling I might find you here."

My breath catches. "This was your first stop? That's impressive."

He shrugs. "No. First, I called Hannah."

I smile. "And she told you I wasn't responding to her texts."

My phone was blowing up, so I turned it off a while ago. I'm surprised that Tyler reached out to the guys. He keeps his emotions so close to the vest. I figured he'd shut down rather than ask for help. Maybe if he were the only one hurting, that's what he'd do. But knowing Tyler, he contacted them out of concern for me. There isn't a thing he wouldn't do for me, even if it's asking for help.

"What's going on? Why are you hiding here watching"—Beckett winces at the screen—"that?"

"Tyler found out about Andrea. That she died."

Turning to assess me, he frowns. "He didn't know?"

I shrug, then let my shoulders sag. "No one knows." Now he's really confused. "I didn't want to be known as the girl whose sister died. When I met the girls, they were fun and carefree. So different from what I was used to. They'd talk hot guys and dating and sex—"

Beckett's face scrunches.

Grimacing, I lower my gaze to the blanket again. "Sorry."

He shakes his head. "Believe me, I spend enough time around Sara to know what you girls talk about. It's amazing, really, how good she is at her job. The woman is the most unfiltered person I've ever met."

I chuckle at the thought of her and all the ridiculous things she says. I sober quickly, though, realizing that now they'll all know. About Andrea and that I've been keeping secrets from them for all these years. And for what? They would have been supportive. There's no question. Our friendships are based on more than just gossip and fun conversations. The whole group rallied around Sara when we learned about her affair with the Bolts' former coach. And when Aiden revealed he was having anxiety attacks, the guys stood by him and made sure he got the help and medication he needed.

And when I broke down over Josie time and again, they sat with me in my sorrow and comforted me.

They probably knew from the beginning that Tyler and I didn't get married for love, yet they said nothing. They let me find my way, they teased me, and they showed up.

Swallowing past the lump in my throat, I meet Beckett's gaze. "I really screwed up."

With an arm around my shoulders, he pulls me into a side hug. "We all do. So how are you going to fix it?"

Heart aching, I bite my lip. "That's just it. I can't. Tyler and I got married so that the judge would be more likely to approve the adoption. I would have done anything for her." I glance up at Beckett. "I still would."

He gives me a small smile. "Of course you would. Because you're her mother."

I drop my head into my hands. "Maybe I wanted to be, but I never truly was."

"Why? Because she's not your flesh and blood? What the hell does any of that have to do with it? Winnie, Finn, and Addie are just as much my kids as June and Maggie. Sure, I may not have been there when they were born, but there isn't a thing I wouldn't do for them. Just like you said."

"Yeah, well, you didn't completely fuck it up. No one was telling Beckett Langfield he couldn't be those kids' father. The judge is going to take one look at the text messages to my sister and know that not only am I mentally unstable, but I'm a liar."

"Do you love Tyler?"

Incredulous, I scowl. "What does that matter?"

"Answer the question."

"Yes, of course I do."

"And do you love Josie?"

I roll my eyes. "Obviously."

Silently, Beckett arches a brow, and for the space of a few heart-beats, he only watches me. "My marriage was also a contract."

Stunned, I gape at him.

"It isn't anymore," he says, almost affronted. "Livy is my entire world. Our family is my entire world. But yeah, the way our marriage began was a little suspect." He smirks, like maybe he's remembering the times before it became the real thing. "And her ex tried to go to the press about it."

"But I never—"

"Because I have the best fixers in the world. And the best family." Beckett laces his fingers, forearms resting on his knees. "Lucky for you, you're one of my people, and I always take care of my people."

"Beckett." Tears fill my eyes. I doubt he can really do what he's offering, but the sentiment is beautiful, nonetheless. "It's too late." I shrug. "The judge already knows."

The glint in Beckett's eye means he's certain he'll get his way. I've seen it time and again when Liv is fighting him on something at work. And honestly, he does get his way a lot. Though in the end, he's usually gotten Liv on his side. He's pretty good at making sure she's happy. "It's never too late, Ava. You just have to be willing to fight. So tell me, are Tyler, Josie, Scarlett, and Brayden worth it?"

The answer is easy. Even if I still don't believe it'll fix anything, Beckett is right. I may have lost my sister, but I fought for her until the end. How could I not do the same for the people who are just as much my family as she was?

Hours later I'm lying in Hannah's spare bedroom, exhausted. As expected, the girls showed up and loved me hard. I hold my phone in one hand, not quite ready to talk to Tyler yet. Not when I don't know how tomorrow will go.

I open the message I received from my sister's number and reread the words.

> Andrea: I know I haven't always been the person you need, and for that, I'm so sorry. But I love you and I'm so proud of you. When you're ready for me to come meet your babies, I promise I'll be better to them than I was to you.

Throat clogged with emotion and tears clouding my vision, I type out what will likely be the last message I ever send to this number.

> Me: Mommy, I need you.

CHAPTER 49
TYLER

THE SOUND of Scarlett calling for her mama from her bed guts me. I've been up for most of the night, lying in our bed, trying to figure out how the hell I'm going to get through this day. Hoping that Ava's okay. Beckett texted to tell me he found her and that he brought her to Hannah's, but I can't help but worry that she's still bottling everything up. Hiding her emotions from everyone.

I scrub a hand down my face. Fuck. I can't avoid the inevitable any longer. Rubbing at the tattoo around my ring finger, I take a deep breath, then another. This symbol only solidifies that this woman is out of her mind if she thinks I could ever move on from her. Even when I thought this was a necessary arrangement, I was crazy enough about her to ink her name and our wedding date on my skin. She's my endgame, whether she believes it or not.

But I have to make it through this hearing before I can fight for my wife.

An hour later Scarlett is snuggled on the couch with Maria—thank god for her—Josie is ready for school, and Brayden is already on the bus.

"Ava will take me to dance tonight, right?" Josie has asked for Ava no less than five times since she walked down the steps to have breakfast and didn't find her here.

I don't want to lie, but what the hell do I tell her? That I don't think Ava will be home tonight? That'll destroy her. I have to remain focused on the hearing for now. Then I'll fix the rest.

"I'm not sure, fighter. But if she can't, either Maria will take you or I will. You know how we roll. Someone will always be here."

Josie eyes me in that way that tells me she's not buying my bullshit, but the sound of a car door slamming outside has her swiveling her head, causing her braids to whip against her face. "Who's here? Is that Ava?"

I rub at the ache in my chest. The way she keeps asking for her is breaking my heart.

"No idea." I head for the door. When I spot Brooks's oversized blue truck and Gavin's dad-mobile—it's really just a van, but we love to tease him about it—my lips tick up at one corner.

One by one, my best friends file out of the cars. It's like a circus. The people just keep coming. First it's Brooks and Sara. Then Daniel, Aiden, and Lennox climb out of the back.

Gavin pops out of his van and Fitz slips out of the passenger seat. Next, the sliding back door opens, and Gavin helps Millie, who's carrying a bundled up Vivi, climb out.

I step outside and stuff my hands into my pockets because it's damn cold out here. "What's going on?"

Brooks raises his brows like I'm an idiot. "The girls are here to take Josie to school, Millie and Vivi are here to hang out with Scarlett, and we're here to take you to court."

"But how—" I shake my head and close my eyes. How did they know I needed them? Like in this exact moment. Because I really fucking did. Two more seconds of Josie's eyes pleading for Ava and I might just have cracked wide open and fallen to the floor.

"Ava asked us to come," Sara says softly.

I swallow, the ache in my chest only intensifying. "Is she—"

Sara squeezes my arm. "Not yet. But she'll be okay. I can't believe none of us knew what she was going through all this time."

My heart stumbles. She told them? That makes me feel a modicum better. If I can't be there for her, I'm glad she has her friends.

"Okay, Ms. Josie," Lennox says, brushing past me, though she does give my shoulder a pat as she goes. "You have a date with Sara and me. What do you say we stop at Starbucks on the way to school for a pink drink and one of those cake pops?"

"It's eight a.m.," I grumble.

Lennox whips her head around, pink hair flying, and hits me with a glare. Apparently even being left by my wife won't save me from her attitude. "It's never too early for pink."

Aiden chuckles as he pulls me in for a bear hug. "Come on, I want to stop for a cake pop too. The ones with the little dogs on them are my favorite."

"They only have those at the Starbucks inside Target," Sara tells him.

"Oh my god, I love Starbucks in Target. Shopping and pink drinks. Can you think of anything better?" Lennox is already holding Josie's coat, waving it around in a silent request for her to hurry.

"Do they ever breathe?" I mutter to Brooks.

He shakes his head, but he's wearing a dopey smile. "Nope. But he's right. Go say goodbye to Scarlett so we can stop for coffee. You look like shit."

I chuff out a laugh. "Thanks."

When we pull up to the courthouse, I almost expect to see the press sitting outside, cameras and microphones at the ready, fighting for quotes and soundbites for articles called "Liar Exposed" and other equally shameful titles.

Fortunately, despite the roller coaster I've been on for the last twenty-four hours, life isn't that dramatic.

Or maybe I'm not as big a deal as the Langfields.

Either way, it still feels as if all eyes are on me, weighing me, judging me.

He doesn't deserve to be a father. He's not worth the court's time. Told you he'd screw this up.

In reality, these people don't know me or my situation. More than likely, they're wondering why most of the Boston Bolts' first line is in family court today.

"Oh, thank god," Madi mutters when we step into the lobby. "I was nervous you wouldn't show up."

Frowning, I give her the side-eye. "This is the most important hearing I'll ever attend. How could I not show up?"

She sighs. "I don't know. People do strange things when they think they'll lose a child."

Given her history, I can understand her thought process. "I'm here. No running."

"And your wife?" She tilts her head and peers past me, as if my petite wife with the long, beautiful red hair is hiding amongst a group of hockey players.

I clear my throat. "Uh. She's not coming."

Nodding, Madi looks at me. Or maybe she's looking through me, coming up with a plan. I'm glad one of us has all their faculties, because I have no fucking idea what to do.

"Okay," she sighs. "Let's go in there. Remember, unless the judge asks you a question directly, don't speak." I take an exasperated breath. I'm not an idiot. "And no eye rolling," she adds.

I guess I did that as well, if the way she's glaring at me is any indication.

"No shaking your head, no mouthing of words. Just sit still, palms together on the desk, and let me do all the talking."

"You got it."

I absolutely cannot listen to a word of advice my attorney gave me moments before we stepped into the courtroom. Not when the judge goes off on a tangent about the concerning text messages she's received.

"I find it extremely concerning that one of the petitioners was sending messages of this nature to someone who is deceased—"

Even as Madi places a hand over mine, which is balled into a tight fist on the table, to keep me seated, I stand and clear my throat.

"Excuse me, your honor, but I can't sit here and let you talk about my wife like that." The judge's surprised glare and the overall whoosh of air the collective room sucks in doesn't stop me. "Respectfully, you have no idea what you're talking about. My wife is too good. So incredible, in fact, that it's hard for her to let go of the woman she was literally created to save. Can you imagine that? She was brought into this world for the sole purpose of saving her sister.

"And that's exactly who Ava is. She cares so much for the people she loves. She'd do anything for us. And now we're sitting here, *judging her*, for caring so deeply. As if it's too much. But is there such a thing?"

The older woman on the bench gapes at me, as if I've stunned her. Actually, I think the entire room is watching me in either wide-eyed horror or wonder.

"All because some faceless person has weaponized what was essentially her only connection to the person who, for years, meant everything to her." Arms spread wide, I continue. My voice is too loud, but I don't care. "My mom died when I was twelve. Do you know what I do when I miss her? I talk to the sky. Would you judge me for that?"

Her head tilts and I take that as her acceptance.

"Exactly. Of course you wouldn't. Because collectively we've all agreed it's acceptable to believe that our loved ones are looking down on us. Others visit the grave of the person they miss and spill their secrets there. They can rant and rave, and that's normal. My wife texts her sister's number." I shake my head. "My wife is a smart woman. She knows her sister isn't holding a cell phone behind a pearly set of gates. It's just her way of working through her thoughts and emotions. Who are we to judge that?" I pound my fist against my chest. "Who are *we* to judge the way a person cares?"

"I am the judge," the woman says, though her tone isn't rude or combative. She honestly looks baffled. As if she doesn't know what to make of my outburst.

I don't blame her.

Madi stands at my side and appears ready to speak, but the judge glares at her, so she sits back down.

"I know you're the judge. I know it's up to you whether Josie stays with us. And I can assure you that is all my wife and I care about. So I'm here to beg you. No, I'm here to *tell* you, there isn't another person in existence who could be a better mother to Josie than my wife."

"You keep calling her your wife, but these messages indicate that your marriage isn't real."

"I assure you it's as real a marriage as that of any person who pledges their life to another in this courtroom. Did we have a contract? Yes. Do I love my wife? *Yes.* I love my wife more than I ever imagined possible. Did I the day I married her? Also yes. I didn't know her well enough to love her the way I do now, but I loved the way she loved my little girl and the way she never let me get away with anything. I loved the way she'd get red when I pissed her off. My love for her may look different now, but our marriage has been based on love since day one. It was based on our shared love for a little girl who we would do anything to care for and protect and make happy. So much so that we pledged to stay together, no matter what, to raise our kids."

"Until your youngest is eighteen," she points out, holding a sheet of paper in front of her.

Probably the post-nuptial agreement Madi had us sign, which details what would happen should we separate.

"What's the issue there? In most marriages, two people pledge their lives to one another without considering what will happen to any future children if they divorce. What happens then? A long, drawn-out fight? How is that in a child's best interest?"

The judge almost appears to hold back a smirk at my response.

"Ava and I made a plan so that our kids would be in a safe, happy household until they're adults." I point at the paper. "That contract protects them. Isn't that what parents do? Isn't that what you're charged with determining? Whether we'll put them first? You can guarantee we will. Josie and her siblings will always be our first priority. That contract guarantees that."

"I understand your devotion, Mr. Warren. But it started with a lie to the court."

"Where is the lie?" I bellow, my body temperature ratcheting up several degrees. Fuck. I wish I could tear my tie and suit jacket off. "Everything we've told you is the truth." I hold up my fist and lift a finger as I count off each truth. "We're married. *Truth.* We love Josie. *Truth.* She'll always come first. *Truth.* She'll always have a home with us. *Both of us.* We'll raise her together, no matter what. Where is the lie?" I'm breathless by the time I've finished my tirade, desperate to make her see our side in this. To see Josie's side. Because truly they are one and the same.

Frowning, she studies me, as if actually considering my argument. "That's all well and good, Mr. Warren. And maybe you'll get your way. But you're the only one here. Why is that? Where is this wife who cares so much?"

My heart pounds as I garner my energy to go another round to defend Ava. She's broken, but I know that, if given the chance, she'll pick herself up and be here for our girl. I just need to fight a little more today so she can have that chance.

"I'm right here."

My head swings around, and when my eyes take in the woman I've pledged my life to, all the adrenaline drains from me, and my whole body sags in relief.

I'm right here. Three words have never sounded so beautiful.

She showed up.

Every head turns toward the back of the room where Ava is now scooting past Beckett, who's sitting in the last row. He shoots me a wink.

With a quick nod at him, I zero in on my wife as she approaches. Green eyes swimming with apology and tears meet mine, and she offers me a shaky wave and a smile. Then she steadies her breath and steps through the gate that separates us from the gallery.

"I'm sorry, your honor. I didn't want to interrupt court once you started, but I've been here the whole time, sitting in the back." She turns and nods at Beckett. "Though I know I owe the court an apology for how I've handled this, I stand by everything my husband said."

She reaches over and brushes her pinky against mine, as if she's nervous.

I can hear her words, can feel the promises she's back to fulfilling. Her pinky promises.

Without hesitation, I grasp her hand and squeeze, my chest tight with emotion. As I clutch her hand like it's my lifeline, my head falls and a sob slips out.

She showed up. My vicious wife came back to fight with me.

To fight *for* me and our family.

Chapter 50
Ava

RUNNING ON PURE ADRENALINE, I stand before the judge, feeling flayed open. Strangely, though I'm exposed and vulnerable, I'm wrapped in so much love I just might burst. The courtroom is packed. Each row behind us is lined by people who love Josie and want the best for her. Tyler's teammates, my coworkers, our family, and our friends.

And my mom.

Thanks to Beckett, she flew in on a private jet overnight. No hug has ever been as healing as the one she gave me. Falling apart in my mother's arms this morning, admitting that I'm lost and afraid, that I'm the one who needs help this time, gave me the strength to fight again.

Beside me, Tyler shakes with silent sobs, but his grip on my hand never wavers. Just like his love never wavers. This man, who loves with his whole heart, who willingly threw himself in front of the court and laid himself bare, gives me the strength to do the same.

I square my shoulders, raise my chin, and meet the judge's narrowed gaze. "We would do anything for Josie. No one will ever love the way my husband loves his family. The way he loves her. I told him the night I proposed to him that you'd be crazy not to choose him to be Josie's parent. I didn't even like him then, but I loved the way he loved that little girl. He bought a house so she would have a home." I shake my head as my eyes fill with tears. "Did you know he painted her bedroom pink with little birds because he knows she loves Taylor Swift? Or that he enrolled her in dance classes despite his ridiculous schedule because she wanted to learn ballet? He built her a dance studio and took her to Disney. He braids her hair every night, and when she's scared of going to the doctor or the dentist, he's the first one she turns to—her safe place. *Her father.* He's deserving of the title of Dad all on his own. He doesn't need me. But I'm so glad he married me so I could be her mom. That role has saved me. Like my husband said, I was made with a purpose, and without my sister, I've been a shell of my former self." I shrug, suddenly exhausted. "Maybe that's why I clung so hard to her through texts. Maybe it's why my messages became less frequent once we got married. I don't know. None of that really matters, though, right? Because I truly believe the moment I met Josie two years ago, I found my purpose again."

Sniffling, I run a knuckle under one eye, then the other.

"Even if I'm nothing more than a friend, I'll always be here for her. But please, don't let our desperation to do all we could to keep her in a safe home, where she is loved and cherished, be the thing that makes you take her from us. We'll do better, but I promise everything we've done up to this point has been with our love for her at the forefront."

With nothing left to say, I force myself to remain standing, even though I could easily crumple to the floor.

Lowering her head, the judge gives it a shake and lifts the papers in front of her. She taps them against the surface of the bench, then sets them down again. "I appreciate your situation. It's clear you both love Josie, and the reports from the guardian ad litem have all made it clear that she loves you too and wants to stay in your care."

For a moment I allow myself to feel hopeful. I turn to look at Tyler, who's grinning at me. He wraps an arm around my waist and squeezes me tight. It feels like we've finally made it. We've been honest and open, and the judge gets it. Loving her is enough.

But when the judge holds up her hand, I deflate.

"This is only a status conference. I'll take what you've told me into consideration, and we'll review the matter in April as scheduled. For the time being, Josie will remain in her current placement." With that, she calls the next case.

A relieved breath whooshes from my lungs. The war may not be over, but we've won this battle.

"Oh god, did that really happen?" I murmur.

Tyler tucks his chin and blinks back tears. "I think it did."

"Come on, guys. Let's chat outside," Madi says as she puts a hand to each of our backs and guides us past our shell-shocked friends and teammates.

The moment we make it to the hall and I spot Beckett, I let go of Tyler and throw myself into his arms. "Thank you so much."

This man has the uncanny ability to be exactly where he needs to be. It's rare, finding people like Beckett Langfield. People like Tyler Warren. Or maybe it's not. As I pull back, I realize I'm surrounded by a sea of people who have shown up time and again for me, for Tyler, for our family.

Hannah, Sara, Brooks, Lennox, Aiden, Gavin, Fitz. Even Daniel.

I suck in a lungful of air, trying to steady my pounding heart, and meet my mother's eyes. She's standing behind Beckett, with tears staining her cheeks. She's got the same red hair as me and the same green eyes. Andrea's green eyes. Though hers are dull from the years of heartache she's endured. Her face is heavily lined and so damn wary, like she's not sure if she should insert herself in this moment.

"*Mommy.*" I crumple in her arms, unable to support myself under the weight of the last twenty-four hours. The excitement from Disney, the flight, the news from Beckett about naming the theater after my sister, the phone call that changed everything, Tyler's heartbreak, my running, the desperation to figure out how to stand back up again and fight for our family that consumed me. Then there was the last half hour, where I sat and listened to the judge recount all my crimes and then watched as my husband stood up for me.

I release my mother and clutch my husband's hand. "This is my mother," I say. Then, turning back to my mom, I add, "Mommy, this is my husband."

Tyler wraps his arm around me, as if he knows I need his strength.

With a kiss to my forehead, he holds out his other hand. "Tyler Warren. It's nice to meet you, ma'am."

"Oh, I know your name," my mother says, giving him a genuine smile. "You're the boy who brought my girl back to life." Then she wraps her arms around us both.

When she releases us, I peer up at Tyler. "Now what?"

Humming, he squeezes my hips. "I don't know about you, but I really want to pick the kids up from school early and just hold them. And you."

"I'm not sure how Bray will feel about that."

Tyler chuckles. "Too bad. The kid's going to have to deal with a man hug or two tonight. I'm all sorts of needy right now."

"Aw, Tyler Warren, did you miss me?"

His eyes soften and the smile falls from his lips. Hands cupping my cheeks, he shakes his head, brushing his nose against mine. "You have no fucking idea, Vicious. Please don't ever leave me again."

His words sober me. "I'm so sorry I ran."

"All that matters is that you came back." He presses his lips to my forehead. "And you're not leaving again."

"Never."

Blue eyes twinkle as his lips tip up. "Pinky promise?"

A rush of relief washes through me as he holds up that finger that has become such an important symbol for the both of us.

I loop mine through his and kiss our joined hands. "Pinky promise."

CHAPTER 51
TYLER

"DON'T YOU DARE," Aiden hollers as Brooks leaves the goal wide open.

I throw my head back and laugh when my center falls to his knees, dramatically pouting over Brayden's goal. We're on the pond, playing the Langfield brothers—minus Beckett—versus Bray, Hall, and me.

If we win this game, then Aiden can't sing during practice for a week. We're not crazy enough to stop him before games—hockey players are superstitious as fuck.

Brooks, clearly on board with less singing, has been diving from the goal each time we get close. Hall is playing goalie for our team, but thanks to Gavin passing the puck to me instead of Aiden every time he gets it, Hall hasn't had to do much work.

From the snowy sidelines, the girls cheer, Josie and Sara being the loudest. We picked the kids up after court and came straight home. Millie ordered pizzas, and Beckett and Ava's mother stopped to pick up drinks on the way here, giving us a few minutes alone before we checked the kids out of school early.

I've never seen a smile as big as the one Josie broke into when she spotted Ava. My wife tried to keep her emotions in check, but as our girl hugged her like she thought she'd never see her again, we were both blinking back tears.

Josie knows that the adoption isn't finalized yet, but that's the extent of her knowledge. And I'd like to keep it that way. Until it's a done deal, I don't want her to worry or get her hopes up. But on days like today, I have to fight the urge to hold her tight and tell her we'll never let her go.

Ava appears with a bundled-up Scarlett in her arms. Her mother follows, and Millie and Vivi trail behind.

"Best of three games?" Aiden says, drawing my attention.

Gavin shakes his head. "No. We're going to eat pizza, then head home. We've got a game tomorrow. I don't need my stars getting hurt during a game of pick-up because you're a sore loser."

"I wouldn't be if you two weren't throwing the game," he whines.

Brayden barrels into me and gives me a good squeeze. "That was awesome!"

I hold him tight and choke back the emotion threatening to overwhelm me. This might be the first time he's initiated affection since he moved in. There's no way I'll let him go too quickly. "Let's eat. After everyone is gone, maybe we can get Ava and Josie out here later. Sound good?"

When we make it over to the fire where our crew is all keeping warm, "Belong Together" by Mark Amber is playing on the speaker and the atmosphere is light. Ava's mom is holding Scarlett, which means my wife is seated in one of the Adirondack chairs all by herself. I stalk toward her, and without a word, I lift her up, then sit and pull her onto my lap.

With a contented sigh, she snuggles against my chest. Then she tips her head up and smiles. "Hi, husband."

"Hi, wifey."

"You know, that's a really great idea," Sara is saying.

"What is?" I ask.

"In April, the Bolts and the Revs will both be playing in Arizona," Hannah says. "We could rent a house and hang out for the weekend."

"I'm in," Daniel says as he settles into an empty chair, beer in his hand.

Hannah eyes him. "Who said you're invited?"

He grins. "I'm always invited. Besides, you couldn't possibly want to go away with all these couples alone. You need me."

Head thrown back, Hannah guffaws. "Oh, Baby Hall, you have so much to learn. I don't *need* anyone."

"I don't know if we could make it work," Ava says as she watches Josie and Bray head for the house.

I squeeze my wife. "Maybe Maria could stay with the kids for the weekend. Have a few nights to ourselves for once."

Lip caught between her teeth, Ava eyes me, unsure.

"I could help," her mother says from where she's cuddling with Scarlett on the other side of the fire. "If you're comfortable with that. Your father and I could come down a few more times before that and get to know the kids. I'd like to be here as much as you'll let me," she says quietly.

With wide eyes, my wife looks from her mother to me, her every thought written on her face. She wants this. She wants a relationship with her parents, a fresh start. But she's afraid to say so without checking in with me. I press a kiss to her forehead. "I trust you, Vicious. If you're comfortable, that works for me."

Those gorgeous green eyes that sucked me in two years ago search my face like she can't quite believe all that's transpired between us in that time. Or maybe just in the last twenty-four hours. Then her lips lift into a smile. "Yeah. I'd like that."

"Yay! Family vacation," Lennox cheers.

Chuckling, I look around the fire at the guys who started as teammates and have become my closest friends. I may not have been born a Langfield, but this group of guys, including Hall and Fitz, are the best brothers a guy could ask for.

This group of people—my wife's best friends, her family, my guys, and our kids—are the only family I'll ever truly need.

TEXT MESSAGES FROM AVA'S AND TYLER'S PHONE

Hannah: I found a house! <link to Arizona house>

War: What is this chat?

Lennox: Oh my GOD, is this a group chat with EVERYONE I LOVE?!

Sara: squeals and claps hands. This is so exciting.

War: Take me out of this chat.

Brooks: Love this for us.

Aiden: I'm with Lex. Best chat ever.

Ava: Oh, it has a hot tub!

Hannah: None of you couples can get naked in it.

Hall: What about us singles?

Hannah: 😊 You wish, Baby Hall.

War: Fine, I'll stick around.

Hall: You can't let her talk to me like that, Daddy War. Tell her to be nice.

Fitz: Why am I in this chat again?

Dad: Tyler, I just want to let you know that Xander has been fired. I can never apologize enough for what he did.

Tyler: He almost cost me my child. I'm not sure how you and I move forward from here.

Dad: What he did was unforgivable. I'll never stop trying to fix our relationship, though. I've left Dory. I'm not sure what else I can do.

Tyler: Keep trying. I'm not closing the door on a relationship. We just need time to rebuild.

Dad: Whatever you need.

Beckett: <link to an article> Xander Warren of Warren Financial was arrested on Friday morning after the IRS received an anonymous tip. According to sources, Warren has been defrauding dozens of clients in the largest Ponzi scheme Boston has ever seen.

War: Ava always said you were her favorite Langfield. You're officially mine. Thank YOU!

Tyler: One more night until I'm back home with you and the kids.

Ava: Have an awesome game. The kids and I will be wearing our number 7 jerseys while we watch.

Tyler: Picture or it doesn't count.

Ava: <pic of Ava, Scarlett, Josie, and Brayden from behind, smiling over their shoulders >

Tyler: Just saved it to my home screen. Want that blown up in the living room.

Ava: I love you.

Tyler: Love you more.

Ava: Pinky promise?

Chapter 52
Ava

"SO THIS IS where you disappeared to," my husband mumbles as he appears behind me. I bite my lip as I take in his strong form in the mirror. I can't help but appreciate the way his black T-shirt stretches against his muscles. The black lines of the tattoos that cover his toned arms. The flex of his jaw as he catches me ogling him. Those blue eyes that always light a fire inside me, so bright and hopeful in comparison to his menacing form. "See something you like?"

I bite down harder, trying to fight a smile, but it's no use. "Very much so," I tease, remembering the words uttered between two strangers who had no idea where that conversation would take them.

It brought us here. To a ballet studio in a house this man purchased for three children he probably couldn't have imagined raising back then. With me, the woman who works to drive him mad on the regular.

Tyler steps closer, the heat of him at my back, but his eyes never leave mine in the mirror. "You smell like heaven." Angling lower, he kisses my neck and nuzzles against me in a way that sends shivers cascading through my body. The goose bumps that erupt are visible since my arms are bare. I'm comfortable in my own skin in a way I never was until him.

He snakes a hand down my side and cups my breast, then settles the other on my stomach. "I missed you."

"Me too, Ty," I rasp, my body already hot from dancing. He's been gone for another ten-day stretch, and I've been antsy. The more time I spend with this man, the more I miss him when he's gone. It's a far cry from how I used to wish he would disappear.

His flight was delayed because of weather, so instead of getting home late last night, he's just now made it in. We've got about two hours until the kids wake up and the chaos of a regular day around here begins. Bray has two hockey games today, though I can only go to one because Josie was invited to a birthday party. This is a first for her, so to say she's excited would be an understatement. She hasn't stopped talking about it since we got the invitation two weeks ago.

"Did you miss me or my fingers, pretty girl?" With a nip to my shoulder, he tweaks one nipple. I never wear a bra under leotards at home, and it drives him wild.

"Definitely your fingers."

His responding chuckle causes the hair at my nape to tickle my skin, and then the hand on my pelvis dips lower. "Keep your eyes on the mirror, then, wifey. I want to watch you watch me take you apart with these." He taps his fingers gently against my core.

Whimpering, I buck my hips.

He corrects me immediately, pulling me back against him, forcing me to feel how hard he is. "Now, now. That's not good form."

God, I love it when he plays with me like this. When he's not gentle. When he expects me to fight him. He makes me stronger. Makes me vicious. Turns me into the person I am only with him.

"Hmm, that's not what Benoir said at practice this week."

Blue eyes narrowed, he digs his fingers into my hip. "Are you teasing me, wifey?"

There's no stopping the smile that splits my face. "Always."

"Strip."

I cough out a laugh. "Excuse me?"

"You heard me." He steps back, releasing his hold on me. "He got to see you at practice this week. I want to see more. Do your dance for me right now. Naked. I want to watch you spin, bend, *pirou-fucking-ette* with nothing on. Dance for me, Vicious. *Please.*" He tacks that last word on with a smug smile. He knows what that does to me. How I yearn to please him. How I live for that cockiness.

I spin on my heel, but before I can face him, he grasps my shoulders and forces me around again. "Face the mirror."

My chest grows heavy with excitement as I fix my attention on his reflection and slide the straps off my shoulders, then pull the leotard down over my hips. "I need music."

Tyler grabs his phone. "Song?"

I smirk. "'Bed Chem' by Sabrina Carpenter."

The laugh that leaves his lips is raspy and sexier than anything I've ever heard. As soon as the first verse begins, I straighten and move. This isn't the routine I've been working on for our show. No, this one is for Tyler only. I'm seducing my husband. My breasts feel heavy under his gaze, my nipples hard, my legs tingling as the ache grows between them. I watch my form—wide arms, pointed toes—knowing he's enjoying every second.

When the song comes to an end, I take a bow, knowing precisely what he's seeing now. My ass, bent over, too enticing for him to ignore.

Tyler doesn't disappoint. With a low growl, he clutches my hips. "Hold still." Then he's crouching behind me and running his tongue between my legs. "Hands on the mirror, baby. You're going to need to hold on, because you're going to be here for a while."

With every swipe and swirl of his tongue, my breathing gets heavier, causing the mirror to fog. When he adds two fingers and pulls back, meeting my reflection, he fucks me slowly like that. "My beautiful, vicious, perfect wife. Fall apart for me."

"I need—"

"I know what you need." And he doesn't deny me. Quickly, he stands and drops his pants. Then, in one swift move, he lifts me into his arms, lines up, and thrusts into me. He kisses me. Fucks me. Makes love to me.

He does all the things. That's how we do everything. We're both soft and hard when it comes to one another. Rough and easy. We love and we fight and we play. As long as we're together, we're happy.

"I love you, Ty," I whisper between gasps.

"I love you so much that sometimes I hate you," he says as he bites down on my lip. "You make it impossible to think of anything else. When I'm away from you? Fuck, Ava, you're my obsession." He fucks up into me, sending me over the edge when his piercing hits that spot inside me no one else has ever been able to touch.

I squeeze him tight, forcing a cry from him and milking his orgasm pulse by pulse.

I place my hand against his heart, reveling in the steady rhythm. "I'm equally obsessed," I whisper, holding my pinky up between us.

He glances at my hand, his eyes narrowing when he catches sight of the design.

"Promise," he whispers as he reads the word I had inked along my pinky. Next to it, in the spot where my wedding ring sits, is a tattoo that matches his. Our wedding date and three letters beneath it.

W-A-R. It's a reminder of what he'll do for me. Who he is. And who I am because of him.

He didn't play by the rules in order to win me, and I sure as hell threw the rules out the window when it came to our marriage. But let's be honest: all's fair in love and war.

Epilogue

Two Months Later

Tyler

"DADDY!" I swear that might be the sweetest word in the English language. Especially when it's spoken by the girl with strawberry-blond hair who I can now officially call my daughter.

"Yeah, Josie?"

"Mommy is almost done getting ready."

"Is there a reason you're screaming at me?" Grinning, I pull the casserole dish out of the oven and place it on the counter.

"Because it's Mother's Day, and I finally have a mother to celebrate."

Well, shit. When she puts it like that, I wonder if I've done enough to honor Ava today. It's not just a first for Josie, but for Ava too. Then again, the only thing my girls will want is to be together. That's when they're happiest. Also when they're shopping. More so Josie than Ava. Josie loves a good shopping spree.

And vacations.

I've got another one of those planned for summer break. Unfortunately, the Bolts season ended after a string of losses in the first round of the playoffs. It wasn't how I wanted my first season as captain to go, but I won't lie and say my heart wasn't in it. The stress over the last hearing weighed on me heavily, and my focus was here on my family, not on the game. And I wasn't the only one with a lot on their plate. I also know that we'll come back stronger next year. Right now, though, I'm not sad about spending more time with my kids and my wife. We need this time to bond, and I'm pumped to break the news that we'll be spending a few weeks in Canada this summer. I want to show them where I grew up and introduce them to my mom—because introducing my family to a headstone is acceptable, just like texting a loved one who's passed on. I won't change my mind on that. And honestly, I just miss my first home.

"Want to go tell everyone brunch is ready?"

With an excited nod, she does a ballerina spin and darts out of the room. She's been practicing nonstop for her show next week, and I couldn't be prouder of her.

My wife is also performing, but I'm pretty sure her performance will be a little less risqué than the ones she's been giving me in our basement after the kids go to bed. Even so, I'm looking forward to it. I'm also looking forward to the end of her classes with fake Frenchie. She's only taking the summer off, and I'll gladly support her when she goes back. She loves dancing, and I'd never stop her.

"Is that bacon?" Bray asks as he saunters into the kitchen and plucks a strawberry off the top of the casserole.

"Don't eat with your hands."

He laughs. "Okay, *Dad*." The word slips out in a sarcastic tone, and for a moment he goes quiet. He was only giving me shit, but suddenly, the moment feels important. But it also feels like if I make a big deal out of it, he'll get weird on me.

I accept the joke with a simple shrug and smile. "That's me, Daddy War."

"Oh god, babe. Don't refer to yourself as that," my wife says as she steps into the kitchen with Scarlett in her arms.

"Good morning, mon chou." I press a kiss to Scarlett's cheek, then give Ava one too. I woke her up with a happy Mother's Day surprise between her thighs, so this isn't the first time I'm seeing her today.

"Go sit down, Mommy. I've got French toast casserole and bacon. You do like meat again, right?"

With a snort, she shakes her head. "Yeah. Remember, only pig."

Once the casserole dish is on the table, ready to be passed around one bite at a time, I lift my glass of orange juice. "To our Ava. Happy Mother's Day, beautiful. The best decision I ever made was agreeing to your crazy proposal."

She coughs out a laugh. "Glad we're sticking to that story."

I wink at her. "You did ask first."

She closes her eyes and blows out an exasperated breath.

Like every time I irritate her, I feel all sorts of gooey inside. I love nothing more than pissing off my wife.

"Seeing as how we're stuck together for the next however many years—"

I glare at her and she blows me a kiss.

"I have a present for you."

Frowning, I tilt my head. "Aren't I the one who's supposed to be doling out the presents today?"

"Let me go first." She turns to our kids. "You guys want to show Daddy his surprise?"

I look from her to each kid, confused.

When Brayden points at the words on his shirt, I read them aloud. "Big brother."

"Now me," Josie says, pointing at hers.

"Big sister." Warmth blooms in my chest at the pure joy radiating from her. I read Scarlett's next, and that's when it dawns on me. "Did we get the final decree from the court? Is it official? Josie's ours?"

Last week, the judge approved the adoption, though we're still waiting on the paperwork. We celebrated with a pizza night followed by a marathon of all the *Zombie* movies. Then we slept in the living room in a fort Bray and I made.

Josie giggles. "Read Scarlett's shirt again."

"Big sister," I say aloud, brow furrowing. "Wait, you're the big sister." I point at Josie. "Not Scarlett."

Ava bites that lip of hers and shakes her head. "Not anymore."

Then her smile turns mischievous. "Scarlett's been promoted to big sister too."

My heart takes off at a sprint as all the pieces fall into place. "We're having a baby?"

She nods as tears fill her beautiful green eyes. Eyes that feel like home to me. They're the color of the trees outside my first home in Canada, the color of Christmas—the first holiday we spent together as a family. They're a color so hauntingly similar to that of the eyes of the first woman I ever loved—my mother.

In that moment I pray to any deity that can hear me that our child gets those eyes. Then I fall to my knees at my wife's feet and press my cheek to her stomach. "Hi, baby. I'm your daddy."

Stroking my hair, Ava smiles down at me. "He or she is just a little bean, Ty. I don't think they can hear anything."

I gaze up at my wife, knowing we can't always see or hear the ones we love, but we can feel them.

I can feel my child. I can feel his or her spirit. This is the first moment I'll spend with our child, and somehow I know my mother is here with us too. And Ava's sister.

The ones we love never really leave. They're always with us, even if it's just in our hearts.

"I love you, Ava Warren. Happy Mother's Day."

EXTENDED FUTURE BONUS EPILOGUE
FIVE YEARS LATER

Tyler

"I can't believe this is it." Aiden shakes his head, his lips turned down and his face a mask of emotion.

There won't be any tears from me. I'm ready. Two weeks ago, I was considering signing on for one more year. Gavin knew it. My wife knew it. She supported my decision, said she was good either way.

Ava's incredible like that. She let me come to this decision on my own, knowing I needed to be at peace with the moment I hung up my skates.

Gavin, on the other hand, gave me just the push I needed.

"I can't believe this is it either," I say to the boy standing next to me. Though this "it" couldn't be more different from the one Aiden is grieving over. This is the moment the dark-haired kid at my side begins his career in the NHL. A career that is sure to rival mine or Aiden's.

With the number 77 on his back—he lives to one-up me, so he went with two sevens compared to my one—and Hawke emblazoned across his shoulder blades, he's a hair taller than me. Has more meat on him too. Though he's been waiting for this moment for a long time, he hasn't waited as long as I have. I knew he'd be in the NHL, well before he even dreamed it could happen, but he put in all the work.

I couldn't be prouder.

The cocky motherfucker turns to me with a sly grin. "Sure you can keep up with me on the ice tonight, old man?"

Aiden arches back and barks out a laugh. "It's like looking in a fun house mirror. You guys are the same damn person." With a shake of his head, he jumps up onto the bench. "All right, guys. Let's do this. One last song for the best captain the Bolts have ever had."

This time tears do coat my lashes. I survey the group of guys who are the best damn brothers I've ever had. Brooks looks just as emotional as I feel. He's not hanging up his skates just yet, but I have a feeling that he'll be joining me in the stands in another year or so. Aiden and the rest of the guys still have a few years to go, which means the kid beside me will have the best mentors a rookie could ask for.

Aiden shimmies his hips, then breaks into an original song set to an older Taylor Swift tune.

"Our captain's got a date
He's doing other things
That's what he says, mm-mm
That's what he says, mm-mm
He's no longer going to play
He says that he can't stay
At least that's what he says, mm-mm
At least that what he says, mm-mm
But we'll keep winnin'
Can't stop, won't stop winnin'
Because he left us with the next best thing
And he promises we'll be alright
'Cause the Bolts are gonna play, play, play, play, play
And Hawke is gonna slay, slay, slay, slay, slay
And Cap, we're gonna skate, skate, skate, skate, skate, skate
Skate it off, skate it off."

I'm laughing by the time Aiden finishes his Bolts rendition of "Shake it Off."

Gavin enters the locker room and looks from me to the man beside me. "You guys ready?"

We nod.

He cocks a brow. "Any last words?"

I turn to the guys and inhale deeply. "Before coming to this team, I didn't have a clue what family was. These last seven years have meant everything to me. And you're not getting rid of me. Ava and I will be at as many games as we can manage with the kids' schedules. For every one of you, I'm only a phone call away." I eye Aiden, whose depression still spikes every now and again. Then I turn to the rookie and grasp his shoulder. "I'm so fucking proud of you."

Though his eyes swim with nervousness, Bray laughs. "Language, Dad." But then he pulls me in for a hug. "I'm so fucking proud of you too."

We skate out onto the ice, and when they welcome number 77, Brayden Hawke, into the Bolts family, I choke back tears.

I'm the last one announced. My family stands at center ice, here for the small ceremony management has planned for my last game. As I get close, I bark out a laugh.

"Really, Vicious? I say, taking in her jersey. "Wearing another man's name and number on your back?"

Ava's lips wobble and tears drip down her cheeks. "I'm just so proud of him," she whispers.

"Bray!" Beckham yells from her side. Our youngest son is four and beyond obsessed with hockey and Brayden, so I'm not at all surprised to see he's also wearing his brother's name and number.

"Seems like you've already been replaced," Gavin teases as he steps up to the microphone.

"Not by me, Daddy!" Scarlett says, reaching for me. At almost eight, she looks so much like her older sister. Josie is fourteen and is giving me a run for my money.

"Ah, my girls are still wearing their Daddy's number." I hug them both but as I stand, my cocky winger is right by my side again.

"Not after tonight, old man. You better get used to wearing 77 on your back."

Gladly.

When Gavin told me he wanted to call Brayden up for my final game, I nearly broke down in tears. I understand why so many guys hold on, hoping for one more Stanley run before announcing retirement, but that's not in the cards for the Bolts this season, and I've made peace with that. We've had a few cups in my career, but not a single one of those wins can hold a candle to what it feels like to take the ice with my son on Aiden's other side.

When all the celebrations are done, I'll go home with my kids. I'll get into bed with my wife, and I'll wrap my arms around the only woman I'll ever need.

I'm happy.

My career may be coming to an end, but the best is yet to come.

"Who's ready to play some hockey?"

SNEAK PEEK

Want to find out what happens when War takes Daniel to the tattoo parlor? Continue reading for a sneak peek of *Playboy.*

CALLIOPE'S COLUMN

The real heroes: Men who get pierced for their women's pleasure

I'm going to be *real* real this week, ladies. I'm riding the struggle bus lately, while all my friends are riding their significant others. Being single has never bothered me. I've done the marriage thing; it's not for me. Until recently, I truly believed monogamy was a mere fable. How could one person truly commit to spending their life with another when I can't commit to wearing the same style jeans for more than a season? In high school, it was the widest bell that dragged on the ground, tearing at the seams. Then there was the low rise style, the pants that barely covered my pubic bone. A year later we were wearing jeggings. I'm sure I'm not the only person who packed on a few pounds because I didn't have to worry about a button or a zipper. Then jeans were gone completely, replaced by black leggings. The jeans have returned, and currently, not only do we need one button, but apparently, we need an entire row to do up the high-waisted style that comes up to my boobs.

My point being, if we can't commit to one style because we're continuously changing, how am I expected to commit to one man who may not change with me?

Until recently, I stood fully behind that sentiment. Why the change of heart you ask? Well, I'll tell you it's all because of a little bling. And not the kind that goes on my fingers. No, I don't need a man to buy *me* flashy jewelry, I can purchase that all myself. But a blinged up dick? Now we're talking. Recently, quite a few of my friends started dating men who are pierced and I just want to stand up and clap for these men.

Let's be clear, ladies: if a man gets himself pierced, he's proven that not only will he be good in bed, but he's willing to do the hard work. Because a pierced penis is for our pleasure, not theirs.

And there is nothing hotter than a man who is willing to do the work, am I right? Now let me tell you about each piercing, and what they tell us about the men who get them.

ONE

DANIEL

"Calliope, guys." I shake my head. I pulled up her article on my phone and immediately inhaled the entire thing. If not for practice, I'd read it again and take notes.

Calliope is a genius. Her articles changed my dating game and my sex life. The woman is honest and direct, and though her column is catered to an audience of women, time and again, it gives me direct insight into how to please the opposite sex. As a man who's determined to give 110 percent a hundred percent of the time, I take her word as gospel.

So far, she hasn't steered me wrong.

Our captain, Tyler Warren—War to his teammates and Bolts fans— groans. "Could you at least try to make it one day without mentioning her name?"

Brooks, our goalie, chuckles as he laces up his skates. "Leave him be. What was the article about today?"

Here's the tricky part. Calliope is absolutely a genius, but if I tell them about what she's pushing, they'll be on my case again.

War, Brooks, and our center, Aiden—who's one of Brooks's brothers —all have blinged-out dicks. It's been a bit of a sore subject for me—no pun intended—because though I really want one, I chicken out every time we walk into the tattoo shop to get it done.

The three guys got their piercings before I was drafted to the team. It sounds ridiculous, but it's like the event bonded them, and I feel left out. But I can't quite get past the idea of a man sticking a needle through my precious jewels.

Before I can decide whether to tell them about the article or make something up, our coach walks in, all business.

All chatter dies at the expression on his face. Gavin Langfield isn't a hard-ass coach. As part owner of the team, he played a role in scouting most of us. Two years ago, though, he took over as coach as well. His unique position means that he not only knows the team inside and out, but he's got to do a lot of schmoozing. He's a genuinely nice guy, too, and that translates to his relationship with all of us. We respect the shit out of him, but also think of him as a friend friend.

He and my dad have been best friends for years, and since he married my twin sister last year, we're exceptionally close. So the formal expression on his face throws every one of us. Especially knowing that the trade deadline hits at midnight. Is he coming in here to break some bad news?

I scan the locker room, studying my teammates. Our team is good, though there's always room to be better. This season especially. Something has been off, and I can't quite put my finger on it.

Normally, I wouldn't be concerned. I've played on the first line since I was drafted during college. While War is known for protecting the guys on the ice, taking the hits when a fight breaks out and instigating them when necessary, I have a different set of skills. As the other winger, I have to anticipate War's moves, as well as those of our center, Aiden. I've got to be ready to make the play or put Aiden or War in position to make it. It's why the guys started calling me Playboy—despite the other obvious connotation. I always find a way to make a play work. Essentially, my goal has been to be good at everything. In turn, though, that means I'm not particularly fantastic at one specific skill.

War, Aiden, and I are one hell of a line, but I've heard the rumors about Noah Harrison, and if they're true, they won't lead to anything good for me.

Harrison is one of the best snipers in the league. He's a winger like I am, but he's just as adept at scoring as his center. The whole league knows it. If he gets the biscuit, even from the most improbable angle, the man somehow finds the back of the net.

He's a coach's dream and is well liked by everyone he's ever played with. His college team called him Beauty, and that name stuck when he was drafted to the NHL.

In hockey that's the gold standard. A player who is talented and well liked.

And his nickname is the kind a player should be proud of. The kind that commentators can't make jokes about. He's Hall of Fame worthy.

If I wasn't already playing with two of the best guys in hockey, I'd be pumped about the possibility that the guy has been traded to the Bolts. Passing the puck to a player like Noah Harrison would be a dream.

But I am playing with two of the greats. I am the weakest link.

And if I were Gavin Langfield and I had the opportunity to trade for Noah Harrison, I wouldn't hesitate.

"I've got some exciting news," Gavin says. He glances in my direction, a quick acknowledgment. He doesn't look ashamed or guilty. And he shouldn't, whether he's done what I'm pretty sure he did or not. I may be his wife's twin and his best friend's son, but he's never shown favoritism to anyone in this locker room, including his own brothers. Outside this arena, the dynamics between all of us are different, but here, we are his players and he's our coach. And he's a damn fair one. He decides who plays and how hard we practice. And we listen. Every one of us wants to please him since it's up to him whether we do the one thing we love the most—play hockey.

"Noah Harrison—" I don't hear the rest of his sentence, but from the cheers going up around me, it's easy to guess what he's just announced. We've secured Noah Harrison in a trade.

And whoever Gavin traded for him isn't in this locker room. Our coach-slash-owner is far too respectful to make an announcement like this before notifying the player affected by the negotiation. He would have thanked them for their dedication to the team and wished them luck ahead of time.

I take in the faces around the room, and once I've accounted for all the guys I'm close with, I breathe a sigh of relief.

"This is fucking awesome." Aiden rubs his hands together, budging War in the ribs with his elbow. "Don't you and Harry have matching tattoos?"

War glances at me, his eyes full of concern. He knows I'm secretly freaking the fuck out. "They're not matching tattoos. It's our college team's logo."

Oh did I forget to mention that Brooks, War, and Harrison played together in college? That they've been friends for years? Yeah, this just keeps getting worse.

War tips his chin at Brooks. "This guy was too chicken shit to get one."

Without shame, Brooks says, "Always knew I was going to be a Bolt. No need to put some other logo on my body."

"Spoken like a Langfield." In the next breath, War's eyes light up. "But you don't have a Bolts tattoo."

Brooks rolls his eyes. "What is it with you trying to get everyone tatted?"

"Your fiancée would think it's hot." War raises a brow.

"Does Harry have a dick piercing?" The second the question is out, I want to punch myself in the face. What the fuck is wrong with me?

The guys' faces scrunch up in various *what the fuck?* expressions.

I double down. "Well, does he?"

"No, that's a Bolts thing," Brooks says, eyeing War. "That's *our* Bolts thing." His voice is stronger now, like he just found his way out of getting inked. "No need for a fucking tattoo when I have Bolts-blue bars through my dick."

I wince. Fuck, that sounds painful. But it's a Bolts thing. Their thing. *Our thing.*

"After practice," I say, forcing the words to sound resolute.

"After practice, what?" War watches me, his lips twitching like he knows where I'm going with this. So what if I'm insecure about Harrison's impending trade? So what if I'm acting like a fucking toddler having a temper tantrum and trying to hold on tight to my friends. They're *my* friends. Anyone would be a little territorial.

I meet War's eyes, determination setting in. "After practice, we're going to the tattoo shop."

"You really think you'll go through with it today?" War sounds all sorts of skeptical.

"Yeah, Calliope says that real heroes pierce their dicks for their women's pleasure."

"Fuck yeah, they do," Aiden says, wearing a too big smile. "Can't wait to use that line on Lex later." He holds up his fist for Brooks to bump, but his brother just glares at the outstretched arm. He shrugs and holds it out to me instead.

"Fuck yeah, they do." I bump him back. "And real friends have matching dicks."

My stomach bottoms out. *What the fuck, Playboy?*

I have two choices here, punch myself in the face or own the comment and hold a fist out to War to complete the assholery.

I go with the latter, leaning into this moment, a moment that, with any luck, will bind these guys to me for life.

War chokes on air. "You need help, Playboy. So much fucking help." He shakes his head, but with a laugh, he bumps my fist.

TWO

DANIEL

"Are you going to hold my hand when he does it?"

War blinks at me, his expression one of disbelief. "You're going to need to start over, and do not repeat that question."

My stomach twists. "I really hate blood. I'm a lover, not a fighter."

Chuckling, Brooks slaps me on the back. "Come on, Playboy, I'll hold your hand."

Behind us, Aiden lets out a *humph*. "You wouldn't hold my hand when I did it."

"Because I was too busy holding my own damn dick." Brooks grabs himself as if he's experiencing phantom pain. "You sure you want to do this?"

"Oh my god, stop babying him. If I have to hear him cry about not having a blinged-out dick one more time, I'm going to personally stab a bar through it for him." War glares at me as if he's imagining doing just that.

Suddenly, it's all I can picture. The instigator coming at me with a needle, holding me down and—

With a shudder, I cup myself and will away the mental images before they get more graphic.

"I have no idea how you got sweet Ava to marry you."

His wife is the sweetest woman. The exact opposite of War. She's the head of charity relations for Langfield Corp, the parent company of the Boston Bolts. I bet she knits sweaters for the homeless in her downtime.

"It was the glitter dick." Aiden laughs. "It's how I got Lex, and how Brooks got Sara."

Sara, Brooks's fiancée, is the head of PR for our hockey team, and Lennox works with Ava, handling the party planning for the charity events. The three of them, along with my sister and Hannah, are close friends. Hannah is quite literally the hottest woman I've ever met. She's gorgeous, sure, but her beauty and sex appeal come from so much more than just her looks. It's her attitude that really does it for me. The way she talks down to me. Maybe it's sick, but I fucking love it.

"Speaking of Sar," Aiden says as he lifts his phone.

"Why is my fiancée calling you?" his brother grumbles, pulling out his phone. "I don't even have a missed call."

"It's 'cause I'm the fun one," Aiden says as he taps the screen. "Hi Sar."

Brooks snatches the device from Aiden's hand and taps the speaker button. "Why are you calling my brother and not me, crazy girl?"

"Brookie, are you getting jealous?"

His response is an unintelligible mumble.

Sara's voice softens. "I only called him because he's not replying to my texts."

"Why aren't you replying to Sara?" I swear Brooks looks like he'll fight his brother for ignoring his fiancée. He is the definition of *touch her and die*, only its more *make her sad and die*. He'll do just about anything to keep a smile on that woman's face.

"Because I'm sitting here being a good friend to Hall so he can finally get the glitter dick."

"Oh my god!" Sara screeches, her tinny voice piercing my eardrums. "He's finally going to do it?"

Head dropped back, I groan. "Seriously."

Aiden shrugs. "They'd all find out anyway. You know we don't keep secrets from the girls, and they don't keep secrets from one another."

"Oh, Hannah and I planned to get our nips pierced when you finally did this. Should I call her? We can be there within the hour."

"Nipples pierced?" My mood lifts instantly at the idea of Hannah's nipples.

"Yeah, your sister suggested them."

And there goes any and all excitement surrounding nipple piercings.

"Ya know what? I think we're going to keep this activity for the boys only," Aiden replies, giving me a knowing look. He holds out his hand for his phone.

Sara huffs. "Fine. But could you please send me the link to the house Lennox booked? She can't find the email, and I want to show it to the girls."

"Okay," Aiden says, tapping at the screen of his device, "it's sent. I'll talk to you later." After they disconnect the call, he holds the phone out. "House is sick, right? Just think, if you get pierced tonight, you might just be ready to test it out the weekend we're in Arizona."

Alarmed, I straighten. "That's almost two months away."

"Have you not done any research since you started whining about not having your own?" War says with a laugh. "You can't have sex for six to eight weeks."

I frown at Brooks, who just shrugs. "Didn't matter to me. I wasn't going near anyone back then."

Aiden shakes his head. "I'd rather not think about when I was with Jill, but I can promise that if I'd been with Lex at the time, it would have been impossible."

I swallow slowly. Do I really want to do this?

Calliope's words replay in my mind. *If a man gets himself pierced, he's proven that not only will he be good in bed, but he's willing to do the hard work.*

"Ya know," Aiden says, leaning against the brick wall outside the tattoo shop. "We ended up here because of a game of truth or dare."

War nods. "Yeah and?"

"Maybe we need a little truth or dare to get him motivated."

Brooks nods. "Yeah, I only went through with it because I didn't want to admit that I was a twenty-nine-year-old virgin saving myself for Sara."

I can't help but laugh. Thankfully, the tension in my shoulders dissipates a little as I do. "Worked out well for you, I guess. You ended up fake dating her not too long after that, right?"

Brooks nods. "And I asked War why he wasn't honest with Ava about missing the charity event at the YMCA when we all knew he had a perfectly good reason."

"Oh yeah?"

Our captain just shrugs. "Brayden called that day. His mom didn't show up to get him after school. But at the time Ava hated me, and I was tired of wasting my breath trying to explain to her that I wasn't a bad guy. My vicious wife never would have believed me." Brayden is fourteen now, and War and Ava are raising him, along with their two daughters.

"You're leaving out that part where you refused to admit you were obsessed with her at the time," Brooks adds.

"And then you ended up in a fake marriage with the woman," I point out.

"My marriage isn't fake," War grumbles.

Brooks arches a brow.

"Fine. It started out *kind of* fake. For her. I was always all-the-fuck-in."

"What was the truth you refused to give them?" I ask Aiden

Jaw tight, Aiden nods at War. "He asked me why I hated shamrocks."

"Back then, none of us knew that Lennox used the word when she broke your heart back in high school."

"And after getting pierced, you ended up fake engaged to her." I'm beginning to sense a pattern. *Fuck.*

War laughs. "That's about right. After getting our piercings, Brooks fake dated Sar, Aiden ended up fake engaged to Lennox and I ended up"—his voice dips, and he grits out the words—"fake married to Ava."

I swallow and nod. "Yeah."

"What's the worst that could happen, Playboy? You take it one step farther and get a girl fake pregnant?" He laughs.

My balls have officially ascended into my body. "None of you are faking anything."

Brooks rubs at his face, trying to hide a smile. "Yeah, Sara likes to say it's the glitter dicks that got us all together."

"Except I'm different. I'm not getting this for anyone." *Except them, but we won't tell them that.*

War smirks. "Calliope."

Rolling my eyes, I laugh dryly. "Yeah, as if I'll ever get to meet her."

"If you do, better be prepared to knock her up, Playboy."

"I don't remember a truth being lobbed my way."

"Fine." War fixes me with a hard look. "Truth or dare?"

I stare right back, refusing to back down. "Truth."

He folds her arms across his chest. "Why do you really want to get pierced? Why today? What changed?"

I think of the article. I think of Noah. Both are part of my why. But I refuse to admit either fact out loud.

Because what kind of man gets their dick pierced with the hope that one day he'll impress a faceless woman hiding behind a pen name who writes articles about improving a person's sex life?

And who gets pierced so they can prove they're closer than some other guy is to a group of friends?

Not the kind of man who admits to it, that's for damn sure.

"Let's go inside."

"Yes!" Aiden hollers. "This deserves a song."

"No singing," War growls.

"Can't stop it," Aiden says as he pushes off the wall and holds a hand up in front of him like he's got an invisible mic. Before we can stop him, he dives into his own version of Taylor Swift's "Don't Blame Me."

Don't blame me, the bling made Lex crazy
Playboy wants it and he's doing it tonight
Oh, Brooks baby, the bling made Sara crazy
Playboy wants it, he's giving up the fight.

Playboy's—"

War clamps a hand over his mouth. "If you use my wife's name in your song about Playboy's glitter dick, I'm going to put my fist through your face."

Aiden blinks.

"So you're going to stop singing, right?"

Aiden nods, his dark eyes wide.

War angles in closer, and I'm pretty sure he's growling. Finally, he releases Aiden. "If we're all ready to act like big boys now, can we get this over with?" He motions toward the door

I give myself one final pep talk before heading in.

When I walk out of here, I'll finally have the glitter. And considering I can't have sex for months, no one is getting fucking pregnant. Fake or otherwise.

Find out if the curse continues and preorder *PLAYBOY.*

ACKNOWLEDGMENTS

Since I first wrote the name War on the page, I knew this book would be a favorite of mine. I just didn't expect I'd love them the way that I do. Finishing the Langfield brothers felt like a bittersweet ending because I have loved writing in this world, but knowing the hockey boys were still coming was a comfort. Now as we get closer to saying goodbye–only two left–I know I'm not ready. So thank you for reading my books, loving my characters and sharing this world with me. I will forever be grateful for this career you have given me.

None of this would be anywhere near possible without quite a few people. Sara, truly, I wouldn't be where I am today without you. Thank you for your neverending support, assistance and friendship. Jenni, this next adventure will be our best yet. I don't want to do life–or writing– without you. Andi, Jess, Anna, Charity and all of the ladies in my swoon squad and street team, I appreciate your help, your love of my books and most of all your friendship.

To my beta readers, Emily, Glav, Nikki, Courtney and Becca, truly, the amount of changes I made in this book because of your notes is epic. But each change made this book better and I'll forever be grateful.

Beth: don't kill me–I've got another book coming to you! JK. But thank you for always squeezing another chapter into your schedule because my books (including those spicy scenes you all like so much) wouldn't be the same without Beth's help.

A big thanks to the amazing artists who designed the cover and commissioned exclusive artwork.

And finally, to my family who I have had the best year with, traveling the world and making memories.

Whether you are a new to me reader or a day one girl, thank you for reading. If you'd like to be the first to know what comes next, make sure you follow me on instagram, join my facebook group, and sign up for my newsletter!

And for exclusive content and special editions, join my patreon!

ALSO BY BRITTANÉE NICOLE

Bristol Bay Rom Coms

She Likes Piña Coladas

Kisses Sweet Like Wine

Over the Rainbow

Bristol Bay Romance

Love and Tequila Make Her Crazy

A Very Merry Margarita Mix-Up

Boston Billionaires

Whiskey Lies

Loving Whiskey

Wishing for Champagne Kisses

Dirty Truths

Extra Dirty

Mother Faker

(Mother Faker is Book 1 of the Mom Com Series, but is also a lead in to the Revenge Games alongside Revenge Era. This book can be read as a Standalone, or after Revenge Era and before Pucking Revenge)

Revenge Games

Revenge Era

Pucking Revenge

A Major Puck Up

Boston Bolts Hockey

Hockey Boy

Trouble

War

Standalone Romantic Suspense

Deadly Gossip

Irish

Made in the USA
Columbia, SC
31 March 2025